MW00641766

A TIMELESS *Romance* ANTHOLOGY

Happily Ever After

A Timeless Romance Anthology

Happily Ever After

Jessica Day George
Julie Wright
Sarah M. Eden
Julie Daines
Heather B. Moore
Annette Lyon

Mirror Press

Edited by Jennie Stevens, Haley Swan, Cassidy Wadsworth, and Lisa Shepherd

Cover design by Mirror Press, LLC
Cover Photo Credit: Deposit Photos #91893194
Cover Photo Copyright: Cherry Daria

Published by Mirror Press, LLC
TimelessRomanceAnthologies.blogspot.com

ISBN-13: 978-1-947152-18-2

TABLE OF CONTENTS

More Timeless Romance Anthologies

Winter Collection
Spring Vacation Collection
Summer Wedding Collection
Autumn Collection
European Collection
Love Letter Collection
Old West Collection
Summer in New York Collection
Silver Bells Collection
All Regency Collection
Annette Lyon Collection
Sarah M. Eden British Isles Collection
Under the Mistletoe Collection
Mail Order Bride Collection
Road Trip Collection
Blind Date Collection
Valentine's Day Collection

Mail Order Princess

Jessica Day George

One

Elise arrived in the New World with nothing but two trunks and a very large wooden crate. The trunks were full of gowns of satin and velvet, trimmed with costly lace. The crate contained seven live swans. The clothes were her trousseau.

The swans were her brothers.

Her stepmother had decided it was time for her to be married and had found an ad in a newspaper posted by a former count who had made his fortune in the New World but wanted a bride from the old one.

"I can't kill you, you know," Elise's stepmother had said merrily. "You or your brothers. I'd lose all my power, including my hold on your dear father, and we can't have that, can we?"

So instead her stepmother had packed her trunks, and Elise had packed her brothers. She wanted to be away from her stepmother just as much as her stepmother wanted to be rid of her.

Elise had summoned the swans from the forest and shut them into the crate. She had built the crate herself and put the hatch in the top that she could lower food and water into and the holes along the sides where she could sluice water through to clean out the filth.

But now she was here, in what the train conductor had called Big Sky Country. She was out of food for her swans, she had sailed across an ocean and ridden a train across a country.

And there was no one to meet her.

The porters unloaded her things, and she climbed atop the crate to wait. She felt like a statue on a plinth. Surely this would alert her soon-to-be husband that she was there. Her stepmother had sent him a picture, and he had bought Elise's tickets; he knew when she would be arriving.

But there was no one to meet her. No one who looked like an impoverished count turned prosperous farmer.

During the long days on the ship, and then the train, Elise had practiced her English on her fellow travelers, fed her swans, and enjoyed the freedom of being out from under her stepmother's influence. This enthusiasm was undimmed by people whispering in scandalized tones that she was a mail-order bride. She could not find the phrase in her English primer, nor would any of her new friends tell her what it meant. One lady patted her on the head like a dog when she asked.

Elise was confused. She knew she was to be a bride, it was the mail-order part that confused her. She had not traveled in an envelope! She decided that she had misheard.

Two weeks later, she stepped off the train, climbed on top of her crate of swans, and waited to meet her bridegroom.

He didn't come.

Two

Elise's nervousness gave way to anger. Why had this count sent for a wife if he wasn't going to bother to collect her? No doubt his duties to his farm had kept him from going all the way to the coast to meet her. But now?

Elise stood up atop her crate, fists clenched at her sides. The people bustling about on the station platform all slowed down, turning to look at her. She supposed she must be quite a sight, in her gown of plum-colored silk, standing atop a box full of large, loud birds.

"Spricht jemand hier Deutsch?" she called. *"Aber ich brauche hilfe, und schnell!"*

The bustling resumed, only now people were avoiding looking at her. The woman who had patted her on the head on the train gave her a little wave before going off arm in arm with a younger woman who was clearly her daughter. All around Elise, people shook hands or hugged and then went off with whomever had come to meet them.

But there was no one to meet Elise.

Long after the train had pulled away. Long after she had

sat down atop the crate and dumped the last of the food through the hatch. Long after she had convinced herself that she was too angry to cry, someone came.

He was tall and broad-shouldered and wore a worn blue shirt with brown canvas trousers, heavy boots, and a brace of pistols in tooled leather holsters. His broad-brimmed hat shadowed his eyes and concealed his hair at first, but as he got closer Elise saw that his black hair hung well past his shoulder blades.

Her heart sank. This wasn't her betrothed. He was probably just coming to gawk at her.

"Princess Elise von Hohenschwangau?"

His accent was dreadful, but it was still recognizably her name. She nodded.

"Welcome to Big Sky Country," he said. "My name is Daniel. I'm here to fetch you."

"I have swans," Elise said, stupidly. She pointed to the crate beneath her feet.

"Yes, ma'am," Daniel said.

Elise gathered up her satchel and went to the edge of the crate, but before she could jump down, Daniel grabbed her by the waist. He swung her down to the platform as though she weighed no more than a child. Elise stood, flustered, while he signaled to a porter.

She supposed that this Daniel was a servant, but what kind of servant? She did not understand how farms were arranged. He was not dressed like a butler or valet. He looked more like one of the gunfighters her old nurse had warned her about before she left.

Perhaps he was kidnapping her?

As long as he brought the crate of swans along, Elise found that she didn't much care. She was exhausted in body and mind. She was hot and hungry, and on top of all that, she still wasn't sure she had found the cure for her brothers' curse. She wasn't a witch like her stepmother, she was just a girl with a second-hand spell book, which she had read almost to pieces on the long journey.

But Elise was not one to swoon or have hysterics.

So she waited silently while her things were loaded in a large wagon. She followed the swans and made sure that they were placed just behind the seat so that its meager shade fell over the crate.

The two horses that pulled the wagon were large, dark gray beasts with feathery white hair around their enormous hooves. She paused for a moment to admire them. Their harness gleamed, and the wagon looked new.

"Yes, this is all your husband's," Daniel said.

Then he grabbed her around the waist again and lifted her up. She scrabbled with her high-heeled boots and finally made it over the side of the wagon to the seat. He didn't let go until she had steadied herself, which she appreciated, though she was hoping that he thought her blushes were from the heat.

"How is he?" Elise asked as the cart rumbled away from the station.

"What was that?" Daniel, sitting tall beside her with his brown hands holding the reins, cocked his head to the side. "You mean, what is he like?"

"Oh. Yes. That."

"He has a good house, a lot of land. It produces well."

"But he is . . . is he . . . such a nice man?" Elise repeated something the motherly woman on the train had said about the conductor.

"He is honest," Daniel said.

They drove on in silence. The sun beat down on Elise. She could feel it beginning to burn her nose. Her beribboned traveling bonnet didn't offer any shade, and she was slowly roasting beneath her layers of petticoats.

"My aunt Mary keeps house for Mr. Ludwig," Daniel said a little while later. "She'll help with . . . that." He pointed to her clothes with an elbow. "You'll need better shoes and different . . . things."

"I am a princess," Elise said.

"I know," Daniel said. "But I'm afraid you're a long way from your kingdom."

Three

They passed endless fields of wheat, barley, and corn. Here and there trees provided a windbreak, but right now there was no wind, only heat and sun and the endless fields.

Hours later the wagon turned down a long lane. Ahead some trees partially obscured a long, low house. Elise's heart began to pound.

Now beyond the house and trees she could see the barn and some smaller outbuildings. But it was the house that held her attention. It wasn't grand, but it was pleasant looking, with a sloping roof and a long porch running across the front and down one side and pink roses blooming against the porch rail.

As they rumbled up into the yard, the door opened, and Elise thought she might actually faint. But a woman came out, shaking a cloth. She froze when she saw them, then she tossed the cloth onto her shoulder and waited with her hands on her hips as Daniel stopped the wagon right at the foot of the porch steps.

The woman was tall with graying brown hair piled high on her head and a blue-sprig dress mostly covered in a large white pinafore. She was studying Elise just as frankly as Elise was studying her.

Elise moved to climb down from the wagon, and Daniel was suddenly right there. He lifted her down, setting her on her feet at the bottom of the steps.

"I'm Mary Gardner," the woman said, looking down at Elise.

"Elise von Hohenschwangau," Elise replied.

"That's quite a mouthful," Mary said.

"What do you want me to do with the swans?" Daniel asked Elise.

"Swans?" Mary asked.

Elise rubbed her forehead. It was so very hot.

"She brought swans," Daniel said, as if it were the most natural thing in the world.

"Live birds? All this way?" Mary came down the steps. She was very tall.

"Yes," Daniel said.

He climbed into the wagon while the women watched. He unloaded Elise's trunks before tackling the crate. At last he pulled a long knife out of a sheath beneath his jacket and began to pry up the nails.

"Pass auf!"

The swans exploded out of their confinement. All seven of them shot into the pale sky, scattering feathers across the yard.

"The pond is that way," Daniel shouted, gesturing to the back of the house with both arms. He chuckled as he shoved the empty crate out of the wagon.

"Why swans?" Mary asked as a feather drifted toward her.

"Why not?" Daniel said. "Kirsten Jorgenson brought

goats all the way from Sweden. We already have goats," he told Elise.

"Goats are useful," Mary said. Her eyes flickered over Elise's traveling ensemble.

Elise felt herself coloring. She was clearly not useful. Her clothes were impractical and covered in dust besides. And she hadn't brought chickens or pigs or even goats, but swans. She looked down at the pointed toes of her shoes, where they peeped out from the hem of her gown. They, too, were not useful. They had high heels and were made of very thin leather.

"I had to bring them," she whispered.

"Mr. Ludwig will be home soon," Mary said. "And you need a bath."

Elise's head drooped further.

"I have been traveling a long time," she whispered.

"Aunt Mary!" Daniel said sharply.

Mary's whole demeanor changed. Still much taller than Elise, she nevertheless stopped looming over her and put a hand on her arm.

"Of course you have," Mary said gently. "And, if memory serves, there are no baths on trains."

"No," Elise whispered.

She felt sticky from head to toe. She had for weeks. She had washed as best she could, but with the dirt and smoke and sweat of travel, it had seemed so futile. She had washed that morning in the tiny train washroom and changed into a clean gown, but she still felt dirty.

"I have a bath waiting," Mary said. "I'll just put some hot water in."

Elise blinked up at Mary. She wasn't smiling, but she didn't look quite as terrifying.

"Come along!" Mary led the way into the house.

Daniel followed behind with the first of Elise's trunks, but Elise only had eyes for the house. Her new home.

The front door opened directly into a spacious parlor, with plain but solid furniture and a large stone fireplace. They walked through the parlor into a short hallway with three doors.

"That's my room," Mary said, pointing to the left. "That's the kitchen." She pointed ahead of them. "And this is your room," she finished as she opened the door on the right.

There was a large four-poster bed and a tall dresser with a tiny looking glass perched atop it. A large square wardrobe, a pitcher and basin on a stand, a dressing screen, and a wooden rocking chair completed the room. The floor was covered in a heavy round rug of a type Elise had never seen before, like a flattened coil of rope. The quilt, too, was strange—a pattern of rings made of flowered calico fabric—and the bed had no curtains.

It was a handsome room, but it smelled like a man's room. Elise froze in the doorway as Mary strode ahead and folded back the screen to reveal a copper tub.

"I cannot," Elise said, suddenly immobile.

"What, of course you can," Mary said. "This is your room."

Elise shook her head. It was not her room, it was *his*.

The stranger she was going to marry. The stranger who slept in that bed and expected her to sleep in it with him now. Elise had been so caught up in getting her brothers here, in breaking their curse, that she hadn't allowed herself to think about anything beyond reaching the farm.

"You don't want the water too hot in this weather," Mary was saying. "The kettle on the back of the stove, that should be just about right."

She bustled out, pushing past Elise, who still stood in the

doorway. Daniel tapped her on the shoulder, and she moved aside, back into the hallway, so he could bring in her trunk. He set it on the floor with a grunt.

Mary bustled back in with a large kettle. Elise didn't move. Mary bustled back out, muttering about a towel. Daniel came in with her other trunk, setting it beside its fellow.

As he straightened, he saw Elise's face. She knew she was staring at the bath too intently. Part of her wanted to plunge right in; she longed to be clean! But maybe if she hadn't bathed when Mr. Ludwig arrived, he wouldn't want to marry her.

"Mr. Ludwig has moved his things to the barn," Daniel said.

"What?"

"And he asked me to stay," Mary said, coming back in with a towel and a pitcher of water.

"You do not live here?"

"No, I have my own place," she said. "My husband is dead, and my children are nearly grown and can do for themselves for a bit.

"I usually come two days a week, clean, bake the bread, and such. But I'll stay full-time until you've got yourself sorted."

"Oh."

"And now Daniel is leaving, and you are getting into that bath!"

Daniel left, and Elise got into the bath. Elise had a feeling that very few people argued with Aunt Mary. By the end of the bath Elise was calling her Aunt Mary out loud, not just in her thoughts.

While Elise bathed, the older woman unpacked the trunks. She hung the gowns and folded the stockings and underthings. Then she told Elise the bad news.

"Not one of these gowns is suitable for life here."

"Oh."

"The hats won't keep the sun off in the summer, or the snow in winter, and your shoes are meant for city streets, not a farm."

"My stepmother ordered my clothes," Elise said.

"I'm sure she did her best," Aunt Mary said. "She didn't know any better."

Elise shook her head. She couldn't keep her mouth from twisting into a sort of pained smirk. Mary looked startled.

"She did not want me to look poor," Elise said. "If I look poor, she looks poor."

"Oh, I'm sure—"

Elise shook her head even harder and took the undergarments that Aunt Mary was holding out. She went behind the screen to put them on.

"But you're a princess," Aunt Mary began.

"Of Hohenschwangau. Hohenschwangau is so small, it is not even on the map," Elise said. She laughed. "Unless that map was made in Hohenschwangau."

"Where *is* Hohenschwangau?"

"In a forest. By Bayern."

"Bayern?"

"Bavaria, I think you say?"

"Ah," Aunt Mary said.

"We are small. A forest. A lake. A village." Sudden tears pricked Elise's eyes. "A castle."

"We don't have any of those things," Aunt Mary said, handing a corset around the screen. "But we have plenty of land. Enough land to build new castles on, if people wanted. But first: this."

Elise stepped out to see Mary shaking the creases out of Elise's finest gown. It was pale blue silk with tiny seed pearls thickly sewn onto the bodice, the hem and sleeves dripping costly lace.

"That is my marriage gown," she explained.

"I know," Aunt Mary said. "Mr. Ludwig's gone to bring the preacher."

Elise felt like the floor was dropping out from beneath her feet.

"Daniel said Mr. Ludwig was living in the barn?"

"So he is," Aunt Mary said. "But the Homestead Act is a precarious thing, and—" She stopped, seeing Elise's confusion. "I'll let him explain."

Mary got Elise laced and hooked into the gown. It still had creases, but it had been carefully folded, so it wasn't too bad. Elise sat on a low stool while Mary did her hair, which was still wet. She parted it down the middle and braided it into two braids in the front, which she looped in front of Elise's ears and wrapped around a knot at the back of her head. Feeling numb, Elise opened the small jewel box. Aunt Mary put Elise's gold-and-pearl tiara in her hair while Elise slipped on her bracelet and earrings.

Aunt Mary made Elise stay on the stool while she brought a thick slice of fresh bread liberally spread with butter and strawberry preserves. Elise was very hungry, so she ate it, but it would have tasted much better if she hadn't felt like crying.

Men's voices came from the front of the house. Elise let her hands fall, scattering crumbs across her skirt. Mary tutted and brushed her clean, then she helped Elise up.

"No sense waiting here," she said, squeezing Elise's hands. "Let's introduce you to Mr. Ludwig."

Four

Mr. Ludwig was a big man, broad and solid-looking. He was tan from working outside, and he wore a black wool suit that must surely have been too hot in this weather, but he showed no discomfort as he met Elise's direct gaze without wavering. His eyes were as blue as her own, but his hair was white, shockingly white, and thick, combed back from a broad forehead.

"You're very young," he said.

Elise didn't say anything. What could she say? That he was very old? He appeared to be older than her father.

"I didn't know you kept swans," the preacher said. He was a pale, lanky man, with only a fringe of pale hair around his ears, despite his youth.

"Swans?" Mr. Ludwig stopped scrutinizing Elise and looked confused.

"Are they back?" Elise looked past Mr. Ludwig to Daniel, who had just come in.

"They're back," Daniel said. Then he saw her, and his eyes widened. "They're, um, in . . . in the pond."

Elise put her hands up and made sure that her braids and tiara hadn't slipped. "Thank you very much," she said. "You are too kind."

"I didn't . . . I didn't do anything."

"Why are there swans?" Mr. Ludwig asked.

"I brought the swans," Elise said.

Everyone looked at her. Elise did her best to stand straight. She was used to the scrutiny, but it was generally from peasants bowing to her, their princess. No one here was bowing, and they were all very tall.

"I brought the swans," she repeated.

Mr. Ludwig reached out and took her arm. "We should talk for a moment, before we marry."

The preacher looked sour. "Yes, you *should*."

Mr. Ludwig led Elise out through the kitchen, onto the long porch. Elise felt trapped despite the broad yard and open fields beyond. She heard flapping and splashing and turned to see her brothers playing in a large pond beside the barn. She smiled in relief.

"Why *swans*?" Mr. Ludwig asked in German.

"Our kingdom is known for our beautiful swans," Elise said.

Mr. Ludwig grunted.

"Your stepmother said you were pretty and in good health. She said you were a good girl."

"She should know," Elise said, and couldn't keep the bitterness at bay.

Her betrothed looked at her in surprise. His eyes lingered on the tiara.

"These are all the jewels I own," she said. "We are not a wealthy kingdom."

"But you do have swans."

Elise shot him a glance, thinking he mocked her. A smile twitched the corners of his mouth, but it was a good-humored smile.

"We do have swans," she agreed, smiling herself.

"And you are a princess?" Mr. Ludwig looked her over from tiara to kid slippers.

"Yes?"

Elise was confused as to why this mattered. There were no kings or queens in this new country. She was holding out hope that it meant there were no witches, either.

"I am a count, but I had nothing in the old country," Mr. Ludwig said. "My king wanted my estate for a hunting lodge, and he took it.

"I came to this new world to see what I could carve from its rock. Make myself a new estate, a new earldom." He made a gripping motion, his face fierce. "The land is free, but you have to tame it: fences built, stumps pulled, furrows plowed, seeds planted. It is isn't easy, but I am not afraid of work."

Elise didn't know what to say.

"But there are no women here, not women like you." He looked again at her jewels and silk gown.

Now Elise understood.

"You need a countess," she said.

"You even brought swans."

"I did."

He took her hand. His was calloused and powerful, completely enveloping her small, soft one.

"Princess Elise, will you marry me?"

"Count Ludwig, I will."

They went inside where Mary, Daniel, and the preacher were waiting.

Five

Daniel and Mary's doubts about Elise's clothing made her worry that she would be working in the fields alongside her husband, but that fear was soon lain to rest. Not that she was afraid of hard work, but she had never done farm labor before.

However, Ludwig had a handful of farm laborers working the fields, and he did not even like her to gather eggs or milk the two cows.

"You are a princess," he had said severely the first time she stepped inside the barn.

"Aunt Mary will return to her own home soon," Elise protested.

"I will hire a girl," Ludwig said.

Elise asked Aunt Mary to teach her to milk, churn, and bake all the same. Mary showed her all the intricacies of the big nickel-plated stove in the kitchen. She taught Elise to pluck and roast a chicken and to bake bread and biscuits. Daniel laughed when he saw Elise with a flour-sack apron over her silk gown, but she was too proud of the loaves she had made to care.

And Mr. Ludwig continued to live in the barn.

Elise didn't mind. And when at last she served a meal that was good enough that Mr. Ludwig complimented Mary, and Mary revealed that it had all been Elise, Elise had beamed around the table, heart bursting with pride.

"I'll be heading home tomorrow morning then," Mary said.

Elise felt the smile drop from her face.

"Thank you for staying so long," Mr. Ludwig said. "I'd like to hire a young girl to live in. Who do you think?"

"The Sullivans have a number of likely daughters," Mary commented.

Neither of them noticed that Elise sat frozen, fork halfway to her mouth. If Aunt Mary left, would Mr. Ludwig move into the house? Into the bedroom?

Elise knew that it was only a matter of time before her husband asked to share her bed, and she was getting used to the idea. But even more worrying: nighttime was the only time she had the privacy to study her book of spells. If she didn't study her magic, how would she turn her brothers back into men?

She got to her feet, mumbling about taking Daniel his supper. Mr. Ludwig spoke with great respect of Daniel's hard work, but he wouldn't let him eat in the house for the same reason that Daniel was not allowed to farm land of his own: his father had been Aunt Mary's brother, a respected lawyer from Boston.

His mother, however, was a Crow.

When Elise had first heard this, her heart had leaped. If Daniel's mother had been transformed into a crow, then he must surely know about magic! Perhaps he could help her transform her brothers.

But then she had learned that Crow was the name of a tribe of native peoples, and judging from the looks on both Daniel's and Mary's faces when she dared to ask about it, people turning into birds was not something they were familiar with.

Daniel couldn't help Elise. No one could. So she spent her days learning to cook and her nights learning to conjure. But if Mr. Ludwig moved into the house? What then?

Daniel was sitting on the back porch, staring at the sky. He took the plate and set it on the porch rail, pointing to the horizon.

"Storm coming," he said.

Despite the heat, there were dark clouds boiling on the horizon.

"Tell Mr. Ludwig I'll secure the animals after I eat."

"Have you seen a plant?" Elise blurted out.

Daniel raised one eyebrow.

"A . . . it has . . . it is sharp?" she finished lamely.

Speaking English was still difficult, though she understood most of what was said to her. But her magic book was in German, and her primer did not have most of the words it contained.

Apparently students of English didn't commonly need the words to magic spells.

Elise held up a finger and then ducked back into the house to retrieve her magic book from its hiding place. She could hear Aunt Mary and Mr. Ludwig in the kitchen, talking about a new breed of milk cow. It occurred to her that Mary would have made him a better wife, but Mr. Ludwig had wanted a princess. Elise was still shaking her head over this folly when she rejoined Daniel.

There was a ribbon marking the spell she hoped would work. She wrapped the ribbon around a finger while she pointed to a faded ink drawing of a plant. It was the only ingredient she would need for this spell.

"*Brennessel*?" She looked at Daniel.

"This looks like what we call stinging nettle," he said. He frowned. "Why would you want it?"

He tried to read the opposite page of the book, but it was handwritten in German. He put his finger into the book to save her place as he flipped through, looking at the worn corners, the stains that marred several pages, the spidery handwriting, and the pictures of herbs and flowers, trees, and birds.

"What is this? Recipes?"

Elise paused and then nodded. Daniel looked at her as though he knew that she was not telling him the whole truth.

"You can't eat stinging nettles," he said. "I've heard of nettle tea, but these aren't the same."

"I won't drink them," she assured him.

"Then why do you want them?" He squinted at the page again. "What kind of recipe is this?"

"It is the beauty . . . it is for the face," Elise said, tapping her cheek.

Daniel stared at her for a minute.

"Past the south field," he said finally. "They've been cleared off the land, of course. But some still grow among the trees down along the creek."

"Many thanks," Elise said.

"You should go tomorrow night," he said. He pointed to a small circle in the corner of the picture. "That's a full moon, isn't it?"

Elise frowned at the page. She flicked to an earlier spell, and then another. Many had a little circle in the corner, but sometimes a sliver of it was shaded in. It was showing the proper phase of the moon for working the spell. She flushed.

All this time studying the book, and someone who couldn't even read German had seen it in a moment!

"My mother deals in herbs and remedies," he said, as though sensing her embarrassment. "Many herbs or plants are harvested at certain times to preserve their potency."

"Oh."

She hadn't quite gotten all the words he had said, but she had gotten enough. She wondered if his mother could help her after all, but didn't dare to ask. If Daniel's mother knew herbs, she would surely know that *brennessel* wasn't used for any sort of beauty treatment.

And then what? Should Elise explain? In the best case they would think she was mad for believing that her pet swans were really her brothers. In the worst case they would assume that she was the witch who had transformed them, and hang her or burn her—whatever they did to witches in this country.

In Hohenschwangau they were burned, Elise's stepmother had told her. This was just after Elise had discovered her stepmother's secret and had met with her brothers in the woods. They had been able to take their human forms briefly, to beg her for help.

"What luck that *I* am not a witch," the queen had said, holding Elise's hand far too tightly, until the nine-year-old had cried out. "Your dear father, the king, my loving husband, is so devoted to me that no doubt my death would cause him to go mad!" And then she had laughed her sparkling laugh, the laugh that Elise's father said was the first thing he had loved about her.

Despite her age, Elise had understood the threat. Her

brothers had displeased the queen simply by being male, and so they had been disposed of. Elise couldn't inherit the throne of their tiny kingdom, but she could tattle to the servants, or worse, the village priest. Elise was not at all confident that the priest, good man though he was, would be able to capture the queen, try her, burn her, and restore Elise's father's will and her brothers' humanity.

And so Elise had bowed her head and remained silent.

Six

The storm came in the night and raged all the next day. Elise wondered if it would stop in time for her to gather the nettles. It didn't matter if it was overcast: she knew the moon was full. But if the storm were too severe for her to venture out, she would have to wait another month. And although her brothers had waited years to be freed, a voice inside told her to hurry, hurry, that she must begin.

She and Aunt Mary made sure the windows and doors were fast, and Mary showed her how to roll up towels and place them against the bottoms of the doors to prevent rain from coming in.

A few hours in, Daniel knocked on the kitchen door, but before they could get it opened he shouted to Mary that he was going to her farm.

"Well, that's both a worry and a relief," she said, turning away from the door.

"How will he go to there?" Elise asked.

"That's the worry," Mary said grimly. "But if he makes it, that's the relief."

"I am sorry that you have to be here," Elise said.

"I agreed to come," Mary said. "And my boys are old enough to do for themselves. For a little while, anyway."

She looked toward one of the windows. They could still hear the wind, which seemed like it would never stop.

"Well," Mary said briskly, "let's do something about these peaches."

They spent the sleepless, stormy night making a pie with a filling of late summer peaches. There was enough crust left for a chicken-and-mushroom pie that Mary said would make a fine dinner.

"Dinner?" Elise asked. "Why are we thinking about—Oh!"

"Morning already," Mary said. "Might as well plan ahead."

She pointed to the kitchen window, which showed a view that was marginally lighter than before. As Elise watched she saw something flapping across the yard.

When it got to the porch, she realized that it was her husband.

Mr. Ludwig came in through the kitchen door, pushing aside the rolled towel with his foot and dripping water from an oilcloth cape. His boots were thick with mud, and under the cape he was soaked through.

Mary hurried to take his cape and hat, while he fell into one of the chairs.

"You look worn out," she fretted.

Elise got him a towel. She went to the stove to make tea and warm some of the broth they had made for the chicken pie.

"I'll toast some of yesterday's bread," Mary began.

"I'm too tired to eat," Mr. Ludwig said.

"You need to warm up," Elise said firmly, in German. "Drink this."

As she handed him the mug of broth, he took hold of her wrist and looked at her hand. She had a red burn from the oven on the side of her palm and a small nick in her thumb where she had chopped carrots with rather too much enthusiasm. He frowned.

"You shouldn't be working," he said.

"Do you want tea or not?" Elise snapped.

Mary and Mr. Ludwig gave her startled looks. She apologized, but not sincerely. Mr. Ludwig was shaking with chills now, his skin grayish.

Despite her reluctance to share a bedroom with him, Elise was fond of Mr. Ludwig. He was kind, and she respected the hard work that he did every day at the farm. Elise wasn't very good around sick people—all she could do was offer tea.

"You'd better get out of those wet things," Mary said.

"I ought to go back out," Mr. Ludwig fretted. "The wind pulled down some shingles. I rigged some canvas underneath, but the animals are restless, and—" He sagged, dozing.

"My swans!" Elise yelled, then clapped a hand over her mouth.

"What?" Mr. Ludwig jolted awake. "No, Daniel brought them in first thing," he said muzzily. "Awful creatures. Biting and hissing."

He stood suddenly and staggered. Mary and Elise both rushed to catch him, but he shook them off.

"I should lie down," he mumbled.

"This way," Elise said.

Without hesitation she led him to the bedroom—her bedroom, his bedroom. She helped him take off his boots, but after that he waved her away and fell back on the bed.

"Undress myself," he slurred.

Elise carried his boots back to the kitchen and exchanged worried looks with Aunt Mary, who was preparing a tray with tea and toast. Elise grabbed the warming pan and scooped some coals into it.

She carried it to the bedroom, but Mr. Ludwig was still sprawled atop the coverlet. His limbs stirred and twitched as though he were swimming in his sleep. Elise got a spare quilt and tucked it around him. As she did, she noticed that his face was still grayish, his lips tinged with blue.

Suddenly he grabbed her wrist.

"*Es tut mir leid*," he rasped. "*Ich hab' mein besten getan.*"

"*Das weiss ich doch*," she said. "*Schlaf!*"

She went back to the kitchen with the warming pan and a frown.

"He is not well," she told Mary as she emptied out the coals. "He just told me he was sorry, that he did his best." She shook her head. "I said I knew, and he should sleep."

The other woman nodded. When the weather began to clear, Mary said they should check on the animals.

Inside the barn, her brothers greeted her with hisses, their fierce beaks stabbing at the door of the stall they were locked in. She looked them over, but they seemed fine, so she shushed them and moved on.

She checked on the two cows. One of them needed milking, but the other had a calf. She made sure that they had hay and stroked the calf's broad forehead.

The great cart horses were a matched pair named Stark and Stern. The only difference between them was the white star on Stern's forehead, hence his name. There was a pretty little chestnut mare, as well, named Schatzi. She searched Elise for sugar, and finding none, retreated to the corner of her stall to sulk. Elise brought them all water and oats.

There was a wet stain down the back wall, and Elise could see how the high stacks of hay had been shifted and covered with tarps. The hole was patched with oilcloth. She was sure that Daniel had done his best to help, but it was more than enough work for two men, and Daniel had left partway through.

She checked that the patch was holding and closed the barn up tight. The rain had finally stopped, but it was chilly, and the sunlight was weak and watery still. The yard was a mire, but she slogged her way over to the pig shed, where the sow seemed happy enough with the situation, and past her to the coop, where the chickens were not. She managed to get some eggs from them nevertheless.

"How is it?" Mary asked as soon as she came in. She was looking out the windows and pacing.

"Fine," Elise said. She put the eggs in a bowl.

"Good, good."

Mary paced to the front of the house and peered out.

"Go, go," Elise said, shaking her skirt at the older woman. "Take Schatzi!"

"Oh, I couldn't possibly," Mary said. "When Daniel comes back I might slip away, but . . ."

But she already had her apron off. Elise tiptoed into the bedroom where Mr. Ludwig still slept, restless. She opened the wardrobe and pulled out a beautiful shawl of deep blue cashmere. She tiptoed back out and handed it to Mary.

"Oh, child, I couldn't—"

Elise tossed it around Mary's shoulders. To her surprise she felt tears well in her eyes.

"I'll be back," Aunt Mary said. She wrapped the shawl around her shoulders and tied it behind her. "Don't you fret." She kissed Elise's cheek.

Seven

Elise didn't fret. She got ready.

She baked bread. She gathered up the towels blocking the doorways, pleased to see they were dry. She put them away before checking the animals again. It was still too muddy to let them out, which her brothers didn't like, but she didn't care what they did or didn't like.

Tonight was the full moon. If her brothers were to be her brothers again, and not just a flock of hissing, biting swans, she would have to begin tonight. She put on her plainest gown, taking her things into Mary's room to change, though Mr. Ludwig didn't seem to notice her comings and goings.

The watery sun was fading, and Elise began to worry. Mary was still gone, and Elise also did not dare leave Mr. Ludwig. He had slept all day, and had not eaten since dinner the night before.

She was listening for changes in Mr. Ludwig's labored breathing when someone knocked. She was halfway to the front door when she realized it had come from the kitchen. Elise raced to the kitchen, a greeting on her lips for Mary. She pulled the door open and froze. A girl a few years younger than Elise stood there, wearing a nubby gray shawl over her calico dress, her straw bonnet much the worse for the rain. Two long red braids straggled out from under the bonnet.

"Er," Elise said.

"Hello there, Mrs. Ludwig," the girl said. She tilted her head up, revealing a very freckled face and very white teeth.

She pushed past Elise and threw her shawl on the back of a kitchen chair.

"Glory be, I'm wetter than a mad cat," she announced, as she began to untie her bonnet.

"Who are you?"

"I'm the new help," the girl said.

"This is Mary Katherine Sullivan," Daniel said, coming in through the still-open door. "But—"

"Everyone calls me Kitty," the girl finished. "And you can, too, Mrs. Ludwig."

"Elise."

"Mrs. Elise," the girl amended.

"Aunt Mary had me bring her," Daniel said. "Their cellar flooded, she isn't sure when she'll be able to get away."

"I could use the money, that's for sure!" Kitty said.

"You'd better go," Daniel said.

"I've only just got here!" Kitty protested.

"No, not you," Daniel said. "Your mistress."

"I will show Kitty around and help her keep an eye on Mr. Ludwig," he went on, as Kitty gaped. "But you have work to do."

He stood aside so that Elise could go. She grabbed the bag

she had prepared and left. She had no hat or shawl, as Kitty loudly observed, but she didn't care.

"Kitty's horse is still saddled," Daniel called after her.

Elise changed direction and went to the barn. Daniel's Minnow had her saddle off, but there was a shaggy chestnut mare tied to a ring in the center aisle of the barn, looking longingly at Minnow's dinner.

Elise scooped some oats into her bag and mounted the red horse, trusting that Daniel would see to the animals and lock up after.

It was dark, despite the full moon, and the wind was starting to blow. The shaggy horse was a sturdy beast, however, and doggedly went where she told it. The horse was the one who found the nettles, and stopped short, refusing to walk through them. It wasn't until Elise tried to turn the horse and felt her skirt snag on something that she understood what had happened.

"You're a good girl," she said as she dismounted.

She tied the mare to a tree and dumped out the oats. Elise had thought about bringing the book, but she knew there was no point. She knew what she had to do.

It was just that there was no going back, once she started.

She stretched her neck and arms, paced in a circle, and called the mare a good girl a few more times. It felt like there should be something more, an incantation or ritual, but there was nothing—just the gathering of the nettles.

And the beginning of the silence.

In order to turn her brothers back into men, she would have to pick nettles and weave them into cloth, shape the cloth into shirts, and put one on each of them. And from the moment she picked the first nettle until the moment she put the last shirt on the seventh swan, she could not speak a word. Not in German, not in English, not a word.

Elise looked around. She had nothing profound to say and no one to say it to but the horse. She grabbed the first nettle.

It hurt. It hurt like a thousand sharp sewing needles stabbing her fingers. She gasped but managed to bite back a curse word.

Tossing that nettle down, she went on to the next, using more care. But if she pulled too lightly, the nettle broke off at the top, which was useless. Gritting her teeth, she got down on her knees and began to pull them up by the roots.

The spell didn't say how many she would need for one shirt, let alone seven. It also didn't say how one went about weaving nettles into shirts. She supposed that they didn't have to be very fancy.

But the patch wasn't very big, and she needed to gather them all at once. So she kept pulling and pulling. The pain went from nearly unbearable to where she could no longer feel it; it was just too much.

It began to rain, and the wind still blew, slashing at her face and soaking her through. She was soon slipping in the mud as she gathered more and more nettles. The pile tumbled over and started to slide down the bank toward the nearby creek. She grabbed at it and screamed, wordlessly, as the pain broke through again.

When she had them secured she looked up and saw a woman standing across the creek. Water streamed down her black hair and the heavy wool blanket she wore. Elise sat on her heels, her mouth open.

Was it the pain making her see such things? Or was it a ghost?

"Don't speak," the woman called to her. "But tell me: how many?"

Elise gaped for a moment more, and as a flash of lightning lit the sky, she saw the woman's resemblance to Daniel. Elise held up seven fingers.

"You have enough," the woman said. "You need to go home now."

Elise looked at her handiwork. She had pulled almost every nettle. And how was she to get them home? The flour sack she had brought seemed woefully inadequate, but she didn't dare leave any of them behind.

"That skirt is ruined," the woman called across the ditch.

Elise saw that she was right. She had ground mud into the skirt of her dress as she knelt and crawled through the nettles. It was torn in several places, making it easy for her to rip it free of the bodice and step out of it.

She spread out her skirt as best she could and piled the nettles on it. Then she tied the whole thing into a big bundle, using hairpins to hold the edges together. Across the ditch, Daniel's mother watched as Elise awkwardly mounted with the shifting, bulging bundle under one arm. It immediately fell to the ground, and one side came unpinned.

Under the scrutiny of the Crow woman, Elise bundled the nettles again, her hands throbbing and shaking. Clutching the bundle to her chest, feeling the sharp, hair-like thorns through the fabric, scratching her arm and neck, she managed to get on the horse again. She pinched the bundle together with her elbows and picked up the reins.

The horse, though she was good enough not to buck or rear, did not like what was happening. For several minutes she wouldn't move, but then another crack of lightning came far too close to them, and the mare bolted into action.

Somehow, through the wind and rain and darkness, they got back to the farm. At first Elise wasn't sure if it was the right farm. All the lamps were lit, and there was an unfamiliar carriage out front, the horses still hitched to it.

Elise had planned to go straight to the barn to hide her nettles there. Elise had planned to pretend the rain had given her a sore throat, and that was why she couldn't talk.

But in the end none of it mattered.

When Elise reached the barnyard, Kitty ran out to meet her. The girl grabbed hold of the reins, her face white between her freckles. She opened her mouth, but like Elise she was mute. It was Daniel, coming out of the barn, who told Elise that she was a widow.

Eight

The next few days passed in a dream. Even had she not been forbidden by the spell to talk, Elise could not have uttered a word. She couldn't cry, either, but only sit in shock. She hadn't known Mr. Ludwig long enough to mourn him, but his death turned the world on its head—a new world, a new life, that she had only just begun.

It was Kitty who became Elise's greatest support. Kitty, whose only moment of silence had come when she could not find a way to tell her new mistress that her husband had died, soon found her voice again.

And as she talked, she worked. She cared for Elise as tenderly as she might have her own sisters: helping her wash and dress and doing her hair, even as she kept up a flow of compliments for Elise's thick hair and her beautiful gowns.

It was Kitty who stitched a black armband onto Elise's midnight-blue velvet gown for the funeral. It was Kitty who took charge of the food the neighbors brought and spread it out on a damask cloth for the funeral lunch.

When Mary arrived, one look at that poor woman's reddened eyes and down-turned mouth, and Elise knew. Mr. Ludwig shouldn't have sent for a princess. Elise held out one hand to Mary, who took it. Kitty brought the older woman a chair, and Elise and Mary sat together by the coffin, silently holding hands.

Daniel drove them to the church. Mary's children came in their wagon, bringing Kitty with them. Elise sat in the front pew of a church so new that it still smelled of raw boards, with Kitty on one side of her and Mary on the other.

Dr. Goode, the preacher who had so recently married Elise, now eulogized her dead husband. Elise didn't bother to try and understand his endless words. Under her veil she let her eyes wander; the church was full of strangers. Some of them wept openly for Mr. Ludwig, which gave her a pang of guilt.

She couldn't find Daniel and felt a moment of panic. By pretending to ease her back she managed to turn enough to see him sitting in the back pew. He wasn't paying attention to the preacher, either, but looking straight at her. When he saw her veil turned toward him, he gave a slight nod.

Then it was back to the house, where Kitty served both Elise and Mary, who again sat side by side. Kitty brought them plates loaded with the best tidbits, but neither of them had an appetite. They picked at things while Kitty fussed.

When the guests had gone, Mary hesitated. Her oldest son had already taken the others home, but Mary stayed until it was just Elise, Kitty, and Daniel. Although Mary had not shed a tear all day, Elise could see that the woman's grief was still very close to the surface. She knew that Mary would stay if she asked. But instead she silently embraced the older woman and gave her a gentle push toward Daniel.

"I'll stay with the poor little lady," Kitty assured them as they left.

So Mary left, and Kitty stayed. She led Elise to the large bedroom, and when Elise hesitated in the doorway, she told her how she had changed the linens and blankets, turned the mattress, and scrubbed the floor and furnishings.

"Even though it was his heart that gave out," she said. "No harm in giving things a good scrub."

Elise squeezed the girl's elbow in thanks and went in. She undressed and washed and turned down the bed. Then, when she was sure that Kitty was asleep in her own room, Elise pulled on her boots and went out to the barn.

Daniel was waiting there.

"I took care of the animals," he said. "Thought I'd sleep in the loft. I'll stay . . . as long as you need me."

She nodded.

He pointed to a stack of hay bales. "I hid the nettles when the guests came. The mourners."

She was standing beside her brothers' stall. Huddled together in sleep they looked even more like ordinary birds. They didn't seem unhappy. She flexed her sore hands, hidden by kidskin gloves. Kitty had said she would make an ointment for them, but Elise suspected it would only get worse.

Would her brothers care? Would they rather be swans?

When she had discovered it in her spell book, sitting in her tiny cabin on the ship, she had cried with relief. There was a way to break the curse, and fix her brothers! But Elise was no witch, and for all she knew, the book itself was a fraud.

There was nothing else to do but try, she decided.

Elise pulled the hidden bundle free. Her skirt was ruined, and the nettles were wilted and had an unpleasant odor. She looked at the swans again.

"You can do this," Daniel said.

She looked at him sharply. How much did he know?

"You can do this," he said again.

She tried to feel as confident as he did as she carried the bundle to the house. Back in her room, she lit the lamps and spread out the mess.

How do I make a shirt out of this? She wondered again. There were no instructions in the book—only that the shirts must be made in silence. And she only had one year from the day she picked the first nettle to the day she put the shirts on her brothers, all of them at once.

Sighing heavily, she folded her legs tailor style and leaned her elbows on her knees. Her reddened fingers gingerly plucked up one nettle, then another. She laid them out in ranks. She didn't know how to make a shirt out of them, but she knew how to make a cloth of sorts, she supposed. Her old nurse had showed her how to make mats out of rushes, and she thought this might work along the same lines.

She laid out a row of nettles, trying her best not to do further damage to her hands. But it was futile. She had to weave in the crosspieces, and as she did so she felt the tiny thorns going deep into her already-raw flesh. Tears dripped down her face as she did her best to weave the dreadful nettles.

When she was drooping over her work and her eyes felt as red and raw as her hands, she stopped. Not knowing what else to do, she scooted everything under the tall bed, taking great care with the placement of her fragile mat of nettles—so miserably small after such a long night's work!

She fell into the bed and went to sleep at once, where she had nightmares of the nettles wrapping around her, pulling her down to drown in a pit filled with swan feathers. When Kitty shook her awake, Elise felt as though she had barely slept. Judging from Kitty's expression, Elise looked it.

"I'm that sorry to wake you, ma'am," Kitty said. "But there's a man here to buy the farm."

Elise almost blurted out, *What?* She stopped herself just in time.

"Here you've just yesterday been burying your husband, and he wants to see you at the crack of dawn! It's unnatural," Kitty went on.

It was not exactly the crack of dawn, as Elise found when Kitty threw open the curtains and let in the bright sunlight. She winced, and then winced again when she tried to push back the blankets.

"Oh, ma'am," Kitty said when she saw Elise's hands. "They look even worse than before!"

Elise just took up her dressing gown and put it on. It had long, ruffled sleeves that hid most of her hands anyway.

Wishing that she could fetch Daniel first, Elise shook back her unraveling braid and marched into the parlor. Her slippers were so quiet that the man didn't notice her for a minute or two, which allowed her to observe how he looked at every stick of furniture and knickknack and clearly afforded them a price.

When his gaze fell on her, he started. She smiled.

"Ma'am," he said, then he gave a little cough and took off his hat.

He wore a fine gray suit and was tall and slender, with a proud, handsome face and dark brown hair just beginning to gray at the temples. She thought he had been at the funeral yesterday but wasn't entirely sure.

"I know you've suffered terribly."

Elise let the smile seep off her face.

"And I know that now you're all alone here."

Kitty appeared at Elise's elbow, but the man went on talking as though she weren't there.

"My name is James Sylvester. I'm your neighbor to the north. I have one of the largest farms around here. I hadn't been looking to expand—"

He stopped as Kitty snorted softly but then continued, still without looking at her.

"I can't stop thinking about your plight. Newly immigrated, newly widowed, and with this big parcel of land to work alone." He shook his head. "I've known Ludwig since he came here, and I would be ashamed of myself if I didn't repay his many kindnesses by helping his widow in her time of need."

He smiled and held out his hand for Elise to shake. She put her damaged hands into her pockets. What did he imagine they were shaking on? She knew from things Mr. Ludwig had said that a handshake could represent a contract here, where paper was scarce and many were illiterate.

She frowned at Sylvester.

"Does she speak English?" he asked, turning to Kitty for the first time.

"Yes," Kitty said. "But she's had a shock, and she's been real quiet since."

"Maybe she's not sure how much 'help' is, in cash," Daniel said from the doorway.

Sylvester whipped around. "So you're still hanging around?"

"I'm the overseer."

"Since when?"

"Since Mr. Ludwig hired me to be the overseer," Daniel said.

"And now he's dead," Sylvester said.

"Which makes it even more important for me to stay," Daniel said.

Sylvester turned back to Elise. "Sell the farm and go home, back to your family. You don't want to stay here, trying to keep an eye on this half-breed. You want to live in comfort!" He smiled at her.

Elise turned her back on him.

"My mistress is exhausted," Kitty announced. "Thank you for coming, all the same." She shepherded the gaping Sylvester out the door.

Elise walked into the kitchen and slumped into a chair. She was tired, but she would never get back to sleep now. And there was much to do, besides.

She was, after all, now mistress of a large farm.

Kitty began making breakfast while Daniel sat down across from Elise. He looked at her.

"Did Mr. Ludwig really hire you full-time?" Kitty asked as she gave them each a bowl of porridge and made one for herself. She put butter and brown sugar on the table.

"He spoke of it," Daniel said.

"So you'll stay on?"

Daniel put sugar and butter on his porridge. "It depends."

"On?" Kitty prompted.

"On whether M—Elise—wants to stay, or whether she does want to go home."

Elise looked up from her own porridge and saw that both of them were waiting on her. She could take her swans and go, she realized. But where? Back to Hohenschwangau and their stepmother? Elise couldn't do that. She had no home.

Daniel seemed to understand.

"You want me to stay on as overseer? You want to stay here at the farm?"

She nodded.

"Do you want me to stay and take care of the house?" Kitty asked.

Elise nodded again. She held out her reddened, sore hand. Daniel took it gently in his warm, calloused one, and they shook on it. Elise turned to Kitty, but Kitty drew back.

"Don't touch me! I don't want to catch that rash! I'll stay, just . . . don't touch me!"

Nine

Kitty stayed on, and so did Daniel. He made himself a room in the stall next to the swans. He brought in men, and they began the harvest.

Elise and Kitty sewed a black gown for Elise to wear to church. Kitty consulted with her mother, with Mary, and even with Daniel's mother about salves and ointments for Elise's hands. She was baffled that nothing seemed to help. Elise took over the baking, since kneading dough and shaping loaves or rolling out crusts felt soothing, while Kitty had to do the chopping and the fine sewing.

None of Kitty's never-ending words were about Elise's silence. After a few days, Elise noticed that Kitty chose her questions carefully, never asking anything that required more than a nod or a headshake in answer. She wondered if Daniel had told Kitty why she couldn't talk, and felt a flush of anger. She didn't want them gossiping about her.

But when Mary stopped by a few weeks later, Elise heard her asking Kitty if she had started speaking yet.

"I've never heard of a widow grieving like this," Mary whispered as Elise listened from just outside the kitchen door. "And she only knew poor Ludwig a week."

"I don't know that it's grief," Kitty said. "I think she doesn't *want* to talk."

"But why?"

"I don't know," Kitty said. "But I'm not going to question it. I've never had such a good audience!" She laughed, and Elise took the opportunity to come in with the eggs she had gathered.

"Elise, dear," Aunt Mary said, with a worried line between her brows. "Are you embarrassed by your accent?"

Elise shrugged and shook her head. She put the eggs away and sliced some cake for Mary, who gasped in horror when Elise handed her a plate. She nearly made Elise drop the cake, grasping her wrist in her own strong, calloused hands.

"What have you done to yourself? Is it poison ivy?"

"I can't figure it out," Kitty said. "This is why I asked you for that salve recipe. I've tried everything!"

They chattered away about tonics and creams while Elise calmly ate her own piece of cake. She was used to getting only a few hours of sleep a night, and she was getting better at weaving the nettles. She was accustomed to nodding and shaking her head, raising her eyebrows or shrugging, and never opened her mouth to answer by accident anymore.

The only thing that truly bothered her was her hands. They hurt abominably. It never went away. No matter how wilted they became, the nettles continued to sting. It was fresh pain every night and swelling and throbbing all the next day.

And the next day. And the next.

Aunt Mary brought homemade remedies and patent medicines. She stopped trying to get Elise to talk and knitted her a warm shawl instead.

When Kitty and Elise ventured to town to buy Elise sturdy boots and a warm wool coat for winter, they overheard some men marveling at how well "that half-breed" had done in bringing her crops. Elise bought apples to make Daniel a pie as thanks.

Winter came, more horrible than Elise had thought it would be. The snow was so deep that it was piled to her shoulders on each side of the path Daniel dug to the barn. The swans hated the cold and snow and the ice on their pond. They huddled in their stall and bit anyone who came near. The other animals seemed used to it and went on as usual.

For Christmas, Elise bought three pairs of skates and taught Kitty and Daniel to skate on the pond Christmas morning. Kitty gave Elise a wonderfully warm flannel petticoat that she had sewn herself, and Aunt Mary gave her mittens and a matching scarf.

Aunt Mary's gifts were black, since Elise had so little mourning to wear, but they were beautifully made, and Elise never minded wearing black. Kitty opined that it drained the color from her cheeks, but that was the least of Elise's worries. Besides, she wasn't out to catch a new man.

Elise and Daniel took a final spin around the ice while Kitty put up her hair for Christmas dinner. They crossed hands to glide across the ice. He and Kitty had been laughing and falling all over, but now he moved smoothly around the pond with Elise's black-mittened hands held fast in his leather-gloved ones. When Kitty called that she was ready to leave, Daniel twirled Elise around, finishing with a bow.

"Were you dancing?" Kitty asked as Daniel hitched the big horses to the sleigh. "It looked so fancy!"

Elise just smiled. She smiled all the way to Mary's, despite the cold.

Mary had invited the entire neighborhood, and the entire

neighborhood had come. Elise added gingerbread and *spaetzle* with rich gravy to the heavy-laden table; other neighbors brought homemade pies and cheeses, sausages and roasted chickens. Mary's daughter Sarah banged out Christmas carols on the piano while everyone strolled around, balancing full plates and mugs of hot cider.

After they had eaten, Daniel tapped Elise on the shoulder. She managed to smile and nod and back away from an elderly neighbor who took her silence for an invitation to describe her kidney problems in glorious detail.

Elise followed Daniel out to the back porch. The night was cold, but the sky was so clear and beautiful. The reflection of the moon on the snow made the world seem bright and full of magic.

She hugged her new shawl around herself and stared out at the landscape. When she had first arrived, she had thought that the land was so parched and ugly, but there was a different kind of beauty to it in every season.

"This is for you," Daniel said.

He held out a small package wrapped in brown paper. Elise took it in hands that shook, and not because of the nettles. She folded back the paper to reveal a small swan carved out of wood. It was delicately detailed, unpainted except for its black eyes.

"Maybe you don't actually like swans," he said. "But I found this knot of wood that looked like it was meant to be a swan."

She let the paper fall away as she held it up to the moonlight. It was perfect. She smiled at Daniel. His lips parted like he was about to speak.

"Am I interrupting something?"

Elise clutched the swan so tightly that its beak jabbed one of her swollen fingers, and she gasped. A distant look came over Daniel's face, as though he had been turned to wood as well. Elise turned to see Mr. Sylvester watching them.

"Dear lady," he said, holding out a hand. "Merry Christmas to you."

She nodded.

"It must be so lonely for you," he said. "In a strange land, without your family, at this time of year."

She shrugged.

"I wondered if you had time to consider my offer? It would be a great blow to me, financially, but as a friend of your *late husband's*—" He looked pointedly at Daniel. "Well, I consider it a duty to see you safely back in the bosom of your family."

Elise was already shaking her head, and she kept shaking it. She could not imagine anything more horrifying than being back in the bosom of her family: her stepmother with her cruelty and her curses, her father, his eyes glazed with sorcery. And if she returned to Hohenschwangau, she would never see Kitty again, or Mary.

Or Daniel.

Sylvester sighed. "What a shame," he said. "What a terrible shame."

Ten

The winter was not as pretty when it dragged on after Christmas. Elise began to hope for spring when the snow melted at last, but the drab, brown grass and mud was hardly the change she had wanted. The wind never seemed to stop howling, and the weather was still freezing, despite the melting snow and overflowing pond.

She had finished half the shirts, however. By dint of much experimentation, she had figured out how to fold the mats and knot the edges to make a rough shirt that held together as well as could be expected. To prevent Kitty from finding them, Elise had hidden the completed shirts in the barn.

The swans were a lot happier now that their pond wasn't frozen. They honked and chased one another through the farmyard, splashing in the water and sliding in the mud. Kitty thought they were hilarious until one of them slid into her and made her fall flat on her back.

She managed to save the basket of laundry she was

holding, but her hair and dress were coated in muck. Elise and Daniel laughed until they cried, especially when one of the swans tried to help her up by biting her apron and backing away, wings flapping. Kitty, who thought that the bird was attacking, screamed even louder, while Elise and Daniel clung to the rails of the porch, weak with laughter.

"I'll get my revenge," Kitty threatened when she was back on her feet. "Just you wait."

She stalked into the house, muttering about mud pies while Daniel and Elise tried to compose themselves. They caught each other's gaze, and that set them off again. As Elise straightened, she saw something moving beyond the barn. She stopped and squinted.

"What is it?" Daniel said, sobering at once.

She pointed, and he leaned out from the porch, trying to see what she had seen. They both started as they saw a man, crouched low, run into the copse of trees past the farm's outbuildings.

Daniel cleared the steps in one leap and was off after the man in a heartbeat. Kitty came back out to see what was happening and waited with Elise until they saw Daniel coming back.

"I don't know who he was," Daniel said. "But he definitely didn't want to get caught. I'd better check the barn."

At dinner he told them he hadn't found anything unusual except the man's boot prints. Kitty thought it might be one of the O'Conner boys trying to spy on her. She flushed as she said it and didn't look displeased.

That night the barn started on fire.

Elise was just about to go to sleep and had gone to the window to fix the curtains, which had to be pinned or the sun shone directly on her face in the morning. She glanced out through the gap in the fabric and let the pin fall.

Flames licked across the roof of the barn. The doors were

wide open, and as she watched, Daniel ran out, shooing the cows in front of him.

Elise ran out of her room, pounding on Kitty's door as she went by, and then she was out the kitchen door and across the yard. Her feet were bare, and the mud sucked at the hem of her dressing gown, but she didn't care. She grabbed the halters of the horses as they came out and steered them quickly to the house, tying them to the porch rail as a confused Kitty came stumbling out and then screamed.

But she screamed only a second before grabbing buckets and pumping water. Daniel grabbed the buckets as soon as she filled them and ran in to douse what he could. Elise ran after him, holding a sleeve over her nose and mouth.

The door to the swans' stall was open, but they were milling around inside, honking and being disagreeable. She clapped her hands, and they hissed at her. Finally, she grabbed a shovel and chased the foolish birds into the yard.

She hoped they would have more sense as humans.

"The animals are all out," Daniel said. "But the barn . . ." He shook his head. "Let's soak the coop and sty. We can save them at least."

Elise grabbed a bucket. She could mourn the barn later, but she was not going to lose any of her chickens the way she had almost lost her foolish brothers.

She froze. Daniel bumped into her.

"Are you all—"

In a panic she grabbed the front of his shirt. She shook the cloth and pointed to the barn, willing him to understand.

"What is it?"

She yanked on his shirt again, but he looked baffled. She let go and ran back into the barn. The smoke blinded her instantly, and there was a cracking sound and a crash as part of the roof collapsed.

"Elise, no!"

She wasn't sure if it was Kitty or Daniel who shouted it, but it hardly mattered. She had to get her nettle shirts!

The side of the stall was on fire, but she clawed at the old cracked bits of leather and rusted rakes propped in the corner. Something stung her hand, and she found the shirts. She snatched them up, counting in her head with relief.

Then someone snatched *her* up, and she was carried out of the barn. Daniel didn't stop until they were on the porch. He deposited her on a bench and ran back to help Kitty. They soaked the coop and moved to the pig's pen.

A flurry of white, glowing with orange streaks in the light of the fire, swooped across Elise's blurry gaze. Two of her swans flew down and gathered up the buckets that Kitty had already filled and flew them over the burning barn. They twisted in the air to dump the water out and then flew on, not to the pump, but to the pond to refill them.

Elise tossed down the nettle shirts and ran into the kitchen. She got her biggest soup pot and threw it out the door into the yard. Then she got the dishpan and the washbasin and threw those out, too.

Kitty filled up everything she could, as fast as her arms could pump. The swans couldn't hold the washbasin, so Elise and Daniel lugged it back and forth.

Mary and her children arrived. They had buckets, and soon there was a line from the pond to the barn, with everyone passing the filled buckets from hand to hand and Mary's youngest running the empty buckets back to the pond. They pretended not to see the swans swooping past them, carrying buckets of their own and dropping them down on the broken roof.

By dawn the fire was out, but the barn was a ruin. Elise slumped on the porch steps. Kitty sat beside her with a groan.

"Our nightgowns are goners," Kitty said.

Elise gave a tired laugh. She would give Kitty the pick of her own embroidered, lace-trimmed nightgowns.

A wagon rolled into the yard, pulled by a pair of fine bay horses. Mr. Sylvester was driving with Dr. Goode sitting beside him. Elise's spine stiffened.

"What a tragedy!" Dr. Goode exclaimed as he climbed down. "You poor women!" He hurried over to Kitty and Elise.

"Thank heavens Daniel was here," Mary said, coming up behind him.

"And that *he's* safe," Kitty said.

Elise looked at her with gratitude. She had been thinking how terrible it would have been if Daniel had not woken up.

"He sleeps in the barn," Kitty explained.

"Exactly. Where the fire started," Sylvester said, coming up behind the minister. "So lucky that he wasn't killed in his sleep."

Elise gritted her teeth.

Dr. Goode turned to Sylvester, his mouth open. "Surely not!"

Sylvester spread his hands, inviting them to draw their own conclusions. "Young girls, living alone, at the mercy of a strange man . . ."

"Young Daniel is a fine—" the preacher began, but Daniel was suddenly there.

"Are you saying that I started this fire?"

Mr. Sylvester just smiled at him.

Daniel's fists were clenched. He stepped up, toe to toe with Sylvester. Dr. Goode bleated ineffectually, plucking at Sylvester's sleeve.

Panic rising in her breast, Elise looked around. Daniel couldn't strike Mr. Sylvester, as much as she wanted him to. He would go to jail for attacking a white man!

Elise was about to try to separate the men when her brothers did it for her. Hissing, wings extended, they charged across the yard, heading straight for Sylvester. Sylvester leaped back as they bit at his legs.

Daniel stepped back much more coolly.

"I didn't start the fire," he said. "But yesterday someone was sneaking around. They ran off in the direction of Mr. Sylvester's land."

"How dare you!" Sylvester said, as he backed toward his wagon, herded by the swans.

"That's the truth," Kitty raged. "If you feel guilty . . . maybe you are!"

"Now, now," Dr. Goode said, also backing toward the wagon, though the swans weren't paying him any attention. "Perhaps young Daniel smokes and hasn't been too careful—"

Mary drew herself up. "My nephew does not smoke," she said. "Nor is he careless with matches or candles."

"Well, of course not, Mary—ma'am," the minister said. Now that Sylvester was on the seat of the wagon, the swans had turned their attention Dr. Goode. "So sorry about your barn," he gasped to Elise. "I'll just, we'd better—" He turned and clambered into the wagon. Sylvester whipped the horses into a trot before the preacher was seated.

"Well!" Aunt Mary said. "This went from bad to awful!"

"So," Kitty said. "Who wants breakfast, and what are them grassy things on the porch?"

Eleven

Slowly but surely the fields were plowed and planted, and the new barn began to take shape.

Elise and Kitty spent every minute they weren't cooking for the field hands hammering nails into squeaky new wood under the eye of Kitty's father, who was far better at building than farming. He left the care of the Sullivan farm to his wife while he oversaw the rebuilding of Elise's barn.

In the meantime they housed the animals in lean-tos, and Daniel slept on a bedroll on the kitchen floor. At church the week after the fire, Mary had told Dr. Goode that Daniel slept at her house, and Elise and Kitty had nodded earnestly.

Sometimes Daniel would hover in the doorway of Elise's room at night while she worked on the shirts. She would scowl at him and look purposefully at the clock. He would throw up his hands and retreat, and she would shake her head. He couldn't help her, and they both knew it.

One night he ignored her head shake, however, and came

into the room. He slumped in her rocking chair, his long arms hanging down, and started to talk.

He told her about his parents' grand, scandalous love affair and his father's death in a mudslide one spring when Daniel was five. He talked about how he had trained his mare, Minnow, and how it was Aunt Mary, not her husband, who had taught him to shoot.

"My guns were Uncle Jason's," he confided. "But he wasn't much of a shot. Aunt Mary? Don't ever cross her." He laughed while Elise rolled her eyes and pointed to the door.

"Am I bothering you?" he sobered.

She mimed drooping eyelids. The last of the planting was to be done tomorrow, and they would need to be up at dawn.

He pointed to the sleeve she was knotting on to a shirt. "This one's almost done?"

She nodded.

"That's number six?"

She nodded again, stood up, and stretched. She took her magic book out from her bureau drawer. It fell open to the right page, the binding broken where she had pored over the spell so many times. She pointed to the row of symbols at the end of the instructions. He had been so quick to spot the full moon at the beginning of the spell; she wondered if he saw anything she had missed.

"Just a minute," he said, and hurried to the kitchen.

He came back holding a fat, gray book, almost as worn as her spell book. He searched the pages, and Elise leaned over his arm, curious. To her shock, she found that it was a German primer.

He found the word he was looking for and switched back to the spell book to compare. Elise was looking full into his face now, and his brown cheeks were turning dark with a subtle blush, but he kept looking at the books and ignoring her for fully three more minutes.

"All right," he said, closing the primer. "You have to put the shirts on the swans between the time when the lower edge of the sun touches the horizon and when it sets completely."

Elise pressed her lips together. That was what she had thought as well, but she pointed to the symbols, wanting to make sure.

"That's a mountain," he said, indicating the triangle at the bottom of the spell. "And that's a sliver of sunlight, and a star. Easy enough."

She raised an eyebrow.

He blushed a little darker. "It's true," he protested. "The hardest part now will be waiting, since it has to be a year and a day since you started."

She shuddered. She wanted to ignore that part. Four more months of silence. Four more months of the neighbors gossiping.

Although she supposed they would gossip more when she suddenly broke her silence and produced seven older brothers.

Assuming the spell worked.

Elise put the shirts in the box under her bed for the night. Daniel had made it out of odds and ends from the new barn. No one had explained to Kitty what the things on the porch were, after the fire, but there had been so much confusion in the aftermath that she hadn't pressed for an answer.

She and Daniel waved to each other, awkwardly, to say goodnight.

Twelve

Spring turned to summer.

The cows kept getting loose, until one of them slipped on the bank of the creek and drowned. Elise was greatly relieved when the barn was finished, though it meant that Daniel slept outside again and no longer checked on her at night.

She finished the last shirt and blissfully began going to bed when Kitty did. Her hands didn't heal, however, and the waiting for the summer to be over gave her troubling dreams.

Sylvester never stopped asking about buying the farm. Elise began to keep track of both his offers and the tragedies that befell her farm, and a pattern soon emerged. After the cow died, after a coyote killed most of the chickens, and after a "wild animal" ruined a corner of the south field, without fail the next Sunday Sylvester would stroll up and offer to end Elise's "difficulties."

"He's not even *pretending* anymore," Kitty said one Sunday in July.

Elise gave her a look.

"I'm not blind," Kitty said. "He knows everything that happens to us, and tries to turn it to his advantage."

"There weren't any coyote tracks around the coop," Daniel said. They were riding back from church, all of them blinking in the bright sun despite the women's deep bonnets and Daniel's broad-brimmed hat. "There were boot prints."

"You think he caught a coyote and shoved it in?"

"The wires had been cut," Daniel said.

"We should tell the sheriff," Kitty said.

"We need solid proof," Daniel said. "I can prove that someone is doing this on purpose, but not who."

"It's so frustrating!" Kitty grimaced. "Maybe I could bring some of the younger kids to stay," she said after a minute. "Have 'em hide around the farm, keep watch."

"I don't think your mother would appreciate your putting them in harm's way," Daniel pointed out. "Not when killing livestock and setting fires are some of our enemy's tricks."

"We could hire someone," Kitty suggested.

Elise shook her head. After paying for seed, feed, a new barn, a new cow and chickens, plus the field labor, she was afraid to open her bank account until they got the harvest in. Her gaze met Daniel's, and he raised his eyebrows.

"I think we might get some help," he said suddenly. "We just need to wait another week or two."

"Who might that be?" Kitty wanted to know.

"Just . . . we'll see what happens in a couple of weeks."

By then they entered the farmyard, their horses scattering the swans except for one. The largest of them was a special pet of Kitty's now. Kitty had asked if the swans had names, and Elise had written them down for her. She herself could hardly tell them apart, except for the big one, who was also the youngest.

"Come along, Peter," Kitty said to him now. "I'll get you some corn."

He waddled along behind her mare.

"She's in for a surprise very soon," Daniel muttered.

Elise snorted, but her heart was pounding. What *would* Kitty do when the birds she alternately coddled or shouted at, the birds that flapped around the pond eating bugs and hissing at visitors, turned into seven grown men? Elise planned to say that her brothers had just arrived from Hohenschwangau, but Kitty would not be fooled. Elise sighed. She hoped that her dear friend wouldn't be driven away by the evidence of real sorcery.

Assuming it worked.

The next two weeks passed in a haze. Elise spent most nights wide awake, staring toward the ceiling and worrying about everything that might go wrong.

Daniel looked as horrible as she felt. He had dark smudges under his eyes and wore his guns all the time. Elise thought about writing him a note, telling him to get some rest, but selfishly she decided not to. It made her feel safer, knowing that he was keeping watch.

But even with him keeping watch in the barn and Elise wide awake in the house, neither of them heard the swans being taken. It was Kitty who roused them both with her screaming. When Elise ran out to the kitchen, she found Kitty at the back door, pointing out at the barnyard.

When she looked, Elise understood the younger woman's hysterics.

A number of horses and men in heavy boots had churned up the dirt of the barnyard. The swans were nowhere to be seen, but white feathers were everywhere, ground into the muck of the yard.

Elise ran barefoot across the mess and threw open the barn door just as Daniel staggered out, holding his head.

"They hit me with something," he said groggily. "Didn't see who." He lowered his hand; there was blood on his fingers.

"Sylvester," Kitty said, as though the name were a swear word.

"I'll get the sheriff," Daniel said.

"*I'll* get the sheriff," Kitty said. "You get that head fixed!"

Kitty dressed while Elise helped Daniel into the kitchen and pressed him into a chair. She stood behind him and gently parted his long black hair. She drew in her breath when she saw the wound. There was a swollen lump and the skin was split.

"I'll be back," Kitty said, and rushed off.

Elise cleaned the wound and then soaked a fresh cloth in cold water and held it to the bump. Daniel sat for a long time with Elise standing close behind him, holding the compress to his head. Her other hand rested on his shoulder. He reached up and put a hand atop hers.

She winced despite the lightness of the touch.

"We have to get those swans," Daniel said.

He took the cloth from her as he stood. He checked it for blood, grimaced at the streak he saw there, then tossed it aside.

"Stay here," he ordered. "I'm going to have a chat with our neighbor."

The moment he and Minnow were out of the barnyard, Elise scrambled into her clothes. She wouldn't—and couldn't—argue with Daniel, nor would she sit at the farm while he got himself killed. In minutes she was riding Schatzi toward Sylvester's.

James Sylvester had one of the largest farms in the county. Elise had expected there to be *some* signs of life, even if her swans were hidden. But there was nothing, not even a chicken loose in the yard.

Elise knocked on the door of the house. She could hear rustling inside, the scrape of a boot, but no one answered. She ran to the barn, but the door was barred. Elise kicked the door before remounting Schatzi and turning the mare toward Mary's.

Mary's farm looked almost as abandoned as Sylvester's. But as soon as Schatzi halted by the porch steps, Mary's youngest came trotting out as though she had been waiting.

"Mrs. Elise," Frances said, clasping her hands and getting ready to recite. "Please go to the church. Everyone is waiting there."

Elise gaped at her.

"Please go to the church. Everyone is waiting there."

When she got to the church, Elise felt a flash of confusion. Was it Sunday? There were certainly enough horses and wagons tied up out front. But no, it was Thursday, the day her ordeal was supposed to end.

Minnow was tied next to Mary's horses, which were still hitched to their wagon. She tied Schatzi next to her stall mate and went into the church.

"Ah, you found us!" Dr. Goode smiled.

He was standing at the front of the church next to a large wooden crate. Sylvester was next to him, and in the pews Elise could see Mary, her arm around Daniel, and several of their other neighbors. She slowly started up the aisle.

Daniel turned his head and looked at her, a strange expression on his face, and Elise realized that Mary was holding him down with her grip around his shoulders. Her oldest son, on his other side, looked to be doing the same.

"It's all right." Dr. Goode came forward and took her hands. "You poor girl." He tugged off her gloves and looked at her swollen fingers. "It will all be better now."

Elise looked at him in shock. How could he know about the curse, or that today was the last day? She looked wildly at Mary, at Daniel, but Mary only looked troubled, and Daniel was trying to pull free of his cousin.

Elise turned back to Dr. Goode for an explanation, but it was Sylvester who spoke. He took a letter from his breast pocket and unfolded it with a theatrical flourish.

"I was so concerned about you, living alone on that farm, that I took the liberty of writing to your family," he said, oozing false sympathy. "Your dear stepmother is so relieved to learn where you are, and that you're safe! She told me everything: how you had escaped from her care, your elaborate daydreams."

Elise could only look around again, bemused. A squawk came from the crate, and she realized that her brothers were inside it. She moved to free them, but Dr. Goode blocked her.

"Elise," he said loudly. "They are *birds.* Not your brothers. Your brothers are dead."

She reeled back. Daniel made a noise, but Mary shushed him. She was crying.

"I was very curious about you," Sylvester continued. "A beautiful young girl, coming halfway around the world to marry a stranger. And mourning him so dramatically, going mute in grief, after only a *week*?"

Mary let out a sob, and Daniel pulled his arm free of his cousin's grip. He started to rise, but Elise gave him a warning look, and he put his arm around Mary instead.

"When you didn't return home after Ludwig died, I thought it was a little strange. Ludwig left a fine farm, but surely a princess would want to return to her palace and her servants, not milk cows alongside a half-breed in a stinking barn!" He chuckled, but several of those watching gave him dirty looks, and now Daniel's cousin looked like he wanted to punch Sylvester.

"So I wrote to your family in Honshwingo, or whatever it's called," Sylvester said. He widened his eyes in a pretense of shock. "Imagine my horror at learning that my poor friend Ludwig had married a madwoman!"

Elise opened her mouth, about to shout that it was lies.

"No!" Daniel interjected.

Startled, Elise snapped her mouth shut. But it was Sylvester that Daniel was shouting at.

"She is not mad, and you all know it!" He pointed around at their neighbors, who wouldn't meet his eyes. "Her stepmother sent her here. Her stepmother is the reason why she won't go back."

There was a loud *cark* from the crate, and again Elise began to edge toward it. Dr. Goode looked like he might throw himself across the crate to stop her.

"This obsession with the birds is just a symptom of your fevered brain," Dr. Goode said.

"Mad as her mother was," Sylvester said, unable to hide a smirk. "So sad."

The stained glass window cast red light over Sylvester and the crate. The day was passing all too swiftly, and these people thought she was mad. Thought her mother was mad. Her mother, who had died bearing her. Her mother, whose chief lady-in-waiting had turned out to be a witch. A witch who had killed the queen and cursed Elise's father and brothers. Who had now given Sylvester just what he needed to take away her life: her brothers, her home, her friends.

Elise's rage burned through her.

"What's that, dear? You look as though you'd like to say something." Sylvester cocked his head. "You *can* talk, you know."

"Stop that," Mary said. "No need to taunt the poor girl."

Elise glared at Mary. Mary had known her for a year now;

could she really believe that Elise was a madwoman, based on a letter from a stranger?

Mary looked away first. "The swans, dear," she mumbled. "Your hands. Kitty says you make doll clothes out of stinging nettles."

Kitty. Where *was* Kitty?

Daniel plucked at his shirt as she looked around, and Elise felt her heart plummet to her shoes. She barely heard Dr. Goode urge her to sit down, didn't bother to listen as he prayed for her mind to be whole. She did listen to Sylvester nobly agreeing to take over her farm and Mary's objection to this plan.

Dr. Goode tried to keep her in her seat, but when the sheriff came in with Kitty, Elise bolted off the pew and faced them. They were carrying the coverlet from Elise's bed like a giant basket. And in that basket were the shirts for her brothers. They laid them down next to the crate, and everyone gathered around to look.

In the daylight they looked even more awful than they did by lamplight. The nettles had withered, the weaving was lumpy and uneven; they were barely recognizable as shirts, and only then if you knew what you were looking at. Certainly none of the others seemed to know what to make of them.

"Poor, poor girl," Mary whispered.

"I'm sorry," Kitty said. There were salty tear tracks on her cheeks. "I couldn't believe it until I saw the letter."

"If you think Elise is mad," Daniel said, his voice taut with rage, "then why attack me? Why steal the swans?"

"My dear boy," Dr. Goode said, in the same slow voice he had used on Elise. "She was dragging you down into her madness. We all saw it happen." He smiled at Kitty. "Praise God that dear Mary Katherine did not catch it."

Kitty flinched and looked pleadingly at Elise. Elise moved away from her. She moved away from all of them. Across the pile of nettle shirts, Daniel stood near the crate. He dipped his chin, then glanced at the shirts. When Sylvester opened his mouth to say something smug, Daniel moved.

He whirled toward the crate, drawing one of his pistols. Dr. Goode and Kitty both screamed, but Daniel didn't shoot. Instead he used the butt of the pistol to break the lock on the crate. The swans burst free and attacked Sylvester.

"Come on!"

Daniel grabbed one side of the coverlet. Elise grabbed the other, and they ran for the door. They had to press close together to pass through it, and Elise winced to think of the damage to the fragile shirts. But then they were throwing them into the back of Mary's wagon anyway, and Daniel was heaving her onto the seat and leaping up after.

"We'll go to my mother," he said. "She'll hide us, and we can pray the swans follow!"

Elise was sure that the others would catch them immediately, but her brothers must have been truly effective at stopping the pursuit. The wagon barreled down the road, and Elise saw no signs of anyone following.

Daniel took her north; farther than she had ever been from the farm or the town. After a while she stopped checking for the sheriff or Sylvester and concentrated on the rocky terrain in front of them. They had to leave the road, abandoning the wagon and the big draft horses to continue on foot, carrying the blanket sling between them.

The Crow village was high among the hills, tucked away safe. By the time they reached it they were gasping for breath and bathed in sweat. Daniel's mother came out of her house with a dipper of water in her hand and gave Elise and then Daniel a drink.

"Are those the shirts?" She wrinkled her nose at the mess they carried.

"Yes," Daniel said.

"Where are the swans?"

"Coming, we hope."

His mother nodded, and they sat on a bench in front of her house while she made them food. If she had not been so tired, Elise would not have been able to sit down at all. The sun was low in the sky now, and the trees were too thick for her to see its exact position.

"I'll tell you when it's time," Daniel's mother said, bringing them bowls of stew. She shooed away some children who had come to gawk. "But first we need your brothers," she added grimly.

Elise set aside her bowl and got up. She would have to go back and look for them. She was trying to signal this to Daniel when her brothers came, gliding down out of the sky to land in front of them.

Elise began to cry with relief, but her tears dried the moment the sheriff, Sylvester, and the others entered the village. Her brothers clustered around her and Daniel.

"Young lady," the sheriff said. "I know that you're . . . confused. But you need to come with us now." He was nursing a large gouge on one forearm.

Kitty clapped her hands. "Peter, you naughty thing! Move away now, good birdie!"

"Start with him," Daniel advised, picking up one of the shirts.

"Oldest to youngest," his mother said sharply. "And wait . . ."

"Daniel, Elise, please," Aunt Mary said. "I don't believe . . . this isn't helping." This last was an appeal to Daniel's mother.

"Now!" the Crow woman shouted in reply.

Elise grabbed the shirt from Daniel and waded into the

birds. She took hold of her brother Karl's neck with one hand and forced the nettle shirt over his head with the other. He flapped his wings, which fortunately forced them into the sleeves. Kitty was crying for her to leave the birds alone; the sheriff was shouting that he would arrest her.

And Elise was scrambling backward as the swan at her feet changed into a tall young man wearing nothing but a rough tunic of nettles. Mary screamed. Dr. Goode fainted. The Crow villagers gathered in a ring around Elise and her flock.

Elise kept going.

She found Georg, Wilhelm, and Stefan and put their shirts on. Her hands burned worse than they ever had. Daniel's mother was shouting at her to hurry. Sylvester swore and then fled.

Elise snatched up another shirt and then another. Albert, Einhart, and last of all Peter, who waited, expectantly, at her feet. She reached for the last shirt and froze.

The last shirt was stained with soot from the barn fire, and its edges were ragged. One sleeve was hanging askew, courtesy of their wild flight from the church. She picked it up carefully, but it crumbled even more.

"There is no more time," Daniel's mother snapped.

Elise said a silent prayer, then she thrust it over the last swan's head.

It barely fit around Peter, who was the largest of her brothers. The damaged sleeve came off entirely. But he convulsed and straightened, and a handsome young man stood there, grinning.

He turned to Kitty, and Elise saw that his left arm was still a swan's wing. Kitty didn't seem to notice, however. Her eyes were locked on his face, her cheeks bright pink.

"You're very . . . your eyes are so blue," she murmured.

But Sylvester had noticed the swan wing. He had noticed

all the young men, standing where the swans had been. His face was ghastly pale.

"They are . . . the birds . . . witchcraft!" He ran into the woods.

One of the Crow men made to follow him, but Daniel's mother called him back.

"Let him get lost in the mountains," she decreed. "No one will miss him."

Elise swayed, and Daniel gathered her into his arms.

"You did it," he whispered. "It's over."

"Oh good," she croaked, and then fainted.

Thirteen

The second time Elise was married she wore a pink silk gown, though she stood in the exact same spot in her parlor. The Crow chief married them, since poor Dr. Goode had never quite recovered from what he'd seen that day, and the sheriff had taken to drink.

Kitty's gown was a gift from Elise. It was heavy satin, the same rich blue as Kitty's groom's eyes. Mr. Sullivan gave away both brides under the watchful eye of his wife, Aunt Mary, Daniel's mother, and six of Elise's brothers. The seventh brother only had eyes for his bride and had to be prompted by the chief at every turn.

He kept his remaining wing tucked tight to his body, beneath his shirt and coat. Mrs. Sullivan had pinned up the empty coat sleeve.

"I never thought I would see such a thing," she had said.

"But I suppose if your bride doesn't mind, neither do I!"

The chief spoke the ceremony in his own language, switching to English for the vows. Kitty and Peter said their I do's, and then it was time for the other couple.

"I do," Daniel said, smiling down at Elise.

"I do, too," she said.

Daniel laughed at how loudly she said it, and they came together in a kiss without needing to be told.

While the chief prompted Peter to kiss his bride, his brothers all hooted and clapped, making a sound almost exactly like the flapping of a swan's wings.

About Jessica Day George

It's all about the books. Friends, family, school, "real jobs", they were just obstacles to be tackled so that I could return to my true love: books. All I have ever wanted in this world is to read and write books. My criteria for choosing a purse is that it must be able to fit a paperback book inside. I took books on my honeymoon, and bought more while we were there. I picked my major because it looked like I would get to read a lot of books, and also I thought it would provide me with interesting background information for my own books (which it did), so I now have a BA in Humanities - Comparative Literature with a minor in Scandinavian Studies. From the time I was twelve on up, I told people that I wanted to be a writer. When they said, "So, you'll teach and then maybe try to write a book?" I would just shake my head.

No, I was a writer, and that was all I wanted to do. Over the years I have lived in Idaho, New Jersey, Delaware, and now Utah, because it doesn't matter. I can read and write anywhere. I've worked at a wedding invitation factory (Bet you didn't know they made them in big scary factories, did you?), at a video store (back at the birth of DVD), at libraries and bookstores, and even been an office lady at a school while I waited to get published. I knew that I would be published eventually, because . . . well, I just had to be.

Now, don't get me wrong, I have other interests. I took eight years of German, four of Norwegian, and even studied Old Norse so that I could read the great Viking sagas in the original language. I knit like a maniac: hats, scarves, sweaters, dog sweaters, socks, felted purses, you name it. I play the piano and viola, love to travel and to watch movies. I have a husband and three kids and a dog . . .

But mostly, it's about the books.

Visit Jessica at: JessicaDayGeorge.com

The Miller's Daughter

Julie Wright

One

Isa first saw him as she opened the gate at her grandmother's house. She'd been absently thinking of how her shoes were a bit too snug and wondering how long it would take to save the money to buy new shoes when her eyes landed on him.

Isa actually gasped at the dark-haired young man standing with her grandmother. At her noise, her grandmother and the young man both turned in her direction.

"Isa!" her grandmother called. "Come see how well my door swings on its newly fixed hinges!"

Isa hurried to greet her grandmother and the stranger. She dropped a small curtsy to the man and gave a kiss to her grandmother before saying, "New hinges, you say?"

"Yes, this kind young man showed up this morning, and when he saw how poorly the door fit into its frame and how hard it was to open and close, he went straight to work to fix it. Not one in a hundred men would do such a service for an old woman like me."

The young man's face pinked up in a way that made Isa's heart stutter in her chest.

"It was nothing," he said, clearly embarrassed.

"My grandmother never lies, good sir. If she says you have done a great service, then surely she is right. Who do I thank for that service?"

He tugged his cap off his head, realizing he'd entered the beginnings of a formal introduction. "My name is Thomas Rumple."

His accent indicated a proper education. Not many in her village could boast a proper education. Not many could speak in the clear, perfect tones of one who knew how to read. That he knew to remove his cap showed he was higher born, likely to a noble family somewhere closer to the seat of the kingdom in Aridel. He certainly wasn't from anywhere close to the village of Davenport. Isa would have recognized such a face.

She lowered into another curtsy, trying to match his good manners. "I am Isa. Thank you for helping my grandmother. How may we repay such a generosity?"

Thomas Rumple smiled. "Meeting you, my lady, is payment enough." He dipped his head to her grandmother, actually bowed to Isa as if she were a lady of some rank, placed his cap back on his head, and bid them both farewell.

"Leaving so soon?" Grandmother demanded to know. "Before I can offer you some water? I have the best well in the whole of the village."

He laughed. Had Isa ever heard a sound so musical? "Thank you, Miss Allyson, but I've work that cannot be neglected. Maybe I shall come again sometime and fix the hinges on your shutters." He spoke to her grandmother, but his eyes stayed on Isa.

Grandmother nodded, her lips twisting up in a knowing grin. "And when you do return, I will make certain Isa comes to pay me a visit so you have company while you work."

"I think I would like that," Thomas said.

Grandmother slumped against her doorframe. "Walk him to the gate, Isa. My legs are tired today. It's the least we can do to show gratitude."

Isa's cheeks burned, but she lifted her chin. Grandmother wasn't fooling anyone with her little display, but Isa was certainly up to the task of showing a handsome man to the gate.

"Goodbye, Allyson," Thomas said to her grandmother.

As they walked, Isa asked, "Do you make a habit of helping old women with repair work?"

"I do when they're as sweet as your grandmother. Out of the memory of my own grandmother, I could do nothing less."

It was a good answer.

"Thank you." Isa unlatched the gate and held it for him.

"While I worked, she told me you might be coming today. She told me you had hair like spun gold."

Isa rolled her eyes. "All grandmothers say such things."

"Yes, but very few can say such things *honestly*."

Before Isa could blush with the realization that he paid her a compliment, he added, "She also boasted of your great wit and good heart. So are those things grandmothers boast, or are they as true as the golden hair?"

Isa couldn't help it; she laughed. "True enough, I suppose. I am adequately clever, and my heart, well . . . it is acceptable by societal standards. But I suspect every heart has a shadow or two lurking within; don't you agree?"

"Only one with very few shadows would be so modest," he observed. "I believe I might return to fix those shutters, and perhaps return another time to repair windows, and perhaps yet another to chase away shadows. I cannot tell you how sorry I am to have pressing duties this day. Perhaps we shall meet again."

Isa felt warmth all over under the gaze of his interest. Had anyone in the whole of the village, or even the kingdom, smiled like that ever, with such confidence and genuine happiness?

Isa didn't think so.

"Perhaps we shall."

She knew they both lied. Strangers seldom came to Davenport. And even fewer ever bothered to return. Whatever brought him to the village was unlikely to bring him back. Isa knew she would never see him again, which was why she dared watch for so long as he swung his leg over the saddle of his horse. The saddlebags bulged with whatever burden they carried. Thomas added a small sack to one of them, clucked his tongue, and trotted away.

"He's pretty, isn't he?" Grandmother asked from behind her.

"I've seen better horses, Grandmother," Isa answered.

Grandmother swatted Isa's shoulder. "Teasing girl! You know what I mean!"

Isa looped her arm in her grandmother's and strolled back to the house. "I do know what you mean. But he's a stranger here, and if he stays long enough or returns often enough, he'll learn the rumors of the miller and his foul temper and fondness of drink, and he will want nothing to do with the miller's daughter—just like everyone else."

Grandmother insisted Isa was wrong the entire time Isa carried flour bags from her cart to her grandmother's house. The whole time Grandmother yammered about the good luck of meeting such a lovely boy, Isa worked to forget the meeting.

But the meeting was hard to forget.

Because Isa saw him again later that day while she watched out the window and waited for the baker to measure out the flour she'd brought from the mill. "Pretty," she murmured and then looked at her too-snug shoes and felt ashamed at herself for the start in her pulse and fire in her chest, but she looked right back up again. She couldn't help it.

He tilted his head at some passerby she couldn't see from where she stood and smiled broadly as he doffed his cap and revealed his dark hair.

Dark like wood from a walnut tree.

And a smile that could melt ice from mountaintops.

Grady, the baker, returned from the back room, his smock powdered in the fine dust of flour from measuring. He looked grim and worried as he handed her the coin satchel she'd waited for. The weight of coin in her hand was far lighter than she had expected, and it jingled far less than it ever had before as she moved the bag from one hand to the other.

"What's this?" Isa asked. Someone entered the bakery behind her, but the fact was something she only barely acknowledged in the back of her mind as she tried to comprehend why Grady would pay her so little when he owed her so much.

Grady held up his hands as if to placate her. "That's all I can spare. The king's collectin' taxes t'day. I know it's not enough, but I need this flour, or the shop will have t' close, and then I'll never be able t' pay the rest that's due. You've got t' have mercy on me."

Isa sighed and rubbed the heel of her hand at her left temple. "But you will make it up, won't you?" she whispered. "The collectors will be coming to the mill as well. And we desperately need the coin."

"I'm sorry, Isa. I know you're trying to make it all work.

And I'm sorry about the money. I will make it up. I promise. It's just with—"

Though he trailed off, Isa knew his thoughts. He paid a doctor from a neighboring village to tend to his sick wife, and it cost them dearly.

She took a deep, shuddering breath, rubbed her hands over her eyes, and nodded. "I know, Grady. And I know you'll make it up. Give my love to Janette. Tell her I hope she feels better soon."

His eyes filled with gratitude.

She pocketed the coin and felt vexed. She'd have to run home if the collectors were to come. They had a way of taking more than their share if no one was there to keep an eye on them. She turned to leave the shop, prepared to spring into a run as soon as she was out the door, when she smacked into the person who'd come in after her and fell back hard enough on the bakery's wood floors to shoot pain through her entire spine.

"Forgive me!" the voice insisted as a hand came into her view. "I'm so sorry to have been in your way."

She took the offer of help and scrambled to her feet, her waspish feelings magnified by this person who'd managed to step right into her path at just the wrong moment. She opened her mouth and lifted her eyes to the stranger to give him the rough side of her tongue for lurking in doorways when her eyes actually focused on him. Her mouth closed again with a click of her teeth.

"You!" The one word came out as a breathy sigh of wonderment. She hoped he mistook the heat crawling over her cheeks as embarrassment in having fallen down rather than embarrassment in being knocked down emotionally by her interest in him.

At least she'd stilled her hands so they didn't nervously

brush back the strands of unruly hair that escaped her braid. Her golden hair was a much-admired feature—even among those who despised her father. But calling attention to it after her grandmother already had and after they'd already shared light flirtations would make her look foolish. The gesture of playing with one's hair always made girls look the part of a desperate flirt to her. Isa didn't have the time to be a desperate flirt, not even for this agreeable man who made her heart bruise itself on her rib cage. Not today.

Not now when the tax collectors were in town.

"I never dreamed of such fortune as a day where you came twice into my life." He frowned as she peered around him to the door. "Is something wrong?"

How did she explain all the many things that were wrong when the tax collectors could arrive at the mill at any time?

The late hour guaranteed her father already had settled his rump on the worn, polished wood bench in the tavern. She could not count on him to keep the tax collectors honest.

She stepped to the side to indicate her intentions to leave. Thomas stepped in her way again and put his hand out, not to help her up this time, but to stop her from leaving. "I didn't mean to cause you injury. Please don't go."

She couldn't help the warmth blossoming in her chest all while resenting its presence. "Sir Rumple—"

"Please call me Thomas."

"Thomas, I am sorry, but I have matters that need tending. I cannot stay longer in town."

"But then"—he moved in her way to keep her from walking forward—"can you at least forgive me, Isa, for not paying better attention to where I walk?"

"There is nothing to forgive," she said. "Neither of us watched our steps very carefully this day. That puts us on equal footing."

There were so many meanings to her words, and she thought of all of them as she hurried away. If she'd watched her steps carefully, she would not be so intrigued by this man who could have no effect on her future. And they were on equal footing for guilt, certainly, but they were far from equal in status.

Isa wanted to look back, to steal just one more glance at that agreeable face and walnut hair, but she'd wasted enough time on a flirtation with no possibility. She opened the door and left.

Why did he have to be a stranger to Davenport? He would likely never return to the village—not with his easy eyes and quick smile, not with words falling from his lips like soft rose petals rather than the harsh, thorny language of the uneducated. Isa was uneducated. Did her tones offend him? Did he think her simple and small-minded? But he'd given her the smile of an interested man, of a man who liked what he saw and enjoyed the words he'd heard. Maybe if they'd grown up together, he would have looked past her father and the intensive work involved in the mill, and he would have seen *her.*

Of course, if he had been a local boy, he surely would have been snatched up by one of the meddling mothers anxious to secure their daughters' marriages. Since Isa had no mother to stand up for her, and since her father discouraged any man who might approach her on his own, she could plan no marriage.

Since Thomas would not be hers in any reality, Isa could spend no time mourning him.

She untied her mare and hopped on, turning her horse in the direction of the gristmill. She did not look back to the bakery.

Except once.

Isa looked back once.

But he no longer stood near the window where he could be seen.

She clucked her tongue to spur her horse to speed. But, by the time Isa neared the mill, she swallowed her disappointment. A carriage marked with the king's colors already waited at the mill's front entrance. Several fine horses were tied to the fence, where they happily munched on the flowers her grandmother had planted years before her spine crippled too much to allow her the pleasures of gardening.

Isa wanted to shoo them away from the flowers, but no one trifled with the king—not even with his horses. Isa slid off her mare's back and slapped Nagga's rump to encourage her to find the barn on her own. Isa then turned her attention to the mill and the collectors who'd already gone inside even though they had not been properly invited.

She squared her shoulders and followed after them.

Two

The noise inside cut off as if she'd snipped it with her old shears as soon as she opened the door and stood surveying the people in her place of business and home.

She knew it was proper to curtsy, to show some humble deference, but her knees would not bend. Anger boiled through her veins. She said nothing because the few things she could think to say were the sorts that would have her swinging from the gallows by morning. So she stood and gazed on the three men inside her mill, her home.

"So good of you," the shortest of the three began with an ingratiating grin, "to offer us shelter from the hot midday sun while we waited for you."

She wasn't a fool. She'd offered nothing, and they waited for nothing. The one of average height, but with a substantial width, stood holding her father's strongbox.

They had to have been inside the mill for a long time to have been able to find where her father stored the strongbox.

She'd been looking for the last week and hadn't been successful.

She quivered in rage but remained silent.

The short one followed her gaze to the strongbox and tsked. "Yes, well. We did take the pains to get on with our business to keep from delaying you in yours." He took the strongbox from the wide man and then approached her as he opened it for her to see inside. "Clearly your business isn't going so well these days."

The box was empty.

Which meant her father had taken the whole of its contents to the tavern. The emptiness of the box was the entire reason she'd been looking so hard for it all week. She knew it had been long enough since the last time he'd gambled away their finances that he was likely to be doing it again soon. She'd hoped to drain the box before he had the chance.

The short man snapped the box closed and dropped it on the floor at her feet. "You must know we're here to collect the king's taxes, but it seems as though you've not understood the importance of setting aside the proper funds for such things." He'd stepped impossibly closer to her. His breath smelled of wine and rotten fish, a combination that turned Isa's stomach.

While sneering up at her, he shouted to his men, "Take what you need, and then take a little extra as a fine for their rebellion against the king."

The wide man and the tall man dove into action, overturning pots and baskets. They shoved Isa aside so they could pass through the doorway as they hauled off sack after sack of already-milled flour to their wagon. Isa started forward when they loaded the silver candlesticks, but the short man stopped her. "You wouldn't begrudge the king what is fairly his, would you?"

Isa's breath came hard and fast, jagged ice ripping in and

out of her throat. She ground her teeth together and gave her head a single shake.

"I'm sorry," the short man said. "I didn't hear you."

"No," Isa said. "Of course not."

"Of course not."

The short man's eyes dropped to the neckline of Isa's dress, and he smiled in a way that made Isa wish she had a cloak or a blanket to wrap herself in as another layer of protection. She fell back a step. The collectors could be stealing far worse things. It was only a matter of time before her father lost the candlesticks in a gamble anyway. She valued her own safety far more.

Her breath stuttered in her throat as he reached for her, his hot, thick fingers brushing against her collarbone.

"Please no," she whispered as his finger trailed down from her collarbone to the neckline of her dress.

"It's a pretty bauble," he said, lifting her necklace away from her skin.

Relief that his fingers were no longer on her and that he commented only on her necklace flooded her until his words registered in her mind.

The necklace.

Her mother's necklace. The only thing she had left of her mother. And the collector's fingers were wrapped around it, proof he'd already claimed it as his possession.

He gave one solid tug, snapping the chain at the back of her neck. Isa gasped at the shock of pain. "But it's my mother's!" she protested as one hand flew to the back of her neck to check for blood and the other reached out to try to take the necklace back from the collector.

He held it out of her reach. "And now it's the king's. If you'd had proper payment ready and waiting, we wouldn't be forced to such base methods. Perhaps you'll be more prepared next time."

Her father had done this to her. As much as she wanted to hate the collectors, this was the result of her father's choices. If they had found the strongbox full, they would have simply emptied it and left.

She planned to pummel him when he returned from the tavern. She would never leave the strongbox in the gristmill again.

Finally, the vile tax collectors departed. All heirlooms were gone. They'd even made it to the stables and taken the mare, though they'd left the cart.

The short man had said he left the cart to allow the miller family to continue business, and that it would do them good to remember every time they pulled the cart into town that they did it by their own labor instead of with the use of a horse because they had tried to cheat the king.

Not that they would have any reason to take anything in the cart to town. Most of the flour they desperately needed to sell was gone. And not all of it had been theirs to lose. Much of it belonged to several farmers who'd brought their wheat in for Isa to grind into flour. They would have paid her for the service, but now she would have to figure out how to compensate them for their lost wheat.

Would they understand about the tax collectors?

No.

They would not count her problems as their problems. They would expect compensation. Isa paced around the grinding stones for a long time before the fury bubbled up in her. Her father had not yet returned from the tavern.

Stupid man.

This was his doing.

This was his problem.

But would he spend even a moment toiling over how to resolve it?

No.

Because he was a stupid man.

The more she thought about it, the angrier she grew until she realized she'd had enough. She'd been a silent, obedient daughter for long enough. She'd be silent no more. She ducked into the back room to snatch up her cloak—one of the few things the tax collectors hadn't taken. By the time she made it to town and back to the mill again, it would be night, and the air would have cooled. She didn't care how long it took, she'd be dragging her father back by the ear, and she'd be filling that ear with all the reasons things were going to change around the mill. He had lost the right to be in charge of anything. He'd lost it when they took the necklace and lost it again when they took the horse and lost it with every sack of flour they loaded up into the king's wagons.

The walk into town did nothing to temper her anger. If anything, every stomp of her foot to the earth drove her anger deeper into her belly until it raged like a summertime bonfire.

"Father!" she shouted as soon as she swung the tavern door open and spotted him with his arm curled around his mug of ale as if it were a babe in his charge.

"I think she means you, miller." The man seated next to her father elbowed him, forcing her father to finally look up at her through bleary, blinking eyes.

"It's just Isa." He lifted his mug to his lips and wiped at where he dribbled down his chin on his grimy sleeve.

"You!" Isa spat out. "You spent it all!" She should have cared that she stood in a public place where anyone could hear, but her anger overrode her sense. "The tax collectors came today, but you'd already emptied the strongbox. So they took everything else. We've nothing left to us but grinding stones and a roof that needs thatching."

"What's this?" Nate demanded to know. Isa's financial declaration finally brought his attention to the dilemma of getting her father out of his tavern. "You still owe me for the last round of drinks."

"Round of drinks? He's been buying for everyone here?"

All eyes fled from her gaze as each man took a sudden interest in what might be hiding in his mug.

"How could he have spent all we had and still owe more? Even if he bought the whole kingdom a mug?"

No one answered, but she felt sure a game of dice had been involved. So she stomped to where her father sat and took hold of his arm to yank him off his seat, but he tugged his arm back with the declaration that he wasn't ready and aimed to have another two or three before he would consider being ready.

Her father's considerable bulk made him impossible to move if he didn't feel any inclination to help her. And with drink in him, he would not only be not helping, he would be fighting her. But Nate had apparently heard enough to know that the seat her father took could be more profitably used under someone else's rump because he came around from behind the bar and shoved her father from the seat. "Time to go, miller."

"I'm not finished!" her father protested.

"You're finished with what you've actually paid for. Come back when you're on your own coin." With that, Nate pulled him to the door and out into the street.

Isa almost thanked the man but realized she'd be thanking the one who allowed him to spend all his money in the first place. If he'd been moral, he would've sent her father home before an entire season's earnings could be squandered.

She straightened her spine and stalked out after her father. Laughter followed as the door to the tavern closed. She closed her eyes briefly before latching onto her father's arm to help him up. Once he was on his feet, he started shoving at her. "I don't need your help."

"Help? You think I'm here to help you? It's not help I'm aiming to give!" she yelled at him. "You spent everything, and today the tax collectors took everything, even the flour. All of it. We have no way to pay back the farmers for the flour taken. None. The season's near over, and you think I want to help you?" She shoved back her hair from her eyes. "Help off a bridge is the only help you'll get from me."

He pulled his arm back to swing at her for her disrespect but threw his own weight out of balance and fell back into the street just as a carriage approached.

"Father!" she shouted.

"You've been a waste of coin and food for your entire life!" he shouted back, not seeing or not caring about the approaching carriage.

"Father! Get out of the road!"

He raised his fist and shook it at her. "How dare you tell me what to do, you ungrateful, useless—"

The horses reared up and whinnied as the driver of the carriage yanked hard on the reins. Only then did her father notice where he stood and what happened around him. He lifted his arm as if that might protect him from the hooves of the huge animals and fell back several paces.

Her father didn't deserve it, but the driver stopped in time.

Even with everything, Isa released a shaky, relieved breath that he didn't die before her eyes.

The carriage door flew open, and a red-faced man exited. His body quivered with rage. "What is the meaning of this?" he demanded to know from his driver.

The driver pointed at her father, who, shocked by near death and slow from the excessive drink, continued to stand in the road.

The red-faced man whipped his cloak over his shoulders

and approached her father. It was only then that Isa noticed the finery of the clothing the man wore and the livery on the driver and on the second man who exited the carriage after the angry man.

"King Tevis." She barely pushed the word through her lips on a breath that felt like ice. Her father had unwittingly stepped into the path and notice of the king.

The king sized up her father for a moment before narrowing his eyes. "And what is this insignificant dog scuttling about the legs of my horses?"

Her father scratched at his nose and sniffed with a great deal of disdain at his king. "I'm the miller, and if you want bread on yer table, I suggest you speak with some respect t' me."

The king laughed.

Her father, uncertain, also laughed.

The driver did not laugh but shot Isa a look that might have been a warning to run or a warning to stand still; Isa couldn't tell which.

The king's laugh broke off, and he leaned low over her father, enough that her father stopped laughing as well. "You should keep laughing, peasant. For tomorrow, you'll be hanging from the gallows for *your* disrespect."

"You're the king," her father breathed. His eyes widened, his newfound terror sobering him to some extent.

"Guard!" roared the king. "Let's make this one comfortable this night since it is the last he'll ever have."

Her father lifted his hands in protest. "I'm sorry, my lord, your greatness, my king. I meant no disrespect. I was only—" Her father's eyes roved the landscape until they fell on Isa. "Only fetching my daughter from the hands of those who would do her wrong."

Isa startled at being singled out and tried to back up into the shadows of the tavern's walls.

"My daughter," her father continued. "You should take her instead. She's of much more value than me, my lord."

Isa's mouth dropped open. Did her father really suggest she go in his stead to hang?

Apparently, the king felt her same shock because his face went slack with disbelief.

Isa's father stammered as if he'd lost his train of thought in his drunken, muddled mind, but then he perked up. "Yes! Take Isa! She is beautiful. She can spin straw into gold!"

The king got over his surprise and narrowed his eyes at her father. "You lie."

Her father hadn't lied, exactly; he'd only gotten the words twisted in his mind. Everyone compared her hair to spun gold. She felt certain her father had tried to bargain off his offense to the king by offering her beauty as payment.

The very idea infuriated and shamed her.

Her father's face looked like ash as the words he'd said unscrambled in his mind. But he didn't admit to the error, which horrified Isa all the more. "No! I don't lie. She's what I said." Though he did not repeat what he'd said, likely because he couldn't be sure he'd be able to say it again in the same way.

The king stared from her father to Isa before saying, "Fine, we'll take the girl. If she is what you say and can spin a room full of straw for me by morning, I'll let her live and consider it payment for your trespass against the crown. If she cannot do as you say, she'll hang in your place."

Isa was taken by surprise when the guard latched on to her arms and pinned them to her sides.

"No!" Isa yelled. "Father! Don't let them take me! Tell the truth!"

The king narrowed his eyes at her. "If he changes his story now, you'll both have trouble. Can you spin straw into gold or not? If you can't, then we'll slit both your throats here and now."

She looked from the king, to her father, to the driver, whose eyes were sad and full of pity. He had been warning her to run; she was sure of that now.

There was no one on the street who could come to her aid or change her circumstances. So Isa, with no other choices left to her, did the only thing she could think to do.

"I can spin straw into gold," she said quietly.

The king's face split into a malicious grin. "Well then, I do love a bit of gold, don't I?"

He was mocking her. Of course he knew she couldn't do such a task. No one could do such a task. All the magic in the woods was not enough for such broken and illogical alchemy.

She lifted her chin. "Your love of such things is well-known, sire."

The guard, recognizing her insult to the king, squeezed her arms tighter to her sides until she cried out in pain as the king said, "Get the little gold weaver out of my sight."

And then he was dragging her away to a cart far behind the royal carriage—a cart filled with the spoils of the tax collectors and watched over by a handsome man with hair dark like walnuts.

Thomas Rumple.

Three

Thomas startled when he saw her but straightened when the guard made a noise in his throat. "Take this one to the livestock cart," the guard said.

"Why? What has she done?"

The guard lightly stroked her hair and brought the end of her single braid to his nose and inhaled deeply. She was sorry she had bathed, sorry she didn't smell like swill water. "Doesn't matter what she's done. What matters is what she'll do. King thinks she might be a witch. But what I know is she hangs in the morning. Get her situated quick-like and catch up. King Tevis isn't waiting." The guard shoved her into Thomas's arms, a place she'd imagined being earlier that day. But she'd never imagined it like this.

And she suddenly hated Thomas. Hated his educated tones and his dark hair and easy smile. Hated his kindness to her grandmother. "You're a tax collector," she said through gritted teeth when the guard had returned to the carriage.

"And you're a prisoner of the king. I'm so glad we met before under more favorable circumstances, or we would likely think terribly ill of each other." He looked her over as if checking for something.

"Why did you have to be a tax collector?"

"Why did you have to be a prisoner?" He asked the question as if he expected an answer.

So she gave him one. "My father stood in the way of the king's carriage. Instead of taking responsibility for his folly, he offered me up to the king with the boast that I could spin straw into gold."

Thomas's eyes widened. "Well then. That's a fine talent. You really should have told me that detail about yourself earlier. I might have run away with you, and it would have spared us the mess we're currently in."

She snorted at him. "You know I can't."

"Run away with me? I don't see why not. I'm a pretty decent fellow once you get to know me."

"I mean I can't spin straw," she said, furious that he seemed to be making a joke out of everything.

But just as she reached the end of patience with him, he sobered. "Don't tell anyone else that. Best to stick to your story." He held a length of rope in his hands, looked at her some more, shook his head, and then pulled a length of cloth from one of the many packs on top the cart.

"So I can hang in the morning?"

"Better a hanging in the morning than a slit throat tonight." He pulled her hands out and lashed them together with the cloth.

"Are you really tying me up?"

"If I don't, then Jarrel will, and he'll use the rope, which will cut into your wrists. The blood will alert the wolves as we travel."

"How nice." She didn't cringe when he tightened the

cloth a little too much and it pinched at her wrist. He loosened the knot as she said, "Jarrel sounds like fine company."

Thomas met her eye with a stern and serious look. "He isn't. Stay out of his reach as much as you can this night. And don't call attention to yourself by disobedience. It'll only make matters worse for you."

The anger from before with her father and then the king and then with Thomas for not being who she had daydreamed him to be finally drained from her and was replaced with a fear unlike any she had ever known. "Then why send me to him? Why not let me stay with you?"

"I am only here to help collect taxes and to keep track of the monetary goods for the night while my master is keeping watch over the palace coffers. Jarrel is the keeper of the living goods. You have to go to him."

"Living goods? There are other people?" she asked, horrified.

"A few. They've been taken to work off their taxes. When the debt is repaid, they'll be freed. There's also the livestock."

He walked her to the back cart in the vast caravan. If she'd entertained any ideas of coaxing Thomas into releasing her, she finally realized just how impossible such a thing truly was. Guards lined the road for what seemed a mile.

They both stayed silent on the long walk to the end. The one time she opened her mouth to ask a question, Thomas tightened his grip on her arm. Speaking would not be allowed.

When they arrived at the last cart, filled with several people who were bound like Isa had been, her eyes fell on the guard.

It was the short tax collector from the gristmill—the one who'd stolen her mother's necklace along with everything else. He sneered when he saw her. "Guess I get to keep everything worth keeping in that mill, after all, eh?" the short man said.

"She's not for you," Thomas said. "She's the king's newest alchemist. She can make gold. Or at least she's going to pretend to until the king has her killed in the morning if she can't."

"If she's being hanged in the morning, why can't we enjoy her tonight?"

"King Tevis has forbidden it. If I find anything amiss in her, I will take the matter directly to the king."

"I'll tell yer master to switch you for being disrespectful. You're not in command of me, pup. Yer nothin' t' me."

"I am not giving commands, Jarrel, but relaying the commands of your king. A man who remembers to obey his king is a man who lives to breathe another day."

Thomas released Isa to Jarrel, but he waited until she was up in the cart with those who had not paid their taxes before he left her to return to his cart at the front.

After a brief delay, the caravan moved forward. Horses, goats, and cattle were tied to Isa's cart, and they plodded along behind it, taking their part in the procession. The animals were why Isa's cart went last. The smell from them overwhelmed her. She tucked her nose into her sleeve so she could breathe without gagging. She wanted to obey Thomas's direction to not call any attention to herself where Jarrel might hear. The less he noticed her, the better because Isa could not be certain Jarrel would heed a warning not to touch her even if it did come from the king.

The fact that it did not *really* come from the king put Isa in great debt to Thomas. She might be hanged in the morning, but she would not be tortured first.

Funny to think of debt when her hands were lashed together and she bumped and rocked alongside the impoverished from her kingdom when she knew she would be dead by sunrise. A debt that would last only a night. She looked at those who were captives due to taxes. Their debt would last much longer as they labored to pay the king.

She rolled her head back and looked up at the thick cloud of stars that banded the nighttime sky like a scarf. Maybe dying wouldn't be so bad. Her mother was dead. Maybe she would join her mother in the stars. Maybe.

To lose the necklace would be nothing if she regained her mother.

She would miss her grandmother, but there was little else in Isa's life to mourn except perhaps sunrises and sunsets, but she felt certain such things kept happening even after a person died.

In spite of the jarring motion of the cart and the discomfort she felt among the people in the cart with her, Isa fell asleep. The day had been long and hard and filled with enough to exhaust her for a week.

She startled awake at the end of their journey while the horses pulling her cart nickered and shuffled. Isa felt shame. When a person had only a few hours to live, it was a waste to sleep away those hours.

Once across the bridge and through the gate, Isa's eyes felt like they could get no wider to take in everything she saw. Gardens like she'd never seen before lay in organized, clean patterns. The castle loomed ahead with stones that seemed like each one might be bigger than her gristmill. And they were all piled on top of one another until they formed a palace as big as a mountain. She gawked like the country girl she was and felt grateful for the half-moon that offered enough light to allow her to see so much. It would have been a pity to come on a night where there was no moon.

Isa was glad that guards other than Jarrel came to fetch her and lead her to whatever the last night of her life held for her.

They guided her up stone palace steps, their boots stomping hard on the stone in comparison to the whisper of her own soft leather-soled shoes. She was led through long halls and even longer flights of stairs. How was so much all under one roof?

At the top of a particularly steep flight of stairs, King Tevis waited on the landing just outside a thick iron-banded door with a lock that looked as if it might bite if one were to try to open it without a key and a proper curtsy.

"Your room, my little gold weaver," the king said with a sneer.

The room held a large pile of straw next to a spinning wheel.

Isa halted at the door, unable to make herself enter, and she found she really didn't want this night to be her last. She didn't want to spend her last night alone among all that straw.

Thinking of her father's bungled attempt to trade her beauty, she also tried and hoped she would succeed where he failed. "My king," she said, clasping her bound hands together in a plea for mercy. "I know my father offended you and was very wrong to do so, but I cannot weave this straw into gold." Isa thought about Thomas's warning to not admit such a thing to anyone else, and she quickly amended, "For if I do, the magic will steal years from my life. So much straw will be a poison to my beauty." She felt sick for resorting to such a ploy, but she knew she was pretty. She could have made a match for herself already if she'd had a father who didn't make all eligible young men turn away.

The king laughed at her. "What care I for your beauty? Half the women in my kingdom are pretty, and the other half are tolerable. One less pretty woman is nothing to me."

Isa had nothing more to say to that. It wasn't like she wanted to tempt him. She loathed everything about him. But she didn't want to die, either. Instead of pleading her cause further, she squared her shoulders and entered the straw-filled room.

"If there isn't gold by morning, then you hang," the king said before he waved to the guard—the same one who'd caught her over by the tavern—to shut the door.

From all the clangs and clacks, Isa knew no escape could come from the door. And though reason told her it was useless, she strode across the room over the straw to peer out the window. The ground was a long way down from the tower they'd placed her in—not so far that a rope wouldn't have worked, but far enough that to jump would be as likely to snap her neck as the noose would.

She turned away from the window to pace the room, testing the walls, hoping for any kind of passage that might lead her away from this mess. The walls were solid, immovable.

So, Isa did the last thing to be done in her situation: she sat at the spinning wheel and tried to spin the straw. She laughed, the noise as brittle as the straw snapping in her fingers as she tried to thread it into the spindle.

"I'm going to die in the morning," she said to the empty room before kicking off her too-tight shoes. Her final hours would not be spent in the misery of pinched toes and aching arches.

And then she covered her face with her hands and cried.

She should have stayed longer at her grandmother's house. She should have held her grandmother longer and tighter and told her how much she loved her. She should have told Grady not to worry about the unpaid-for flour. She should have told him she understood his financial plight and that she forgave the debt. She should have wished him a good business in his bakery and thanked him for making such wonderful tarts. She should have left her father in the tavern to rot forever.

Noise from the direction of the window startled her out of her self-pity. She mopped at her eyes and stood, wondering if a bat had lost its direction and flown into the shutters. Another thump at the shutters made her cross over the straw to unlatch them and peer into the darkness, thinking perhaps a bat might be dizzy on the ledge and in need of help.

To her surprise, a large metal hook had its tip wedged tight between the stones in the ledge. From the hook hung a thick rope. "Thomas?" she whispered, not believing her eyes at all.

He climbed higher as she watched, each hand reaching out toward a knot placed at regular intervals in the rope. A shushing sound came from his lips, so she did not call out to him again, but when he reached the ledge, she pulled and tugged at his clothes to help him over and into the room. A heavy sack hung low down his back from a smaller rope over his shoulders.

He spread himself out on the floor and panted and heaved for several moments before she dared whisper, "What are you doing here?"

"This tower is a lot higher than it looked," he said instead of answering her question.

"It looked plenty high to me when I considered jumping," she responded.

He still gasped and wheezed for air, but he pulled his arms from the loops of the small rope at his shoulders before rolling to his side and sitting up.

As he rolled, he looked down at her stockinged feet and said, "Where are your shoes?"

Too bewildered by his presence to consider why he would ask such a thing, she answered, "I took them off."

"Is it decent to be barefoot in the king's palace?"

She stared at him, opening her mouth to form some sort of answer and then closing it again before she finally asked, "Are you serious? They're killing me in the morning. Decency is not exactly my top concern here. And *you're* a tax collector."

"Actually I'm one of the apprentices to the overseer."

She eyed him warily, not sure if this excused him for being part of the tax collection process. "And you're here because?" She glanced at the rope still hanging from the large metal hook.

"To help."

She fixed her eyes on him. "How?"

He squatted in front of the sack bulging on the ground. He opened the top of the sack, and gold coins tumbled out.

Isa gaped.

"It was quite a job finding coin not marked with the king's crown, so it took longer to get to you than I'd hoped."

"I don't understand," Isa said finally.

"I'll take the straw down with me. You have the gold here as proof you did your part, and in the morning, the king will have to set you free."

"He won't set me free. He'll know I'm lying because no one can accomplish such a task. No rational man would believe in such things."

Thomas scratched his hand through his dark hair. "That's where we find ourselves in a fortunate position. King Tevis is very superstitious. He'd walk a mile to avoid a fairy ring. He'll believe this."

She reached out to touch a coin. "Where did you get all this gold?"

"It's collection day. This gold hasn't been entered into the ledgers. Not yet, anyway."

"You stole gold from the king?" She snatched back her hand.

Thomas squirmed. "Not really. It's not stealing when he's getting it right back."

"Wouldn't it be better just to let me climb down your rope rather than risk him knowing you stole his gold?" She was certain the king would definitely consider Thomas's actions as stealing, no matter what Thomas said.

Thomas shook his head. "The only way off the king's property is through the gate and over the bridge. You could take your chances with the rope and get a guard's arrow in your back, or you can tell him you spun some gold and that a deal is a deal and be set free."

"But—"

"Besides, Isa. He knows who you are and where you come from. You could never go back to your village and be the miller's daughter. He'd send for you, probably hang you right in your own town as an example. He'd string your father and grandmother up beside you for good measure. If you do as he says, he'll have no reason to go looking."

The weight of Thomas's words brought Isa slumping down on the ground next to him. He was right. She looked at the gold coins. They were the only way. And even though the king might see through the lie, it was the best chance.

Isa stared at Thomas. "Why are you doing this?"

Thomas smiled. "We had plans to fix windows and discuss shadows. I was looking forward to those plans. I hate to be disappointed."

She laughed, threw her arms around him, and cried again.

He let her cry and even put his arms around her.

She finally pulled away and settled her hands in her lap, feeling foolish for her impropriety. "Thank you, Thomas. I'm sorry I wasn't nice to you earlier."

"It's not your fault. The tax collectors are hard people to like when they take more than the tax due. When I signed on for my apprenticeship to the overseer, I didn't know this was part of the job. I'm sorry I was a tax collector today."

"Is that what you were doing at my grandmother's house?"

"Yes. But don't worry. I didn't rough her up." He smiled.

She did, too. After he'd gone to all the trouble to haul the gold up the rope, she let him rest while she emptied the sack and then restuffed it with straw. They talked as she worked, and she found there weren't many places she'd rather be. The situation was less than ideal, but the company was excellent. He told her of how he came to be an apprentice and how his apprenticeship was nearly over. He talked about his sister who cared for their aging parents while he was away and about how much his sister would probably like Isa.

There was a lot more straw than what fit in the sack, so Thomas removed his shirt and tied up the bottom of it so they could stuff it, too. She tried not to stare at his bare chest. She'd seen men without shirts before, but somehow in this setting with no chaperones or witnesses, the action felt intimate.

She turned and talked to distract her from what he made her feel. She told him about her mother and the necklace Jarrel had stolen. She told him about her drunken father and the mill and how she actually liked the work of grinding wheat to flour.

They talked about stars and sunsets and their best memories as well as their worst. They talked about plagues and tricks and neighbors they liked and didn't like.

They talked.

Slivers from the brittle straw sliced into her palms and fingers, but she only packed it in tighter, trying to fit every scrap in case the king tried to claim she had missed anything.

"I didn't know," she said once the floor had been entirely cleared.

"Didn't know what?" Thomas asked.

"I didn't know how heavy gold truly was."

Thomas must have realized she stared at the red chafing marks the ropes had cut into his shoulders, because he tried to smile. "It was nothing."

"It was everything. You saved my life. And I'm a stranger with no claim on your goodness."

Thomas's finger touched her chin, lifting it so she met his eyes. "You are no stranger to me. I knew you the moment you slid from your horse's back at your grandmother's house. You took care to check your animal to assure its comfort before you ever approached the gate. Later, I knew you the moment you forgave a poor baker for a debt you could not afford to carry. I know kindness when I see it. I know a gentle heart when I see it for all your talk of shadows. I knew you in all the moments I was able to watch you."

His light touch on her chin sent a shiver of warmth unlike any she had ever known through her.

She thought he might kiss her. They'd already broken so many rules of society; what was one more? But he pulled away and moved to the window while tying his shirt and the sack around his waist.

"I'll see you free in the morning," he said before clambering over the window ledge and disappearing from view.

Isa glanced about the room to be certain no single straw hid in any crack between the stones. But they had been thorough. The job was done.

Isa stacked the gold into tiny piles near the spinning wheel and almost wished they hadn't been so thorough. There were no blankets or anything she could sleep on, and the straw would have provided her with some bedding. Now that she felt assured she would not hang at first light, exhaustion consumed her.

She curled up next to the spinning wheel, tucked her arm under her head, and smiled at the thought of Thomas climbing the rope.

She was certain she dreamed of him, for, as the sounds of the door locks clanking outside her tower room roused her from sleep, her head was still full of him. But she barely had time to think of Thomas or of anything, because the king was in the room with his soldiers, and the soldiers had swords drawn.

Four

Isa hurried to get her feet under her, determined to face the future bravely.

"What is the meaning of this?" the king cried out as his eyes wildly roved the room, his face a mask of blatant disbelief.

"The meaning, sire?" Isa had to be calm, to not be afraid. That was the only way she could make this plan work.

"What is going on here?"

Isa schooled her face into the most innocent look she could muster: with her eyes wide and her mouth opened in surprise. "Why, sire, I've only done as you've asked. I'm sorry I slept when you entered. As I mentioned before, the work takes much out of me."

"Where is all the straw?" The king demanded to know.

"It's here, my lord," Isa said.

As if he hadn't heard her, King Tevis stomped over to the window to peer down to the ground below trying to find evidence of her throwing it out the window. When he saw none, he returned his glare to her. "What have you done with it all?" he asked.

"I speak in earnest when I say it is here, sire." Isa waved her hand over the tidy piles of gold near the spinning wheel.

King Tevis actually took a step back when he saw the gold. He stared at it, took another step back, then finally raised his eyes to hers. His stricken look would have made her laugh if she hadn't been so desperate to leave the tower and never return.

"What mischief is this?" King Tevis barked.

Most of the guards took several steps back behind their king as if the impossibility of the accomplished task filled them with fear of her. That fear on the men's faces said everything.

Thomas's plan would work.

"There's no mischief, sire. You gave me a task, and the task is accomplished." Isa couldn't quite bring herself to say *she'd* accomplished the task.

King Tevis scratched at his beard, frowned, and mumbled. No one else moved. "Where did you hide the straw?" he asked finally.

"I've not hidden anything."

"You could've thrown it out the window." The king lifted his chin, a stubborn child refusing to see reason.

"But then it would be on the ground below, and Your Majesty has already seen nothing lies below."

His gaze finally drifted to the piles of gold. "There's not very much gold, is there?"

His words infuriated her to the core. The rope Thomas used to carry all that gold sliced ribbons into his flesh from the weight, and the king dared complain it wasn't enough? "It's the proper amount for the straw you left me. Sire." She almost forgot herself in her anger and hoped she remembered his title soon enough to appear respectful.

"Well then." His eyes took on a different sort of glint. And to make up for the steps he took back, he circled her like a wolf might a wounded animal. His hand whipped out and latched onto her wrist. He forced her palm up and inspected it carefully. "Those slivers look like they hurt," he observed, his voice sweet and gentle. "You must have worked the straw diligently to acquire such wounds."

Isa was not swayed by the kindness. She did not believe he cared about her pain. But she responded truthfully. "Yes, my lord. They do hurt. And there was much work done."

"We'll have to make sure you have more straw for tonight. You'll want to be more careful as you spin, won't you? It would be a pity to slice your hands further."

Isa felt the blood drain from her face and into her stomach, and she thought she might vomit all over her too-tight shoes. "Tonight? But you said if I did this, I could go in the morning. It's morning, *now*. Sire."

He waved away her protests as he dropped her hand to return his focus to the gold. "I need another night to assure myself this isn't some sort of trickery."

"Trickery, sire? I can't begin to imagine—" But she could imagine and wasn't able to finish the sentence.

He stooped and picked up a coin, feeling the weight of it and peering closely at it. "Is this real gold?" he asked.

"It's as real as anything in your coffers, sire," she said through gritted teeth.

He nodded, accepting her words as truth, which they were truer than he knew. He lifted a tendril of her hair between his fingers and twirled it around the piece of gold. "Fitting for your hair to match your talents."

Isa grasped the only thing she could think of: a desperate lie already told. "I cannot bear another night. I will age with such magic. It could kill me."

He watched her carefully, and in his eyes passed something she'd never seen before: a cold, calculated apathy. There was interest in those hard eyes, too, an interest that hadn't been there the night before. An interest she didn't like. "It doesn't seem to have harmed you yet. You look as well as you did last night."

It was Isa's turn to take a step back. His eyes stayed on her, traveling over the length of her in a way that made her hunch her shoulders against his visual assault.

"Another night will drain me. Age me. If it goes too far, it will—" She floundered for any story that sounded true. "It will turn the gold to lead, and I will fall dead in a pile of ash."

"I'll make sure you're fed to replenish your energies." He turned on a heel and strode to the door. He motioned to the soldiers. "Order food and drink from the kitchens and have it brought up. I would hate for her to lose her strength when she has such a task before her. And make certain to bring up plenty of straw. Twice as much, I think. It will be interesting to see what the little witch can do with twice as much straw." Most of the soldiers filed out.

King Tevis glanced back at Isa and said, "I'll release you in the morning if fortune continues to favor you as it has." He glanced at the gold again, smiled, and swept out the door.

Isa could not allow herself to feel the meaning of her situation or his words. The guards who were left plucked up the gold and stuffed it into bags. As those soldiers left, other guards re-entered with three large bags of straw. They didn't bother removing the straw from the burlap bags but instead left the bags in the middle of the room by the spinning wheel.

The king had said to double the amount of straw, but from the looks of the bags, they had decided to triple it instead.

Isa stood and watched silently as the soldiers went about their tasks of bringing in straw and food for her. She did not move until her door closed and the locks clanked into place from the other side. Only then did she let herself think about everything and feel all of it.

If she threw the bags out the window and stacked them just right, she might be able to jump and let the straw break her fall. She tugged at the knot at the top of one to lift it. It was heavy but not too heavy for her to pick up and move.

She couldn't count on Thomas. Chances were good he didn't know she'd been detained for another night due to the horrible king saying she might be involved in trickery.

Of course, she *was* involved in trickery, but that wasn't the real reason he kept her. She saw the gold reflected in his eyes. He believed her when she said she could spin straw into gold. He just wanted her to make more of it.

She peeked through the thin slat between the shutters. A jump might be possible. It was high up but not absurdly high. If she managed to land the jump right, she might survive. She sighed. Of course, there was that other rather weightier problem of getting off the castle grounds. Chances of getting out of the tower were much higher than the chances of making it over that bridge without an arrow between her shoulder blades, as Thomas had already warned her.

She went away from the window and quietly tiptoed to the door. She listened hard for a long time until she finally frowned at what she heard.

A scratching sound.

And then a long, thick nail bent at an angle and a slip of parchment slid under her door.

Five

A moment later, a long, thin rope slid under the door as well. The parchment had a drawing of her tower with the nail shown coming out of the stones on her ledge and a rope slung over it with a bag tied to the rope. A pulley. Thomas must have heard the king hadn't let her go. And he must have known she couldn't read and was kind enough to leave an illustration.

"Thomas?" she whispered in case anyone else was out there instead.

But no one answered.

This plan can work, she thought as she reviewed the drawing while she ate. She curled up on one of the sacks of straw so she could sleep in preparation for the upcoming night's activities. *This plan can really work.*

She awoke in time to watch the sunset. Then she watched

the stars come out. Once she'd wedged the nail into the stones of her window, she waited.

She waited long enough to worry he might not come. Perhaps the overseer caught him pilfering gold from the coffers. Perhaps the king himself caught him, and Thomas had already met up with a blade's punishment. Perhaps Thomas had decided she wasn't worth the risk.

Stop worrying, Isa. He'll come. Or he won't. And worrying doesn't change it either way.

She considered her options if he didn't come. The bags holding the straw were quite large and sturdy. If she emptied them and lashed them together, she could use them as a rope to the ground. Then she would just have to take her chances with the bridge and the gate.

As she considered these thoughts, she heard a low whistle from below. Relief flooded through her.

He had shown up.

He was not caught and killed, and she was not abandoned.

Before she knew it, the bags of gold rose up via the pulley system, and the bags of straw lowered. Then a bag the size of a peasant's coin purse came up the pulley. The bag was full of ashes. And attached to the bag was another drawing of a face with black under the eyes. He must've heard her story about aging.

She was sad Thomas did not come up to her tower but understood he had to figure out how to return the straw to the stables without getting caught.

With the task completed, Isa lifted the thicker rope from the nail and let it drop. She pried the nail from out of the stones and returned it to the pocket in her smallclothes. Then she dipped her fingers into the little bag of ashes and combed the ashes through her hair. She did it carefully to keep the ashes from clumping and becoming too obvious. She then dragged a line of ash under each of her eyes. She hid the bag inside her clothing.

Isa spent the rest of her wait watching the moon dip back below the horizon and watching the shadows of bats chasing night bugs. Isa thought of her mother and what her mother would think of such a man as Thomas.

She was certain her mother would approve.

The sky turned from black to bruised to gold as the moon left and the sun took its place.

She felt calm as the bolt slid back and the locks clicked from the other side of the door. She remembered to add a slight stoop to her posture as she waited for the door to swing open.

The king entered first. "Well done, indeed!" He didn't bother to suppress his pleasure at the pile of coin by the spinning wheel. He swept up a handful of gold and let it slide through his fingers to the floor. "What a wonderful gift you have!"

He didn't once look around for the missing straw. He believed in her magic. Once the gold had been gathered and removed from the tower, he fixed her with his stare, taking in the loss of luster in her hair and the dark circles under her eyes. "A little maturity looks well on you," was his only response.

She gritted her teeth and waited for him to release her from the tower, for him to say the magic words, "You're free."

But he didn't say those words.

Instead, King Tevis said, "Tonight, I will fill this tower with straw. If you can spin it all into gold for me, I will make you the envy of every woman in the kingdom. I will make you my bride."

Isa cried out in her shock and horror. "You must be mad! I can't spin an entire room full of straw!"

The guards froze behind the king as if they'd never heard anyone deny a request from the king before. She was glad she hadn't refused the marriage part out loud. King Tevis lowered his voice, his anger at her declaration a fiery whisper. "If you cannot spin the straw, then I will have your head cut off in the morning."

Six

Isa couldn't believe what she'd heard. Once alone in her tower again, she paced and fumed and ranted to the walls. Her choices were to marry the king or have her head cut off. She had somehow imagined a marriage proposal to be a little more romantic than a beheading threat.

And did he really say a little maturity looked well on her? Dark circles under her eyes and her hair full of soot were becoming?

It would be nice to be married to a man who saw past a woman's beauty enough to not care about anything more than the soul she was inside, but Isa was no fool. He only looked past her beauty to the gold she might produce for him.

She wanted to wring his neck for his threat to remove her head from *her* neck.

Her tower door opened twice for meals, but no messages or drawings were slid underneath.

Her tower door opened a third time as the sun sank into the horizon, and sacks of straw filled her room. Not just three sacks but a dozen. That decided things for her. Better to die in an attempt to escape on her own terms than by a beheading at the pleasure of the king. There was no way so many sacks of straw wouldn't break her fall. She could figure out what to do next when she was back on the ground.

She snuffed the light from her lamp and waited for the moment between sunset and moonrise when the night promised to be the darkest to begin stuffing the sacks out her window.

From the night before, she had practice on how best to maneuver the heavy, bulky sacks over the ledge and through the tiny window. Isa dispatched the fourth sack when she heard a "Careful!"

She peered out the window and saw two shadows. She didn't recognize them and wasn't sure she hadn't been caught until she heard, "Get the nail set up. We have a delivery." Thomas.

Isa wanted to answer, to explain she didn't want a delivery because that would mean she had to face the fate of marriage to the king and she'd rather be dead, but she didn't answer because the few words already spoken aloud by the people below were too many already. They might have been heard, and the only thing worse than Isa's current circumstances would be for anyone else to suffer because of her.

She kept her silence and put up a nail, and when the thin rope was tossed up, she caught it and tucked it behind the nail under the curve so it wouldn't slip off as Thomas pulled the rope to deliver her a small sack.

In it was gold coins—likely the same gold coins they'd used for the past two nights. The king really did need a more attentive overseer. Isa had every intention of sending the coin back down to the people below with the admonition for them to leave and forget all they'd done and seen, but before she could return the gold, the thick hook Thomas had used the first night was suddenly in the room with her and dragging back until it caught on the stone ledge and pulled tight.

The rope attached to the hook vibrated with motion. Isa peeked over the ledge to peer into the darkness and saw a large, shadowy mass, too big to be a person, ascending the tower wall.

When the form reached the top, she realized it was too big to be a person because it was two people: her grandmother and Thomas. She didn't let her shock delay her action because the idea of her grandmother hanging from the tower filled Isa with dread. What if her grandmother fell? She rushed to grab at her grandmother's clothing and tug her over the ledge and into her room. Thomas and her grandmother spilled out over the window ledge and flopped down on her floor in a puddle of heaving exhaustion.

How her grandmother got onto the palace grounds and how she found Thomas were all questions that could wait.

"What are you doing, bringing my grandmother into all this?" she whisper-yelled at Thomas.

"Have you met your grandmother? Because when I refused to help her, she insisted in a way I couldn't refuse. She has a plan."

"What? A plan to get killed alongside me?"

"I won't be alongside you, child," Grandmother said as she caught her breath from the climbing ordeal. "I will *be* you."

"What does that even mean?" Again, Isa addressed the question to Thomas.

But her grandmother would not be left out of the conversation. "Don't you yell at him, Isa. This was my idea, my doing, and I will not be moved from my decision. Rumor has it you told King Tevis you would grow old if you spun again.

You look enough like me when I was younger that I daresay you will look like me when you get stooped with age. So you are leaving tonight, and I am staying in your place."

"He'll kill you!" Isa cried, horrified Thomas would ever go along with a plan that endangered an old woman's life.

"He won't kill me. You told him his gold would all turn to lead if the magic was overtaxed. I'll tell him it will turn to lead if he kills me."

"I think it'll work," Thomas said, his voice gentle as if trying to soothe her anger to keep her from shouting. She was aware that guards passed the bottom of her stairs regularly and would hear if she was too loud.

"What about crossing the bridge and getting through the gate? Or can you make us disappear the same way you make gold appear from nothing? Can you do magic after all, Thomas Rumple?"

Thomas ignored her anger. "There is a wagon loaded with fabrics to be taken to Austick, a city not too far from here where the fabrics are to be dyed. There is space under the fabrics to keep you alive and well and breathing until we are past the guards."

But Isa would not be placated with the knowledge that he had planned so far in advance. She was still far too angry he'd brought her grandmother into her peril. "So you think you've thought of everything. But how do we return to our prior lives? The king knows who we are and where we live. You said so yourself!"

"There will be no going back for you, Isa. You'll have to find a remote part of the kingdom where we can start over together. Your life before now will have to be forgotten. It won't be easy, but we'll get through it."

"Wait." Isa could not believe what she heard. "You're coming with me?"

He nodded. "If you'll let me."

"Why would you do that?"

He scratched the back of his neck. "I think my sister would like you. I think she'd like the chance to meet you and talk to you and be friends with you. We can go to her and get ourselves settled. We can keep you safe."

She wanted to ask why, but she knew why. She'd spent an entire night talking with him about dreams and stars and life. In the course of one night, she knew there was no one else she'd rather have at her side.

"You don't have to stay with me if you choose otherwise," he said once her silence dragged on for too long.

"I need to think," she said, turning away from the way his features fell.

Of course she wanted to go with him but not like this. Her grandmother taking her place was unacceptable. What could she do? What should she do?

"Is there lead down in the king's coffers?" she asked finally.

"Not in the coffers, but there are bars of it in the armory, where they melt it down for various things they need. Why?"

"As you said, I didn't just tell him I would age. I told him the gold would turn to lead and that I would turn to ash. No one's staying in this tower. We're all leaving in that wagon. And the king will find he should've listened better."

"What is your plan, exactly?" Thomas asked.

"First, we need to get all this straw out."

Without wasting more time with demands and explanations, they went to work on getting all twelve sacks of straw out the window. Then, Thomas had her grandmother get on his back again and hold on tight as he descended the rope. Isa was grateful for all the sacks of straw. If he should lose his grip, her grandmother had something to break the fall.

Isa followed them down on the rope, grateful for the years of hefting large sacks of flour that gave her strength enough to hang on to the rope.

Once down, Isa got her grandmother to the wagon full of fabric and left her there to wait. Isa did not want her grandmother near anything else that might put her in danger, and she planned on giving Thomas a good talking to once they were free of their current mess.

With her grandmother safe, Isa helped Thomas dispose of the straw, which turned out to be much easier than she had imagined. The king kept many such sacks in a large barn near the stables. The inventory was often replenished to make sure the king's animals were never without fresh bedding. The bags would not be out of place so much that they'd draw attention to themselves.

Thomas then tried to take Isa back to the fabric wagon to stay with her grandmother.

"No!" she whispered in the dark after they'd managed to lug the last of the sacks of straw and then cleared up the path of any stray bits of straw. "You are not going to the armory by yourself. What if something happens to you?"

"Nothing's going to happen," he said, sounding almost as stubborn about it as she felt.

"I'm going. The end."

And so she did.

The armory was as complicated as the straw sacks had been simple. The convoluted route was filled with detours and long ways around that would keep them out of the sight of guards and palace staff who would question the wandering of two young people in the middle of the night.

While they waited for a change in guard that would allow them to access the armory without intervention, they managed to tighten into a small crevice where the walls didn't meet together properly. Their bodies were pressed together so tightly, Isa was sure she could feel his heartbeat against her shoulder. His breath, hot at the back of her neck, sent shivers through her. She decided if they were caught at that moment, well, there were worse ways to die.

"I think it's time," Thomas whispered. "We should go now."

Isa hated to leave her snug little hideout but knew they had to take the chances given to them; they had to get moving.

But didn't taking the chances given mean for her to take all the chances?

As Isa edged out of the small space, she whirled to face Thomas, pushed up on her toes, and pressed her lips to his. She caught him by surprise, making him slow to respond, but when he did respond, it was if they had melted into one person. Fire ignited in her belly and flamed to her extremities. When she finally pulled away only because she needed to breathe or she would suffocate in so much fire, she whispered, "No knight has ever known more bravery than you are showing and have shown since the moment I met you."

He didn't respond with words but instead pressed another kiss to her lips that made her feel dizzy with the need to stay there forever tracing kiss after fiery kiss over his lips.

It was Thomas who forced them forward, progressing them toward the armory where the lead bars were kept.

Isa opened the satchel she brought to carry away the lead but grunted when she picked up the piece that was roughly the size of her palm. "It weighs as much as a small sack of flour!" she whispered. Though by the time she'd placed several in her bag to equal that of a bag of gold in bulk, she realized the lead was about half the weight that the gold had been. Thomas had to be exhausted doing this for three nights in a row.

With what felt like the weight of a full grown woman in lead over her shoulders, and with Thomas carrying at least as much if not more, they made their way to where the gold was kept. Thomas made quick work of making a believable-looking exchange. He buried some of the lead under a few piles of gold so it looked like it had turned right where it was.

Once their work in the armory and coffers was through, they made their way back to the outside and around to the side of the palace where her tower waited for them.

"Let me go up and make the changes." Thomas had repeated this statement several times, and each time Isa refused to hear of it.

"If something happens and anyone checks on the tower, it will go better for me than it would for you," she replied.

He didn't argue further, but he also clearly didn't like her answer.

She wrapped her fingers around the first knot in the rope, but he stopped her and kissed her again.

"Just in case," he said.

She nodded and gave a smile. "Just in case."

Once she'd made it to the top and pulled herself over the ledge, she peered down at him, waiting for her with a loyalty no woman had any right to. She hoped they both got out of this situation alive because she knew she would never grow tired of kissing that man.

He used the pulley system to get the rest of the lead to her. She placed small stacks of the lead around the spinning wheel and scattered the rest of the ashes over the seat of the spinning wheel and around it in a way that she hoped looked convincingly like the shape of a human body. She stuffed the bags back into her clothes so her hands were free for the climb, removed the nail and rope from the pulley, and descended the thicker rope to where Thomas waited.

He buried her into the fabrics next to her grandmother and promised she would be out soon.

And then the wagon was moving, clopping over flagstones and then wood and then the hard-packed dirt of the king's road.

She didn't sleep at all for the many miles it took to get to Austick, where the fabric would be dyed. She waited for the moment when the fabric would be cleared away and Thomas would be grinning down at her and probably prepared to kiss her again.

As the sun climbed higher into the sky, the heat under the cloth became nearly excruciating. The stale air felt like it scoured her lungs more than refreshed them. She held her grandmother's hand, only letting go when the heat became too unbearable for human contact.

The wagon came to a stop with a jolt and a cluck of the tongue to the horses. Finally, the cloth was pushed aside, and she was breathing in the fresh air of freedom. But as she blinked at the person standing over her in shadow under the midday sun, she came to a horrible realization.

The person was not Thomas.

Seven

"Grady!" She didn't mean to spit out his name like venom, but her surprise at seeing him there instead of Thomas made her sick. "How are you here? Where is Thomas? Did he get caught? Did he get hurt?" She asked these questions as she thought another altogether: *did he change his mind about her?*

Her grandmother met Grady's gaze with one of resignation. "Grady was who told me you were in trouble and who got me into the king's palace. He knew the king's baker. That was how we found Thomas. Grady agreed to drive the wagon."

"But where is Thomas?" Isa demanded to know.

"He said you'd be mad," Grady observed as the two women shoved aside bolts of cloth and scrambled out of the wagon.

"Where is he, Grady?" Isa begged to know.

"He said it would look strange if an apprentice went missing at the same time things went funny in the coffers. He said for you to take this and go to Norandy and give it to a woman named Gabrielle. He said she'd keep you until he can safely leave and come for you. He said to wait for him."

Her grandmother nudged her. "You go to where he says. You can't come home with me or the king might hear about the miller's daughter returning to Davenport."

"But what about you?" Isa asked.

"I'll go home and watch my garden turn to weed and look like a grandmother properly mourning her granddaughter. But you know I won't be mourning. In my heart, I will be rejoicing because I will know you are safe and loved."

When Isa's gaze slid to Grady, he shook his head. "I'll check on her. She won't be alone."

Isa realized this was how things had to be. Maybe later she could go back privately to visit, but for now, this was how it had to be.

Grady handed Isa and her grandmother each a small satchel and shook his own pocket, which jingled with the weight of coin. He shrugged. "Thomas said he couldn't put this part of it back. Said it would mess up his numbers in the ledgers somethin' awful. Said it was the least he could do after all the tax collectors took from you when they weren't supposed to."

Inside her own satchel was a variety of unmarked coins of various metals and sizes. But Isa barely saw it because her mother's necklace lay on top. Thomas had found it and returned it to her.

She hoped he, like the necklace, would also return to her.

With his promises of silence and his expressions of gratitude, Grady left Isa and her grandmother alone at the edge of the city so he could deliver the fabric as Thomas asked.

Isa and her grandmother stood together watching him leave. "You need a bath," her grandmother said as she finally got a good look at Isa's ash-soaked hair and ash-stained face.

Isa bundled her old grandmother into a tight embrace. "You could've been hurt, coming for me the way you did, climbing into the tower the way you did. Don't ever scare me like that again."

They both turned and walked farther into the city of Austick together. They paid for a night in the inn, baths, and food, and spent the night talking and laughing because they knew they would spend the next day pushing away tears and saying goodbye.

The next day, Isa went shopping and bought clothing that befitted a lady. It was the best way she could think to disguise herself. She tried to buy clothes for her grandmother as well, but her grandmother waved off such frivolous notions. Then Isa hired her grandmother a carriage back to Davenport. Isa waved for a long time after the carriage was no longer in sight. With nothing left to do, she turned and set her sights on a land she did not know and a life she could not yet imagine.

She took the first step in that direction.

Isa arrived at the home of Thomas's sister, Gabrielle, and was met with hugs so engulfing and complete, Isa felt like she might drown in them. Whatever Thomas said in the letter she delivered to his sister must have been very favorable in regard to Isa because his sister acted as though she could not do enough to help Isa.

Neither woman rested easy as they waited for word from Thomas because the king might have been angry. He might have taken it out on the apprentices. Or Thomas might have been caught outright.

Isa walked a little farther each day down the road leading back to the king's palace knowing that if Thomas didn't show up soon, she would end up not turning back as she had been doing each evening.

On one such day, Isa walked past the place where the rivers split, past where the trees gave way to fields, past where the soft soil turned to crumbly shale and sand until she stood and wondered if this was the day she would keep walking until she found Thomas. As she considered her options, a shadow emerged from the scrub oak. The familiarity in the shadow rooted Isa to the spot where she stood. "Thomas?" she whispered.

And then she ran to him.

He caught her and held her so tight, it felt like he pressed all the places that felt unhinged back together again. She smiled and thought of the first time she saw him fixing the hinges on Grandmother's door.

"Did you come to fix shutters?" she asked after he loosened his grip on her.

He dipped his head close to hers so she could see into his dark eyes. "I've actually come to chase shadows." And then he kissed her in a way that felt like a good start to sweeping all hint of shadows away.

About Julie Wright

Julie Wright started her first book when she was fifteen. She's written over a dozen books since then, is a Whitney Award winner, and feels she's finally getting the hang of this writing gig. She enjoys speaking to writing groups, youth groups, and schools. She loves reading, eating, writing, hiking, playing on the beach with her kids, and snuggling with her husband to watch movies. Julie's favorite thing to do is watch her husband make dinner. She hates mayonnaise but has a healthy respect for ice cream.

Visit Julie's website: JulieWright.com
Twitter: @scatteredjules

The Pebbled Path

Sarah M. Eden

One

Once upon a time, far away and long ago, a man and his daughter lived in a meadow at the edge of a forest. The man loved his daughter, and she loved him. They were not wealthy, neither were they important in the eyes of the world, but they were happy.

Yet time marched on, as it always does, and the man was forced to admit that his daughter could not remain so isolated forever. She had, with increasing frequency, spoken wistfully of meeting a handsome young man, falling in love, having a home and family of her own. He could not deny her that dream.

With winter gone and spring making herself known, the man gathered food and supplies enough to see them to the nearest village, where he hoped to introduce his daughter to families with young people her own age with whom she might form friendships. Perhaps among them she might find a suitable young man. He had no expectations of an immediate match; indeed he earnestly hoped for the opposite. This, he told himself, would simply be their first journey of many. In time, she would find her future. For now, they would focus on improving her present.

He led their pony cart along the narrow and seldom used path through the forest. He knew the way well. They ventured to the village twice per year, though only to replenish supplies and sell goods of their own. This time, their purpose was more personal, and the journeys would, from this moment forward, be more frequent.

Gretel, his beloved daughter, was aware of their reasons for journeying. A nervous smile hovered unchanging on her lips. Her eyes were wide with anticipation. "Will there be a great many young people my age?" she asked.

"Have you been lonely, Gretel?"

"No, Papa." The eagerness in her expression belied her declaration.

"The village boasts many families," he said as they traveled deeper into the forest. "You have met them in years past. Surely you remember."

She leaned against him, a warm buffer against the chill breeze. Winter no longer held the forest in her grip, but warmth had not entirely returned.

"I do remember," Gretel said, "but I wish to hear again. Never before were we going there with the sole purpose of making friends."

He told her of the families he knew, the size of the village, its many prospects and enjoyable activities. She asked more questions than he'd heard from her at any one time. His darling child was excited. Her anxiousness added to his. Though he knew this journey would signal the beginning of the end of their time together, he found he could look on the pending change with increasing happiness.

They reached a familiar fork in the road. He made to guide the pony in the appropriate direction, but hesitated. Indeed, his indecision led him to stop their forward progress altogether.

"Papa?" Gretel asked, eyeing him with confusion.

"Forgive me." He eyed both paths ahead of them, no longer certain which was the correct one. "I believe we must go right."

"No, Papa. I remember this well. We are to go left."

That, he now felt certain, was wrong. "No. We are meant to go right."

"But, Papa—"

"Gretel," he answered firmly. "I have never been more certain. We are meant to go right. We *have* to go right."

He guided the pony to take the right side of the fork, even as his daughter more loudly insisted he was mistaken. He would not be deterred. The farther down the road they traveled, the surer he was of his decision. This was the right path, the best path. It was important that he travel it. Turning back would never be an option.

He flicked the reins, urging the pony faster. Reaching the end of the road was paramount. The need to do so quickly filled every thought, every thud of his heart, every breath. On and on they went. Faster and faster.

"We have gone the wrong way," Gretel insisted. "Please, Papa. We must turn around."

Her pleas only served to urge him forward, a desperateness to prove her wrong. This was the path he had unknowingly been looking for all his life.

"Please, Papa."

On and on.

"Please."

And on. Until, quite without warning, a cottage appeared

before them. He had been looking for this very place, this very spot. He felt certain he had been, though he could not say with any confidence when he had begun looking for it, nor how he knew it existed, only that this was where he had to be.

"I do not like this," Gretel said.

"I must go in. I must."

"What of our trip to the village?" Worry laced her words.

He eyed his daughter, baffled that she felt none of the excitement, none of the pull that he did. How could she not? He'd never felt anything so powerful.

"I must go in." He alighted from the cart and walked with swift steps up the flower-lined path. Every step felt more right than any step he'd taken before.

He knocked frantically on the cottage door, desperate for it to be answered. He knocked again. Footsteps sounded inside. Relief surged through him. Closer the steps drew. Louder. Only his pulse sounded with greater volume.

The handle turned. The door pulled open.

There in the doorway stood the most alluring woman he had ever seen in all his life, the most exquisite woman who had ever lived. He could do nothing but stand in mute awe of her beauty.

"Welcome." Her voice warmed him through, pulling the very breath from his body.

He stepped inside, his eyes never leaving her. Such beauty. Such grace. He stopped in the middle of her sparsely appointed home, words eluding him. The woman walked in a circle around him, looking him over. He straightened his posture, held himself proudly, all the while quaking with fear that she would find reason to disapprove.

"You are handsome," she said, "though not so young as I might have hoped."

"Forgive me," he begged. "I would have come sooner, but

I knew not how to find you. I knew not that I ought to find you."

"It is of little matter." Her smile pulled a sigh of utter relief from him. "You've youth enough."

She closed the gap between them. The tip of one velvet-soft finger traced a path along his hairline, down his jaw, brushing lightly along his neck. Her touch was mesmerizing.

"I hope you mean to stay," she said, her words deep yet airy.

"I could never leave you," he insisted. "No one could ever make me."

A single golden brow arched in pleased amusement. "You will do whatever I ask of you?"

"Anything at all."

She gave half a nod. "Very good."

"Tell me what it is you wish."

She leaned close, her face near enough his for her breath to tickle his face. "I wish you to take your supper with me."

"I will take all my suppers with you."

"Yes," she whispered. "All of them."

She kissed him quickly, lightly. As she broke the contact and stepped away, he felt as though some of his breath and a few beats of his heart left with her. He watched, ready to beg her to return should she move too far away.

"Come, sit," she bade. "I will prepare our supper."

He followed, desperate to do whatever she might ask of him. Somehow, everything depended upon her happiness. Everything.

"Papa?" a small voice interfered.

Frustration bubbled. He did not wish for interruptions. Distractions would only mean he might miss a request or a moment of his lady's company and affections. He turned to bid the one interrupting to leave, only to realize that he had, somehow, forgotten Gretel. His own daughter.

"Gretel." He bade her step inside. "You must meet—"

He knew not the name of his lady love. She did not supply it.

"Why have you come?" she asked Gretel. "I've no need of you."

"My papa and I are journeying to the village on the other side of the forest." She spoke to his love with disapproval. How could she?

"Gretel," he scolded.

But her eyes did not leave the vision of beauty before them, a vision she appeared to dislike intensely. He would not countenance such rudeness.

"You must apologize," he insisted. "I mean to stay here from now on, and you must not be rude."

"Stay here? You cannot," Gretel said. "We have a house of our own. We are visiting the village." She looked back to the beautiful woman once more, revulsion filling her expression. "We must go."

"*You* must go." He knew it to be the truth the moment he said the words. Gretel did not belong, but he did. He always had, always would. "I will remain here with this enchanting and beautiful woman."

"Beautiful?" Gretel repeated the word as if it made no sense. "Do you think she is beautiful?"

Could she not see what was right there before her? "No one has ever been more beautiful." He returned his gaze to the vision before him, determined to never look away again.

His daughter and his newfound love continued to speak to each other, though the longer he stood there, the less he cared what they said. All that mattered was remaining in his love's company and doing whatever she asked him to do.

"You are a witch," Gretel said.

The woman laughed lightly. "An enchantress. There is a difference."

"What do you mean to do to him?"

For a moment, his enchantress looked at him, and his heart sped with hope. But she looked away again, back to Gretel. "We are to have supper together."

"And tomorrow?" Gretel pressed.

"We will have supper again, then again the next day, and the next, for however long it takes."

"However long *what* takes?"

Again, a golden eyebrow reached upward. "You ask a great many questions, child."

"I suspect you intend to kill my papa," Gretel said. "That entitles me to a few questions."

He adjusted his position so the beautiful woman upon whose favor he depended remained in his sight.

"You have pluck," she said to Gretel. "I like that. And you are young, able-bodied."

He did not like that she had lost interest in him. His very purpose was to bring this beauty whatever might give her joy, but she had turned away from him. "Dearest one."

"Hush," she instructed.

He immediately and silently vowed not to speak again until he was bidden to do so.

Once again speaking to Gretel, she said, "You are also clever. Not many realize so quickly the fate that awaits men who arrive at my door."

"Only men?" Gretel asked.

She shrugged a shoulder. "An oddity of the magic. Still, it does make things more fun."

"That does not sound like fun."

The woman laughed. How he wished *he* had been the one to make her laugh.

"I might be willing to spare your father," she said, still to Gretel. Would she never speak to him again? The possibility spread fear in his heart. "You would have to do something for me, though."

"What would I have to do?" The girl did not even seem to be enjoying their conversation. How could she not realize the privilege it was to have this woman's attention? He would have given anything to have it back.

"I am in need of a servant," she said. "Someone to fetch water and firewood, clean the house, care for the gardens."

"You are offering a trade? My servitude for his life?"

A simple nod.

"How do I know I can trust your word?"

"Clever girl."

She ought to have been offering *him* compliments. He would have said as much, but she'd not given him permission to speak again.

"Ours is a mutual agreement," she said. "I will bind us to it on a talisman, one that will annul our promises should either of us break our word. Should I cause harm to your father, you will be freed from your servitude."

He waited impatiently for her attention to return to him.

"And if something were to happen to you?" the girl asked his lady love.

The answer began on a laugh. "Foolish child. Do you think me so weak as that? I am protected by magic more powerful than you can imagine. I cannot simply be killed, so you had best put that idea from your mind."

"What is to stop me from fleeing or refusing to live a life of servitude?" The girl spoke a great deal.

Even as the woman's gaze narrowed in apparent anger, she remained exquisite. "Your father would be lured back."

His love stood in silence, watching the child, waiting. He did not look at the girl to see what she felt. Only this vision before him mattered.

"What if he comes looking for me?" the girl asked.

"He won't."

He moved to close the distance between them, but his love waved him away. He obeyed.

"I will send him away, and he will agree to go. Upon returning to the fork in the road, the spell will be broken, but he will remember nothing of what is here, and that includes you."

"He would forget me? His own daughter?"

"There is a price to be paid for cheating fate. Are you willing to pay it?"

He did not see her answer. He did not look.

A moment later, his love turned to him once more. She snapped her fingers. Confusion settled over him. He still knew he wished nothing more than to remain, yet he could not remember why.

"Go," the woman said. "Climb into your cart and drive home."

"I will do whatever you ask," he said. He indeed would, but the declaration sounded odd to his ears. He turned and walked toward the door. The younger woman stopped him with a hand on his arm.

"Pardon me," he said and pushed on.

Go. The instruction repeated in his mind, forceful, unignorable. He climbed into his cart and set the pony in motion. All his attention focused on the path laid out before him. It was very important that he reach home quickly. He flicked the reins, setting the pony at a faster clip. Onward and onward. Faster and faster. Until the path he rode merged with another.

A cool spring breeze rustled the trees all around him as he made his way home. Trips into the forest were enjoyable, but he always looked forward to returning home to the quiet solitude that awaited him there. Many might think a man alone would be lonely, but he wasn't.

He'd always been alone, and he found comfort in it.

Two

The days passed and grew into weeks. Gretel thought often of her papa, though doing so broke her heart. The enchantress's required forfeiture meant that Papa had no recollection of her. He did not miss her as she missed him. He did not mourn her or grieve her. In his mind, she never existed.

No one would ever know how miserable she was. No one would ever come to rescue her. She was not afraid, though. She intended to rescue herself.

Gretel worked hard without complaint. She did all that was asked of her, knowing that maintaining her part of the bargain was essential to protecting her father. But as she worked, she thought and plotted and reminded herself that she was clever and brave. When the solution presented itself, she would be ready to take advantage.

Being the enchantress's servant meant Gretel could not leave the forest. Doing so would invalidate their agreement.

The enchantress always slept late, allowing Gretel the morning to see to her chores indoors, then escape to the outdoors once her mistress was awake.

She had responsibilities in the garden, something she had expected to enjoy. But the garden was an unnerving place. The tall wall, built of stone columns taller than she was, formed a semi-circle at the far end of the garden. It was an imposing structure, made even more so by the constant trickle of water seeping from the rock and spilling into the soil. The wall must have been built upon a spring of some kind. The drip, drip, drip of water echoing around her as she saw to the weeding and tending of plants pricked at her nerves. Gretel never remained in the garden any longer than she had to.

That left her but one temporary escape: the forest itself. The enchantress insisted that she fetch their water from the stream some distance away. Gathering it from the stones in the garden was expressly forbidden, something for which Gretel was grateful.

In the forest, she found some peace.

At the end of her first month of servitude, as the enchantress barked complaints and instructions, Gretel noted how very tired and haggard the woman looked, which was something of a feat unto itself. For, though her father had insisted he saw a woman of unparalleled beauty, Gretel saw nothing of the sort. Her mistress, she would wager, was a monster of some kind. Her skin was a sickly green and her eyes yellow. Her hair was silver, but not in the pleasing way a person's hair whitened as life marched on. It nearly glowed, crackling with something very like the residue of a lightning strike. Her fingers more closely resembled claws than a human hand. Beyond her appearance, she inspired in Gretel an undeniable and almost irresistible urge to run, to hide. She hadn't that luxury.

The enchantress looked less vital of late. Her green coloring turned to a greenish gray. Her lightening hair sat flat and dull. Her yellow eyes faded to the point of being almost colorless. Perhaps she was ill. Gretel was not usually one to wish illness on another, but escape would be far more likely if she were not contending with one in possession of such powerful magic as she had seen the enchantress wield.

That night, Gretel, whom the enchantress banished each evening to the dank and dim basement, was sent below earlier than usual with instructions not to emerge until sunup. The enchantress would not be requiring anything of her until then.

She had never been granted a reprieve from her chores. Grateful, she took advantage, secluding herself below. She lit the single candle she was permitted to chase away the shadows, and she sat and pondered and planned.

Except she had no real plan. She hadn't yet sorted out any means of ridding herself of her vow to the enchantress. To simply break that vow would cost Papa his life. Her only hope was magic, but she had none of her own.

The talisman the enchantress hung over the cottage door, the one that bound them both to their agreement, was the closest thing to obtainable magic Gretel could think of. Would breaking it break their vow as well? She would be free, but Papa would no longer be protected.

No. That would never do.

What she needed was a means of accessing the enchantress's powers. A magic spell of her own or a potion, something of that nature. Did her mistress keep her magical knowledge entirely inside herself or had she a book of some kind where she read and studied her art? If Gretel could find that book . . .

She stopped her pondering, certain she heard a deep,

rumbling voice. She listened more closely. Nothing but silence. Odd, that. A moment later, the tiniest bits of words spoken by the enchantress floated through the floor. That wasn't entirely unusual; her mistress often spoke to herself while preparing her food. The enchantress only ate food she made herself—an unusual approach, considering she made Gretel do everything else.

When no more sounds met her ears, Gretel returned to the subject foremost in her thoughts. If she could find a book explaining how she might undo the spell while still protecting her father, she would not hesitate to make the attempt. But where ought she to look?

Again, she thought she heard a deeper voice, but upon listening more closely only heard silence. The same baffling sequence of events occurred repeatedly as the evening wore on. Perhaps the enchantress's voice changed as much as her appearance could. Perhaps the thickness of the ceiling above Gretel's head distorted the sound.

She did not manage to sort out the puzzle before weariness required she extinguish her candle and rest. She did, however, firmly resolve to spend her mornings, while the enchantress slept, in a determined effort to find a spell book.

Gretel did not mean to live out her life trapped as she was. Somehow, she would be free.

When the first rays of dawn streamed in through the gap around the door, Gretel lifted the trapdoor to the basement. All was still and quiet above. She would see to her duties quickly and efficiently and, if she were truly fortunate, would have time enough to search for the enchantress's spell book.

The table had been moved—not drastically, but enough to be noticed. So had the bench that usually sat in front of the fireplace, and the enchantress's throne-like chair. She had never known her mistress to rearrange the room. This did not look intentional, really, more the result of things being pushed out of the way and not returned to their rightful place.

Had the enchantress undertaken a ritual of some kind? Perhaps she'd required more room to prepare a potion or spell. Worry clutched Gretel's heart at the possibility. The last spell she had seen the enchantress cast had been the very one keeping Gretel with her, and it had followed a spell cast over her father, one intended to end his life.

The sooner Gretel discovered the location of a spell book or some other form of written instructions, the better. Her future was not the only one in need of securing. Any man the enchantress lured, as she had Gretel's father, would be killed.

She swept and scrubbed the floor. She washed the windows. The fireplace was swept, the furniture returned to its original locations. All the while, she looked in cupboards, behind the sideboard, in the backs of shelves. She found nothing resembling a collection of spells. The house was not large; there were few places such a thing might have been hidden.

Her gaze moved slowly to the two closed doors at the far end of the small cottage. One was the enchantress's own bedchamber. The other had no occupant, but Gretel had not been permitted the use of it. She could not search the enchantress's room, especially not while she was in it. But if Gretel was very quiet, she might manage to look in the other.

With careful steps, slow and deliberate, avoiding any floorboard that might squeak, she crossed the room, all the while eyeing with trepidation the door to her mistress's bedchamber. It did not open. The distinctive buzzing of the enchantress's snores echoed quietly within.

Gretel took a shaking breath and reached for the handle of the other door. She turned it downward and gently pushed. The door did not budge. She tried again. When a third attempt proved futile, she tried pulling it instead. Still, nothing happened.

The door was locked. But Gretel had never before seen a key in the house. How was she to find what she needed if doors were locked with no means of opening them?

Something rustled in the enchantress's room. Gretel swiftly returned to the fireplace and pretended to be just finishing sweeping up the ashes. Behind her, the door of the enchantress's bedchamber opened. Gretel took a slow breath, reminding herself to remain calm.

She stood, dustpan in hand. Keeping her expression neutral, she turned, intending to offer a small dip of her head in acknowledgment, as she always did. But the sight that met her surprised her so greatly that she could do little but stare.

"You appear to be feeling better," Gretel said. Indeed, the enchantress's yellow eyes glowed with life once more. Her skin had lost its hint of gray. Her silver hair shone brilliantly. She was hideous, as always, but somehow less haggard.

The enchantress declared herself quite well in tones of smug satisfaction, before ordering Gretel back to work. Gretel, grateful for the escape, slipped from the house to tend the garden. Her enthusiasm waned as she approached that corner of the yard. Oh, how she hated the garden with its looming wall of weeping rocks, its dark shadows and dismal corners. She would weed and harvest and tend as quickly as she could.

Just as the house had changed overnight, so had the garden, but in a far larger way than the mere movement of furnishings. A new stone pillar had been added, one as tall and wide as the others. When had it been placed, and by whom? And why was this new rock dripping water like the others if it had only recently arrived?

The enchantress must have placed it there. That, no doubt, was the reason for Gretel's discomfort. Even this secluded corner of the tiny world Gretel now occupied bore the mark of her task master, a master she feared she would never escape.

Three

In the far western corner of the kingdom, a young man named Hansel, who possessed a particular talent for woodworking, both of an intricate and practical nature, determined that, should he hope to find any success in his chosen profession, he would do well to make his home in a place near a large supply of wood. Only a forest would do.

He packed his tools and his few belongings, kissed his mother and father farewell, and journeyed to the large eastern forest. Fate appeared to be smiling upon him, for he found on his first day near the legendary woods a woodsman who lived alone, someone having recently given up claim to an empty room in his house. He did not speak of his recent tenant in any specific terms, but he seemed generally pleased with his situation and asked no money in exchange for a place where Hansel might lay his head. He required only that the younger man help with those chores that age made difficult for him.

Hansel ventured the next day out into the forest, though not very far. The next day, he went a bit farther. The next day, farther still. If these woods were to be his home, he needed to become familiar enough with them to not get lost, and he needed to learn to love them. One could not expect to benefit from the bounty of a forest otherwise.

Farther and farther he went, making note of each variety of tree, discovering which were softest and most easily carved, which were stronger and better suited to the building of furniture. He noted those that were more abundant and those he would need to harvest with caution lest none be left. He spent his days on the winding paths amongst the thick stands of trees. And he did, indeed, grow to love his new forest home.

After nearly two weeks of daily exploring, Hansel came upon a stream. The water flowed cool and clear, tumbling over rocks and twisting around tree roots. Sunlight danced over its ripples, filtering down through the canopy of leaves above.

He found a fallen log, one of a perfect height for sitting on, and allowed himself a quiet moment to take in the beauty of the scene. This would be the perfect spot for working on his more intricate bits of carved art.

Footsteps broke the silence. He turned to see a young woman nearly his own age approach. She had not seen him yet, and he watched her approach the stream. A yoke sat on her neck, a bucket swinging on both ends. She had come to fetch water.

Hansel had not seen another soul in the weeks he'd spent in the forest. He could not countenance missing the opportunity to make the acquaintance of perhaps the only neighbor he had outside of the man with whom he lived.

"Do you come to the stream often?"

His words startled her. The yoke slipped, and she struggled to right it. Hansel leaped from the log and moved to assist her.

"My apologies," he said. "I did not mean to frighten you."

She shook her head, watching him with concern. "I have never seen anyone here before."

"I am newly arrived in this part of the kingdom," he said. "Do you live in the forest?"

"Yes. All my life."

He took one of her buckets and, lowering it into the stream, filled it.

She smiled at him as she filled the other bucket and set it on the stream bank beside the first. "What has brought you here?"

"I am a woodworker. Where better for me to ply my trade than in a place so filled with trees?"

"And what place is more filled with trees than a forest?"

A thought entered his mind, one he spoke aloud. "I imagine you know the forest well, having lived here so long."

She nodded. "The forest is like a friend to me. I know it very well."

Sensing in her one who shared his enjoyment of trees, he asked about the forest and if she liked one variety of tree better than another. She responded with all the enthusiasm he felt. She told him of a fragrant variety of evergreen found along the northern edge of the forest, not far from where he now lived. She spoke of a small bush with a thick trunk, the wood of which was a deep shade of red. His curiosity was not met with dismissal on her part, but appreciation. He felt certain he could talk to her all the day long and never grow weary, never run out of things to say.

Alas, after a time, she took up her yoke and water and began to walk away.

"Must you go?" he asked.

"I must." She seemed to regret her departure.

"May I walk with you?" he asked.

She immediately shook her head. "My mistress is very strict, and she watches me closely. I must return alone."

Her mistress. She was a servant, then.

"Do you come to this stream often?"

"Every day at about this time."

"Perhaps I will see you again tomorrow."

She smiled softly. "I hope that you will."

Hansel arrived at the log near the stream earlier the next day, not wishing to miss her arrival. After a time, his efforts were rewarded. The young lady arrived. Only after they had parted the day before did he realize he had not learned her name. The man with whom he lived was not aware of anyone matching her description who lived in the forest, neither did he know of any household that kept servants. But then, he'd admitted, he did not know everyone who lived in the forest. It was a vast and mysterious place, all the corners of which no one person had ever traversed.

But she was there again. She smiled when she saw him, the expression one of both pleasure and welcome. He returned it and joined her at the water's edge.

"Good afternoon," he said.

"To you as well."

"I neglected to learn your name when we were together yesterday," he said. "And I do not believe I gave you mine. I am Hansel, and I hail from the western kingdom."

"I am Gretel, and I hail from the eastern forest."

He offered a bow and she a curtsy, and they walked together along the banks of the stream. They spoke of plants and trees as they had before but also ventured to other topics. He learned that she enjoyed the sunrise, she liked to read though she hadn't access to any books, her mother had passed away long ago, and her father was far away.

He, in turn, told her of his childhood home, of his

parents, his brothers and sisters. He told her of the carving he did and the furniture he built. He told her of his dream to one day sell his goods throughout the area. However, when he asked her what dreams she had for her life, she gave a vague response, devoid of any real answer. Was there nothing she longed for? Surely there must be.

"If your life could be anything at all," he asked, "what would you choose?"

"I haven't time for pondering such things." She bent and picked up her water pails, they having circled back to the spot where she'd left them. "I must return. My mistress will be cross if I delay."

He helped her balance her yoke. "Will I see you tomorrow?"

"I will try."

She was not there the next day, though she was the day after that. The days passed in that same unpredictable pattern. The time he spent with her drew him ever more to her. He sensed her situation was not a happy one, yet she was not an unhappy person. The burdens she carried, figuratively and literally, were not light, yet she was not crushed by them.

She was a woman worth knowing better. Somehow, he would manage precisely that, even if he had to petition her strict mistress directly.

Four

Though Gretel's trips to fetch water had brought her tremendous joy over the past weeks, her time in the enchantress's cottage grew more miserable by the day. The enchantress frequently grew short-tempered, impatient, and ill. Just when Gretel felt certain her horrible mistress was beyond recovery, she would improve, sometimes overnight, sometimes over the course of a few days.

The transformation always followed the same pattern: The enchantress's health grew incredibly fragile. Gretel was banished to the basement before her usual time. While down there, she heard voices, yet never saw anyone come or go during the day, never heard the enchantress mention visitors. In the mornings, the furniture would be moved about in nonsensical ways.

Always, whether the pattern repeated for days on end or

only one night, the enchantress would improve, returning to her previous state of health and vitality. And Gretel always knew when her early banishment would end by watching the garden. A new pillar of rock would appear in the wall one morning. The enchantress would appear hale and hardy, and Gretel would remain above ground until the usual time.

She did not know precisely what was happening above her during that time, but she worried greatly. What could she do, though? She had not yet found a spell book or a guide to potions or anything that might help her make sense of what she was seeing, certainly nothing to help her escape. Her one consolation in the loneliness and worry was Hansel—dear, kindhearted Hansel.

More than a month had passed since she had first made his acquaintance. They spent more time together than they had at first. She asked him to meet her in the mornings, rather than the afternoon. With her mistress asleep, she need not rush back to the cottage. Her time was more her own. This meant being inside the cottage more often when the enchantress was awake. It was a misery, but she was willing to endure it.

Her papa, she felt certain, would have liked Hansel. Indeed, the man with whom Hansel lived reminded her of Papa. At least, she thought he did. She often grew confused when thinking of him, as if bits and pieces of her memory were hiding just out of reach. Had she been away long enough for that to be possible?

As she walked in the direction of the predetermined meeting place, Gretel attempted to remember how long she had lived in the enchantress's cottage and found, to her astonishment, that she was not entirely certain. Had it been months or years?

"Gretel."

Her eyes darted upward, her gaze having dropped to the path as she pondered the inexplicable gaps in her memory. There stood Hansel. She hadn't yet reached the place they had intended to meet.

He offered her one of his friendly smiles and a deep purple wildflower. "I knew you lived in this general direction."

"Why would you not wait where we had decided?" Worry rendered her question more forceful than she would usually have asked it.

His brows pulled together in confusion. "I thought we might enjoy a bit of additional time with one another."

She could not like the idea of him coming so close to the cottage. The enchantress had laid some kind of trap for Papa. Gretel still remembered the way he had suddenly veered from the route they'd determined to take. Nothing she said had persuaded him to continue down the road to town. She felt certain that, should Hansel come too close, the same spell would lure him into certain danger. Though Gretel managed to bargain for Papa's life, she had nothing to offer that might save Hansel's.

"I would very much like to show you the stand of poplar tress I told you about a few days ago." She hoped the abrupt change of topic did not raise his suspicions too greatly. "They are closer to where we intended to meet. We will have a little bit of a walk."

Hansel carried a bag of tools slung over one shoulder. He offered her his free hand, something he'd done more and more often of late. Happily, she accepted it. He had, over the many weeks of their acquaintance, brought such light into her life. He had shown her unending kindness. The tender flower she carefully held stood as such a simple but loving symbol of that kindness. Should harm befall him at the enchantress's hand, Gretel did not think she would ever forgive herself.

She immersed herself in the joy of their time together in the poplar grove. They laughed. They shared thoughts and stories. At times, they simply sat in comfortable silence.

When the time came for her to depart, she did so by a roundabout path, which she ought to have done from the beginning. Her consistency had very nearly shown him the way to the cottage. That, she knew full well, was a dangerous thing.

The time had come to redouble her efforts to find the elusive spell book and put an end to the enchantress's grip on her life and future.

Gretel arose early the next morning, long before the enchantress would rise, and set herself in front of the door to the unused bedchamber. The book she sought had to be in this room or the enchantress's; there was no other possibility. But how did one enter a locked room without the key?

The door was made of a heavy wood, far too solid for her to break open. Even if she possessed the size and strength for that feat, the enchantress would be sure to hear. Gretel had already examined the outside of the house and knew the bedchamber window was shuttered with the same impenetrable wood.

Oh, there must be a way inside. She leaned against the door, desperately thinking. Though she had done so dozens and dozens of times without success, Gretel tested the handle once more. To her great shock, the door gave way, swinging open on silent hinges. A never-opened door to an unused room ought to squeal, to protest in some way, but this one did not. The door and room beyond were not as neglected as they first appeared.

The space beyond was dark, the window entirely covered by the thick shudders. She fetched a candle, lit it, and stepped tentatively inside. The room was not empty, though only just.

A narrow cot was pushed against the far wall. In the center of the room was a long wooden table, on top of which sat an iron cauldron. Jars of different sizes containing a variety of unidentifiable things—some solid, some liquid, some appearing to be little more than colored smoke—lined the room.

But the thing in the very middle of the table caught and held her attention: a seemingly ancient, leather-bound book. She tiptoed closer and read the gold lettering: *Sundry Magical Enchantments.*

The spell book, at last.

She opened it, her heart pounding. Page after page of spells and potions—some designed to transform ordinary objects into other objects, some designed to impact people's beliefs and actions. She paused at a potion entitled Artificial Beauty. By taking the potion, one would appear irresistibly attractive to a chosen group of people. Adjusting the ingredients allowed the potion maker to decide who would be affected by it. Among the many unsettling options was "children under the age of ten." Gretel's stomach turned at that. Another option was "unattached men." That was likely the variation the enchantress used. It had worked on Papa, who had been a widower for many years and had no romantic attachments. He had described the enchantress as the most beautiful woman in all the world. Gretel, on the other hand, never saw anything but the green-skinned, silver-haired, claw-handed hag she truly was. No instructions were included for undoing the enchantment.

Gretel turned page after page, hoping to find something that might pertain to breaking the spell binding her to the enchantress. The language was old, difficult to decipher. She could not simply skim over the book's contents. Soon enough, the enchantress would awaken, and her time with the book would come to an end.

Her search revealed a spell entitled Allurements, a means of enchanting small objects with the ability to lure a person in a given direction. This, no doubt, was the means by which the enchantress had enticed Papa off the road he'd intended to take. Something near the fork in the road had pulled him toward the cottage. The same fate would, she felt certain, befall Hansel should he draw too close.

The book contained instructions for creating allurements specific to an individual. If she could create ones for Hansel in particular and lay them in such a way as to lead him *away* from those placed by the enchantress, then he would be safe. She need not worry that he might follow her to his doom.

The enchantress's loud, sleep-heavy breathing continued in the next bedchamber. Gretel yet had time to save her dear Hansel. She gathered the items for the potion. Amongst the ingredients was "something bestowed upon the potion-maker by the one who is to feel the pull of the allurements." She pulled from her apron pocket the small wildflower he'd given her, which she had pressed beneath a heavy pot in the kitchen overnight, and dropped it in with the other ingredients.

Lastly, she needed something to carry the allurement, something to place along the path she wished him to take, the one leading away from here.

Whatever they were, the allurements needed to draw little attention to themselves, lest someone remove them. What was unlikely to draw notice in a forest? Leaves, perhaps? No. One gust of wind would undo her efforts. Bread crumbs? No. Birds would most certainly eat them. Pebbles, perhaps?

Yes. Pebbles would be perfect.

She hurried from the cottage and grabbed two handfuls of pebbles, returning with all possible speed. They were added to the concoction, which, to her relief, did not require heating.

To drag the cauldron from the room and to the fireplace beyond would make too much noise.

She stirred according to the directions. The contents swirled long after she stopped. Wafts of steam lifted from within, dissipating in colorless, odorless clouds. Long moments passed before the mists stopped. She peeked inside the cauldron. All that remained was the pebbles. Nothing about them looked different. Had the enchantment worked?

She scooped them from the cauldron and into her apron pockets. She checked once more that everything had been returned exactly to its previous place. The room appeared as she had found it. Though the enchantress's snores continued buzzing beyond her door, Gretel did not know how much longer she would sleep. With all set to rights, Gretel slipped out of the room, closing the door softly behind her. She pulled the pebbles from her pockets and tied them into a rag, hurrying down to the basement. She set the tied napkin beneath the folded blanket on the floor, then rushed up once more.

The enchantress's snores had stopped. She would emerge at any moment. Gretel grabbed the broom and began to sweep. She kept herself calm as her mistress stepped from her room. Gretel didn't look back. Nothing was said between them.

The remainder of the day passed as most did. The enchantress was as unhappy as ever, as difficult. Gretel was as quiet as always.

She settled into her bed that night, nervous but hopeful. She would go to the forest early and place the pebbles along the path leading away from the enchantress's allurements.

Hansel would be safe. Just as her papa was. Even if she never found a way to free herself, she would do all she could to save them.

Five

Hansel's woodworking and crafts were coming along nicely. Gretel wasn't able to meet him as often as she once had. He saw her only twice per week. He worked hard in the days between, building furniture and cabinets and carving decorative pieces for sale. He also ventured into the forest beyond the paths and meadows they traversed together, looking for new and interesting varieties of wood and hoping to find the place where she lived.

He discovered new favorite corners of the vast forest, yet portions of it he did not explore. He would begin to wander in the direction Gretel usually walked, but never made it very far. Why was that?

Two months had passed since he first met Gretel. Only two months, and he did not even see her every day, yet he could no longer imagine his life without her.

He met her on a chill, late-autumn morning in a meadow, one they had declared several weeks earlier was a particular favorite. He brought with him a thick woven rug he had purchased on his one and only trip through the forest to the town beyond. That had been a difficult journey; he'd found himself turned around time and time again. But he'd managed to sell a few things and gain the attention of many people who were likely to purchase goods from him in the future. And he had this rug, perfect for him and Gretel to sit on in their meadow and spend a leisurely morning.

"What are you carving?" she asked.

"A bird." He held it up for her to see. He'd nearly finished it, and, though he hadn't told her yet, he meant it for her.

"You've chosen maple. It's the perfect choice."

He shook his head in amazement. "I never imagined I would meet another person as fascinated by trees as I am."

"And I never imagined I would meet a man who did not think that an oddity in me."

He leaned closer and pressed a kiss to her temple. She blushed, but did not object. Indeed, she rested her head against his shoulder.

"I wish we could stay in this spot always." She spoke with such regret.

"It is lovely, more so when we are here together." He set aside his carving and put his arms around her. "Can you not come more often, my dear Gretel?"

She shook her head without moving away. "If somehow my mistress did not notice my frequent absences, she would surely realize I was not seeing to my duties."

"I could come call on you. If she were able to meet me, to see that my intentions were honorable . . ."

"She does not care about that," Gretel said.

"She fears if you marry, you will leave her employ?"

Gretel sat fully upright. "I cannot leave her employ. I cannot even leave this forest."

Cannot? "You are held prisoner?"

She stood as if to leave.

Hansel jumped to his feet. "If you are in danger, if you are being held against your will, please, you must allow me to help you."

"It cannot be helped."

He closed the distance between them, then took her hands in his. "Gretel, please."

"She is an enchantress, Hansel. A witch. She bewitched my father, blinding him to what she truly was, making him abjectly devoted to her from the first moment he saw her. She would have killed him; that is her design in luring men there. I did what I needed to do to save him."

"You traded your freedom?"

She nodded. "Another of her spells binds me to her home and these woods. I cannot leave. If I try, her vow to spare my father will be erased, and she will likely kill us both."

Fear pushed Hansel's pulse to racing, but determination squared his shoulders. "We will find a way to break this spell."

"I have been trying, with no luck. I am not yet ready to give up entirely, but, Hansel, if she had any idea of our connection, of your very existence, she would stop at nothing to destroy you simply because it would hurt me."

He shook his head firmly. "I will not be threatened into abandoning you."

She reached up and gently touched his cheek. "Continue to meet me here now and then, and I will feel anything but abandoned."

"That is not enough."

She stepped away but glanced back at him. "It will have to be enough."

With one final, fleeting smile, she slipped into the forest.

He waited but a moment before following her. She was quick and more familiar with the twists and turns and branching paths. Farther and farther into the forest they went, he attempting to keep pace with her.

He managed it until, quite suddenly, he stopped. He couldn't help himself. His feet carried him back in the direction he'd come. He turned around with great effort, only to be repelled once more. This happened any number of times. It was almost as if he was being pushed away by . . . magic.

Magic. The enchantress, no doubt.

Hansel, however, was not one to be so easily defeated. Following the path his feet forced him down, he vowed to find a means of reaching the home where Gretel was kept prisoner. Somehow, he would manage it, and together they would find a way to free her.

Six

Hansel did not ask again if he might follow her to the enchantress's house. Their time together began with his inquiries into her well-being and happiness and ended with his pleas that she be careful. The precious minutes in between were spent in pleasant conversation, warm embraces, and periods of comfortable silence. How she missed him on the long, lonely days they were not together.

If not for the spell binding Gretel to the enchantress's home, they might have courted like an ordinary couple, meeting at her home, Papa offering his blessing.

She paused in her weeding of the garden. No matter how hard she tried, she could not form a clear image of her home or her papa. She had not been gone so long that she ought to have so fully forgotten the faces and places she had known all her life. This, no doubt, was the enchantress's doing. Would she eventually forget Papa entirely? Would she forget Hansel as well?

"Your vow requires you to work." The enchantress's

hissing voice echoed off the tall stone wall. "Daydreaming does not count."

The enchantress seldom ventured from the house, which had always offered Gretel some comfort. What had brought her to the garden?

Gretel did not dare ask. The few times she'd inquired of her mistress over some matter or another, she'd been severely scolded and subjected to long days locked in the basement. She had learned to keep her questions to herself, to put her head down and do her work.

She watched her mistress out of the corner of her eye. The enchantress walked beside the wall, an unnervingly satisfied smile on her hideous face. Something about the stones pleased her. A shiver slid down Gretel's spine. Nothing that delighted the enchantress could possibly be anything but contemptible.

The garden, and the wall in particular, had unnerved Gretel from the very start. This moment confirmed that impression.

The breeze picked up, gusting cold. The ever-present flow of water splattered in the wind. The enchantress jumped back. Odd. Never, in the months Gretel had been in the enchantress's cottage, had anything frightened her mistress. Indeed, nothing had even seemed to concern her. But the water *had.* Gretel knew deep in her bones that the water was, in some way, of crucial importance.

The enchantress's head snapped upward. Her eyes pulled wide, searching the area nearby. Her slit-shaped nostrils flared wide. Gretel looked about as well, unsure what had captured her mistress's attention. She saw nothing. She heard nothing.

The enchantress's thin lips spread in an eager smile. "We have a visitor."

Gretel's heart sank. Someone had been entrapped. She suspected others had been, though she'd been banished to the basement and didn't know for certain. There would be no uncertainty now, neither would she harbor any doubts as to the fate of those the enchantress lured to this cottage. She hadn't the first idea how to save whoever had stumbled into this trap.

"To the basement," the enchantress snapped.

Gretel's mind spun as she walked back to the cottage. What could she do? How could she help? She could not simply descend into the basement and leave the poor soul to his fate. But what power did she have?

She stepped inside the cottage and froze.

Hansel.

How had he come here? She'd laid the allurements. They ought to have kept him far away.

The enchantress had not yet arrived.

"You must leave," Gretel said, the words rushing from her lips. "Please. Go now. She will kill you. She has done so before."

She glanced over her shoulder. The enchantress was coming near enough to overhear. There was no time for escape.

"Good evening," the enchantress said as she glided into the cottage. "How wonderful of you to join us."

Hansel watched the haggard witch with utter adoration. Gretel vaguely remembered Papa doing the same. Another enchantment, no doubt. Her actual hideousness was somehow not seen by the men she lured to their doom.

"Gretel," the enchantress hissed. "Why are you still here? I told you to go below."

"I only just stepped inside," she said. "I wasn't certain if you wished me to do something to make your guest comfortable. Perhaps some food or something to drink."

"I will provide his food," the enchantress said. "He will join me for supper, for however long it takes."

She had said precisely that with Papa. The food, then, was part of her devious plans.

Hansel sneezed, pulling their attention to him once more.

"Are you ill?" The enchantress sounded utterly disgusted.

"Only a little." He sounded pleading, as if desperate for her to approve of him.

She circled him, Gretel entirely forgotten. "You do seem hale enough. Young." She ran a clawed finger down his arm. "Strong."

He watched her worshipfully.

The enchantress nodded to herself. "You'll do. But first you must regain your health." She motioned him toward the room where Gretel had found the spell book. "Lie down. Rest. My maid here will bring you food and water until you've recovered. Then you"—she laid a hand on his chest—"and I will have our supper."

He nodded mutely, his gaze never leaving the enchantress's face.

"To the room," she repeated.

He walked in that direction, repeatedly looking back at the enchantress. She waved him on. He stepped into the room and closed the door behind him.

A frown firm on her face, the enchantress turned to Gretel. "Make broth. See to it that he is well soon."

Gretel nodded. Here was an unforeseen bit of luck. The enchantress needed Hansel fully healthy, which he was not. They had time to think of a plan, if only the spell the enchantress wove on men's perception of her was not too strong for Gretel to get around.

The enchantress entered her own room and snapped the door closed. Gretel set to the task of making broth. She did not know precisely what her mistress did to the food she fed the men who came to the cottage, but at least Gretel could be assured that the food *she* would make for him was safe.

The sounds of the enchantress sleeping soon filled the cottage. Gretel stirred the pot of broth simmering above the fire. How was she to get through to Hansel, to help him escape? If she brought a bowl of broth in to him, she would have time to look at the spell book, perhaps find something to free him.

Footsteps sounded behind her. She looked back. Hansel had emerged, no doubt looking for the mesmerizing, engaging woman he thought the enchantress was.

"She is asleep," Gretel said. "You'll have to wait until tomorrow to see her again. For now, you had best lie back down."

His eyes darted toward the closed door to the enchantress's room. "I heard the snoring. I hoped that meant we would have a few minutes."

That was unexpected. "You aren't looking for her?"

He shuddered. "I likely am meant to be. Her appearance fluctuated between beautiful and horrifying. I suspect I was only supposed to see the alluring version, but somehow the enchantment is not working."

Gretel stepped away from the fireplace and directly to him. She clutched his upper arms. "You have to leave. If she is not truly trapping you here, you have to go."

He did not heed her warning but instead wrapped his arms around her, pulling her close. "She means for you to nurse me to health. I can feign a slow recovery. We will have time and plenty for managing both of our escapes."

Though she ought to have argued and insisted that he leave while he still could, she leaned into his embrace, resting her head against his beating heart. "I do not know how you found me. The path leading here is enchanted to make you go the other way."

"I came from the other direction, on my way back from the village."

She hadn't thought that the enchantress might have bewitched other paths leading to the cottage, but she should have. "She kills the men she lures here. I could not endure it if you suffered that same fate."

"We will escape, my dearest Gretel. I have full faith we will."

"I do not know how to break the spell that keeps me here."

His hand rubbed a comforting circle on her back. "There is a spell book in the room she's placed me in."

"I've read portions of it. I haven't found anything yet."

"I will read while I am supposed to be sleeping. You can read while you're meant to be nursing me. We will find the answer."

She pulled back enough to meet his eye. "Will you promise me you will be careful?"

"If you will promise me the same."

She took a fortifying breath. "I will ladle a bowl of soup and meet you in the room. We can search the book."

The enchantress's snores continued; she was no doubt confident in the spell she had cast over Hansel. That would grant them time to read through the book.

Gretel carefully carried the bowl into the room where Hansel was kept. She placed it on the very table where she had turned the pebbles into allurements. Hansel sat on the cot, the spell book open on his lap. Gretel quietly closed the door.

"You should eat," she said quietly. "The food the enchantress will give you is tainted somehow. It is part of what kills the men who come here."

He watched her. "They are always men?"

She nodded. "I don't know if they are because they have to be or because she simply prefers them to be."

He gave that some thought. She sat beside him on the cot. "Allow me to read while you eat."

He rose and crossed to the table where the bowl sat. "Are there any other patterns you've noticed?" he asked before sipping a large spoonful.

"She always insists they eat supper 'for however long it takes.' She often looks quite ill and exhausted before their arrival, but by the time they are . . . gone—dead, I assume—she looks healthy again, energetic, though never pleasant."

He smiled a little. "Hers is a rather horrifying visage, isn't it?"

"I suspect she is something otherworldly."

He continued to eat as she read spell after spell.

"It seems to me," he said, "that something in the food transfers the life from her prisoners to her. She gains their strength and vitality."

That fit what Gretel had seen. But how did the enchantress manage it? And how did they stop her from doing so again?

Hansel finished his soup and rejoined her. "Have you had any luck?"

She began to say no, but the word caught the moment she turned the next page. "'New Life.'" She read the title of the spell aloud, followed by the description. "'The transference of vibrancy for the purpose of attaining immortality.'"

"You've found it, Gretel."

"But what do we do about it?"

He put his arm around her. She set her head on his shoulder, continuing to read. The potion created by this spell was to be mixed into the food of the victim. How, precisely, that gave the enchantress these men's lives, the spell did not make clear, only that the end result was what Gretel had feared.

"'Once all life is claimed by the one who executes this spell, the one from whom it is claimed will, in tears, be rendered a thing cold and inert, all remnants of consciousness filling a pool of mourning.'"

"Merciful heavens," Hansel whispered. "And this is the monster whose servitude you cannot escape."

"But this is also the fate from which I saved my papa and from which we will save you."

He kissed her temple, then her hairline, then her cheek. "Go rest, my darling Gretel. Build your strength while I continue to feign a lack of it. We will find the answer, and we will find a means of deliverance."

Seven

Hansel needed very little effort to appear less than well. He spent the next two nights awake, reading through the spell book. Gretel had almost no opportunity to do so herself. The enchantress worked her all day and banished her to the basement at night.

For a few brief moments each morning, Gretel slipped into his room. He quickly told her anything he'd discovered the night before, and they spoke of their plans for that day. She also fed him soup and bread a few times each day, though the afternoon and evening meal was not undertaken in any degree of privacy. The enchantress watched him be fed, checked on his health and progress. He was careful to appear as though he was, in fact, improving, though slowly enough that she would not yet deem him truly recovered and ready for stealing his life away.

The fourth morning of his pretended convalescence, Gretel came in with a bowl of gruel, the usual morning offering. He was, as always, eager for her company, her presence, and the way his heart both sped and calmed when she was nearby. But this morning, he also had a discovery to share with her.

"Good morning." She set the bowl of gruel beside him, having closed the door already.

He pressed a gentle kiss to her lips, the greeting that had become customary between them. She usually smiled softly and leaned into his embrace for a long moment. Today, however, she pulled back, worry hanging heavy in her expression.

"Darling?" he pressed.

"We cannot continue this way much longer. She will realize the ruse."

He shook his head and guided her to the cot. They sat beside one another, his arm around her. He had never known her equal for strength and determination. To see her struggling sent an ache clear to his heart. "I discovered something last night," he said. "Two somethings, in fact."

She turned a hopeful gaze on him.

"The first is not good news, I am afraid."

She nodded. "The more we know, the better able we will be to decide our next step."

"I believe I found the spell she used to bind you to her," he said. "It is not breakable. It cannot be undone."

Though a flash of disappointment crossed her features, she replaced it almost immediately with acceptance.

But he would not give up on freeing her so easily. "The spell does, though, bind you to *her* and not to this place. If she is destroyed, the spell no longer holds."

Her brow pulled in thought. "I have always known her death would free me, but her magic protects her from being killed."

"I read more closely the spell she uses on the men she traps here," Hansel said. "It prevents her from dying or even aging."

"Then *that* spell is the key."

He nodded. "None of the descriptions I have read of the effects of spells or potions is figurative. This spell says the victim becomes something cold and inert. I believe that is literally true."

"Her victims become inanimate?"

"I believe so. The spell also references tears."

She rose and paced away, her right forefinger and thumb fussing with her lip. "Inanimate but tearful."

He shook his head in confusion. "It makes little sense."

But she spun about, eyes pulled wide. "I know what it is. The weeping stones in the garden. There is a wall made entirely of stone pillars. The pillars drip water in a constant trickle."

A wall made of the crying remains of the enchantress's victims. A chill shivered down his spine.

"I believe she is afraid of the water," Gretel added. "I saw her jump away when a bit of it nearly splashed on her. She also insists I gather water from the stream in the forest, despite the presence of water in her own garden."

"The question, then, is does the water make her uncomfortable because of its source, or would it actually harm her? Would it harm you or me?"

She shrugged. "I haven't the first idea."

"Yet it is the only weakness of the enchantress's we've found."

Gretel took up the bowl of gruel once more and gave it to him. "You need to eat. I will read through the book while you do."

He knew better than to argue with her when she was

being so entirely sensible, no matter that he felt painfully close to the answer they were seeking.

Gretel spent a few moments looking over the spells beyond the ones they had already read through, but then she returned to the New Life spell. "The answer has to be here," she said quietly. "We know what the potion does. We know the men are turned to weeping stones. But what of the tears? Why does she—?" Gretel leaned forward, reading more closely. "A pool of mourning."

Hansel had pondered that bit himself, though he'd not sorted out its significance.

"Perhaps the tears flow into a pool containing her victims' remnants of consciousness," Gretel speculated. "Those tears are what they are reduced to."

The idea was both disturbing and a bit of insight. "The water knows her crimes. That is why she fears it."

"If she were forced into the pool, her victims could have their revenge?"

He nodded. "It is at least plausible."

"But how do we force her into it?"

He finished his gruel, then joined her in pacing. "The pool is in the garden, isn't it?"

"It is."

"Then we must get her to the garden, but how?"

"She goes there now and then," Gretel said. "But she is very careful of the water. I could not, on my own, get her into it."

"The two of us together might manage it."

"I could create more allurements," Gretel suggested.

He had read the allurement spell, the one they felt certain the enchantress used to draw men to her cottage. "She would likely realize she was being drawn forward. I do not believe we can rely on our use of magic to defeat her. I believe we must use hers against her."

"The pool of tears."

He nodded. "The pool of tears."

"The only way the three of us will be together in the same place is if you are well enough to take supper with her," Gretel said. "And I must be required to serve it. She has never allowed me to be present during her suppers, let alone required it of me."

"If I feign an ever-deepening infatuation with her and insist that I cannot bear the thought of losing even a moment of her company and plead with her to leave the serving of the meal to you, do you think she would agree?"

"Possibly." She pressed her fingertips to her mouth as she thought. "You could also insist that you'd like to have a meal outdoors, for the fresh air or the beauty of the surroundings. Make it sound as though you wish the setting to help you woo her. While she is not the least interested in being courted, I do think she thrives on the attention. And your enthusiasm for her helps her schemes. I believe she will encourage it."

The plan was not without risks, but it was the first promising moment they'd had. "I will plead for a more 'romantic' supper and the convenience of a servant . . . if you'll pardon my referring to you that way."

"Pardon?" Gretel actually laughed. "Should you refer to me in any other way, she will likely suspect you of being less than enamored of her."

Hansel took Gretel's hand in his and raised it to his lips, kissing her fingers. "Once we have managed the impossible and defeated this foe, remind me to tell you just how enamored of *you* I am."

She set her free hand lightly on his cheek. "And I of you."

He turned his head enough to kiss her hand. "I will make my request of her this afternoon. With luck, our supper tonight will mark our last night of imprisonment."

Hansel must have made his appeal very convincing. Gretel was pulled from her usual afternoon duties and charged with moving a table, two chairs, and two place settings to the garden.

She had wondered if the enchantress would find the request annoying. Far from it. Undertaking yet another bit of heinous magic while surrounded by the monoliths of her previous horrid deeds seemed to please her immensely. As expected, she insisted on preparing the meal she meant to take with Hansel.

Gretel stood in the garden at a bit of a distance from the table, where the enchantress waited when Hansel arrived that evening. He made a good show of being healthy but still a little worn. No one looking at him would doubt that he had recently recovered from a prolonged bout of illness or that he saw a beautiful woman when he looked at the hideous enchantress.

He offered a bow. "I feel I have waited a lifetime for this moment," he said to the enchantress, watching her with adoration. "I am so pleased you were willing to meet me in such an appropriately beautiful setting."

"Of course." The enchantress motioned to the table. "Shall we begin our meal?"

He held out her chair. She sat, and he made for the other side, pausing before sitting as well. "This table is rather too bland."

"It is the girl's fault," the enchantress snapped. "She is not a very reliable servant."

Hansel did not show even the tiniest bit of surprise. "Have your girl begin serving the meal. I know precisely what will make the setting perfect."

The enchantress leveled Gretel with a look of bone-chilling disapproval. "Serve quickly," she said. "And remain near at hand should you be needed. I will not abide laziness."

Gretel nodded and did as she was told, all the while keeping an eye on Hansel. He had bent low on one side of the pool of tears, tugging at a wildflower. He seemed to be struggling to pull it, though she knew it likely gave him no trouble at all.

"Flowers will be the perfect touch," he said from his position at the edge of the pool. "I'm still weakened by my illness. Will you pull it?"

"Will *I*?" The enchantress looked shocked at the very suggestion. "The girl can do it."

"But this is our special supper, not hers. I wish it to be perfect."

The enchantress sighed and stood. "I am not at all certain you are going to be worth the effort."

"Do not say that," Hansel pleaded. "I will do all I can to please you."

That appeased her enough to gain her cooperation. She crossed to where he was, quickly eyeing the wall and the pond. "Which flower?"

"The purple ones, just there." He stepped back, giving the enchantress room to place herself in front of the flowers at the pond's edge.

Hansel looked at Gretel, his gaze pointed. She did not require further prompting. With quick, quiet steps, she joined him directly behind the enchantress and held her breath. Should they manage to get the enchantress into the water only to discover it had no effect at all, they would surely pay with their lives.

The enchantress bent low, reaching for the small flowers. Hansel nodded firmly.

In unison, they pushed the enchantress from behind, putting all their force behind the effort. Her arms flailed. Hansel slipped one leg in front of hers and swept it backward, knocking her feet out from under her. Gretel gave one final shove, and the enchantress toppled over into the pond.

For one horrifying instant, nothing happened. Then, great ripples of bubbles began, as if the water simmered.

"What have you done?" The enchantress's growl rang with anger.

A waft of bright green mist rose from the water. The enchantress swatted at it, attempting to push her way through. It clung to her, holding her back, yet she made progress.

Gretel watched in horror. "She will escape."

"A stick or something." Hansel looked around. "Something to push her back in."

What did they have? What could they use?

The enchantress clawed her way to the edge of the pool. No matter what she had to do, Gretel would not allow the enchantress to escape, knowing she would take more lives. She rushed toward the pool, launching herself at the enchantress. Kneeling at the pond's edge, she grasped the enchantress's shoulders, holding her back, preventing her from climbing out of the pool. Green mist enveloped them both, blocking out all but the shadows of the world around them.

"Gretel!" Hansel shouted from beyond the edge of Gretel's vision.

She would not allow the enchantress to escape. She would leave the safety of solid ground for the horror of the pond if need be.

An ear-piercing crack shattered the air. Then another. And another. The world around them grew darker.

The enchantress forced her way upright again, clutching Gretel's wrist painfully. Gretel fought for freedom enough to prevent the enchantress's escape. As they struggled, shadows enveloped the pool, blocking out every ray of light. The enchantress cursed and screeched in the blackness.

Something grabbed hold of Gretel's arm, yanking her away from the pool of tears and out into the light once more. Hansel pulled her farther from the pool. Gretel looked back, terrified that she'd see the enchantress close on their heels.

The garden had transformed. The stone wall no longer stood where it once had, but now fully encircled the pond. The high tops of the wall bent forward, closing off the top of the circle they'd formed and creating, in its place, a large dome. The sides rippled like liquid, though they were made of solid stone.

"She is still in there," Gretel breathed out the realization. "I would be as well."

"The wall was closing in on you," Hansel said. "I couldn't leave you there."

An almighty rumble shook the ground, then an upward explosion of the same green mist that had risen off the pond shot forth from the top of the mountain like a volcanic eruption.

Gretel clutched Hansel, and he her, as bits of rock shot in all directions. They remained thus for some time after the shaking stopped and silence descended on the garden. She hadn't the heart to look, to see if they'd managed their own redemption or if the enchantress was simply waiting to enact her punishment. Gretel held fast to Hansel and hoped against hope.

"Open your eyes, darling," he said. "I believe we have done it."

She opened only one, and tentatively at that. Where the pond had once stood, there was a mountainous rock with a deep crater at its top.

"Can she escape?" Gretel wondered aloud.

Hand in hand, they walked to the rock's edge. Stretched on his toes, Hansel looked inside the dome. "It is solid rock," he said. "There is nothing left of her."

"She is dead?"

He looked at Gretel once more. "I believe so."

"And we are free?"

He nodded quickly, yet she was still unsure. To let herself hope only to discover she still could not leave would break her heart.

"The talisman," she whispered. The answer would be found in the talisman.

She pulled her hand free and ran back to the cottage. She stopped in the doorway and glanced up where the talisman hung. Where it *had once* hung. It was no longer there, neither was it on the floor nor set aside. It was simply gone.

Hansel caught up to her.

"We have done it," she said, hardly believing the words even as they fell from her own lips. "We have done it. We are free."

He pulled her into his arms and spun her about. She had dreamed of this day, but had feared it would never arrive.

Freedom. A future. And love.

She now had claim on all three.

Hansel and Gretel walked to the edge of the forest, hands clasped, hearts glad. They'd made certain the spell book, potions, and other implements of suffering had been utterly destroyed. They could do nothing to undo the pain and loss of life the enchantress had been responsible for, but they would not allow others to be hurt by the trail she'd left behind.

As they reached the clearing that led to the forest home where Hansel had been living, Gretel stopped, staring.

"This is—" She shook her head, attempting to clear it. "My memories are returning slowly, but I believe this was my home. My papa lives here."

"*I* live here as well," Hansel said.

"This is the home of the man who took you in? My papa?"

He smiled. "It appears fate brought us together in more ways than one."

A man stepped out of the humble house. "You were gone for some time, Hansel. I'd nearly given up on—" His gaze fell on Gretel, confusion settling there.

Her expression likely looked the same. She knew him. She knew she did, and yet . . .

"Gretel," Hansel said. "I believe he is your father."

"Papa," she whispered.

Hansel cupped a hand to the side of his mouth and called out to the man. "This is Gretel. Your daughter."

The moment the words left his mouth the last remnants of fog left Gretel's mind and, if her papa's sudden intake of breath was any indication, from his mind as well.

"Oh, my darling Gretel." He rushed to her and her to him. His arms flew around her, holding her tightly. She held to him as well.

"I am free, Papa. I am free."

Hansel was invited into the embrace. By that evening, he was fully invited into the family. By week's end, his place among them was official and binding.

Hansel and Gretel spent their days happily wandering the now-peaceful paths of their beloved forest, building their life together, and never taking for granted the very real miracle of their freedom.

About Sarah M. Eden

Sarah M. Eden is the author of multiple historical romances, including the two-time Whitney Award Winner *Longing for Home* and Whitney Award finalists *Seeking Persephone* and *Courting Miss Lancaster*. Combining her obsession with history and affinity for tender love stories, Sarah loves crafting witty characters and heartfelt romances. She has thrice served as the Master of Ceremonies for the LDStorymakers Writers Conference and acted as the Writer in Residence at the Northwest Writers Retreat. Sarah is represented by Pam Victorio at D4EO Literary Agency.

Visit Sarah on-line:
Twitter: @SarahMEden
Facebook: Author Sarah M. Eden
Website: SarahMEden.com

Black Fern

Julie Daines

One

Rós stopped at the gate and peered through the heavy iron slats hanging bent and covered with rust. Sharpened spikes along the top of the wall called out a warning, while the crooked gates, draped in moss, whispered neglect. Which voice to listen to, she did not know.

"This is it?" she asked Finn.

He nodded, pointing up the darkly wooded mountain path. "Black Fern Manor."

Every fortnight Finn carried a load of food here and left it, coming away with a coin for his troubles. No one knew for certain who lived up there. A man. A monster. A demon. All had been seen by someone or another. But Finn got paid, so there was money to be had. 'Twas this that brought Rós to the forgotten gate. It was her last hope.

She lifted her small bag of belongings—the few things she'd brought with her—and shimmied through the gap in the broken gate.

"It's not too late to turn back," Finn whispered.

"Where else am I going to get money? I cannot let my family starve."

Finn gave the iron rods a kick. "I'm sorry we cannot do more. We are barely getting by as it is."

He would have given her work at his parents' inn had there been earnings to spare, but the inn saw fewer and fewer visitors these days. Finn wanted nothing more than to escape their little village of Muine Bheag. He dreamed of Kenmare, or better yet, Dublin. But he did not have enough money for that, for it was on the other side of the country.

"I know, Finn." She reached through the gate and took the parcels he was delivering. "I'll see you here in two weeks."

"Yes."

She turned and walked away.

The overgrown path wound up the mountain in a tunnel of shadows. Thick tree trunks supported the branches overhead like great columns in a cathedral, blocking out all sunlight. Up and up she followed the narrow trail through the ferns and brambles.

At last the house came into view. A great structure of dark stone, all slate and timber. Bigger by far than anything she'd seen before. More like a castle than a manor.

On the door hung a knocker with the face of a lion. Rós lifted the brass bar and pounded it three times. Even through the thick oak door she could hear the knock echo inside. Empty, it sounded, and alone.

She waited. And waited. Dreading what might answer. Or worse, no answer at all. She would have peeked through a window, but they all were shuttered.

She knocked again, then paced the stone stoop, wringing her hands. Someone—or something—must live here, or Finn would not need to traipse up the mountain with supplies.

Five more clacks with the brass knocker. A wind whistled

around the corner of the castle, fluttering her skirts and brushing through her hair, wrapping its fingers around her like a hidden specter. A watcher stroking her features, desperate for a closer look.

A moment later, the door opened, wide enough for her to pass, but not enough to welcome.

Not a soul was there.

"Hello," she called into the empty hall. Nothing good could come from a place where doors opened on their own.

"What do you want?" a voice growled from the dark. A dragon guarding his lair.

Rós turned toward the sound. No candles burned. Nothing shone through the windows. The only light was the square of sun coming in through the open door. She could see no one.

"I'm looking for work." If his voice was a dragon, hers was a mouse. She cleared her throat and spoke into the darkness. "I'm looking for work. Sir."

"There is no work here."

Rós peered harder into the darkness, but still she could see nothing.

"Please, sir. I'm a good worker. I can—"

"Leave." The deep voice had risen, swelling until it shook the stones beneath her feet.

She wanted to leave. She'd never wanted to come here in the first place, but need had won out over wants. "I am desperate. I'll do anything. My father is unwell and cannot work. My mother, long dead. My sisters are starving. I have nowhere else to turn."

She'd not meant to tell all, but there was not much lower she could go. Begging for menial labor like a waif. A stray. Waiting for coins to fall from darkness and shadow.

The hall was silent. Even the dust motes drifting in the

meager rays of light seemed to pause. She waited, again. And waited.

"Sir?"

"Your father sent you?" he snarled.

"No. My family does not know where I am." Again, she told more than she should.

"I do not take outsiders."

She'd failed again. Her family would starve. "I understand." She motioned to the sack on the ground. "Here are your things from Finn." She turned to go. A breeze brushed past, settling over her.

"Wait," he said, his voice now the breath of falcon's wings, soft but sharp enough to sting. "I will give you work. On two conditions."

She peered into the darkness. Seven sisters and her father needed food—she would accept whatever terms. "Anything."

"You must promise to stay 'til harvest moon."

Four months away. She glanced around at the gloom. The dragon's lair. But if it would put food in her sisters' mouths . . . "And second?"

"You must not set foot off Black Fern during that time. Keep only to the manor and grounds."

No visits to home. No walks down to the village. Stuck here with a creature she'd not even seen. There was no sign of other servants, but there must be someone else here, helping to care for the place. What little care they'd afforded, at least.

A monster, some said. A dragon, she thought. What sort of creature was she making promises to? "Are you a man?"

He grunted. "Yes, I suppose that's what I am."

Four months. She could endure anything for four months. "All right."

"You must give me your word." He'd found his voice again, and she shook at his command.

"I p-promise." Only four months.

The door slammed shut behind her, filling the hall with shadow upon shadow. "What is your name?"

"Rós," she whispered.

"Come, Rós. I will show you to your quarters."

"I cannot see to follow, sir." Perhaps her first task would be to render some tallow for candles. Yet, if he couldn't afford candles, how could he afford to pay her? "You have candles, I presume."

"I do not use candles."

She tried to follow the sound of his voice, waving her hands in front of her, stepping slowly, carefully, not to bump into anything.

"For pity's sake," he grumbled. "We'll never get there at this pace."

"Then for pity's sake, let there be light. I am not a bat that can see in utter dark."

Another soft gust of wind rustled her hair, and she could have sworn she heard a breath of laughter. He took her by the hand and pulled. No claws. No talons. It felt like a man's hand. Warm and strong. At least that ruled out dragon.

"There are stairs here," he warned, gripping her hand more tightly.

She followed him up, feeling for the uneven steps as she went. Then she missed a step and fell forward. His other hand grabbed her waist as she stumbled into him. A solid chest, shoulders. More reasons to assume man.

"Sorry." She peered into what she thought should be his face and saw nothing.

He stood still for a moment, then released her. "You will get used to the darkness." He started again up the stairs, guiding her along.

"Why must it always be dark?"

"There is little worth seeing here," was all he said.

He stopped abruptly, and she bumped into him. A door opened, at least it sounded so. "These are your quarters."

She stepped forward, running her hand along the wooden door and into a room she could not see. The door closed behind her.

She turned. "Hello?"

He did not answer. She was alone—or so she presumed. Across the room, the unmistakable outline of a window glowed with the faintest shimmer.

The master—for she did not know his name—had given her two rules, neither of which prohibited her from opening the shutters in her own room. She fumbled along the fittings until she found a latch. The window was stiff. She pulled and tugged until at last it opened. Then she heaved against the shutters until they flung out.

Light flooded in. Rós shielded her eyes. The master was right; already she was unused to the brightness, even though it be only the last of the twilight.

She looked up, uncovering her eyes. A grand bed stood in the center of the room, the posts intricately carved. The ceiling was painted in a red-and-white diamond pattern. Moth-eaten tapestries covered the walls. The master had said there was nothing worth seeing here, but this room was exceedingly fine, even if it had fallen into disrepair.

These were not servants' quarters. With a little dusting, scrubbing, and mending, it would be fit for a king. What other treasures must lurk in the darkness of this place?

If nothing else, she would get the light back. She would convince him to put candles in the chamber sticks. To open the shutters and let the day in. Keep the night to its own. He would see that it is better to dwell in light.

Two

Rós woke the following morning famished. She'd not dared leave her quarters last night to find supper for fear she'd never find her way back. She pulled her hair up, tied her apron on, and opened her chamber door, surveying the hall.

"Did you sleep well?" asked the master, his voice coming from beyond the reach of her window. It seemed this morning he was somewhere between falcon and dragon. Perhaps she was in for a scolding for opening the shutters. He had made it clear he preferred the dark.

"Well enough. Thank you, sir." She curtseyed for propriety's sake. She was the servant, after all. She waited for her reprimand, perhaps even her dismissal, but none came. "Sir?"

"Yes?"

She looked back through her bedroom door at the window, the glass closed, but a beam of light streaming through. Still he said nothing. Perhaps he wasn't as set on darkness as she thought. "What would you have me do?"

"Do?"

"Yes, sir. What work would you have me do?"

"Of course." Yet he seemed uncertain. "Any work is fine. It matters not to me."

"Perhaps I could prepare your meal. If you could direct me to the kitchens."

"Yes," he said. He sounded almost like a man now. Like the innkeeper or the tanner or the smithy. He took several steps toward her, down the hall. Ten or eleven perhaps. And on the twelfth he crossed from darkness into light.

Rós let out a gasp. His eyes were the color of blustering clouds. As if someone had taken a sky full of storm and trapped it behind his lids. His face was covered in scars. They puckered his cheeks, warped his brow, twisted his lips. But it was his unnatural eyes she could not drag her gaze from.

He took her hand to guide her, but she pulled away. Perhaps he was a monster after all.

"What?" His voice had an edge like a wolf now, a warning growl rumbling deep in his throat. He turned and walked into her room, straight to the window. His hands ran over the glass until he found the latch, just as she had last night in the dark, when she could not see. He pulled on it and then spun around. "You opened the shutters."

She nodded.

"Did you see me?" The wolf was circling, an attack imminent.

She nodded again.

"Did you see me?" he growled, and a rush of wind nearly blew her off her feet.

He was blind. He hadn't seen the beam of light pouring into the corridor. He hadn't seen her nod. That explained his empty eyes.

"Yes," she whispered.

The word hung in the air, unsure where to go. But she had let it out, and so it went where it must. To him.

He roared, his strange eyes swimming with anger. He picked up a chair and threw it across the room. It burst into pieces. Rós backed up against the corridor wall.

"I warned you about the light." He yelled so loud that she covered her ears. "But you would not listen." He stormed out of the room, leaving naught but smoke and fire behind, then disappeared into the darkness.

Rós stayed still. Was he gone or still lurking in the shadow? She could not tell. She tiptoed silently into her room and shut the door.

Four months was a very long time. Too long. And when his anger turned on her instead of the chair, what then? There must be other servants somewhere in this great place. She could not imagine a blind man—or whatever he was—living completely alone. Was it he who walked down the mountain path to retrieve the supplies left there by Finn? It seemed unlikely, but perhaps.

She reached for her bag, ready to pack up her few belongings and leave. Except that she had given her word. This might be more difficult than she'd expected, but a promise was a promise. And if it brought her money, she had to stay. For her family.

She straightened her apron and left her room. Wolf or no, she had work to do.

She went into the corridor and turned toward the stairs. The kitchen first.

It was slow going. She dared not open any more shutters to let in light.

At last she came to a room that could well enough be called a kitchen. From what little she could see, it had a hearth, a larder, and a set of cracked and rusted pots. This man had been living like a bear, holed up in his cave. But spring was here now. Time for him to come out of his night and remember the day.

Despite his outburst, he could not possibly expect her to live in complete darkness. She opened the door that led to the garden, for she needed at least some light to work. His appearance had startled her, to be sure. But now she was prepared. Next time she would show him he need not hide.

She found the supplies from Finn and dug out a few potatoes, some turnips with wilted tops, and a portion of salted beef. It would serve for a pottage of sorts. She'd worked with less. A rusted knife was all she could locate for the chopping, and a wooden spoon with a broken handle to stir with.

More and more she came to believe that the master lived here utterly alone—and completely blind. Perhaps he would allow her to hire some help from the village to put the manor back to rights. She would not dare approach this question until his temper settled down. If it ever did.

It would take all day for the pottage to simmer. In the meantime, she made a few loaves of bread. Once those were raising she took to tidying the kitchen. As she knelt on the floor, scrubbing at the dirt, a breeze blew past. It came from the corridor and swirled around her. Then, as quickly as it came, it was gone.

The day outside was calm and still. This breeze had come from inside. Was it possible that he had opened a window somewhere? She peered down the hallway, but all was as dark and still as ever. Of course not. He would never. He'd made that abundantly clear.

By the time she finished the floor, cleared the cobwebs, and took thorough inventory of what she had to work with, the sun was lowering toward the horizon.

She dipped the broken spoon into the pot and gave it taste. Not bad. She ladled a portion into one of the bowls she'd just cleaned and sliced a thick wedge of bread.

She had no idea how the master had been used to eating. Judging by the state of the castle, he probably hadn't had a real cooked meal in some time. She placed the food on a tray and carried it to the dining room—a vast and unkempt room in near complete darkness. This would have to be a job for another day. She set his food on the dusty table, at the head, with a mug of ale. At least the pottage was warm and the bread soft and fresh.

She fumbled her way to the hall, near the bottom of the stairs. The place had been silent the whole day, but he must be here somewhere.

"Sir?" she called. There was no answer. "Sir," she called again. "Here is your supper."

A soft wind came through a dark doorway. It circled her, stroking her cheek gently, almost hesitantly—if such could be said of wind—and lifting her hair. Then the room went still again. For such a shut-up place, this house was certainly drafty.

The castle fell back to quiet. She almost called out again, but didn't. He had heard her. He must have. For all the silence that pervaded the place, Rós had the feeling he knew exactly where she was and what she was doing. Though she never caught sight of him, his presence tingled her skin as surely as the breeze that just rustled by.

She left the food on the table and returned to the kitchen. If he wanted it, he could come and eat.

After storing the rest of the pottage and bread, and taking a bowl of food for herself, she plodded up the stairs to her room. Her window was still open, making this room and the kitchen the only rooms with light streaming through. Tomorrow she would add to it, but for now she thought only of her bed.

Three

When Rós came down the next morning, the pottage and bread were gone. Eaten. Nothing remained except the tray, empty bowl, and three silver coins. Her first day's wages, she presumed. It was generous payment. More than she'd expected from this place of ruin and neglect. More even than a proper servant could earn in a week.

She lifted the silver into her hands. This would go far to help her family. "Thank you, sir," she said into the air. He was there, somehow, watching. Though he could not see, she felt him watching.

As she began her work for the day, the silence was too much. She came from a large family, and quiet was not something she was accustomed to. So she sang as she worked. Songs of heroes. Lullabies. Anything to take away the dark that lurked in every corner.

Never once did she see his face or hear him moving about, but his presence was always near.

"I know you're there," she said one day. "I know you can hear me."

There was no response. Not even the rustle of wind.

"Did no one teach you 'tis poor manners to lurk in the dark, spying on others?"

She could have sworn she heard a faint laugh echoing from somewhere.

"Fine, then." She opened the shutters of the drawing room, and light flooded in. "If you won't talk to me, I'll talk to you."

Complete stillness settled on her. She looked around the room, certain he must be somewhere, but there was naught but dust and cobwebs.

Now that she'd made the threat, she could think of nothing to say. So she started with her family. "My mother was born in the north, near Dublin. But then she met my father, a sailor, and it was love at first sight. At least, that's how they tell it. I don't know if I believe in that."

Rós positioned a little, three-legged stool under the iron candle holder hanging from the ceiling. No candles were in it, and it likely hadn't been lit for ages. She stepped up and continued her dusting.

"How can you know if you love someone by merely glancing at them? Even devils can smile. You must be able to see the heart, I should think. See if there's room there for love." She stepped down and moved the stool, tasking herself to the cobwebs on the wall sconces. "Not all hearts are willing to share."

This she'd learned all too clearly as she'd watched Finn's father slowly and mercilessly steal away his mother's soul. A bruised cheek. A twisted wrist. There was not room in his heart for love.

Rós would rather die than attach herself to a cruel man. This was the reason she'd kept some distance from Finn. She was unsure about his heart. Would he be like his father? When his interest in her seemed to grow beyond friendship, she'd kept herself aloof.

But this piece of her life she was not willing to share with the wolf of the manor. So instead she talked about other things, simpler things, as she swept the dead moths from the floor.

And so it went for a sennight, then two. She cleaned and cooked for him, and every morning three pieces of silver. More and more frequently, gentle breezes danced around her, lifting her hair or tickling her cheek. And day by day, the house lightened as she threw open windows and shutters. She expected another outburst, but thus far, he had remained silent about the growing lack of darkness.

Four

Rós sat at the small table in her chamber and carefully placed her little pile of silver coins into a square of linen. She folded it over, then wrapped that bundle in a piece of vellum and tied it with string. There was quill and ink, but she did not know how to write. Nor could anyone in her family read.

This was the day Finn was due to leave another delivery of goods. She slipped out the main door, letting the sun warm her.

She followed the winding path through the woods bursting with hawthorn blooms and thrush song until she reached the gate. It leaned crookedly where she had left it a fortnight ago.

Finn was not here yet, so she wandered through the woodland, picking a bouquet of flowers, until she heard the clanking of iron.

Finn was placing a few parcels of goods inside the gate. He looked up and smiled at her.

"Still alive?"

She laughed and spun a circle. “As you see.” To be outside in the sun had lifted her spirits immensely. So much better than the dark and neglected manor. Though with every day it was getting better. More livable.

“And happy. I didn’t expect that.” Finn leaned against the gate, his red hair catching fire in the sunlight. “Tell me, how is the demon of the manor?”

A brisk wind stirred her skirts. “In truth, I have barely seen him.”

“Is he the Dullahan?” Finn asked, drawing his finger across his throat to represent the headless harbinger of death.

“No, his head is quite intact.”

“Perhaps he is Balor?” He stared at her menacingly.

She shook her head. “No, I have seen his eyes and am still among the living.” Balor could kill a person simply by looking at him. “Balor only has one eye, and the master definitely has two.”

“One of the Sluagh then?”

She hadn’t considered this. Though the Sluagh always hunt in packs, it was not impossible that one could be alone. The host of undead was comprised of sinners and the vilest of mankind. They roved in flocks, carried by the west wind, seeking other mortals with black spirits to join their ranks. Black Fern had more than its fair share of wind. Was the master hunting for her soul? Or perhaps the Sluagh were circling the master, waiting to feed upon his dark and petulant heart. Then he would become one of them, and still she would not be safe.

God forbid she had gotten herself mixed up with one of the most dreadful sort of faerie. “You should not speak their name,” she reminded Finn. Speaking the name only summoned them closer.

"I've frightened you," he said. "You need not stay here. Come back with me. Come back to Muine Bheag. You will be safe there. Your sisters are worried."

Rós stepped closer to the gate. The wind that stirred her skirts whirled into a great gust. Finn rocked back, blown by the powerful burst. It pulled Rós away; her hair loosed from its pins and whipped out behind her. With one hand, she grabbed onto the iron to keep from falling over. With the other she tried to keep the hem of her skirt down.

Pieces of bracken and moss swirled into the air, stinging her face. Finn shielded his eyes.

Rós looked back up the hill toward the castle. "Stop," she called, though her voice was swallowed by the wind. "I gave you my word. I'm not leaving."

The wind blew hard with one last gust, then died away. Not even the yarns of her frayed shawl wavered. All was absolutely still. Unnaturally still.

"How . . . how did you do that?" Finn asked. "You spoke, and the gale ceased." He was staring at her as if she was one of the faerie folk. "You have power over the wind now?"

She gave another quick glance up the hillside toward Black Fern, then turned back to Finn. "Don't be silly. No one can have power over the elements, save the Almighty."

More and more, she felt the master's presence in the breezes that blew about the place. But that was impossible.

She thrust the packet of coins into Finn's hands. "Here are my wages. Please give them to my family."

Finn nodded.

"You have not told them where I am?"

"No."

"Good. I beg you, say nothing of my whereabouts. It will only cause more worry. I'm perfectly safe here, and well compensated for my work. Do not worry about me. I'll see you in two weeks."

She gathered up the supplies and set off back through the woods and up the hill.

What kind of man could send his presence in a gust of wind? No man. So what was he? Could he be one of the Sluagh? If he was, she would not stay here a moment longer, promise or no. It was time for him to explain himself. Or at least to show his face again.

She entered through the front door and set the goods down.

"Come out," she said. "Show yourself. I know you are here. You are always here," she muttered. "Come out and speak with me, or I am leaving, promise or no." It was the only thing she thought he cared about. For good or for bad, he did not want her to go.

His form silently emerged from the shadows.

"What are you?" she demanded.

"A man, as you say."

"Are you living?"

He shrugged. "It's difficult to say."

How could it be difficult? Either he was or he wasn't. She crossed the room to him, staring into his empty eyes. Solid gray, yet bottomless. Like gazing into a fog where nothing can be seen and yet something is certainly there.

She'd touched his hand on her first day here, as he'd led her through the dark to her room. He had felt warm and alive. Perhaps she'd been deceived.

"What is your name?"

"Branán," he said quietly. "Branán O'Clyn."

An ordinary enough name. She'd half expected him to say Dragon-wolf. Or Balor. She still hadn't ruled out some sort of faerie demon, with his unearthly eyes and face like a tattered coat that had been mended far too many times.

She lifted her hand and placed it on his chest. He closed his eyes, and his jaw tightened. For all his wolfish ways, he looked very much like a begrudged child accepting punishment.

His chest rose and fell with each breath. A very living thing to do.

"Your heart still beats," she said. The undead did not have heartbeats. Perhaps he wasn't one of the Sluagh after all.

He opened his eyes, and the wall of clouds behind his lids swirled and churned as if driven by a great storm. He slapped her hand away. "Enough of this. You have work to do," he growled. "I do not pay for idleness." He stormed off, taking the stairs three at a time, blind as he was.

Branán O'Clyn. Strange that she'd never heard of him before. Black Fern wasn't so very far away. She should have known of it, and of the solitary wolf who lived here. Solitary and temperamental. She had been called many things in her twenty years, but idle was not one of them. She'd worked her fingers to the bone every day of her life. How dare he accuse her of idleness. Ungrateful man.

Rós gathered up the supplies and carted them off to the kitchen. It seemed like more of the same. A few vegetables, more salted meat, a round of cheese. She would make a fine meal for him tonight. Make him eat his words.

A chicken from the yard, some fresh herbs she'd found growing in an abandoned garden, and a loaf of hot, warm bread from the oven. Turnips basted with the juice of the roasting chicken. She even managed a steamed pudding. It took her the whole afternoon, but it was probably the most sumptuous meal she'd ever prepared. Her family ate mostly pottage and bread.

She carried the food into the dining room, plate by plate, and set it at Branán's place at the head of the table. He never came to eat until she had gone to bed, wasting her efforts, as it would all be cold by then. Perhaps she'd clean up and retire early so he might eat sooner.

She stood over the large cauldron of hot water, scrubbing the grease off the cooking pan, when a soft breeze rustled the back of her hair. She turned around and found him in the doorway to the kitchen. The sun shone in through the garden door, bathing his face and illuminating every scar.

He must feel the warmth on his face, but he made no move to hide. "Have you eaten?" he asked.

She shook her head, then remembered he couldn't see her. "No." She always took her simple meal after the kitchen was finished.

"I . . . Would you . . ." He shook his head. "It is foolish not to eat together, as we are the only two in the place. Will you join me?"

He stood tall, his shoulders broad and straight. Still it was clear by the crease in his brow and the twist of his lips that it cost him greatly to stand in full light and ask her. She glanced back at her dirty pots. It was unbefitting for a servant to dine with her master, but propriety did not reign in this house. If she had to spend the next three and a half months at Black Fern, how much better if they could be friends.

Another gust of wind blew past. When she looked up again, he was gone. He had no patience at all.

"Wait." She poked her head out of the kitchen to see his back retreating down the hall. "I want to come."

He paused and gave her a nod.

"I'll get another setting." She gathered up the plate and cup she usually used for her own quiet meal and hurried to the dining room. Branán was already seated at his place. No candles were lit, and the setting sun dragged what little light there was away with it.

Rós glanced at the large and spacious table. Where would he want her to sit? The lower the station the farther from the head. But it was silly to put miles of space between them when they were the only two. She plunked her plate down on the side nearest to him.

"This is quite a meal," Branán said. "I haven't had roast chicken since—a long time."

Already in the weeks she'd been here, his face seemed a little less gaunt. Still crossed with scars. Some newer looking. Some seemed to have been there for ages. Whatever he had suffered, it had happened more than once.

Rós filled his plate with food and set it in front of him, then dished some up for herself. He said nothing about the windows. If he was going to be outraged with her, she'd rather get it over with quickly.

"Thank you," she said. "For not being angry that I opened the shutters."

He tore off a piece of bread. "You were right after all. You are not a bat."

She grinned. There was more to this man than scars and shadows. If only she could get to know this other part of him better.

A flutter of air curved around her. "Are you not going to eat?" he asked.

Somehow he knew she was sitting there, staring at him. "How do you do it?" She asked. "How do you use the wind to . . . see?"

He speared a turnip. "Don't be ridiculous. No one can control the wind."

"Then how do you always know what I am doing?"

He did not answer.

Perhaps she should let it go, for he clearly did not want to talk about it. But she couldn't. If she was to fulfill her promise and remain with this man, she wanted to know. "I can feel your presence in the drafts that follow me about the castle."

He shrugged.

"And this morning. At the gate. What was that about?"

He shrugged again.

"Why were you so angry?"

"He wanted you to go with him. I thought you were leaving me." The more he tried to look like he didn't care, the more vulnerable he appeared. His eyes clouded, as though the wind itself churned inside them.

"I gave you my word," she said. "I intend to fulfill my promise, no matter how frightening—"

He pounded his fists on the table and leapt to his feet, tipping his chair back with a crash. "I am fully aware of my frightening appearance." In a biting whisper, he added, "I apologize for disturbing your appetite. I will leave you to dine in peace." He turned and stalked off.

That man. It was his temper that frightened her, not his face. Perhaps if she could convince him of that, he would soften. Then he would not need to hide behind his fury. There was more to be repaired here than simply the house.

Five

The following morning, at his place on the table, she found her three silver coins along with a sprig of lavender—the flower of peace. An apology of sorts. She brushed it along her lips and under her nose, letting the musty scent seep in. As she expected, a breeze rustled past.

"I do not fear you," she said. As angry as he got, it seemed a great sadness lay underneath. She placed the lavender in the pocket of her apron with her other herbs. If only she could prove to him that he did not disgust her. Then perhaps she might see more of the man that lurked beneath.

"'Tis a beautiful morning. Will you walk with me?" She opened the back door of the kitchen and stepped out.

She turned her face to the sun, letting its heat seep in to chase away the cold. A tell-tale breeze brushed her cheeks, as soft as any touch. He came into the kitchen, only a few paces behind her.

"I must thank you for one more thing," she said. "The generous wages. They will do much to help my family."

"You have earned it. No one has worked harder." Another attempt to make amends.

Since he was in a mood for concessions, she would try again to understand this half-man, half-faerie. "Are you one of the Sluagh?"

He set off down a path leading into the woods. Rós hurried to catch up. Perhaps he was not so conceding as she'd thought, for his eyes stormed.

"You do not need to remind me that I am vile. I know it full well."

"Sir." She pulled on his arm to stop him. "Branán."

He paused.

"I do not mean that you are vile. 'Tis only, there is something otherworldly about you. Your eyes. The way you move in the wind. I am not repulsed. I am sorry for whatever has happened to you, and I want to understand."

This did little to calm the gales raging in his eyes. "I don't want your pity." He set off again, the stomp of his boots tramping down the plants overgrowing the walkway.

She ran in front of him so that he bumped into her before he could stop. "You don't want me to fear you or pity you. What is it, exactly, that you *do* want from me, Branán O'Clyn?"

A whoosh of wind burst past, almost knocking her over. Then all went still. "I want you—"

"Me to what?"

He closed his eyes for a moment. When he opened them, the clouds inside were dark and brooding. "I want you to stay with me until harvest moon."

She pulled out a bundle of herbs from her apron pocket and removed a long stem of rosemary. If he spoke in the language of flora, she could too. She reached out, taking his hand, turning it palm up. She laid the rosemary branch on it, a symbol of loyalty.

He lifted the herb and smelled it. "Rosemary."

"I said I would stay. And I will."

His fingers closed almost desperately around the sprig. "You must understand, many, too many, have promised the same thing. Yet look at me." He motioned to his face. "It is my curse to be alone."

He set off again along the winding path, and she fell in step beside him. They wound around the trees deeper into the forest. The trees grew taller, thicker, blocking out the sun. The ground was soft to the step, covered with moss and fern. He might be leading her to his faerie world forever.

They followed a stream until a clearing opened up. Water trickled through a hole in a moss-covered rock and spilled almost silently into a pool of glass. The water reflected exactly the canopy of green above it.

"This is beautiful." Rós had never seen anything like it. A breeze rustled past, and she smiled up at him.

"It is my favorite place on the grounds."

She knelt and dipped her hand into the cool water. It trickled through her fingers, sending ripples across the mirrored surface. "You should not have showed me this," she said. "How shall I get my work done when I will wish to come here every day?" She cupped her hand and scooped the water again.

"You do not need to work."

She looked up to find him smiling. Something she thought she'd never see. Though the scars pulled at his lips and wrinkled his cheek, he was—or had been at one time—a handsome man.

"The money is yours, regardless, for all the work in the world will not save me or my manor." His smile was gone, replaced by the dark lines she'd seen that first day, when he'd agreed to let her stay.

"I am not a charity, sir. I will earn my wages, same as anyone."

The grin flicked across his face again.

"Tell me then, what's this about curses? I think it's about time you told me what it is that's going on here. What happened to you?"

He frowned. "It's not any concern of yours."

"It is my concern if I'm living in a cursed house with a person more faerie than man."

He stared into the water for a long time, though his eyes were as blank as ever. "Perhaps you do have a right to some truth. Though you will not like it."

"I've lived through your temper, so I think I'll survive whatever it is you have to say."

Another flash of his elusive smile. He'd better be careful, or she could get used to the way it transformed his face.

"I have not always been an honorable man. A man, though, same as any. Or at least, I was at one time. And though I am not one of the Sluagh, they circle me. Hunt me. They came for me one night." He scrubbed his hand across his face. "I was proud. I told them I didn't belong in the ranks of the host. I pleaded my case, and they laughed at me, telling me I would see soon enough how despised I was. Then they left, taking my sight with them and leaving me as you see, cursed." He smiled at her again, but it was a sorrowful, sad-looking thing. "They are always near, waiting to snatch my unrepentant soul."

Then he would be condemned to become one of them, waiting in the dark places of the world, hoping to steal another soul into their ranks. Rós drew back. No wonder he kept his windows shut tight and his shutters drawn. Anything to keep the Sluagh away.

"Can you not repent?" she suggested, though she knew it would make little difference, for once they have you in their sights, they cannot be dissuaded. But turning to God would surely do something to remove the curse.

He shrugged. "You said it yourself. I am vile."

She stood. "I never called you vile. You said it of yourself."

"Whether by words or your face, they say the same thing."

So stubborn. So decided. Yet for all his watchful wind, he was still blind to many things. "You cannot see my face. How do you know what it says?" She took his hand and placed it on her cheek. "Now tell me what you see."

He took a deep breath, then raised his other hand, cradling her face. His thumbs grazed her cheeks, her brows, then her mouth. She smiled to prove her point. He closed his eyes, as if he might get a better picture.

"Well?" she asked. "Does it say vile?"

"No, it does not." His words floated like thistle down over her head. "Of all my scars, yours will be the worst." And with that, he set off down the path toward the castle.

She clambered to her feet. "Wait. What about your scars? How did you get them?"

He did not answer. He disappeared into the trees. She'd been wrong about him. He was not a dragon or a wolf. He was simply the saddest man she'd ever met. And the most hopeless. Such despair would only make him more vulnerable to the Sluagh. She would do what she could for him, in her time here at Black Fern.

Six

And so it went over the following weeks. She worked her way from one room to the next. He followed, sometimes out of sight, his presence brushing past and fluttering her skirts. Sometimes he worked beside her. Often now he would walk with her out in the gardens, to the mirror pool, or just a wander in the woodlands.

He did not speak again of the Sluagh or his curse, and she did not ask. It would only open his heart to more despair. He was quiet, but he listened to her chatter about all sorts of nonsense. When she thought he wasn't listening she would stop, but he would always ask, "What happened then?"

She met Finn at the gate five more times, always passing on her coins for her family and taking the new batch of supplies. Every time he asked if she would not leave with him, and every time it was easier to decline.

One day she opened a door off the great hall. It was a smaller chamber with nothing more than a few soft chairs. A harp leaned against the wall. One of the few items she'd come across that wasn't buried in cobwebs and dust.

She ran her fingers along the strings, creating a waterfall of chimes.

"Do you play?" Branán asked. He was never far away.

"Heavens no. How would I ever come upon such a fine thing?" She brushed her fingers along the strings again, filling the room with sound. "Will you play a song for me?"

"I do not play the harp."

She crossed the small chamber and took his hand, pulling him toward the instrument. "Of course you do, else I would now be plucking spider webs from it. I've had little opportunity for music in my life. It would please me greatly if you would play a song." She hefted the harp and thrust it into his arms.

"How can I refuse such a plea?" He sat and settled the instrument on a small footstool between his legs. His fingers plucked the strings, and she recognized the tune immediately. The ballad of Tristan and Iseult. He played very well. The music danced around her and settled into her very heart.

She sat beside him and closed her eyes. Never had she heard anything so beautiful. The words ran through her mind. How Iseult was meant for the Cornish King, but her love for Tristan ran deep. Tristan's anguish as he was exiled, parted from Iseult forever. Rós could not help herself: when Branán reached the last verse where Tristan was mortally wounded and sent for Iseult to heal him, she quietly sang along.

If Iseult were willing to come to Ireland and heal Tristan, she was to sail with white sails. If she refused, the ship was to come with black sails. Tristan's wife, jealous of his love for Iseult, lied and claimed the ship had black sails. Tristan's grief overcame him, and he died believing Iseult did not care for him. When Iseult found her love dead, she succumbed to grief as well.

The music stopped, and Rós waited until the last echoes faded away. "Play it again."

"Again?" He smiled, puckering his scars and transforming his face. "I will play if you will sing."

She nodded. "I will."

He started the tune over again. This time she sang from the beginning, when Tristan was sent to Ireland to fetch Iseult to be the king's wife. The king took Iseult's hand, but only Tristan held her heart.

"It is the most beautiful thing I've ever heard," Rós said when the song ended again.

"Yes, it is," he said as a breeze softly grazed her cheeks. He played a few lines of a simple melody—a children's rhyme. Thrice he plucked the same tune, then said, "You try."

"Oh, no. I couldn't." It seemed too complicated to know which string to strike. They all looked the same.

Branán scooted to the side, making room for her in front of the footstool. "It is easier than it looks."

She took his seat, and he placed the harp in front of her, hovering behind her and showing her how to hold it.

"This part rests here." He put the shorter end of the instrument against her right shoulder. He then lifted her left hand. "This one stretches back to reach the farther strings." He stopped, turning her hand in his. He reached around her and took her other hand so that his chest warmed her back where it pressed lightly against her. "Look at your hands."

"What . . ." She found it hard to think about her hands with his breath tickling her neck. His words brushing past her cheek. Much the same and yet also very different from the winds he sent so many times a day. She twisted her head to ask again, but he had turned to speak to her at the same moment. Her lips nearly brushed against his.

He stilled, leaving naught but their breath between them. This close she could see the mist behind his eyes stirring faster and faster. She lowered her gaze but did not move away. He would surely take that as a sign of disgust. Though somehow, the thought of her lips touching his did not fill her with disgust. Rather, it brought a rush of heat to her cheeks, and she drew in a sharp breath.

Branán let go of her hands, stepping away. For the first time his blindness seemed to get the better of him, and he stumbled on the leg of a chair. "You . . . You are working too hard. Your hands are rough and cracked."

"So they have always been." Though she hadn't really worried about it until Branán had touched them.

"You've done more than enough. Let it rest. The other rooms will never be used."

"Are you dismissing me?" She could not help her family if she lost this income. She would never find a post that paid as well. She still had a few weeks 'til harvest moon.

"No." He seemed surprised by her question. Then his scars puckered and creased as he frowned. "Unless that is what you want."

The thought of leaving Black Fern caused her stomach to twist. After all her hours of work, it was part of her now. But it wasn't so much the manor that had found a room in her heart, it was Branán. She wasn't ready to leave him. Not yet.

"I need the money," she said.

"Yes. The money."

"For my family. My father is unwell. His mind is slipping. And there are seven other sisters to feed."

"Of course." He was retreating again. Withdrawing into hopelessness. She almost preferred his rage, for at least then he showed some will.

"Now then," she said in her brightest voice, "are you going to teach me how to play this thing or not?"

At last there was a glimpse of his elusive smile, though it was fleeting and grim. "Yes. And tomorrow, instead of wasting your time on meaningless chores, we shall begin proper lessons."

"Proper lessons?"

He nodded. "I shall teach you to read and write."

She stared at him. The priest's scribe was the only person in Muine Bheag who knew how to read and write. If Branán could teach her, her possibilities for employment were boundless. The townsfolk always needed someone to scribe for them. She could live at home, care for her father and sisters, and still bring in coin.

"Is it difficult? I have only three weeks left 'til Harvest Moon. How much can I learn in so short a time?" Perhaps she could come back for lessons. It would give her a reason to return. To see Branán again.

"Yes," he said gruffly. "I keep forgetting that your term is almost up and you will be leaving me."

It sounded as though he might not want her to return. He'd been so angry at her when she first came. He must be ready to return to his life of solitude. But now he had enticed her, and she did not want to let it go. "But still, isn't there something of scribing I could learn in our last few weeks?"

"Of course," he said. "I'm sure there is much you could learn. We will start first thing in the morning."

"Thank—" She'd almost forgotten what tomorrow was. "But that is my day to walk to the gate to meet Finn." She hated wasting a precious day on this task, but the supplies must be collected and her money sent to her family.

"The day after, then," he said with finality.

"Thank you, sir."

Seven

Rós skipped down the stairs, eager to get her meeting with Finn over quickly and perhaps persuade Branán to give her an early start on lessons tonight. He would likely prefer to work in the dim light of candles anyway.

Branán met her at the door. "You are going down the mountain?"

He knew she was—as she did every fortnight. Perhaps this journey could be more pleasant. "Why don't you come with me?"

He drew his head back. So concerned about his scarred face.

"Finn never steps past the gate. Come with me, and you can wait out of sight, if that is your worry."

He stood silently for a few moments, until a soft wind rustled her hair and swept her cheek.

Fretful man. "See here." She took his hand and placed it

on her cheek so that he could feel her sincerity. "I would very much enjoy your company this morning."

His fingertips grazed softly across her cheek, stroking her forehead and then her mouth. "You will be the death of me," he muttered.

"Nonsense. The air is warm and the birds are singing. 'Tis a lovely morning."

"Indeed, it is." Branán opened the door and gestured for her to pass through, then followed her out.

She slipped her hand into the crook of his elbow. Perhaps it was forward of her, but it really was a beautiful morning, and she did not care. By the way he tightened his arm, tucking her hand up snugly against him, he didn't seem to mind. His face, though, was creased and worn.

"What is it?" she asked.

He shook his head. "How is it, again, that you came to me?"

"I needed work. And Black Fern was the only place left I hadn't tried." She scooted closer to him as they passed through a narrow part of the path, where two enormous tree trunks squeezed out the light from above. "And you were kind enough to take me in."

He snorted. "I don't think I've ever been called kind before. Not by anyone."

"That is because they don't know you as I do." When she met him, she would not have used that word either. "When I first heard you speak, I thought you were a dragon. Then a wolf. But now I see you are naught but a hedgehog. Prickly, to be sure, but underneath there is nothing but fluff."

"Fluff?" He grunted. "I think I prefer to be the dragon."

She tried to recall what it was that was so frightening about him back then. His temper, yes. He'd been so angry. Especially when she'd seen him fully for the first time. What a shock that had been, his face carved with scars and his blank eyes. Now she hardly noticed them.

"Will you tell me now about how you got your scars?" she asked.

He walked in silence for a while, but she'd learned by now to give him time. "They are part of my curse," he said at last. "They are the reminders of all I have lost. And this is where I leave you, for I'll not go all the way to the gate."

She hadn't realized they were so close. "But you will wait for me, here, right? You'll not leave me alone?"

His mouth twitched in a half smile. "I'll not leave you."

"Good. I'll be back soon. Quickly as I can."

She hurried down, around the bend and out of sight of Branán, who waited for her behind the bank of giant oak trees.

Finn was at the gate already, his load of supplies slung over his shoulder. "You are late this morning."

"Sorry." She opened the broken gate as far as she could. "I was enjoying the walk so much, I forgot to hurry." She took the sack of goods and set them on the ground. "How are things in Muine Bheag?"

Finn shrugged his shoulders. "Same as always, I suppose. A new smithy has come to town, but I don't think he will stay long. Not enough business. But he's lodging at the inn for now, so that is good for our coffers."

Finn was wearing a new tunic, one made with a fine, bright blue wool. It suited him. The blacksmith must be paying well. "I'm glad to hear it," she said. A wind blew past, sifting in and out between Finn and herself. Of course he would be listening. She held out her bundle of coins—her wages from the last two weeks. "How is my family?"

"Very well, I should say. I saw Éile just the other day, at market. She was buying a lamb shank."

Her money was going to good use, then. Her father's

mind would surely heal faster with meat in his belly. "And she looked well?"

"Aye, she looked very well. You'd best take care, Rós, or she may surpass you in beauty." He laughed. Another gust of wind swept past, blowing hard against him. "It is always so windy up here. You must be tired of being blown about."

Rós grinned. "Actually, I find I've come to appreciate it."

This time the wind didn't die down. It moved past her and Finn and continued down the mountainside.

"You'll give those coins to my family?" She always asked.

And he always answered the same. "Yes, yes. Are you sure you will not come home with me?"

"Not today. Thank you, Finn."

She closed the creaking gate and climbed the path back toward the oaks where she'd left Branán. His wind was still swirling past her, perhaps following Finn back toward the village.

She rounded the bend and found Branán kneeling on the ground, his eyes a whorl of mist. He didn't move as she approached.

"Sir?"

He did not respond. He must be down the mountain still, in his wind.

"Branán?" She put a hand on his shoulder, shaking him.

"Wait," he said.

She'd never seen him like this. Perhaps it cost him to let his breeze travel so far. She set the sack of goods on the ground and knelt beside him. She waited, as he'd instructed, until the air stilled. He let out a long breath, and the scars on his face furrowed.

"What is it?" she asked. "What did you see?"

He stood, then held out his hand and helped Rós to her feet. "What is your relationship with that man? Finn?"

"He is my friend," she said. "And that is all. Why?"

Branán picked up the goods and held out his arm for Rós. She put her hand through it, as she'd done on the way down. But he was stiff and distant with her as they climbed the path, his face creased in thought.

Finally she could take it no longer. "What is wrong?"

He stopped. "Rós—" he said, his mouth a thin, tight line. But he didn't finish. He turned away, facing into the forest and let out a roar. A dragon again.

She pulled on his arm. "Branán?"

"Finn," he said, turning toward her. "He has betrayed you."

Betrayed? "How?"

"He is not giving the wages to your family."

"What?" Finn would never. She trusted him. He wouldn't keep her money. It must be Branán who was mistaken. "Are you sure?"

He nodded.

Finn would never do such a thing. Yet as she studied Branán's face, it was he she trusted more than Finn.

"That's not all," he whispered. "Your family."

She swallowed hard. Her entire reason for coming to this forsaken mountain was to help her family. "What about them?"

Branán's tall frame seemed to fold. His head hung low, defeated. "I think they are ill," he whispered. "The fever, perhaps. Or plague. I cannot say for certain."

"All of them?"

"Many. Your father. I did not see everything."

She staggered backwards. Without her wages, they must be starving. This was Finn's fault. And hers, for ever leaving in the first place. If she'd stayed, they would still be poor, but at least she would have been there to care for them.

That lying, backstabbing snake. Telling her that her family was doing well. Did he know they were ill, or had he simply never checked on them at all? How had she been so deceived?

"I must go to them." She started back down the path toward the gate, but Branán's hand grabbed at her wrist.

"You promised to stay."

She'd never seen his face so grim. When she'd promised to stay, she'd believed her earnings would go to her father and sisters. To put food on their table. Clothes on their backs. To shore them up against the long winter. Not to a thieving louse. Finn had ruined everything.

"I will come back. I promise." She took his hand. "If I do not go, they will die, and all my time here will have been wasted." Her whole reason for coming to Black Fern was to protect her family, and now they were worse off than ever.

"Wasted." He let go of her. "Then you should go."

She would not be gone forever. He need not look so pained. "I will be back. I will make up the lost time and stay past Harvest Moon. I will return. I promise. But I cannot let them die."

"No, you cannot." He pulled a purse from his belt and handed it to her. "Take this. Get what you need for them."

She lifted it from him, heavy with coin. Before he could pull his hand away, she took hold of it. "You are very kind."

His eyes were empty, the clouds that spun in them still as death. "Go."

A wind swooshed past her as he turned and walked quickly toward his manor. He disappeared into the dark of the woods and thick trees. Something tugged at her heart, tempting her to follow him, but that would have to wait.

Eight

Muine Bheag was quiet as she passed through. Perhaps more families than her own were hit by whatever sickness had swept through.

When she reached her home, she found the door ajar and the sound of crying leaking out. She pushed it open and blinked into the darkness. The smell of sickness hit her like one of Branán's winds. She left the door open to let the air in.

"Hello?"

"Rós?" It was the voice of Brigit, coming from the bedroom.

Rós hurried across the small room and up the narrow wooden staircase to the sleeping chamber above. Her family were all laid out: her father in his bed, Éile and Fiadh in Rós's bed, and the other bed with the rest of her sisters.

"You're back." Brigit said. "We thought you were dead."

"Dead? Did Finn tell you nothing?" That cur. She'd thought a lifetime of friendship would go farther than extra coins in his coffers. If the Sluagh had to go after the worst of men, they should set their sights on Finn rather than Branán.

Brigit shook her head. "You just disappeared." The poor girl's eyes were lost and broken. What she must have suffered trying to care for a sick family at only thirteen years old.

Rós wrapped her arms around Brigit. "It's all right now. I'm here."

Brigit collapsed into her.

"What has happened? Tell me all."

"Father is worse than ever. He barely recognizes any of us." She wiped her eyes. "He dug up half the garden one day, claiming it to be all weeds. There wasn't enough food. So when the fever came, everyone fell ill."

"Except you. You have always been the strongest."

"I made broth out of our last turnips yesterday. There is nothing left to do but watch them die." Brigit's voice broke, and her little body shook against Rós with a sob.

Finn would pay.

"Brigit, dry your eyes. We cannot give up. All will be well." She took Brigit's hands. "Go fetch the doctor."

"He will not come. He knows we cannot pay."

She opened Branán's purse and removed a few silver coins. "Give him one of these. Tell him there is more to pay for whatever is needed."

Brigit's eyes grew wide as she stared at the silver. "Where did you get this?"

"I've been working for a man." She stroked her sister's cheek. "A generous man." They were meant to have this much and more from Finn, but he'd kept it for himself. She pushed her anger down, saving it for later, after she got her family back on their feet. "Use the rest to go to the butcher and get a nice beef bone. We'll make a hearty marrow broth. Then go to Widow Mulligan for comfrey and nettle." She jangled the coin purse. "Get what you need."

Brigit pulled her tattered shawl across her shoulders and scurried down the stairs, her fist clenched around the handful of coins.

Rós filled a basin with fresh water from the well. She built up the fire to take the chill from the house and set a pot over the flames. The house looked like it hadn't been cleaned in weeks. She found a clean scrap of cloth and used it to wipe her father's brow.

He opened his eyes and smiled at her. "Muirín." Her mother's name.

"Father, it's me, Rós. I've come home."

"Rós?" It was as though he'd never heard the name before.

His skin burned. Perhaps that was why she was a stranger.

She did the same for each of her sisters, cool water on their fevered brows. Some opened their eyes, giving her a hug and a brief grin. Brigit returned with the doctor and a basket filled with goods.

"Thank you for coming, sir." Rós said to the doctor.

"You sister assures me you can pay." As if money was more important than the lives of her family.

"Yes, sir."

He nodded at her. "Very well, then."

He examined each of her sisters and her father—touching their brows, listening to them breathe, wrapping his greedy fingers around their pale wrists to feel faint heartbeats. A few slits in the tender skin of their elbows to let the sick blood out. Anga, the youngest, cried out, and Rós held her on her lap.

"It is not plague. A fever." The doctor mixed a syrup and gave each a few spoonfuls. He poured some in a flask and gave it to Rós. "Give them more tomorrow morning. I would also advise you to move them downstairs and get this room cleaned. The air is filled with bad humors."

"Yes, sir."

He named his price, and Rós paid him. He left, his step lighter even though he was weighed down by several of Branán's silver coins.

She and Brigit fed them the marrow broth seasoned with some onions and celery root Brigit had also bought. They managed to get the girls and her father down into the main room and spent the rest of the day washing bedding and scrubbing floors. Much like Rós had spent her days at Black Fern.

Occasionally a breeze ruffled her hair. "Thank you," she would say, softly, wishing there was more than air to embrace.

The following day, once her father and sisters were all settled, she marched off to the inn, ready to flay Finn for his treachery. She wanted her money back.

"Gone," said Finn's mother, the innkeeper's wife. "He packed up his things and set off for Kenmare in a hurry."

"When did he leave?" asked Rós.

"Yesterday." He must have gotten word of her return. No wonder he asked every fortnight if she would come home with him. Not because he wanted her, but because he had to be wary. Wretched worm. That she'd ever considered him her friend made her want to bathe in lye. She hoped he'd fall into the hands of thieves on his way to Dublin.

It took more than two weeks for her sisters to recover. Anga much sooner, but Éile's fever dragged on and on. Her father seemed fine, though Brigit was right, his mind was less and less in the world and turned mostly into his own thoughts.

Rós made her way home from the market, her arms filled with food they never could have afforded if not for Branán. The day was warm, despite the leaves turning to fire and gold. She used her shoulder to wipe her brow. Where was one of his winds when she needed it?

He'd been sending them less and less. Perhaps it was too far to follow her around like he did when she lived on the mountain. She was lonely without them. Seven sisters and a father, yet Branán's absence left a vacancy all of them together could not fill.

Clouds moved in and covered the sun, yet it did not cool. Rós's head pounded from the heat of the day. Even her eyes were affected, and she could hardly see the path to her home. Something was wrong. Now her legs could barely carry her. She sat on a moss-covered rock to rest.

Nine

"Rós," Brigit's voice called to her, but all she could see was black. She was home, for she breathed familiar scents and was tucked into a bed. But her eyes would not open.

A spoon pressed against her lips. "You must eat." Éile's voice this time.

Rós gathered her strength and forced her eyes to open.

Éile sat beside her, on the edge of her bed. "You need to eat, Rós."

She opened her mouth and swallowed the liquid. Marrow broth. Same as she'd made for her sisters.

"Are you recovered?" Rós asked Éile, though to get the words out left her exhausted.

Éile nodded. "Well enough. Thanks to you." She spooned in another mouthful of broth. "The smithy found you collapsed on the wayside. You've been wandering the world beyond for four days. Doctor said you mightn't live. Guess now that you've awoke he'll be disappointed he cannot bleed us for more money."

It was hard to pull her mind out of the clouds and down to earth. "Four days?"

"Aye. And you've been calling for Branán. Whoever that may be." But the smirk on her face and quirk of her brow told Rós she'd already guessed exactly her feelings for Branán.

"Open the window," Rós said.

"You'll get a chill."

"I want to feel the wind."

Éile pushed open the shutter. The softest breeze whispered across her cheek. Rós smiled, lay back on her pillow, and rolled toward it. "I'm all right," she whispered. "I'll see you soon."

Ten

When next she woke, the shadows were on the other side of their little cottage. The day was getting late. Her window was still open, and autumn breezes wandered in, but he was not in them. Harvest moon was only days away. She would like to be back at Black Fern by then, since he seemed so intent to have her there on that day.

She sat up, her head a little light, but overall feeling much better. With a blanket draped across her shoulders, she crept down the stairs. Her family sat around the hearth, a merry fire dancing. Anga played with her rag doll, Éile and Brigit were mending clothes, talking about the handsome new smithy. Fiadh was helping Marga to knit. Ciara and Sarán weaved garlands. Father dozed in his tall-backed chair.

It was the most content she'd seen them in a long time.

"Rós!" Anga called out, running into her arms. "You're awake."

Éile laughed. "Come sit here. Have some pottage and warm bread."

Rós was starving. She took the food from Éile and ate.

"Ciara and Sarán are making wreaths for the festival tonight," Anga said.

Sarán held up her garland. "What do you think?"

"Festival? Tonight?"

Ciara nodded. "For harvest moon."

"It's tonight?" She'd been lost in the fever longer than she thought. It seemed she wouldn't be with Branán as she'd wanted.

She leaned back, tearing a piece of bread and dipping it in the pottage. Though she'd been famished only moments ago, she could barely swallow. Her thoughts flew to the house hidden in the mountains.

She stood.

"Rós?" Éile watched her.

Rós opened the door and stepped into the afternoon light. She leaned against the doorway, weak still from the fever. She closed her eyes, beckoning any breeze to wash across her. Her chemise fluttered, and a few strands of hair blew across her face. It was just wind.

"Where are you?" she whispered.

"Who?" asked Éile, looking up the path.

A raven cawed from high above. Then another.

"Something is wrong," she said to Éile. "I cannot feel him."

"Who? Branán?"

"Aye. And look." Rós pointed at the sky. Bird after bird flew past, twisting and swirling in the west wind. At least, they looked like birds. All of them dark as night and headed toward the mountain. "The Sluagh. I must go."

"Go?" Éile turned on her. "You cannot go. You aren't well enough to leave."

"I must. They are coming for him."

Rós hurried into the house and threw a dress on over her chemise. She found her worn boots and stuffed her feet into them. Éile threw a cloak around Rós's shoulder and fastened it, all the while sermonizing why she should not leave, how she would catch her death. And mostly how if the Sluagh were coming for him, nothing could stop them.

No matter, she had to go. If the host was swarming, it could only mean one thing. Death was knocking at Branán's door.

She stuffed a sack full of every candle she could find and a set of lighting stones. She bade her family farewell, telling them she would come back as soon as she could, leaving what was left of the coins in Éile's hands.

The climb up the mountain path nearly killed her. She tried to hurry, but her breath came in hollow gasps. At last she reached the gate, pushing through the crooked iron and into the darkness of the woods.

The cries of the host grew louder. Their dark shadows swooped through the sky.

"I'm coming," she said, though the wind was desperately empty. What if she was too late? If he was ailing he should have told her. When she'd left him he'd seemed fine. Perhaps he'd had an accident. "Wait for me. I'm coming."

She wiped the sweat from her face, though the evening was cold. Every step sent a wave of dizziness, and she stumbled from tree to tree as she followed the darkening path. Black Fern waited for her, as unwelcoming as ever.

She pushed through the front door as the sun finally dipped into the trees.

"Branán," she called.

All was silent. She was too late.

"Branán O'Clyn. Where are you?"

The softest touch of air stroked her cheek. Her heart leapt. She was not too late after all.

She ran up the stairs and down the long corridor to his chambers. It was dark in this part of the house, for no windows had been opened here to let the twilight in.

"Branán."

He lay atop his bed, still as death, his tunic cast aside. Across his chest was a gaping wound that stretched right across his heart. It looked as though it had been there for some time. She bent over the hearth and lit a fire for both warmth and light.

A patchwork of scars marred his chest. His whole body must be covered in them.

"Are you really here? Or am I dreaming again?" he whispered.

"I am here."

He sighed. "That's what you say in all my dreams."

She lifted his hand and pressed it to her face. "See, flesh and bone. I am here. What happened to you?"

"You left," he said, as if that explained everything.

She found his tunic on the floor and tore off some strips, wrapping them around his open wound.

"I mean how did you injure yourself?" Maybe something went wrong with the ax while he tried to cut wood for the coming winter. He was blind, after all. He managed so well, she sometimes forgot.

He shook his head. "This is how I got all my scars."

"What?" He was not making sense.

He put his hand over hers, where she tied his wrap. "It is my curse. It is how I get my scars."

She leaned closer. “I don’t understand.”

“These are the marks of all the people who have left me. I am a vile man. A sinner. Unrepentant. And so I am cursed. All those who come to know me and forsake me leave their mark.” He paused, his voice tired and slow. “The more I care about someone, the deeper the wound.”

Rós looked down at the gash across his chest. This was because she went down the mountain to care for her family? It was a miracle he was still alive. Her fingers traced the rippled scars that marked his body. What he must have suffered, endured. His body rent time and time again.

“But I did not forsake you,” she said. “I am here with you now.” Rós gathered up another strip she’d torn from his tunic. “We will get this healed up.”

“Leave it,” he said. “It is too late. ’Tis Harvest Moon. They are here for me.”

“No. You will be fine, I just need to—”

“There is nothing you can do. You are here. You came back even though you are unwell, and that is enough.” The clouds in his eye hardly moved at all. He was weak, and growing weaker. “I have one last request.”

“What?”

He lifted his hand and ran his fingers through her tumbled hair. “I wish you would lie here beside me, ’til it is over.”

Life drained out of him, little by little, whether from the host circling outside or from the death wound she had caused, she was not certain. But she was certain of one thing, she was not ready to lose him. She would never lie down and let him die.

She tied off the swath of linen. “That is something I cannot do.”

He turned his head away. So forlorn, her dragon of the mountain. And so sure he was unloved. Such sadness made him more vulnerable to the Sluagh. She must give him hope. Some glimmer of happiness to make it harder for them to pry his soul away.

A brush of air touched her face, soft and sorrowful as the last rose of summer.

She kissed his cheek. "I will stay with you, Branán O'Clyn, 'til it is over. But I will not sit idly by." She kissed his other cheek. "I missed you, while I was away. I missed our walks to the faerie pool. I missed your breezes following me around the house, listening to me as I spoke of nothing. I even missed your temper."

She leaned close, her unkempt hair falling forward like a curtain, cutting off the world around them.

"Rós," he whispered.

She touched her lips to his. Instantly both of his hands cupped her head, pulling her closer, kissing her with more strength than she thought he had left. Until this moment, she'd not understood how completely her heart had turned to him. But as his hand slid to the back of her neck, her fingers twined into his dark hair, and a soft moan escaped her lips.

A crash against the window pane echoed through the chamber. "The Sluagh." She'd almost forgotten about the darkness circling outside. "I won't let them take you," she said, running to the window and securing the latch. "You promised to teach me letters. Would you go back on your word?"

The banging on the window grew louder as the host battered against the glass. She lit all the candles she'd brought, positioning them around Branán's chamber. "I'm setting out candles," she explained. "The host are creatures of dark and forgotten places. The light will lessen their power."

"You cannot stop them," he said, trying to sit up. He groaned but managed to get himself up. "I have known they were coming for me this day since my curse began."

"Hush now," she scolded. "Curses are meant to be broken. You cannot despair, it will weaken your soul."

With a crash, the window burst open. A flock of shadows, roiling and flapping their wings, poured in. The wild hunt of the Underfolk. Rós clapped her hands over her ears to block out their screeching.

One of the dark shapes twisted in the air in front of Branán, landing on the stone floor with its claw-like feet. Tall and slender, like a man, but all brittle bones stretched with desiccated flesh.

Rós stepped in front of him, blocking the creature's path. "You cannot take him," she said. "I have seen his heart, and it is good. His soul is no longer yours."

The creature took a step closer, leathery wings hanging close, like a cloak. A sharp beak for a mouth and a face so dark no other features could be seen.

"Step aside, Rós," Branán said.

She'd heard the only way to dissuade the host was to offer another soul instead. If she could turn them away from him, perhaps she could make a bargain of some sort. "Take me in his place," Rós cried, moving forward.

"No." Branán pulled her back. "This is my fate, not yours. I will not allow it." As he spoke, a rush of wind swept past her, rough and fierce. The creature's wings fluttered in the gust, and it let out a terrible shriek. It leapt backward, away from Branán.

Rós turned to him. "Send a wind."

"What?"

"I don't think it likes your wind," she explained. "The

Sluagh always ride the west wind. Why do we keep the west side windows barred when someone in the house is ill? Why do we cower indoors when the west wind rages? They move on the wind like it is their friend. But yours is not the west wind. I think it is not their friend."

He stared at her—or at least, that's what she would have called it if he could see.

Two more creatures came to light in front of her. Their claws clicked on the floor as they crept toward him.

"Please just try," she begged.

He put his arm around her waist and pulled her close. "Hold on."

The clouds in his eyes swirled, and a mighty gust burst forth, sweeping the Sluagh off their feet. Their screeching cries filled the room like a roar of thunder.

Branán's wind grew and grew. Rós closed her eyes and buried her head in his shoulder. He held her tight, both arms wrapped around her. The wind raged and raged until the shrieks of the Sluagh died away.

The gusts ceased in an instant. Branán's body folded. She lowered him back onto his bed. The room was a disaster of blown linens, chairs, and tapestries, but the Sluagh were gone. With a slam, she closed the window and latched it.

"You did it," she said. How he had managed with so little strength left, she couldn't comprehend.

He did not answer but let out a soft grunt.

Rós smoothed her windblown hair. "They're gone."

He smiled, his eyes still closed and his breathing heavy. The wrap she'd wound around his chest had come loose and now hung at his waist. The lesion was gone. Rós ran her fingers along the place where only minutes ago his flesh had been torn.

Branán's breathing stilled.

"There's not even a scar," Rós said. "Your wound is completely healed. As if it never existed."

Branán ran his hand along his chest. "It must be because you came back. No one has ever done so before."

When she'd found him here, lying on his bed, he was near death. His other scars still covered his skin, but the one she'd caused had utterly vanished. "Does this mean the curse is broken? What would happen if I left again?"

He sat up. "Do you want to go?" he asked, his voice low. "Your time is up; you need not stay."

She should have phrased her question better. Of course he would assume the worst. "Branán O'Clyn. You are a rogue."

A whiff of air fluttered past.

"To kiss me like that, and then dismiss me so easily. Are you trying to break my heart?"

The scars on his face curved with his crooked smile. "Nay, it was you who kissed me."

"Always so contrary." She sank onto the bed beside him, bone weary. She shivered from the cold while sweat beaded her brow. "I didn't hear you complain."

Another brush of air, and he drew her close. "Indeed, I did not." It was he, this time, who placed his lips to hers, soft as dove wings. He'd built a room in her heart, a home where he would always stay.

"You are not well. Your skin burns again with fever." He laid her back on his bed, covering her with a blanket. "Rest."

Eleven

She woke in the morning, tucked into Branán's bed. It smelled like him, of wind and warmth. He sat on a chair beside her, a breeze touching her cheeks. She did not speak but watched him keeping his vigil, his brows creased.

"What is all this worry?" she asked.

He shook his head. "Not worry. Trying to make sense of things."

"What things?"

"You." He shrugged. "I don't understand how you are here."

"You defeated the Slu—the host. Remember?" Better to not speak their name ever again.

"I remember. What I don't understand is how you are here, in my home." He put his fist on his chest and whispered, "And in my heart. I did not think it possible."

She could not imagine all he must have suffered to be so

scarred. And more than his body bore the marks. His wounds ran deep, bruising his mind. His soul.

"I . . . Do you think . . ." He took a deep breath, then spoke with barely a whisper. "Do you think you could find room in your heart . . . for me?" He'd remembered the words she'd spoken when she'd told the story of her parents.

She lifted both his hands and placed them on her cheeks. "You are already there. Never doubt it."

At last his face relaxed, and a slow smile began to spread. But before he could answer, a knock rang through the castle. His face changed instantly to the wolf she'd encountered her first day at Black Fern. He rose to his feet, and a rush of air pushed down the hall.

"It is your sisters," he grumbled. "Two of them, anyway."

"Oh?" Odd that they would come this far. She stood, straightening her dress.

"Send them away," he ordered.

She perched on her tiptoes and kissed his cheek. "Don't be grumpy." Then she darted out of the room and hurried down the stairs.

It was Éile and Brigit.

"We were worried about you," they explained. "There was such a storm last night, up here on the mountain. And you were so weak when you left." They stepped across the threshold, into the pool of sunlight pouring through the open door.

"We did have a terrible wind," Rós said. "But we are both well. Is that not so, Branán?" She walked into the shadow where he always lurked. Hidden. Putting her hand in his, she dragged him into the light. His mouth was a thin line and his eyes a wall of mist. He hated the light, to be seen. But she held tight to his hand.

Her sisters gaped, Éile's mouth falling open.

He was quite alarming, when first seen. Rós was so used to him, she hardly noticed. He may not be the handsome man she and her sisters dreamed about as young girls, but she couldn't imagine her life with anyone else.

Brigit was the first to recover. "We, uh, want to thank you for your generosity, sir," she said, her voice weak but growing stronger. "You have saved our family."

Rós squeezed his hand, and he gave them a nod.

"How is Father today?" Rós asked.

"Well enough." Éile glanced at Rós's hand wrapped tightly around Branán's. "Well, then. We only came up to check on you. And to see when you might be coming home."

Branán went still beside her, his grip now tightening on hers. Curse or no curse, if she followed her sisters home, he would be hurt.

"I'll be staying here." His hold relaxed. "Perhaps in a few weeks I'll come for a visit. But this is my home now."

Her sisters looked at each other, then at Rós.

Branán cleared his throat. "You're welcome to come here any time." His voice was still a bit wolfish, but he had tried. It was not for the benefit of Éile and Brigit he'd spoken. It was for Rós he'd made his offer.

Whatever his past, whatever things he had done to summon the Sluagh's curse, she did not want to know. He was a different man now. He must be, for she loved him.

"I believe that is the kindest thing you've ever said." Rós grinned up at him as her sisters started back down the path.

"Don't get used to it. After all, I am a vile man."

"That is, if you are a man at all."

He laughed. "Perhaps you will never know." And with that, he took her into his arms and kissed her.

About Julie Daines

Julie Daines was born in Concord, Massachusetts, and was raised in Utah. She spent eighteen months living in London, where she studied and fell in love with English literature, sticky toffee pudding, and the mysterious guy who ran the kebab store around the corner.

She loves reading, writing, and watching movies—anything that transports her to another world. She picks Captain Wentworth over Mr. Darcy, firmly believes in second breakfast, and never leaves home without her verveine.

Visit Julie here:
Website: JulieDaines.com
Facebook: julie.daines.7

Scarlet

Heather B. Moore

One

I always take the long way home. No matter the weather. Snow, rain, sleet, wind, sun. I refuse to walk past the stonecutter's house since I never know when his son might be in the yard.

The stonecutter's son, August, teased me as a girl. Followed me to school, tripped me, tugged my braids, stole my lunch.

My mother said boys tease the girls they like.

But I knew August didn't like me. Not in the way Sawyer liked my friend Violet. Sawyer brought her flowers. He wrote her poems. He carried her books. Sawyer's eyes are a soft, kind green.

August's eyes are black as night. His hair is the color of mud, his skin tanned by the sun. His arms are thick as branches, as befits a stonecutter's son. August's gaze is cold, like the wind from the north, and when he looks at me, I tremble.

August is nowhere in sight, so why am I trembling now?

I must pass by his house so that I am not too late to join my mother.

My mother attends to Mrs. Ivy as she labors to bring forth her third child. Two boys she has. This will be a third boy, my mother predicts.

But the labor has been long and arduous. Mother has sent me to fetch more of the herbs we dry over the hearth, at the ready for our midwifery. As the village midwife, Mother attends to the women; I am her lady in training.

I clutch the basket of dried herbs I carefully covered with a cloth to keep out the wind.

Soon, August's house is behind me, and I breathe more easily.

Mrs. Ivy's homestead is not too far now, just around the next bend in the road. Because I have let myself believe all is well, I do not see August beyond the curve of the road until it is too late.

He leads a massive stallion by the reins, and my first impression is that the animal has been hurt.

I stop in the middle of the road, too stunned to speak for a moment.

August's gaze slides over me, over all of me, and I know he does not miss my twice-patched dress, my threadbare sleeves, or the way my hair is barely contained by my only ribbon.

"Halt," he says to the stallion, and the horse's hoofsteps slow.

I walk to the edge of the road, making a wide berth around beast and man.

"You are traveling alone, Little Red?" August says.

I cringe at his nickname. My hair is no longer the bright red of my youth. It hangs in dusky auburn tangles down my back. But my true name is not any more discerning. Scarlet.

"The evening is still young," I say, meeting his black gaze with as much defiance as I can muster.

"You know the wolves are in heat this time of year." His deep voice shudders through me, and I fight a blush. August never minces his words.

It's late summer, and the moon is full. The past few nights, I've heard them crying to the sky, though I've learned to ignore their piercing howls. A wolf in the throes of heat is like a mythical monster. Neither man nor hunter will match it.

The villagers have learned to latch their gates and fasten their doors and windows on nights such as these.

"I am helping my mother with Mrs. Ivy," I say, although it is none of August's business.

His eyes shift with understanding, and this again makes my cheeks warm.

I hate my tendency to blush around him. It does nothing to tamp down his nickname for me.

"Be on your way, then," he says, as if he is lord and master over me.

My hand clenches into a fist, but I force myself to remain calm as I continue along the edge of the road.

His gaze follows me, and it isn't until I move completely around the bend of the road that I hear the horse's hooves begin to move again.

I continue, faster now, and notice the lateness of the hour. The shadows are long and stretch from one side of the road to the other. The trees bordering the road have already changed colors even though the cold has yet to set in.

A rustling sound comes from my left, where the brambles gather in a tight bunch, but I decide I am just nervous after August's warning. I hurry on, nearly running now, my boots clomping on the ground. If a wolf is in the area, perhaps I will scare him away by commotion alone.

Even as I run the rest of the way to Mrs. Ivy's house, I know that the wolves present a true danger. Every few years, someone is injured or killed. Last year, it was a young boy, not more than four years old. His father was returning from a hunting trip after dark when they were surrounded. The father came away badly injured, maimed for life, and the boy was dragged off into the woods. A scouting party found his remains the next morning.

The glow of light in the front windows of the Ivys' house sends a wave of relief through me. I am almost there; almost safe.

I knock on the door, then open it myself, knowing that those in the household will be busy. Mr. Ivy looks up from his place at the kitchen table as I enter. He's cracking nuts, his young sons helping—or, more like making a huge mess.

A cry sounds from one of the back rooms, and I know it can only be Mrs. Ivy. The sound does not distress me though. I am familiar with this, and I know I can help. I close the door tightly behind me and latch it. Mr. Ivy says nothing about me locking his door; he only nods.

I rush through the kitchen and find myself in a dusty corridor. Mrs. Ivy is not the best of housekeepers. The door to her bed chamber is ajar, and I push it the rest of the way open.

My mother, her hair covered in a blue-checked kerchief, motions toward a steaming kettle. "Soak the herbs in there, Scarlet, and be quick about it."

I glance at Mrs. Ivy and wish I hadn't.

Her round face is slick with sweat, and the edges of her lips are blue. These are the classic symptoms of blood disease. I can only hope I brought the herbs in time.

Two

August waited a few moments on the path leading to the Ivys' homestead. He'd watched Scarlet enter the house, so he knew she was safe inside. Still, he was reluctant to leave. How long would she be inside, helping her mother and the laboring woman? Would Scarlet be so foolish to return home in the middle of the night once the babe was delivered?

Normally, he wouldn't bother with so much worry, but tonight would be a full moon. Wolves' appetites were fierce during their mating ritual, and they'd go into a frenzy if they smelled flesh nearby.

The villagers didn't always heed his warnings, yet he continued to give them. August felt a deep well of guilt for every death caused by the wolves. But he also knew the necessity of the wolves.

August had stumbled upon this fact by accident. He was nine years old when he'd followed his father one day into the forest, even though he'd been told to stay home and help his mother.

But his mother had one of her headaches and told August to go outside. She didn't want to be disturbed. August had been learning how to use a bow and arrow, and his father had yet to take him hunting with it.

August hadn't planned on going far, but a few paces into the woods, he caught a glimpse of his father's shirt. Surprisingly, his father hadn't traveled far at all. He was kneeling by a stream and filling up a flask of water. For some reason, August didn't call out to him, but instead decided to follow his father—like a game of trying not to get caught.

August followed his father deep into the forest and up a steep ridge. The wind was sharp and the air cold upon the mountain, but August pushed on, curious as to where his father was going and what he would hunt.

When his father disappeared suddenly, August stopped. And then he heard it.

Growls and yips. Like dogs, but deeper.

August had carefully walked toward the sound until he saw a crevice in the mountainside. He walked through the narrow space, then stopped and stared when it opened up into a haven.

His father was kneeling on the ground and pulling out bits of meat from his pack.

Five large wolves had gathered around, making sounds as if they were ready to pounce on the meat and the man.

Then, his father turned to see August.

Terrified and confused, August had run. All the way back home. It was hours before his father returned, and when he did, August was still trembling in his bed.

"You followed me," his father said in a low voice after shutting the bed chamber door. "Why?"

August had stared up at his broad-shouldered father. "I—I wanted to see where you were going. And I—I wanted to hunt with you."

His father released a sigh and sat at the edge of the bed. "You must never tell a soul in the village, not even your mother, what you saw today."

August nodded.

"I feed the wolves once a week," he said. "If I don't, they will seek food closer to the village." His father folded his muscled stonecutter arms. "There are worse things than wolves that will prey on a small village. Bears and cougars live beyond the hills—and if the wolves are not in our area, those predators will move in on us. If I feed the wolves, they will stay, but they will not prey on us as long as we stay out of their way."

August stared at his father.

"Someday, I'll tell you more, but for now, you must keep this secret," his father said. "Do you understand?"

"Someday" had come three years later when his father had come home from a hunting trip with his thigh slashed open. The wound had festered and turned to poison, despite the doctor's efforts. For days, his father had grown weaker and paler.

Finally his mother called August to his father's bedside when the village doctor had declared the man lost.

August had entered the room to find his father stripped to his waist and covered in lacerations where the village doctor had blood-let him.

"Son," his father rasped, holding out a trembling hand.

August was on the cusp of becoming a man, but it was hard to stomach seeing his father in this condition. He looked nothing like the robust man August remembered.

With a trembling, gray hand his father grasped the necklace he wore at all times and tugged it off. "This is yours now," he said. "You are the keeper of the wolves."

August took the necklace, his own hand shaking. He'd been curious about it and was always told it was a family emblem. The leather necklace held a round, flat rock, upon which was carved a half circle.

"This represents the half-moon," his father said. "When the moon wanes or waxes, the village is safe. Now, turn it over."

August obeyed. A simple circle was on the other side.

"That's the full moon," his father continued. "When the moon is full, the village is in danger. You must warn them then." His dark eyes captured August's. "And you must feed the wolves every week, without fail. Do not underestimate the wolves; they are highly intelligent. If you don't keep them appeased, they will make you pay." His trembling hand rose from the covers and grasped August's arm. "Never let the wolves know what you love. That will be their first attack."

"What do you mean?" he'd asked his father.

"Sometimes, during the full moon cycle, the wolves are not content with the meat I bring them. They want more. At times, they follow me to the village. I would stay overnight in the forest so they'd not trace me to our house. I could not let your mother know what I did each week. I had to protect her completely, but keeping a secret from one's wife is a terrible way to live."

Those were the last coherent words August ever heard his father speak. The man died the next day.

The weight of his father's stone necklace about August's neck reminded him of the weight of his responsibility to the village. He alone had been commissioned with keeping the village safe. So August began to carry meat to the wolves. At first, he left it outside the haven, too afraid to go near the beasts. But as he grew older, August became bolder. Yet, even with the weekly offerings of food, the full moon brought out the frenzied nature of the wolves. Late summer was always the worst. No one was safe. Not even August.

So what if he'd become the village curmudgeon. It was worth it to save lives.

This is what he told himself as he stood outside the Ivys' house, wondering if Scarlet would be fool enough to travel home in the night. Her scent would attract the wolves, and their ravenous appetites would rear their ugly heads.

August pushed back the thoughts about Scarlet that seemed to intrude more and more—thoughts of how her smile could make a man's heart beat fast. Thoughts of how he always seemed to be aware of her presence, and he always felt the urge to warn her, to protect her, no matter what she was doing.

She was just another village girl and would marry like the rest of them. Have babes, scrub laundry, and enter the festival baking contest.

Her fiery red hair was now a deep auburn. Her eyes hadn't ever changed color though—they were still a clear blue, like a summer lake. She was reckless and competitive. She beat most of the boys in the school yard games, except for August. She seemed to resent him for that.

When August's father had died, leaving August to watch over his mother alone, he'd left school and taken up his father's trade. The hours were long, the days exhausting, and yet . . . he still managed to feed the wolves without anyone knowing. Then, the day after August's fifteenth birthday, his mother had died, leaving him completely alone.

A distant howl of the wolves sent a shiver along August's skin. The wolves were awake, and the night just beginning.

The front door of the house opened, and August drew back in the shadows.

Mr. Ivy stepped out, followed by . . . Scarlet.

August exhaled. Scarlet was a foolish girl—no, a foolish *woman.*

Mr. Ivy said something to Scarlet, then she waved and began walking down the path. Scarlet tugged her cloak tightly about her as she looked up at the moon. She was no longer carrying the basket she'd brought.

August watched her come toward him, almost disbelieving that she could be so unguarded. She wouldn't see him in the deep shadows of the night unless he stepped out in front of her. Once she rounded the bend, she'd see his stallion, grazing on the side of the road. But for now, she was completely oblivious. Perhaps it was time to teach the foolish woman a lesson.

Three

I can't believe August is watching me. He doesn't move from his place as I near. I sensed him the moment I stepped out of the door. There is one thing I have always been good at—noticing him. I think even if I wore a blindfold, I'd be aware of him.

I don't know why he's here—does he have business with Mr. Ivy? And if so, can't he wait until morning? Mrs. Ivy is seriously ill now, and Mother is sending me home so I don't have to be exposed to her decline. Mother fears the woman won't live until morning. The babe has been delivered alive, so there is that.

I only have a few hours to fetch the tonic that my mother successfully used on other women in the same condition. The tonic has run out, but my mother refuses to travel into the forest during a full moon, where the apothecary Mistress Zoe lives.

When I offered to fetch it, and Mr. Ivy offered to accompany me, Mother forbade us. "I will not have your deaths upon my shoulders."

But seeing the sorrow in Mr. Ivy's eyes as I left the house made me even more determined to fetch the tonic.

I gaze up at the moon now, wondering if she will, this once, smile down upon me and protect my journey. What are the chances that the wolves will pick up my scent? I am not a small, weak child. I can run. I can scream. I can fight.

August still hasn't moved, and I walk past him, pretending I don't see him either. He is a strange, moody man, with never a kind word for anyone. He doesn't wear a hood, but the brown of his hair that's pulled back into its usual leather tie blends with the surrounding trees. His cloak is dark, blending him perfectly in the night shadows.

I don't know why he is hiding from me. I'm not afraid of him. Yet, I pat the side of my hip to double check the knife I have strapped there. It's in place.

As I round the bend, there is August's stallion.

I almost laugh. Why is August hiding in the first place? His stallion can't be missed, especially on the open road beneath the bright moonlight. I slip my cloak off my shoulders and walk up to the stallion.

He nickers but otherwise isn't bothered by my approach. I touch my cloak to his body and rub it slowly along his side. The cloak will now smell more like horse than human and mask my scent from the wolves.

I shrug into my cloak once again, and I'm about to move past the horse when a hand grips my arm.

"Red," August's harsh whisper brushes over me.

I flinch. He seems even larger up this close. He tightens his grip, and my heart thuds. His eyes are so dark that they look like two vast pools of water. He smells of the forest, wood, stone, pine. I have never been this close to him, at least not since I was a girl in the schoolhouse. When his father died, August stopped coming.

"I told you it isn't safe to travel after dark," he growls out, his voice almost animal-like. "Where are you going?"

Why do you care, I want to ask. Instead, I say, "Home."

His eyes narrow. "Liar."

The words are a hiss, and they cut through me. I cannot see the depths of his gaze; I cannot read his emotions. I step away from him, but his fingers keep hold of my arm, strong and hot.

"You cannot go into the forest, Little Red," he repeats.

"My name is *Scarlet,*" I spit out. "And what *I* do is none of your business." I jerk my arm away, and he drops his hand. Perhaps he is surprised at my vehemence. Clutching my cloak tightly, I turn and hurry down the path.

His footsteps thunder after me, and I grow nervous. August's stride is much longer than mine. He's not a kind man, and, well, it's in the middle of the night, and I am alone. Other than the threat of wolves, I have never been afraid of anything in the village. Until now. Why is August so determined to control where I go and what I do?

He cuts in front of me, and I stop. Even though I can try to dodge him, I know it's pointless. His height looms over me, and I already know he is quicker than me.

"I'll ask you one more time," he says in a low rumble. "Where are you going? And if you lie to me, then I'll drag you home."

His words are like ice and fire on my skin, both competing for sensation. Looking into his hard gaze, I have no doubt that he'll carry out his threat.

I lift my chin. He can drag me wherever he likes, but I'll manage to get the tonic tonight. I have to. "I'm going to the apothecary's," I say in a thin voice. I can't act the coward now. I clear my throat before his stormy eyes can turn into stormy words. "Mistress Zoe has a tonic—one that will help Mrs. Ivy's blood disease."

The harshness in August's features seem to dissolve. He exhales, and his warm breath touches my skin. I have an insane urge to lean toward him, to breathe in his forest-scented cloak.

"Can she not wait until the morning?" he asks.

I blink to clear my thoughts. "Morning will be too late."

He says nothing for a moment. My heart rate slows, and my skin grows cold with the night.

"I will take you," he says eventually.

I am not sure I've heard him right, but he clicks his tongue, and the stallion breaks into a trot and joins us.

August grasps the horse's reins with one hand, then holds out his other hand to me. I look at it, hesitating.

"Scarlet." The way he says my name sends a warm shiver along my skin.

I place my hand on his, and he boosts me up on the horse. A moment later, he swings up behind me and reaches around me to take up the reins, trapping me against his body. And we are off.

The moon offers just enough light as we ride into the forest, and the stallion seems to have little trouble finding his footing among the deep shadows. August's arms might be around me, but I try not to lean against him. The less contact we have, the better. My pulse is already racing, and my breath is short, although I am only sitting upon a horse.

I have not been this physically close to a man. Ever. During the Solstice festival, I danced with several young men in the village, but it felt nothing like this ride with August through the dark forest.

My inexperience is what makes my pulse race, I tell myself. I cannot allow myself to think too deeply about August—the way his breath stirs my hair, the way his chest radiates heat against my back, or the way his muscled arms jostle against me as the horse picks its way through the fallen branches.

A wolf's howl splits the air. I shudder, and August tenses. Then, another howl—this one much closer. My chest feels tight, and I want to grab the horse's reins and make the beast run.

August seems to read my mind, and he clicks his tongue and flicks the reins at the same time. The horse lurches forward, and I tilt to the side. August grabs the reins into one hand, and his other hand wraps fully around me, securing me flat against him.

If it wasn't for the nearness of the howling, I would protest. But I am suddenly thankful for August's presence.

Through the trees, I catch a glimpse of glowing yellow. The apothecary's hut is near, and I have never been more grateful for anything in my life.

"We're almost there," August whispers as if he's felt my relief.

Another howl pierces the night. So close.

"Hang on," August grinds out. His arm about me tightens further. He urges the stallion into a gallop.

The ground is uneven, but somehow the horse manages to avoid the bushes and low branches. Perhaps the beast is as frightened as we are. I grasp August's thighs to keep seated as we plunge on, the cold air streaming through my hair and billowing my cloak.

The howls multiply, and I dare not look behind us—for surely I'll see a pack of silver wolves on our trail.

The stallion bursts into the clearing that surrounds the hut, and we thunder across the space.

"Mistress Zoe!" August bellows.

I wonder if the horse will plow through the woman's door, but August pulls back on the reins. I would lose my balance again if it weren't for his strong grip.

"Inside, now," he says to me, sliding off the horse and pulling me with him.

"What about—"

The door to the hut flies open just as the first wolf bounds within reach. It's a big, silver thing, its eyes yellow-orange in the glow from the hut's open door.

I shriek.

"Inside!" August yells, shoving me toward the hut, then drawing a long knife.

"I can fight, too—" A gnarled, but strong hand clamps around my wrist, and I'm pulled toward the hut.

"He's trained to fight the wolves," the apothecary says in her gravelly voice.

I don't know what she is talking about. But for an old woman, she is extremely strong, and she forces me inside, shuts the door, and locks it.

Four

August stretched out both hands, one holding his knife, the other empty. The leader of the pack had arrived first, and now four others stood at the edge of the clearing. They wouldn't attack until they were all gathered, August knew. Which might give him a full minute, or maybe two, before he'd be defending himself, the stallion, and the two women inside the hut. He might as well be defending the entire village.

If the wolves drew human blood tonight, they would go into a frenzy.

The wolves' howls were the only sound he could hear above his pounding heart. He cursed the wolves, and then next he cursed Scarlet. What had she been thinking? His stallion had backed up, moving close to the hut. August could practically smell the horse's fear. It matched his own.

The leader of the wolves growled low in its throat and

advanced into the clearing. August was surprised it wasn't waiting until the rest of the pack arrived, but perhaps that would give August an advantage.

"I'm the one who brings you meat," August told the wolf. "Yet you follow me here to attack? You're a greedy mutt!"

The wolf's yellow eyes flashed as it kept advancing, growling, bristling.

The stallion pawed at the ground behind August. Women's voices rose above the howls of the wolves on the perimeter. Scarlet was arguing with the apothecary.

August cursed again. The wolf crouched to the ground, its shoulder muscles hunching. August knew what would come next.

But he was ready. If he could fight one wolf at a time.

Just as the wolf lunged, August leapt into the air to take full advantage of his height. The wolf's head collided with August's shoulder. The bared fangs sliced through his sleeve, and August knew he'd been cut, but the pain would come later. For now, he had to counterattack whatever the wolf did next.

He turned just in time to deflect the wolf's next attack with his knife. They began an awkward dance, with the wolf lunging, and August slashing toward the beast. He knew he could only play this game so long. Soon, the other wolves would join their leader.

A piercing scream—a woman's scream—rent the air behind him.

August didn't turn or take his eyes from the wolf, but the wolf froze.

And then Scarlet was in front of him. How she got out of the hut was beyond him. She threw a jug of liquid toward the wolf. A temporary diversion, but nothing that would actually help.

"Get back—" August started to yell when Scarlet knelt on the ground and touched a candle flame to the liquid.

Amazingly enough, the liquid burst into streaks of fire.

August grabbed her arm and yanked her away from the growing flame. The orange fingers raced across the clearing, following the trail of liquid Scarlet had dashed onto the ground. The lead wolf fled toward its companions, who were already backing up from the approaching flames.

Scarlet was either brilliant or very foolish.

He wanted to shove her toward the hut again, but he wasn't entirely sure if the hut would be safe either. Fire was fire. It would burn whatever strange liquid was upon the ground, but it would also burn the trees, the underbrush, and the hut behind him.

He stared in breathless wonder as the wolves abandoned the clearing and ran into the shadows of the forest. Their howls were high pitched, but they grew fainter as the minutes passed.

And the fire . . . burned hungrily at the liquid, then simmered, sputtered, and died.

As the popping and crackling sounds of the flames quieted, August slowly became aware of his own labored breathing and that of the stallion. Then he realized that Scarlet was still next to him, her hand clutching his cloak.

He turned his head to gaze down at her. She was staring straight ahead, a triumphant smile on her face, while tears marked her cheeks.

She was the most confounded woman he'd ever known.

"They're gone," she said in a cracked whisper full of wonder.

Her dark red hair tumbled about her shoulders, and her eyes glistened, either with satisfaction or tears, he couldn't be sure. Her skin was nearly translucent in the dying glow of the fire, mixed with the moonlight coming from above.

She'd saved him.

August couldn't believe it. Was he dreaming all of this strange night? He lifted his hand and touched her jaw line.

She looked at him, eyes wide, but she didn't pull away from his touch.

Her skin was warm, and he brushed away the tears that had nearly dried.

"What have you done?" he asked, and even as he spoke, he knew he wasn't referring to the fire. But to the way he felt when he gazed at her face.

Her lips quirked as if she couldn't decide what he was truly asking either.

"It worked!" Mistress Zoe pronounced, clapping her hands together. "I was worried that the concoction was too experimental."

The apothecary walked about the clearing. She wore her usual black clothing, augmented with dozens of bracelets and leather wraps on both of her thin arms. Her hair was completely white and reminded August of a nest of bird feathers. August stepped back from Scarlet, dropping his hand. He wasn't entirely sure they were all that safe—the wolves could very well return.

Mistress Zoe moved to the stallion and stroked his head. "There, there. You are safe now."

"What was that liquid?" he asked the apothecary.

"Oh, it comes from a tree root," she said in an absent-minded voice. "It has a pungent smell, but it's quite flammable." She shook her head as she continued to stroke the horse. "Those wolves are fierce tonight. I'm surprised you would make the journey to my place." Her eyes focused on August.

"Scarlet needs a tonic for Mrs. Ivy."

"Yes," Scarlet said. "August was good enough to bring me here."

It was perhaps the most civil thing Scarlet had ever said about him. She was simply speaking the truth, but it made him feel a bit weightless to hear the semi-compliment.

"Mrs. Ivy has delivered her babe, but she is afflicted with the blood disease," Scarlet continued. "My mother doesn't expect her to live until morning."

"Well, then," the apothecary said, brushing her hands off. "I'll fetch it and send you on your way." Her eyes narrowed as she regarded August. "You will see Scarlet back safely?"

He nodded once.

Mistress Zoe hurried into the hut, and Scarlet moved as if to follow her. August reached out and grasped her arm. "Wait," he said.

She turned to look up at him. And instead of the annoyance he expected, she merely looked inquisitive.

"You could have gotten killed," he said in a low voice. Her blue eyes were like velvet in the dimness of the clearing. "I told you to stay inside."

Scarlet didn't look chastised at all. Then her gaze shifted. "You're bleeding."

August looked down. The sleeve of his tunic was torn, and blood had seeped onto the tear where the wolf had clawed him. With all the adrenaline, he hadn't felt a thing.

"Come, we must clean it and bind it," Scarlet said, grasping his other hand.

Her hand felt small in his, yet warm and strong. She tugged him toward the hut, and he let the questions and reprimands on his tongue die as they stepped inside.

His first impression was that the place was chock full of junk. Every surface and even every bit of the wall was covered with something hanging, bottled, or stacked.

The smell was enough to knock a grown man over—a

mixture of animal pelt and rotted vegetables. He tried not to breathe too deeply as he followed Scarlet. She joined Mistress Zoe at the hearth, where a healthy fire lapped at the air. Over the fire hung a huge iron pot. Mistress Zoe was mixing whatever was boiling, and a sweet scent like strawberries wafted up in steam.

"August is hurt," Scarlet said.

Mistress Zoe turned from the boiling pot. "Let me see."

Reluctantly, August tugged his shirt over his shoulder to expose the wound. It was bleeding, but not much. The length of the cut was only the length of a finger.

"We need to clean it," Scarlet said, and the apothecary dipped a square of cloth straight into the boiling pot, then handed the steaming cloth to Scarlet.

Before August could protest, she pressed the hot, wet cloth on his wound.

He hissed as the hot mixture touched the wound. It stung for a few seconds, and then, strangely, it felt much better.

Scarlet lifted the cloth and peered at the wound. "Should we stitch it?" she asked.

"We don't have time," August said. It didn't look deep anyway. "I can wait until first light if needed."

"We can't risk it festering," Scarlet said.

August pulled away from Scarlet and took the cloth binding the apothecary had gathered. He proceeded to wrap his upper arm while Scarlet watched with pursed lips. Then he tugged his shirt back up over his shoulder.

"Where's the tonic?" he asked Mistress Zoe while he pointedly ignored the glare Scarlet was giving him.

Mistress Zoe stepped toward a row of shelves filled with all shapes, sizes, and colors of bottles.

August's arm began to throb with new pain, but he ignored it.

"Ah, here it is." Mistress Zoe picked up a narrow-necked, yellow bottle, then held it toward Scarlet.

"Thank you," Scarlet said, taking the bottle, then searching her cloak for something. "I have some coins, somewhere."

"Here," August said, handing over the money to Mistress Zoe. "We need to be on our way." He could feel Scarlet's gaze on him, but he ignored it. "Let's go," he said, turning. The scent of rot was giving him a headache.

He opened the door of the hut to find his stallion waiting. Then he motioned for Scarlet to follow. She spoke a few departing words to the apothecary and came outside.

"I can pay you back," she said, her cheeks a rosy pink from the heat inside the hut.

"Very well," he said, although the few coins were nothing. "We need to make haste." Not only could the wolves come back, but the wind had picked up, which would carry their scent all that much faster toward any predator.

August handed Scarlet up on the stallion; then he followed.

The night was not over yet.

Five

The wolves stay silent as I ride back with August to the Ivys' homestead. His arms wrap around me, but he doesn't hold me as tightly as before.

My fear has abated, making it so I am even more aware of August, the solid warmth of his body and the strength of his arms. We reach the road without hearing any wolves, and I start to relax. But not too much. I am keeping as much distance from August as possible.

When the homestead comes into view, relief rushes through me. We've made it, and I can only hope we aren't too late. A dim light glows from within the house, yet I don't know if this is good or bad.

August urges the stallion all the way to the front door, then reins in the horse and climbs off. He hands me down from the horse, and I pull my hand away once I touch the ground. I must forget about the way his bare hand holding mine sends bursts of fire along my skin.

"I will pay you in the morning," I say, then realize morning has already come with the passing of midnight. "When the day breaks."

August nods, but he doesn't say anything. And he doesn't move away from me or turn and mount his stallion.

"Thank you for helping me," I say. Still, August doesn't respond, but he watches me with those dark, glittering eyes. I cannot wait another moment, so I make my way toward the door of the house.

I don't knock but open it and find it unlocked.

The fire glows in the hearth of the front room. The other children are nowhere in sight, but Mr. Ivy sits at the table, his shoulders slumped, his head bent.

I realize he is sleeping.

I cross to him, although I'm reluctant to know how his wife is. He lifts his head before I can awaken him.

"You've returned?" he asks in a mumble.

"I've brought the tonic for your wife."

He blinks rapidly, then pushes up from the table. "Come with me."

I follow him, even though I know where the bed chamber is. The house is silent except for our footsteps. There are no sounds of a new babe or a woman laboring.

When we reach the door to the bed chamber, Mr. Ivy opens it with a trembling hand.

Inside, the room is dim. A child's cradle is near the fire, and the bundle inside reveals a small pink, sleeping face. My mother sits on a chair next to the bed, where Mrs. Ivy is covered with a quilt up to her chin. Both of their eyes are closed, and I approach quietly, not wanting to startle either woman.

Mrs. Ivy looks like death itself. Dark hollows paint her skin beneath her eyes, and her breathing is shallow through her cracked lips. Her skin looks as if it's been pulled tight across her cheekbones, and around her mouth the blue discoloration is even more pronounced.

My mother stirs, and her eyes open. "What are you doing here?" she whispers.

I hold out the bottle of tonic, and she gasps. "Where did you . . .? You didn't go into the forest, did you?"

"I was fine, and here's the medicine." I cannot tell her of the wolves and the way August fought and how I started a fire. Perhaps later.

My mother purses her lips as if she knows I'm not telling her everything. But she doesn't want to waste time either. She tugs off the cork of the bottle, and picks up a nearby spoon that sits next to a bowl of cold broth.

"Ginny," she says to Mrs. Ivy. "We've medicine for you. Please take it."

The woman opens her eyes a slit, and somehow my mother gets her to swallow two spoonfuls of the tonic. Then Mrs. Ivy closes her eyes again.

My mother recorks the tonic, then looks from me to Mr. Ivy, who is still hovering at the doorway. "Now we wait." She exhales and grasps my hand, then closes her eyes again as if she plans to sleep.

I kneel next to my mother and rest my head on her knees. My heart feels as if it's been racing for hours, and now I can finally stop moving and rest.

"Scarlet," my mother says, touching my shoulder.

I awake with a start, realizing that I must have drifted into sleep. The room is still dim, and the night thick outside. Mr. Ivy is no longer in the room.

"Her coloring is better," my mother says in a soft voice, referring to Mrs. Ivy.

My mother is right. Mrs. Ivy's pale skin has more color

to it, and the blue about her lips is all but faded. The circles beneath her eyes have lightened, and a thin sheen of perspiration borders her hair line.

As we stare at her, Mrs. Ivy opens her eyes. She looks at my mother first, then to me. In a clear voice she says, "Where's my babe?"

My mother laughs—a laugh of relief. "Your son is sleeping."

Mrs. Ivy's mouth moves into a smile. "Wake him, then."

This time I laugh. My mother nods, and I scramble to my feet, then collect the sleeping baby from the cradle. He yawns as I carry him to his mother. We all stare at the tiny being as I hand him over to Mrs. Ivy. The woman shifts her clothing, and my mother helps her position the babe at her breast.

As the child suckles, tears sting my eyes while watching Mrs. Ivy nurse her newborn.

"How are you feeling, Ginny?" my mother asks.

"Better," she whispers, her voice thick with emotion. "Bring in my husband to meet his son."

It's my mother who rises this time to fetch Mr. Ivy. When he arrives, his eyes shining with excitement and gratitude, I back out of the room to give the husband and wife privacy.

My mother bustles into the kitchen with me, then pulls me into a hug. When she releases me, she cups my chin with her hand. "You saved a life tonight, daughter. But never defy me again."

I don't know whether to laugh or cry, or perhaps both. "I had to try."

My mother gives a nod, then releases me and turns away, busying herself. I know she, too, is overcome with emotion, and busy hands help both of us cope. It's then that I notice the stallion outside the window. Has August not left yet? It's been more than two hours, perhaps three, since I came inside.

When my mother leaves the kitchen to return to the bed chamber, I step outside. The stallion tosses its head when he sees me, as if to greet me, but I search for the owner. August is sitting against the house, his knees drawn up, his eyes closed. I shut the door behind me, and his eyes snap open.

He's on his feet in an instant, his gaze locking onto me. For a moment, I don't see a spiteful man who tried to bully me. I see a man who is concerned for others, one who is concerned for *me*. One who risked riding through the woods on a night of a full moon. One who fought wolves while I was safe in the apothecary's hut.

I walk toward him, and he watches me approach through his black eyes. "Did the tonic work?" he asks in a voice scratchy with sleep. He scrubs a hand through his unruly hair that's come undone from its leather tie.

"Yes," I say, unable to stop the smile spreading across my face. Without thinking, I step up to him, and throw my arms around his neck. "Thank you," I breathe against his neck. "You saved a mother tonight."

No doubt I've startled him, and August doesn't move for a moment. Then, his arms slide around me, and he pulls me close.

My heart soars, and my pulse races. I am fully in his embrace. This is new to me, foreign, and I am hyper aware of the hard planes of his body against the curves of mine. He is warm, solid, and so . . . *August*. I want to stay this way, in his arms, breathing in the scent of his skin, the spice that I am sure is uniquely him. But the longer I am close to him, the more I want to . . .

I draw away, trying to clear my senses. He releases me, and I cannot look at him, for I'm afraid of what he might see in my eyes and know that my blood is pumping hard through my whole body as if I've run through the entire village. And it doesn't help when August touches my chin and lifts it, forcing me to look at him.

He gazes down at me, absorbing me with his dark, dark eyes.

"I'm glad she's all right," he says, tracing a finger along my jaw.

I cannot move. I cannot breathe.

"What am I going to do with you?" he continues, and he lifts his other hand to cradle my face.

His warm, callused hands upon my skin make me burn. My heart feels like it will leap out of my chest if he doesn't stop touching me. I need space. I need to pour cold water over my head.

But before I can escape his touch, August's hands slide behind my head, his fingers threading through my hair, and he lowers his head.

Then, he kisses me.

His lips are warm. The scruff on his chin chafes my skin, but it only makes everything tingle. He draws me closer, and then his kisses turn urgent, as if he's coaxing me to kiss him back. And I do.

I have been kissed by a boy or two, but I quickly learn the difference between kissing a boy and kissing a man. August is all man as his mouth explores mine. One of his hands stays in my hair, while the other trails down my back, then settles at my waist.

All of my senses are on alert, and every sense is consumed by him. I don't know if I am even touching the ground or if I exist any longer in this world. For now, my entirety is August's mouth, his hands, his cloak sweeping against my legs, his hair that's fallen forward and brushes my face. The cool night air doesn't penetrate our cocoon of warmth.

His hand at my waist remains firm, yet gentle. Through my clothing I can feel the warmth of his body against mine, and for a moment I wish we didn't have so many barriers. The thought makes me gasp, and I draw away. Cool air rushes between us, and it's like coming back to earth with a hard thump.

August arches a single brow and scans my face, as if my expression will explain why I am so jumpy.

"I must—I must go and check on Mrs. Ivy," I stammer.

August says nothing, though his gaze says he doesn't want to release me. Yet, something shifts in his eyes, and he drops his hands and lets me go.

I waiver where I stand, wanting more, yet feeling the word "fool" scream in my thoughts. Finally, I turn and hurry into the house, putting much-needed distance between myself and August.

I groan with dismay as I open the door. I have been foolish. I have given into a desire that I hadn't even realized was there. Or perhaps I realized it, but successfully ignored it, until now. My lips are swollen, my hair disheveled, and my skin hot as I hurry across the kitchen. Voices come from the bed chamber, and I take a moment in the hallway to smooth my hair back and calm my breathing.

In only the short time I've been outside with August, I have irrevocably changed. For a few moments, I've felt like a woman who is desired by a man.

Six

August waited outside the Ivys' house until dawn had cracked the sky and spilled its gold across the eastern hills. Scarlet hadn't come outside for hours. He'd told himself he'd wait until the first signs of dawn. But when the sky molted from black to gray, then to violet, he remained.

Now, the sun was well on its way to spreading across the entire valley and warming every house in the village. August knew he should go. But he remained, thinking about the way Scarlet had flung her arms around him. Thinking about how she'd kissed him back. Thinking about the way she'd fit into his arms, and how he'd felt . . . *whole*, somehow. As if all the secret work he'd done to protect the village had finally been acknowledged, and the years living alone, as an orphan, had somehow melted away.

He'd succeeded on a quest. He'd delivered Scarlet safely, and Mrs. Ivy was healing. August would fight wolves every night if it meant Scarlet would thank him, with an embrace, with a kiss, again and again . . .

A squall of a newborn from within the house jolted August out of his thoughts.

He crossed to his horse and mounted it. The stallion had grazed half the night and needed exercise. And August needed sleep.

He rode hard through the early morning, trying to shake off thoughts of Scarlet's blue eyes and the way they shone after he'd kissed her. He needed to forget the way his body had responded to her, almost in desperation, and how he continued to crave her touch. He couldn't let himself be distracted, or he would grow careless. He'd promised his father he would protect the village, and he intended to keep that promise. Even though years had passed since his father's words on his deathbed, August had never forgotten them. *"Never let the wolves know what you love. That will be their first attack."*

He had to stay away from Scarlet.

August slowed his horse as he neared his home. Something was different. The gate stood open, hanging on a single hinge. It clattered in the morning breeze, creating an unsettling sound. August slid off the horse, and led him by the reins the rest of the way to the small stable on the edge of the property. After closing the stall door and making sure the horse had fresh water, August continued toward the house.

Strewn along the path leading up to the door were tufts of fur—silver-gray and black—the color of the wolves. August's neck prickled. The front door stood ajar, as if it hadn't been latched properly. August withdrew the knife from his sheath and pushed the door open all the way.

The house was silent.

August stared at his surroundings. The kitchen table had been upended. The sacks of grain and barrel of apples scattered. Someone had been searching for something. Or someone.

He ran outside and hurried around the house. The chicken cages had been ripped apart, and all the chickens were gone. Only their feathers and blood remained.

The wolves had found him.

August exhaled, letting the shock pass through him as he tried to collect his thoughts. The wolves had broken his gate, entered his home, then found his chickens. They'd come right into the village and preyed upon a human. They hadn't encountered someone in the woods—their territory—no, they'd been deliberate. Intent. Destructive.

His father's words echoed in his mind: *"Don't underestimate the wolves. They are highly intelligent."*

How did the wolves know where to target him? And then another thought chilled August to the bone. What if he wasn't the only villager? What if the wolves had attacked others last night while he was sitting outside of the Ivys' house?

August started to run. He made it to his neighbor's, just on the other side of the stone wall, to find Widow Green pulling weeds from her garden.

"Good mornin', August," she said in her usual cheery voice.

"All is well?" he asked, trying to keep the panic from his voice.

Widow Green squinted at him. "Yes, and it's looking to be a beautiful day."

He couldn't give her any cause for alarm if there was none. Perhaps he'd been the only victim.

"A good day to you," he said, trying to keep his voice upbeat. Then he passed through her front gate and strode down the road to the next homestead. Over the course of an hour, he walked by every home. There was no sign of the wolves' intrusion. They had not attacked anyone in the middle of the night. August had been singled out.

August's father had been so careful to keep the wolves from their house, and now, somehow they'd come right to his front door.

Fear and worry urged August to Scarlet's home. The gate was intact. The front door shut. Everything was quiet, serene, and if the women were home, they were likely sleeping.

Regardless, August was sorely tempted to knock. He couldn't leave without knowing if they were all right. He opened the gate and walked to their front door. So easy a wolf could do it. August peered in through the front window. The sunlight splashed across the room—no one was in the kitchen. He moved to another window on the side of the house.

His breath caught as he saw a bed and a form beneath the pale blue quilt. The woman's dark red hair spilled across her shoulders. He couldn't see her face, but undoubtedly it was Scarlet. By the steady rise and fall of her shoulder, he knew she was asleep.

He watched her for longer than he should, and finally he forced himself to leave. She was safe in her home, asleep, and that was all he could ask for now. He spent the rest of the morning repairing his gate, adding a second latch to his front door, and cleaning up the mess. He'd have to buy chickens later.

Finally, when the sun hit its zenith in the sky, he fell asleep on top of his feather-tick mattress.

Seven

My room is bathed in afternoon gold when I awake. I've slept all day, and I hear my mother moving about the kitchen. The memories from the night before crash into me all at once: Mrs. Ivy, the newborn babe, the ride through the forest upon August's stallion, the fight with the wolves . . . the kiss . . .

I am hot from remembering, and I rise from the bed. My face looks no different when I peer in the mirror above my wash basin. My eyes are still blue; my lips haven't changed. No one would guess that I'd been kissed. Would they? Smoothing my tangled hair back from my face, I tie it into a ribbon, then splash my skin with the tepid water.

My mother has let me sleep, and for that I am grateful. I didn't realize how exhausted I was. But now, she will want the full story.

"You're awake," she says simply as I walk into the

kitchen. She sits at the table, peeling a pile of potatoes. She's already peeled a half dozen.

"Are you making stew for a week?" I ask, sitting down and picking up a potato and knife.

"We've company coming for supper," she says.

I look at her closely. Her eyes are bright, her skin rosy. My mother is a pretty woman, or once was, before aging drooped her features. "Oh?" I prompt.

"August," she says, holding my gaze. "It's the least we can do to thank him for taking you to the apothecary's."

I am fully aware that my cheeks burn and that my mother notices my blush. I sincerely hope she doesn't know about the kiss. If I were to admit an attraction to August, I'd need to get in line behind every unmarried woman in the village.

August has never encouraged any one of us. I don't think he's kissed any of the women . . . until now. This doesn't give me hope, though. It just proves me the fool. And now my mother has invited him over for supper—where we must make polite conversation and share a meal?

"Can we not just give him a few coins?" I ask, stumbling over my words.

My mother laughs; then she sobers. "He told me what happened, Scarlet. I went to thank him and found him tending to a wound. He confessed to his fight with the wolves, and how you warded off the wolves with the liquid fire." My mother's eyes are like fire themselves as her voice sharpens. "You were very, very foolish. You could have both been killed."

This time my cheeks burn with shame. "I am sorry."

She sets down the potato she's peeling and places a hand on my shoulder. Her touch is gentle instead of a reprimand. "If something had happened to you, I would have never forgiven myself for bringing you to the Ivy house."

"I want to help you," I say. "I want to train as a midwife through all types of labors."

"I know you do," she says, lightly squeezing my shoulder. "But I won't have you risking *your* life like that."

I nod, my throat tight. In the light of day, and after a long nap, the events from the night before seem like a dream—a terrible dream—and I can't quite believe all that happened.

Once the potatoes are peeled and diced, I tell my mother I will milk our cow while she cuts up the carrots and onions. I need to be alone with thoughts that seem too large for the confined space of the house. I fetch the milk bucket from the corner of the kitchen and carry it outside.

As I make my way to the lean-to where our single cow is lolling in the shade, I know I must come up with conversation items to bring up during supper. I am already feeling nervous about seeing August again.

What will he say in greeting? How will he look at me? Will he watch me like he did last night?

I release a nervous laugh. August is always watching me—at least it feels like it. One part of me wants to tell my mother I am too ill to have supper with her and August. The other part of me wants to intercept him on his way over here and tell him that there will never be another kiss between us.

Except I don't know if that's what I want.

Perhaps *he* thinks it was a mistake . . . perhaps kissing a woman isn't something that keeps him awake at night.

Our cow, Justice, bellows when she sees me. She's unhappy—since neither my mother or I milked her that morning.

I pick up the stool from the edge of the lean-to, then set down the bucket I've brought.

"Sorry, girl," I say in a soothing voice, stroking her sides before I start to milk her.

Justice bellows a second time, then settles as I continue to milk her. The work gives me focus, and I think that perhaps August will say nothing about the kiss. We can both pretend it never happened. Last night was a series of strange events anyway. The light of day has brought new clarity.

"Feeling better, girl?" I croon to Justice. I start to hum and close my eyes as I work. The rhythmic milking relaxes the tension I feel over August coming for supper, and soon I am in a mellow state of mind.

When I am almost finished, my arms prickle with gooseflesh. I open my eyes just as a shadow falls over me.

Without turning, I know it's August.

He doesn't speak for a moment, but my movements slow, as I know he's watching me. I finish with the milking, then stroke Justice's side, and say, "Good girl."

I stand and turn to face August.

He wears a simple cotton shirt, open at the neck and revealing the necklace with a stone pendant that he always wears. His shirt is tucked into his dark gray breeches. He's not wearing his cloak from last night, and it somehow makes him seem more approachable, although his eyes are as black as ever.

He has shaved—noticing this detail makes me blush, since I think of how he kissed me the night before.

His gaze flits over my face, then lingers on my eyes.

I am certain he can see the blush staining my cheeks. "Hello," I say and hate that my voice is barely above a whisper. *I'm not nervous.*

"Your mother told me you were out here," he says, leaning close.

For a moment, I think he's going to kiss me, right here in the yard, in front of anyone who might pass on the road. His arm brushes mine, and he picks up the bucket of new milk, then straightens again.

No, he wasn't trying to kiss me. I exhale, with relief, or disappointment, I am not sure.

August begins to walk toward the house, and I clear my racing thoughts and follow him.

"How's your shoulder?" I ask.

He looks down at me, a rare half-smile on his face. "Better. Your mother gave me a salve to treat it with."

"Good," I say. We are almost to the house, so I take the plunge. "What did you tell her about last night?"

He stops then, the bucket swinging in his hand. Behind him, the orange from the sunset makes his skin golden. I swallow, waiting for him to speak.

"I didn't tell her about kissing you," he says.

My mouth falls open in surprise. Then I snap it shut.

He laughs. It's dark and rich.

I don't think I've ever heard August laugh. He was such a serious boy, and after his father died, I rarely had any contact with him. Partly because I deliberately avoided him.

His rich laughter steals through me, and I don't know what to make of it. I push past him, not caring that I knock against the bucket and milk sloshes out. I'm nearly to the door when he catches my arm with his hand.

"Red," he says, his voice low.

I jerk out of his grasp. "Don't call me that."

"Scarlet . . ." His tone is contrite now.

But I don't care. I open the door, and there's my mother, ladling stew into metal bowls. Supper is ready.

"There you are," my mother says in a cheerful voice.

"Just finished up," I reply, trying to sound normal. My mother has set a vase of wildflowers on the table as a centerpiece.

August enters the kitchen behind me and sets down the bucket of milk. I can feel the heat of his gaze on me, but I refuse to look at him.

When he steps away from the bucket, I pick it up and pour the milk into a pitcher. Then I carry the pitcher to the table, along with our best painted clay cups. Fortunately, our table is a perfect square so we can all sit on our own side. My mother is on my left, and August is on my right. I will live with the arrangement, but I won't look at him or speak to him directly.

My mother grasps my hand for our prayer. With her other hand, she reaches for August's. This leaves me no choice but to hold his other hand with mine.

His large hand dwarfs mine—his warm and callused, mine cold and tense.

"Bless the food, O Maker," my mother says.

I keep my gaze on the table, too agitated to even close my eyes in respect. And likewise, I can feel August looking at me. Does he not pray at mealtime?

My mother prays for our health, our cow, our village, Mrs. Ivy, her newborn babe, me, and finally expresses her gratitude for August joining us for supper.

And ever so slightly, August squeezes my hand. I swallow back a gasp, and as soon as my mother says, "Amen," I pull my hand away from his.

Eight

August wasn't fooled by Scarlet's irritation. He'd seen the desire she tried to hide in her, was still trying to hide, even now, as they ate supper.

Her mother talked about the villagers, her garden, and the upcoming harvest festival, and August responded, trying to act like the interested guest. But he knew her mother noticed Scarlet's silence as much as he did. Scarlet wouldn't even look at him.

It both maddened him and made him want to pull her outside and kiss her again. She didn't know that the pink on her cheeks from her blush only made her more attractive.

August had to stop dwelling on Scarlet, though, and get to the reason he had accepted this invitation to supper. He had a warning to give.

When Scarlet's mother finished her current observation about a new way to bake squash, August said, "Last night the wolves stole my chickens right from their pens."

This caused Scarlet to look up and meet his gaze.

Her mother gasped. "Are you sure it was a wolf?" she asked. "Perhaps it was a dog."

"This attack was more aggressive than a dog's," he said. Scarlet's expression was guarded, as if she didn't quite believe what he was saying. But at least she was looking at him, and listening.

When he spoke next, he directed his words at her. "You need to be extra vigilant about staying inside at night, with your doors and windows locked tight."

She gave a slight shake of her head. "The full moon always makes them more active," she said. "But I'm sure if the wolves actually came into the village, everyone would be talking about it."

She might not believe him, yet. He'd explain more when her mother wasn't around. But he didn't want to start a widespread panic either. His father had warned him about wolf hunts. If the wolves were killed, the village would be even more vulnerable.

Supper seemed to move very slowly after that, and finally, when the lemon pudding had been served and good manners dictated that he could take his leave, he said, "I appreciate the meal. Thank you."

Scarlet's mother nodded and rose from the table. "We appreciate you coming. Scarlet, why don't you walk our guest to the gate?"

Scarlet's eyes shot to her mother, and August nearly laughed. He didn't know what her mother was about, but he liked her well enough.

Scarlet avoided looking at him, and August knew the walk to the gate would be very brief.

He opened the front door and motioned for Scarlet to go through first. She did, reluctantly.

When he pulled the door shut behind them, she folded her arms.

"Are you really so upset with me that you can't even *look* at me?" he asked.

She glanced at him, and her cheeks flushed. He couldn't help but smile. But the smile was short lived because they'd reached the gate, and he still had to tell her what the wolves had done to his property.

"Scarlet," he said with emphasis—using her correct name. "There's more I need to tell you."

Her blue eyes looked up at him, then narrowed slightly. "And not my mother?"

He glanced back at the house, then grasped her hand and tugged her through the gate until they were on the other side of the stone wall, shielded from the house. Thankfully, the road was empty of passersby. Twilight had nearly arrived. The golden light of the afternoon had cooled into a dusky violet.

She pulled her hand from his immediately, but she was at least looking at him and paying attention. "The wolves entered my house," he said.

Her eyes widened. "How? . . . Maybe it was a thief?"

"No, the fur left behind was evidence enough," August said. "I can't warn you enough. Promise me you'll lock everything up at night, and don't go anywhere. Not even with your mother."

Scarlet pursed her lips, then folded her arms. "I can't promise that, and you know it. My mother's a midwife. Two other women in the village are near their time."

August placed a hand on her shoulder, moving closer. She didn't flinch or draw back, and this he took as a good sign. "Women have been giving birth for centuries on their own."

Her cheeks reddened, and she licked her lips.

Was she tormenting him on purpose? "Listen to me, Scarlet. The wolves know who I am. The wolves were bested by the fire, and they came to my home to seek revenge. I don't know how they knew it was my house. Perhaps they've known for a long time."

"They can smell you," Scarlet said.

"What?"

"I mean, humans have a scent, just like animals do."

August knew this, of course. But he hadn't thought of it in regard to the wolves singling out his house. And he knew it was more than that . . . these wolves wanted revenge. And his father had warned him about the wolves discovering what, or who, he . . . loved.

He looked into Scarlet's eyes. "You don't understand."

She heaved a sigh. "You're not making sense."

He lifted his hand and rubbed the back of his neck. He'd have to tell her, everything. It was the only way. Then she'd understand, and he could stay away from her, while at the same time she'd keep safe. He glanced at the sky. Twilight had deepened, the sky a vivid purple streaked with red.

"All right," he said. "Come with me."

She arched a brow. "It will be dark soon."

"We won't go far." He grasped her hand, and this time, she didn't pull it away. He led her along the stone wall that edged her property. He stopped when they were past a copse of trees that concealed them from the road.

The stone fence here was about waist high, and August perched on it, crossing his arms.

Scarlet sat on the top of the wall, too, although about two feet from him. She folded her own arms, waiting.

August began with the story about finding his father feeding the wolves. Scarlet listened, her eyes wide in amazement. She asked some questions, but mostly she listened. Then August showed her the stone necklace about his neck and told her about his father's words on his deathbed.

Scarlet stared at him while he repeated his father's last

words. "Wait," she said. "You've been feeding the wolves every single week since your father died and haven't told a soul?"

"Right," August said. It was nearly dark now, but the glow of the oil lamps inside the house told August that Scarlet's mother was patiently waiting for her.

"Then why are you telling me?"

"Because of what happened at the apothecary's last night," he said. "The wolves will remember you were with me, and they will single you out." He could tell she was trying not to laugh at him.

"Do you really believe that?" she asked. "They're *animals*."

August hopped down from the stone fence and faced her. "They are far more intelligent than we give them credit for. They can only be appeased for so long, and they are more dangerous than ever. So you need to be vigilant."

She leaned forward. "I'm not afraid of the wolves," she said, almost in a taunt. "I mean, if I can handle *you*, I can handle *them*."

August took a step closer. "I hope you're joking, Red."

She didn't correct the nickname. Her blue eyes had deepened in the coming darkness, but the glow of the rising moon gave him plenty of light to see her.

He was close to her now, and he couldn't help the way his blood was simmering. "I care about you," he said in a soft voice. "The wolves know it."

"Hmm," Scarlet murmured, staring at him.

Her lips were red. How was that possible? He took another step and placed his hands on either side of her on the stone fence. She didn't move, and he wasn't sure if he was breathing.

She smelled of wildflowers and lemon. She was intoxicating, and he knew that he could no longer hold back from touching her. He either had to walk away or . . . He lowered his head and pressed his mouth against the curve of her neck.

"What are you doing?" she whispered.

"Kissing you," he murmured against her neck.

"I thought . . . I thought last night was something that wouldn't happen again."

He lifted his head and gazed at her. "Do you want me to leave?"

She didn't speak for a moment. Then she said, "No."

"I don't want to leave either."

She smiled, and his heart flipped over. "So you're going to kiss me, then lock me up?" she said.

He pressed his lips just beneath her ear. "Yes."

"No."

Before he could reply, she kissed him. Her mouth was warm and welcoming. She kissed him deeper and with more confidence than she had the night before, and he didn't mind at all.

The violet sky turned to ink as she wrapped herself around him and pulled him closer. August became completely and utterly lost.

Nine

August is a surprising man. He can be gentle, and the protectiveness I once found exasperating has become endearing. Yet, no matter how much I love to be wrapped in his arms, and to have his lips on mine, and his hands holding me tight, I will not be a prisoner at night.

I know my mother is waiting, and that is likely the leading reason I draw away from August. The other reason is to catch my breath.

He leans his forehead against mine, and for the time being, words are not needed.

He's made his intentions clear through his caressing kisses. He cares for me, yes, but he fully believes the wolves will invade the village. And if I trust August at all, I must believe this, too.

I run my hands across his shoulders, careful not to press against his bandaged wound, and then I run my fingers along his arms, to his wrists. I link my fingers through his, and his tighten over mine.

"We must fight back," I say.

He lifts his head to search my eyes.

"I will not live my life afraid of being attacked by a beast at every turn," I continue, gathering courage and determination. "I won't barricade myself inside a house at night."

August exhales. "The cycle of the full moon is when they're the most aggressive."

I release one of his hands and place a finger on his lips to hush him. He doesn't seem to mind my touch. "I know. You've been warning us for years. It's time we shared the burden."

He straightens fully, and his eyes flash. "No, Scarlet. I can't allow anyone to put themselves in danger."

I tilt my head. "Oh, so you're the only one who can risk his life . . . You're the only one who has to carry the burden?" I place my hands on each side of his face. "You don't have to do this alone. I know your father did. But I'm here. *I* can help you."

Fear jolts across his face, and it's gratifying to see his concern for me, yet it's frustrating at the same time. I have an idea, though.

"We kill the dominant wolf," I say in a quiet voice. "That will mellow out the pack."

August shakes his head. "Another leader will take over, and their need for revenge will be greater."

He might be right. "Then we kill the wolf without the others knowing it was human-caused."

August stares at me in the moonlight. His face is shadowed on one side, and his jaw muscle flexes. I know he's about to argue with me, but I lean forward and kiss the edge of his jaw.

And then suddenly, he pulls me into his arms, crushing me against him. As if he cannot hold me close enough. I sigh into him.

"I don't know," he murmurs. "I don't know."

This tells me he is at least thinking about it.

"We set a trap," I murmur. "The dominant wolf will fall into it, and the pack will be weakened by his disappearance."

He continues to hold me tightly against him. I can feel his thudding heart, and I wait for his answer. Finally, he releases me and traces my cheek with his fingers. "Tonight," he says. "They will be roaming the forests, looking for trouble."

My breath hitches. "Where do I meet you?"

"There's an old well beyond my property that I can lure them into with fresh meat. The well will be the perfect trap. It's on the north side of the burned farmer's house," he says. "I will come for you when I've trapped the leader."

And then he kisses me again. Fiercely this time, as if he isn't certain he'll see me again.

August walks me to the gate of my house, and I feel his gaze on me, watching me as I walk to my front door. I don't know how long he will be, but I am sure I won't sleep at all tonight.

My mother looks up from the kitchen table when I enter. She's working on a stitching sampler by the light of an oil lamp. She smiles when she sees me, and I'm aware that my cheeks must be flushed.

"You were gone a while," she says. "But I knew you weren't far."

I nod, not really wanting to explain anything. "I'll latch everything tight." I latch the front door first, then move to the kitchen window.

My mother sets her stitching down. "I thought he was interested in you."

I turn to her. "You did?"

She smiles. "He watches you a little more intently than he does anyone else in the village."

Heat warms my neck. "He's an intense man."

My mother's brows lift. "That he is." She stands. "And I'm off to bed. See you in the morning."

"Good night," I say, wondering what morning will truly bring.

I latch the windows, then enter my own bed chamber. The moonlight is sharp and cuts a path through my room. I open my own window wide so I can watch. I think of August and wonder what he is doing. The night is still, and there is no wind. The time passes slowly, and I've been waiting at least two hours when the howling starts up.

The hairs on my arms stand up. The howling is distant, though, and I tell myself it's not a threat to the village. But I know better. It grows closer by the minute.

My hands are clammy, and my heart races. I stare out the window into the night. The moonlight splashes across the fields beyond the stone wall, then tops the trees on the other side of the road.

"August," I whisper. Has he already set the trap, but now is trapped himself with the arrival of the wolves? Have they picked up his scent, and are they targeting *him*?

Before I can think of what I'm doing, I grab my cloak and slip a small knife into my waistband. I sneak into the kitchen without a sound and unwrap a bit of dried meat my mother keeps on hand. Perhaps the meat will be a distraction if I encounter a wolf. Then I return to my bed chamber and climb out of my window so that I can leave the front door latched. I tug my skirt free when it catches on the ledge and threatens to tear. I run across the yard and slip through the gate, closing it silently behind me.

Another round of howls starts up, and the sounds skitter across my skin, pooling into a knot of dread in my stomach.

Up ahead, on the moonlit road, I see a dark shape. I immediately know it's not human, and I fervently hope it's a dog. But the animal is too fast. It runs across the road and disappears into the forest.

If it's a wolf, it's by itself, but that gives me no comfort. I run toward August's homestead. His home sits at the edge of the village, and typically it would take me twenty minutes to walk there.

As I run, I realize the howling has stopped, and the only sound is the slap of my feet against the road. My cloak streams out behind me as I run, and perspiration dots my skin. When I reach the gate of August's property, I am panting from running so hard. The place is dark. He's not here.

I lean against the gate, trying to decide what to do next. Is he still at the well? Or is he on his stallion, leading the wolves from the village?

Another howl pierces the night, closer than the other ones. I can't stand here and wait. I need to do something.

I open the gate and hurry across August's front yard. A quick glance into the barn tells me he's on foot. The stallion is in his stall, and he doesn't look happy about it. It takes me only a second to decide.

"Hello, boy," I say, walking toward the stallion. His gaze is wary, but he doesn't back away when I offer my hand. A barrel with a few half-dried apples sits at the end of the stall, and I pick up an apple and hold it out.

The stallion sniffs it, then practically swallows it whole.

I stroke his nose, then open the stall. Moments later, I'm riding the stallion across the property, in the direction of the well.

The horse is fast, and strong, and I barely hang on as he gallops. Before, August had controlled the horse, and now I am second-guessing my decision. Another round of howls, and the stallion seems to bristle. "Find August," I call out to the stallion.

We ride through the adjacent field, toward the edge of the trees. The field is barren, and a shape of a ruined house comes into view. My mother told me a farmer's house had burned down when I was a child. I have only seen the charred remains of the walls that became overgrown with vines and weeds over the years.

Beneath the moonlight, the ruins of the farmhouse walls rise out of their graves like ghostly fingers. I shudder but urge the stallion forward. He doesn't miss a step.

And then suddenly, we've arrived at the well. A chunk of fresh meat sits on the stone ledge of the well, and I'm sure there is more meat inside. But the area is empty. No August. No wolves. I am not fooled. The chill that's spread over my body tells me I'm being watched. I scan the trees on the opposite side of the well. They are silent as well.

I climb off the stallion and begin to walk the last few paces toward the old well. A shovel has been discarded at the edge. Is it August's?

I walk toward the edge of the well and peer down inside. I can only see black, but I know it's empty.

Then I hear a crashing sound from the trees. I snap my head up in time to see August drop to the ground from where he must have been perched in a tree.

"August!" I hiss.

His eyes widen, but he doesn't answer. He brings a hand up, signaling for me not to speak. Slowly I turn my head. To my left, a wolf slinks toward me.

I freeze in fright. The wolf's muscled shoulders gleam silver beneath the moonlight, and its eyes glow a deep orange as its gaze locks onto me. Most frightening of all is the beast's bared fangs. Long, white, sharp.

I want to run, but I know I won't get far. Perhaps I can dive into the well. I cannot see the stallion from my peripheral vision, and I don't blame the horse for leaving the scene.

I reach for the dagger tucked into my waistband, but even as I hold it out in front of me, I can see that the knife will have little effect on a wolf so large.

The wolf growls, and the sound ripples through me. My mind and body thaw, and hot anger shoots into my limbs. This creature will not threaten my village, my loved ones, my family—me.

"Scarlet," August voice whispers in the air. "Move behind me."

I realize he's reached my side. He's somehow crept silently up behind me, and now his hand brushes mine, guiding me to the side of him. The wolf has moved so he is at the other end of the well from us.

"Why did you come?" August says close to my ear.

He's angry.

"Because you've done this alone your whole life," I answer.

He releases a breath, and for a moment I feel the press of his lips against my hair. But then the sensation is gone, and August shoves me behind him while at the same time he hurls a rock toward the wolf.

It strikes the wolf in the shoulder. The beast growls and lunges forward.

Everything happens so fast that I barely have time to move.

Instead of tripping into the well or running around it, the wolf leaps across. My blood chills as I realize the wolf is going to make it. August realizes it, too, and moves to block the wolf's landing.

The two of them tumble to the ground, and I can only see a mass of fur and teeth. I scream.

I grip my knife and rush to them and strike at the wolf. The wolf howls. I know I've done little damage, but the pain is still real. And this gives August a chance to use his own knife on the beast and kick it into the well. The wolf tumbles down, and when it lands at the bottom, it's still growling.

"It's not dead," I gasp, unable to look over the side for fear that it will leap out.

August scrambles to grab the shovel and begins to toss dirt into the well.

I join him on my hands and knees, scooping dirt and throwing it over. We work like mad for what feels like an hour but can't be very long.

After some time, August grasps my arm to stop my frenzied motions. "Scarlet, that's enough."

I realize I've been crying as I've worked.

"It's dead," he says, pulling me to my feet.

I collapse against him, and he gathers me into his arms and holds me up.

"Why did you come here?" he asks in a ragged tone.

"I had to find you," I say in a half sob. "I couldn't let something happen to you."

His arm tightens around me, and he buries his face in my hair. "You're a foolish woman, Red."

I close my eyes and cling to him, breathing him in.

"Come on," he says, one hand rubbing my back. "We must destroy the evidence and leave before the other wolves track their leader." He whistles for the stallion, which returns to us. "You take the stallion back, and I'll start the fire."

I shake my head. "I'm not leaving you."

And so I watch, sitting atop the stallion, as August starts a fire with bits of flint. He tosses dried grass into the well, then drops a burning stick down the hole. The flames leap from the well for a few moments, then die out. The fire will kill the scent of the wolf, and its pack won't be able to locate the leader.

Then August climbs up behind me on the stallion. He pulls me close, and we ride into the night. The howling starts up again, and I tense.

"They're deep in the forest now," August says.

"I wish we could kill them all," I answer.

August's breath brushes against my ear as he speaks. "We need their protection. Our village is safer from larger predators with the wolves around. And I'm hoping the death of their leader will calm down their attacks."

"I hope so, too." I close my eyes and relax into the comforting strength of his body behind me.

"In the spring, I'll take you to their alcove," he says. "From afar, you'll be able to watch the young pups with their mothers."

"How many are born each year?" I ask.

"Usually a single litter, but usually only one will survive from it."

I give a shudder. If more pups survived, we could very well be overrun with the wolf population.

August rides the horse to his barn, where he climbs off the horse, then helps me down. After he settles the stallion inside the stall, he takes my hand and leads me inside his house. He lights two oil lamps, and the front room brightens. I have never been here before, but I am not surprised to see the sparse furniture. August doesn't seem like a man to have more than what he needs.

"Sit," he tells me. It's more of a command.

I sit at the kitchen table, my head spinning with all that's happened. I don't even mind the way he is ordering me about.

He strips off his torn, dirty shirt. His chest and abdomen are covered in scratches and bruises, but when I attempt to rise and examine them, he tells me to stay where I am.

I watch as he washes in a basin, then dries off with a cloth. Next, he approaches me with a jug and a cup. "Drink," he says, pouring me what smells like a strong cider.

I sip at the drink, the spiciness a welcome burn on my throat.

Then he brings another cloth that he's dampened and kneels in front of me. He touches the wet cloth to my face and wipes away the dirt and tears. I close my eyes and let him take care of me. I feel like crying again, but I don't. We've been successful. The leader of the pack is dead. The wolf pack will be weakened.

Together, we can protect our village.

"Scarlet," August says.

Slowly, I open my eyes. He is gazing at me with that intensity I've become familiar with.

"I could have lost you," he whispers.

I swallow back the lump forming in my throat.

He is still kneeling before me, so his eyes are level with mine, and he places his hands on either side of my face. The way he looks at me makes it hard for me to breathe. It's as if he's looking into my soul and that he can see every thought and feeling.

My eyes burn with tears as I remember how he was attacked by the wolf. I almost lost him, too.

"Don't ever leave me," he says and leans forward to press the softest kiss on my mouth.

"I won't," I promise. It's not a difficult promise to make. Somehow, some way, August has become a part of everything I am.

The edge of his mouth lifts in what I believe is approval.

"Good," he says, kissing me again, longer this time, more urgently. And then he pulls back. "Scarlet, I'll be speaking to your mother, if that's all right."

I tense. "About tonight?"

He shakes his head, and a smile lifts his features. "About *us*. About how I can't live without you. About how I want you to be my wife."

My breath rushes through me, and I feel as if I'm floating. "Are you sure?" I whisper.

His brows raise, but only for a moment. "I'm sure." Then he kisses me again. Very slowly.

I wrap my arms about his neck, and press myself against his warm, bare skin. The stone necklace with its moon is cool to the touch. I kiss him back. August is alive. We are together. He is mine. And I am his.

Together, we will protect the village.

About Heather B. Moore

Heather B. Moore is a *USA Today* bestselling author. She writes historical thrillers under the pen name H.B. Moore; her latest are *Slave Queen* and *The Killing Curse*. Under the name Heather B. Moore, she writes romance and women's fiction, latest include *Love is Come* and *Delilah's Desserts.* Under pen name Jane Redd, she writes the young adult speculative Solstice series. Heather is represented by Jane Dystel.

Heather's email list: hbmoore.com/contact
Website: HBMoore.com
Facebook: Fans of H. B. Moore
Blog: MyWritersLair.blogspot.com
Twitter: @HeatherBMoore

So Rare a Power

Annette Lyon

One

"Tell me another story," Stella asked. She sat at her vanity as her maid, Mary, arranged her hair.

"Oh, I don't know," Mary said. "Aren't you too old for such things?"

"A young woman never tires of happy tales," Stella said.

"Your mother doesn't approve." Mary had told plenty of stories over the years. Only in the last few months, since Stella's eighteenth birthday, had Mother decided that such things were nonsense and lies that were better left unspoken. The tales brought a joy to Stella's otherwise monotonous life in a way that nothing besides Patrick, the Kennisens' servant next door, ever did.

The thrill she got from her time spent with Patrick on the balcony linking the attics of their townhouses never faded. Truth be told, only a portion of that thrill came from the sunset palette of roses and watching them grow from bud to bloom. She hadn't managed to get away to their rose garden in several days, and her hands itched to work with her roses at Patrick's side.

No matter the weather, she managed to slip up to the fourth-floor attic, hurry to the window, and hope to spy Patrick waiting for her across the balcony. Every time she saw him, a delicious shiver went through her, followed by a warmth that heated her from the inside out.

If Stella didn't manage an excuse to tend her roses today—something Mother assumed she did alone—she'd be unable to bear it. That was, unless Mary told her a tale. "Tell me about the queen of ice," Stella said. Her chamber door opened at the same moment. Stella held her breath. She and Mary exchanged nervous glances.

The question as to whether Mother had heard was answered posthaste. She strode into Stella's chambers and folded her arms. "I'll have no more of those tall tales, Mary. You've been warned. I will not warn you again. Am I understood?"

Mary bobbed at the knee, her chin lowered contritely. "Yes, ma'am. My apologies. It shan't happen again."

"But, Mother," Stella said, turning in her chair so fast that Mary lost her grip and dropped a piece of hair. "She didn't tell me a single story, though I asked her to. If you are to punish anyone, punish me."

"That is highly unlikely," Mother said. "Mary, I need to speak with my daughter a moment."

"Of course, ma'am." The maid released the rest of Stella's hair and quickly withdrew.

Stella waited to be reprimanded, but instead, Mother wrung her hands and paced the small rug. "Mother?" Stella asked uneasily, then glanced at the door where Mary had exited. "I thought—"

"Forget Mary and her stories. That's not why I came to

your quarters." Mother stopped pacing and looked Stella in the eye. "Mrs. Frandsen will be coming to visit this afternoon. I want your best flowers on display for her. We must have two bouquets in the foyer, at least that many in the parlor. Can you make half a dozen?"

Finally, a reason to visit the garden! Even better, she had an order to go, not merely an excuse she'd invented herself. She remained vigilant about keeping her and Patrick's meetings a secret. A hint of them would see Stella married off to some landed gentleman and Patrick dismissed from his job with no recommendation to help him find another position.

"I'm happy to help," Stella said, trying to hide her excitement. She'd see Patrick today for certain.

Mother turned about anxiously. "Six bouquets isn't too many?"

"Not at all." For some reason Stella could never explain, she could always harvest precisely the number of roses needed.

"I'm so relieved. I have yet to find a bouquet at any of the sellers as pretty as a single one of yours." Mother resumed pacing, which indicated that her nerves were not entirely at ease.

"Have I met Mrs. Frandsen?" Stella asked. The woman had to be important, or Mother wouldn't be so concerned about making a good impression.

"You've seen her at society events," Mother said with a wave of her hand. "Her son is one of the most eligible bachelors in all of the kingdom. He's recently returned from service as a captain in the navy, and he's looking for a wife." Mother looked as excited by this revelation as a child might on Christmas morning, but Stella's heart dropped.

Mother wants me to marry Captain Frandsen, Stella thought in dismay.

"How quickly can you make the bouquets?" Mother asked.

"Um, I-I'll go up at once."

"After Mary finishes with your hair," Mother said. "I'll go fetch her. After that, do hurry."

"Yes, Mother." Stella's voice sounded hollow to her own ears.

I get to see Patrick, she reminded herself as Mary worked on her hair anew. *How many more times will I see him before I'm married to some gentleman I don't know?*

Hair finished, Stella hurried up the flights of stairs with almost no effort at all. She had to see Patrick and tell him of Captain Frandsen.

She went into the attic and locked the door behind her, then hurried to the window. The garden was outside, on the bridge between the two windows, one they'd made of planks, a warped and discarded door, rope, and other haphazard supplies. Together, they'd built a sturdy balcony on which they'd added trellises of blossoming roses and a bench wide enough for two. Their garden wasn't readily visible from the street, but they'd made sure the trellises hid them from public view.

For months, they'd cultivated roses together, usually in the afternoons, when Patrick's employer, Mrs. Kennisen, napped. Sometimes at night, they sat under the dark sky and watched the stars and moon. The night they saw the Northern Lights had been magical in more ways than one: that was the night Patrick first kissed her.

Putting the stars out of her head, Stella donned her broad-brimmed hat and garden gloves, then selected a pair of sheers from her toolbox on the floor by the window. All the while, she hummed the tune she and Patrick had invented together. Several roses began to open as she touched them, but she knew they wouldn't open fully until Patrick joined her. He had a special way with roses, one that had grown as their love had.

Stella remembered when Patrick first took her hand and threaded their fingers together. Love pulsed between them. With his free hand, he reached toward a dying rose. At the touch of his finger, life flowed into the petals, and the rose bloomed. With her free hand, Stella stroked a tiny, struggling bud. Within seconds, it had grown twice the size. It opened into a glorious yellow rose. She could never make the same happen without Patrick at her side.

She moved to climb through the window, but stopped halfway through at the sight of the rose garden blanketed with snow that shimmered in the sun. A swirl of air sent ice crystals spiraling around a figure facing away from her. Stella climbed out the rest of the way and tried to identify the bluish-white, sparkling woman, who seemed to be made of snow and ice. Across the way, Patrick stood outside his window, looking mesmerized.

Magic! It is *real.*

The woman was a beautiful, awful sight with icy hair swaying about her shoulders, her snowy cloak and dress rippling as if it wasn't solid but made of individual snowflakes.

To Stella's horror, Patrick stepped closer to the woman, never looking from her face. "Patrick!"

He didn't hear or see her. Whiteness brushed his cheeks, lips, eyebrows. Frost tipped his brown hair. The woman reached out to touch Patrick. Suddenly, Stella knew that if one slender, translucent finger touched him, he'd be lost to her. Never again would he smile or laugh with her. Never again would he kiss her.

"Stop!" she cried.

Slowly, the Snow Queen turned her elegant self about and shot a glare so cold, so icy, that Stella couldn't move. Her chest felt like ice, and as she gasped in pain, white puffs left her mouth.

"You think you can stop me?" The Snow Queen laughed, a sound that made Stella's bones shake.

Stella took a breath but couldn't move, couldn't feel her heart, or swallow or blink. *I'll die here.* She teetered to one side. The cloudy thought of falling to the cobbled street appeared in her mind, along with how the impact would shatter her frozen body. But as she tilted further and further to the side, she could not catch herself.

When she came to, Stella lay in the garden, alone. The snow and ice had fled. All but three tiny, pink roses were dead. She touched one, but the petals crumbled. Her mind slowly cleared, and her limbs regained some strength. She used the bench to get to her knees and then to her feet, looking for Patrick. She searched his attic, then the street below.

Patrick was gone.

Two

In the Snow Queen's grand sleigh, Patrick whooshed at her side through forests at breakneck speed. Frost swirled about them, far more than could be accounted for by the sleigh's runners. He reached an arm into the swirling snow and felt the Queen's power in the crystals dancing around his hand. She drew winter to her as the moon drew the tides.

At times, he could have sworn that small animals ran beside the sleigh, but they *weren't* animals, not as he knew them. Rather, they were churning snow shaped like heads, bodies, legs, and tails—a frozen entourage. The sight was equally glorious and entrancing. Patrick watched reindeer, hares, foxes, and even chickens made entirely of snow and ice, bounding beside them as he and the Snow Queen flew through the trees on her expansive sleigh.

So fast did they travel, and so smoothly, that at times he wasn't sure if the runners touched the ground at all. If they were indeed flying, how was the sleigh propelled? He didn't recall wings on the shadowy, horse-like shapes hitched to the front of the sleigh. Perhaps they, too, were nothing but charmed snow and ice.

Perhaps this is all a dream. If so, what did reality consist of? He furrowed his brow and settled back against the velvet cushion. Where did he live? What had his life looked like before he'd stepped onto the sleigh?

Try as he might, he couldn't remember anything of life before this ride—nothing before the Snow Queen had slipped her snowy cloak about his shoulders. He looked down at the cloak draped around him. It consisted of thousands of miniature icicles resembling fur, yet he felt warm in its embrace. How? How was *any* of this possible?

How did he know that these things were unusual?

On and on they went, eventually leaving the forest. Winter stretched in all directions for leagues—nothing but ice and snow, not even animals, unless he counted those made of snow. More animals surrounded them than before; several reindeer joined, along with more foxes and a few owls. When the light struck the animals just so, he could see through them. "Real" animals weren't transparent, he felt quite certain. He decided to admire them instead of worrying over whether he could explain them.

The animal entourage sparkled as if sprinkled with glitter and diamonds. He'd never seen the like. He'd never seen so much light during winter. Not that he could recall another winter.

Winter days are short, and we've traveled for days, yet it's never been dark. I don't understand.

"Troubled, my pet?" the Queen asked.

He shook his head and leaned closer. The Queen was tall; she sat a head taller than he did, though Patrick stood taller than his own father.

My father. He sat up with a jolt. *I have a father.* But the sliver of memory vanished like so much snow in the wind.

The Snow Queen rested her arm over his shoulders and drew him closer. He leaned in like a child toward his mother and absently stroked the cloak. Everything was beautiful—the cloak, the sleigh, the animals, and, most especially, the Snow Queen herself. The only thing he wished for was to see her majestic, chiseled form, even while in her embrace.

He continued to stroke the icy fur, lingering thoughts of long-ago history fading to an inconsequential blur. He breathed the icy air, drinking in the pleasure of being near the Queen and wrapped in her warm-yet-frozen cloak. He tucked it under his chin.

She made a pleased sound. "You like my cloak?"

"Very much," Patrick said, though her voice made his hand release its hold. Would she be cross with him for touching her cloak? Perhaps he'd broken off some tiny icicles.

She did not upbraid him, however. She merely chuckled. The sound resonated in her chest and through Patrick's limbs all the way to his toes. "You may touch it all you like."

Patrick let out a stuttered breath, sending a puff of white from his lips. "Thank you." He eagerly brought the cloak to his chin once more. Touching it became even more soothing, as if the Snow Queen had infused more of her magic into the cloak. Without mittens or gloves, his hand didn't feel cold.

"Are you happy?" the Snow Queen asked in a voice that sounded like a pane of ice shattering and falling to the ground—beautiful and sad at the same time.

"Yes," Patrick said quickly, though he didn't feel entirely confident that he knew what *happy* meant. If she wished him to be happy, he would be happy.

"I'm glad." The Snow Queen smoothed the hair above his

ear. Her touch left trails of frost, which were intoxicating and painful in equal measure.

With each stroke, Patrick could feel a piece of himself, deep inside, growing colder and colder. If she continued, he'd freeze solid. The thought merely made him curious. *Do I want to be frozen? Would that be . . . happy?*

The question flitted in and out of his mind with no concern, as he might have once brushed away a fly at the supper table. He could envision a kitchen like the tip of another memory poking through the surface of his hazy mind. A table laden with food. A door on the far side of the room held open by a stone. He tried to see past the door, to see what lay outside. When that didn't work, he tried to remember what the rest of kitchen looked like. He felt on the verge of remembering the room and faces of those who'd worked in the kitchen with him.

I was a servant, I think. Yes, that seems right. What is a servant?

Such thoughts confused him and made his middle feel sour. Certainly, *this* sensation was not *happy.* He wanted to forget, to be happy.

"Where are we going?" he asked, brushing off thoughts of *servants* and *kitchens.*

The Queen pressed a kiss to his temple. She didn't pull away, but traced his hairline with kisses, each chilling his scalp and sinking into his brain. She kissed his forehead, his nose, and finally, his mouth. Every kiss froze part of him with chilling pain.

Yet when she pulled away, he felt the loss sharply, as if he were drowning and needed her kiss to pull him from the dark waters. He reached for her, his lips and tongue too cold to form a full sentence. "More?" His tears froze as soon as they appeared, rendering him nearly blind. Sharp pain shot through both eyes. The searing pain increased, though he tried to thaw his eyes with what little warmth he had in his hands.

"Oh, my sweet," the Snow Queen said, her voice like icicles clattering together. "I mustn't kiss you more, or you'll freeze altogether and die."

"Die?" Another word Patrick felt he should know.

"That's right," she replied, placing her hand to his shoulder once more. "Soon we'll arrive at my palace. There you will feast, for you will be my king."

"I will?" Patrick lowered his hands, now able to see without quite as much pain. She nodded. His cold brain couldn't think clearly. He felt certain that *king* meant something better than *servant*. "Why will I be . . . king?"

"Because," the Snow Queen leaned in and whispered, "you have a special power I need."

"I-I do?"

"You can create beauty and life. I've seen it, my pet."

He faced forward and idly put his hand into the swirling snow again. "I don't remember."

"You needn't fret about that," the Snow Queen said.

He nodded absently. The Snow Queen said he needn't worry, so he didn't. *That must be what* happy *means.*

"My powers are great," the Snow Queen went on, "but with yours, I can rule the earth. You will need never again lift a finger working for another human." She drew him nearer and whispered again, her frozen breath tickling his face. "Never again will you feel the pangs of hunger. Never again will you be without me."

Her breath chilled his nose, then his cheeks, his forehead, his chin. Each breath brought with it a memory of his past life—ones of pain, sickness, and weariness. Images of serving others with money and power. Memories of never having the freedom to make his own choices. Except . . . had his life been one unending series of soul-wearying pains? Hadn't he ever been a little *happy*?

He closed his eyes and pressed his palms into them, both to speed the thawing of his vision and to think more clearly. Yes, he felt quite sure that he'd once experienced happiness as great as what he felt now with the Queen—a warmer happiness. He opened his eyes and looked at the Snow Queen. Her lips were rounded, and she blew her delicious, cold breath onto his face. The almost memory was gone, like so much dust swept away with a broom. He forgot whatever had been so close to returning.

No matter. If it were important, I'd remember.

With one arm, the Snow Queen gestured in a broad arc. "We've arrived."

Turrets of ice stabbed the sky, reaching high into the clouds. The palace was massive, extending to the left and right as far as Patrick could see. It surely had miles of corridors and thousands of rooms. How had he not seen it miles ago? *Magic.* That explained everything.

The Snow Queen stepped from the sleigh, then turned around and held out her hand, which looked translucent and perfect, sculpted from ice. "Come."

Patrick put his hand in hers, and she helped him down. Snow squeaked under his boots. He tried to take in the magnificence of the palace—its intricate designs of snowflakes, spirals, staircases, and more, all formed from glittering ice and snow. The palace itself seemed to create the white-blue glow all around it.

"Let's get you fed," the Snow Queen said. "My servants haven't cooked for a human in some time, but they'll remember how soon enough. They make excellent food."

As if on cue, Patrick's stomach rumbled. He placed a hand over it self-consciously, but the Snow Queen smiled with lips of red so dark they were almost purple. “Patrick, dear boy.”

“Yes?”

“After I see to it that you are fed, you *will* share your powers with me.”

“Yes.” He nodded without meaning to. “I will.”

The Snow Queen made a pleased sound again. Arm in arm, they walked up the grand staircase and into the palace of ice.

Three

Stella opened her eyes to see several faces surrounding her bed—her mother, her lady's maid, and, based on the clothing and the hat she wore, a nurse.

"H-how did I get here?" Stella asked, her voice dry and raspy. She swallowed to moisten it. "What happened?"

"You were found in the attic," Mother said. She sat at the edge of the bed and almost looked compassionate. "Draped over the windowsill, as if you'd fainted on your way inside. When you didn't come back with the bouquets after a few hours, I sent Mary to seek you out." She cupped Stella's cheek, an unfamiliar sensation. "Gave us quite a scare."

Snatches of memories revealed themselves to Stella. The attic. Flowers for bouquets. She did her best to piece them together through mental fog. She'd reached the balcony, so she must have fainted going back inside. Oh, how her head hurt.

Had she seen Patrick? Yes, she had. But . . . what happened? She couldn't imagine quarreling with him. And then she remembered: a woman of ice and snow wearing a glittering crystal crown.

With a gasp of remembrance, Stella tried to sit up. "Where's Patrick? Please—"

The nurse pressed her hands to Stella's shoulders and eased her back down. "You need your rest, miss."

"But—"

"Listen to the nurse," Mother said. But Stella noted something in her mother's face that spoke of more than the need for rest.

Oh, no. I spoke of Patrick.

Where was he? Dismissed by the Kennisens? Taken by the fantastical queen of snow? If so, where? Was he hurt? Abandoned?

Mother raised an eyebrow but said nothing about Patrick. She didn't have to. She addressed Mary. "Would you see if Cook has some broth for Miss Stella?"

"Yes, mum." Mary curtsied and left.

With her memories intact, Stella sat up and threw the bedclothes off before either the nurse or Mother could stop her. They erupted in protests, but the urgency to find Patrick gave Stella strength she hadn't possessed moments before. She had to find him, plain and simple. Urgency flowed through her like a rushing river, pushing her forward.

She opened her armoire and withdrew her simplest frock, one of pale yellow. For the moment, the greatest benefit of it was that Stella needed little help putting it on. She could reach most of the buttons on the back, and if Mother forbade Mary from helping with the two Stella couldn't reach, she'd simply add a shawl to hide the gap.

"What do you think you're doing?" Mother demanded.

Stella removed her nightgown and pulled the dress over her head. For the brief moment that the room was blocked from view, she took a strengthening breath. When the gown lowered, she slipped one arm and then the other into the sleeves in a matter-of-fact manner. Behaving emotionally would convince Mother that Stella needed a harsher hand to keep her under control.

To avoid looking at her mother, Stella smoothed the skirt, then turned to the side and worked on her buttons, deliberately not thinking about the other layers of clothing she was neglecting to don. "I am going to pay a visit next door."

"Not dressed like that, you aren't," Mother said. "You know better than to drop in unannounced. You haven't the slightest idea what hour it is—or what day, for that matter."

At that, Stella's head came around. "How long have I been in bed?" Mother didn't answer, offering only a smug smile and folded arms. Stella turned to the nurse. "How long?"

"Two nights, miss. This is the third day."

Stella backed up to her vanity table and dropped to the chair. "So long?"

She hoped that Patrick was safe and sound next door, even if it meant working long hours for the Kennisens, rather than being stolen away by some creature of magic, never to be heard from again.

Perhaps I dreamed that part. Yet she could recall every line of the Snow Queen's face, crown, and dress. Dream or reality, she had to go next door to be sure.

"Mary, my buttons," Stella said as her maid returned, carrying a steaming bowl. Mary looked warily between Stella and her mother, clearly unsure what to do.

Mother took two steps toward Stella. "I forbid you to visit the servant boy."

"I fear he may be gone, Mother—hurt or abandoned somewhere. I must find out."

"You will do no such thing." Mother leaned in so close that her nose nearly touched Stella's. "I know of your secret meetings. The truth was all too clear when Mary went into hysterics, sure you were dead."

"You saw Patrick?" Stella asked.

"I saw plenty that you should be downright ashamed of. How long have you been meeting him in secret? Did you think you'd be able to pull the wool over our eyes forever, that you wouldn't be found out? How dare you so much as consider having a dalliance with someone so below your station? How do you expect your father to find a suitable match for you when you have so blatantly and deliberately besmirched your good name and that of your family? How heartless and cruel you are!"

Jaw clenched, Stella leaned forward, an action that surprised her mother so much that she took half a step backward. "Patrick is the best man I have ever met. He loves me, and I love him. This is no dalliance, I assure you. I do not need Father or you marrying me off to make yourselves appear successful. I'd rather live in the wilds of Lapland, scraping out a living from the land with Patrick at my side, than endure a loveless marriage arranged by parents who only have their own interests at heart."

Stella had never spoken so many contrary words to her mother in her entire life. The effect of such defiance was remarkable: Mother, Mary, and the nurse all gaped as if she'd lost her mind and they were afraid of her.

Good. Then they won't try to stop me.

She pulled a wrap from the armoire and draped it around her shoulders, leaving the room without looking back. Keeping her head held high, Stella marched into the hall, down the stairs, and out the front door. Only when she stood on the street, with the closed door behind her, did the weight of what she'd done settle on her, including the heaviness of what she might find next door—or *not* find.

Her middle gurgled with hunger, and she felt lightheaded. She wished she'd been able to partake of the broth before leaving. Such was not to be, however, and she had to make the best of it. Stella squared her shoulders, adjusted her wrap, and strode next door, where she used the brass knocker to rap three times.

Moments later, Mr. Andersen, the Kennisens' butler, answered. "Why, Miss Hinks. What a pleasant surprise. How may I help you this evening?"

Evening? Stella looked about and noted that, indeed, the sun was making its way toward the western horizon. What would she do when night fell and the streets were dark? Would Mother let her back into the house, or was Stella forever to be an outcast?

"Miss?" the butler asked again.

"By chance," Stella said, fighting lightheadedness, "is Patrick available?"

"Patrick? May I ask why?"

"It's a rather urgent and sensitive matter." Not even a butler would dare pry further of a lady who proclaimed such a thing. He might make some untoward assumptions, but he wouldn't question her openly.

Let him guess and gossip all he wants. I just need to find Patrick.

"Is he here?"

"No."

Her stomach dropped to her toes. "Where— Where is he?" She cleared her throat, unsure how much longer she could maintain her composure before turning into a weeping puddle right there on the stoop. "Is he out on an errand? Traveling with Mr. Kennisen?"

"Oh, no, nothing like that," Mr. Andersen said. "Patrick isn't trained for the duties of a valet."

"Of course not," Stella said, though her heart raced, and she felt quite sure she'd explode if he didn't say more. "Where is he, then?"

The butler pressed his lips together in thought, then said, "I apologize if it is not my place to ask, but . . . did your parents send you here?"

"I came of my own accord. Please," Stella said desperately. "I must know."

The man must have seen something in her face or heard the crack in her voice, because he finally took compassion on her. He glanced behind himself, stepped over the threshold beside Stella, and pulled the door almost closed. When he spoke, it was a whisper. "He's missing."

"No." Stella's fingertips went to her lips, for while she'd anticipated the response, she'd been praying for another.

"No one knows where is," Mr. Andersen went on. "He finished cleaning the fireplaces, but when Mrs. Jensen—she's our cook, you see—called him to dinner, he was nowhere to be found. It's as if he simply"—the man shrugged—"vanished."

"I must find him," Stella said, more to herself than the butler.

"You look most unwell, Miss Hinks. Please, come inside and have some tea, something to give you a little strength before . . ." His voice trailed off, and then he finished, "before you go."

His eyes told Stella that he knew she wouldn't be going home, that she needed nourishment for a much longer journey than a thirty-second walk home. He opened the door fully and stepped back inside, this time gesturing for her to come in as well. She hesitated only a moment before joining him in the foyer.

"Come," he said, leading her down a hall to a green, felt-covered door—a door only servants used.

Stella almost asked why, but somewhere in the middle of her chest, she knew the answer. Mr. Andersen was Patrick's friend. While she never fully understood servant life, Patrick told her that his fellow servants were like his family. Mr. Andersen surely knew of their relationship, and he, too, was concerned about Patrick. He seemed eager to help her in whatever way he could. For the moment, that meant bringing her to the basement, where the Kennisens wouldn't learn of her visit.

When he pushed the door open, Stella hesitated only a moment. She'd never stepped over such a threshold before and didn't know what lay on the other side.

I don't know what lies beyond my next meal, either, she thought as she stepped into the servants' corridor. *But I will do everything in my power to find Patrick.*

Four

"It has been long enough," the Snow Queen bellowed, rage etched on every sharp line of her face. "Give me your power. Now!"

Patrick's sinews vibrated like the strings of a lyre. He backed away, only to slip on the ice and fall, bruising his hip again.

"You dare try to leave?"

"No, of course not—"

She stood above him, her scepter held high. Patrick tried to back away with his hands and feet like a crab. He managed to get a little distance away, but the Snow Queen reached out with a grasping motion. Her icy fingers seemed to clasp his shirt, though she stood ten feet away and wasn't touching him. She twisted her wrist, making his shirt wrench until it was painfully tight. She yanked toward herself, making him slide forward.

When he came to rest at her feet, he stared at the scepter, still raised. "No. Please." He'd experienced what the scepter could do, and the thought of its punishment shot fear through him.

Her eyes narrowed into dark slits that cut like daggers. "Share. Your. Power."

"I don't know how!" Instinctively, he raised his arms, crossed, to protect himself. He knew how much pain she could inflict when only annoyed. Her dark eyes were far past annoyance today.

"I gave you food, didn't I?" She flicked the scepter like a wand, and a ragged bolt of iced lightning struck on his right.

"Yes." He'd eaten whitefish and reindeer. He'd indulged in rich breads with butter and more cheeses than he'd have believed one stomach could contain. She'd provided never-ending flows of mead and wine. Honey and sweets. "It was delicious. Thank you."

She leaned down. "I didn't have to make your food taste like anything other than shavings of wood." The statement sounded like a threat, made more so by being punctuated by a second ice lightning strike on his left, which grazed his hand. He pulled away, crying out in pain.

"The food was delicious." From where he sat, he was forced to look up as she drew closer. "I thank you. I've never eaten more amazing food." He'd thanked her profusely during and after every meal, and she'd always seemed pleased in the moment. But now, no matter what he did, his actions served only to anger her.

"In exchange for such generosity, you refuse to share anything with me at all."

"No." More than anything, Patrick wanted to please her. "I want to share everything I have." He had nothing *to* share. Everything he had, including the leather and fur clothing he wore, had been gifts from the Snow Queen.

"Yet you will not share the one thing I desire." Her voice

softened slightly, and she leaned over as if she might stroke his cheek with her perfect, cold fingers.

Patrick sat up more fully, eager for her touch and approval. "I want to share my power," he said, infusing the words with as much yearning as he could. "I don't know how."

The Snow Queen yelled in frustration, straightening to her full height. She sent cords of ice shooting from her fingers on both sides of her outstretched arms as her voice shattered ice in the distance.

"Help me, oh Queen!" Patrick cried, hoping she'd hear his plea over the cracks and booms of crumbling ice. "Show me how."

Icy explosions continued around them for a few seconds, but she slowly lowered her arms, and ice no longer shot from her fingertips. She lowered her face to his; he waited to learn whether her expression would be one of fury or adoration. She rarely showed an emotion that fell between.

There—she wore a smile. Patrick breathed out with relief. "Will you teach me?"

At first, the Snow Queen gave no response. She turned to the side and began to pace in a circle, hands behind her back, one of them holding the scepter. "You are willing?"

"Yes," he said, so quickly that he nearly spat the word.

She whirled about. "Then why have you not shared your power in all the time I've had you here as my king?"

"All this time?" Patrick repeated. He had no idea how long he'd been at her palace, only that she demanded what he could not give. A hundred times, she'd demanded his power, and when he'd been unable to give it to her, she'd punished him. He had scars on his back that bore witness to her tortures, along with spots that had frozen solid. Some were white, others tinged with black; some swelled more each day and had turned an angry red. All were painful.

"Your Majesty, I beg you." He held out his arms

helplessly. "I don't know what my power is, let alone how to share it."

The Snow Queen tilted her head as if finally comprehending his words. "You truly don't know your own power?"

He shook his head several times. "Teach me."

"Your power creates life and beauty." She'd said the same words a thousand times. They meant no more to him now than before.

"Yes, but I don't remember how I used my power or how it works, or"—his voice dropped with sadness and dread, knowing she'd unleash her temper again—"or how to give it to another. Truly. I don't remember."

This time, the Snow Queen tilted her head back as she looked down at him. The heat of anger ebbed as she pondered. He could almost see her thoughts swirling like flurries of snow. "You don't . . . remember." She resumed her pacing, this time tapping her lower lip with a slender finger.

Oh, he hoped she could find a solution. He wanted to share his power with her. He desired nothing more than to please her.

The Snow Queen stopped right before him and spoke slowly. "You don't remember." Her tone held something he'd never heard from her before: wonder.

"Do you have an idea?"

"I think so." She nodded, tapping her lip again. "I must help you remember."

Horror welled up in Patrick. She'd always said that his past held only misery and sorrow, that to have forgotten it was a fate worth celebrating. Now she would force him to remember? "But— But—"

"Shh." She bent down and pressed a finger to his lips. "You needn't remember much. Only enough to give me your power."

Patrick shuddered. His skin broke out in gooseflesh. "Only that much?"

"Only that much," the Snow Queen said, her voice smooth like mead. "Afterward, I can make you forget it all over again. I'll wipe away the pain. And you will be happy once more."

He got to his feet and stood as tall as he could manage. He wanted his queen's admiration and respect. He'd been groveling. And a king didn't grovel.

"Help me remember, my Queen."

Five

Stella received much more than tea from Mr. Andersen and Mrs. Jensen, who fed Stella a virtual feast. She eagerly partook of new potatoes with dill and butter, meatballs, and lingonberry sauce. She ate until she felt ready to burst.

Near the end of the meal, she looked up at the two elderly servants. "I don't understand. Why are you helping me? You don't know me."

"We know enough." Mrs. Jensen patted the top of the table. Her eyes grew misty.

"Patrick loves you, Miss Hinks," the butler said. "Ever since the two of you began growing roses upstairs—"

"You know about that?" Stella's fingers tightened around her fork. Anxiety wormed through her. She'd never forgive herself if Patrick was terminated from his job because of her.

"Yes, dear." Mrs. Jensen chuckled, shaking her portly frame, and wiped her eyes with the hem of her apron. "Patrick has been happier loving you than we've ever seen him. That speaks volumes about who you are."

Emotion tightened Stella's throat. "Have you told anyone about us?"

With a shake of her head, Mrs. Jensen said, "No one upstairs, if that's what you mean. Your secret is safe down here."

Mr. Andersen rested his arms on the table. "Now, tell us everything you know about his disappearance."

"I don't know anything," Stella said.

Mrs. Jensen clucked her tongue. "That can't be entirely true. I'm sure you know more than you think."

Stella looked dubiously from the cook to the butler. Even so, she related everything she knew—how she'd gone up to cut roses for bouquets, as they were expecting guests, and how she'd wanted an excuse to see Patrick. Speaking those things aloud was freeing; Stella hadn't realized how bottled up she'd been. Simply speaking of Patrick warmed her heart and made her love for him bubble up and overflow.

"We were up there together, and then . . . he disappeared. I fainted, and when I came to, he was gone." She didn't want to look up and see disappointment in the eyes of the friends who were as dear to Patrick as family, so she stared at the wood grain in the table.

Mrs. Jensen reached across the table and took Stella's hand. "Do you remember anything from before you fainted?"

Stella shook her head. "No, not really. It's all vague and blurry, like a strange dream. I'm quite sure it was a dream, because it couldn't possibly . . ." As she focused on a knot in the wood, she remembered—vaguely at first, but more clearly as the seconds ticked away. A woman. A tall, beautiful woman in white and blue, with dark red lips. And a cloak. And . . .

"What is it?" Mr. Andersen asked. "Do you remember?"

"It can't be real," Stella said, as much to herself as anyone. "Can it?"

"Tell us what you saw," Mr. Andersen urged gently.

Stella did, though she was sure they'd think she'd lost all reason and was living in children's stories like the ones Mary told her. But when she finished her account and looked up, sure they'd send her home and lock the door behind her, they did no such thing. They were looking at each other intently, as if they were holding an entire conversation in silence.

After a time, Mrs. Jensen spoke. "Tell her," she said quietly.

The butler nodded soberly. "You saw the Snow Queen, Miss Hinks. She must have taken Patrick."

"I saw the—wait, who?"

The butler explained what little was known about the mythical creature known only as the Snow Queen—about how she sought to rule the world. While she was powerful, she lacked a final step that would allow her to cover the world in ice and force all of humanity to serve her. "Most people think she is a creature of imagination," he said, "but she is most real. I have family stories about her that would scare the skin right off you."

"And you think she took Patrick?"

"We do," Mrs. Jensen said. "Everything you described fits what we know of her."

"Where does the Snow Queen live? I must find her."

"I'm glad you think so," Mr. Andersen said. "Only someone who loves Patrick as you do could find the Snow Queen and save him."

The servants had another silent exchange, after which Mr. Andersen got up and left the room. Mrs. Jensen began packing food—a round of rye bread, a hunk of cheese, a few cookies, and some apples. She wrapped the whole in a large piece of newsprint and slipped the package into a burlap sack, which she tied with a short length of twine.

"Take this with you," she said, pressing the sack into Stella's hands.

Mr. Andersen returned with a pair of heavy boots and a thick coat. "Take these. You'll need them where the Snow Queen lives."

As Mrs. Jensen helped Stella put on the coat and boots, she sniffed. "You're a mighty brave one to go looking for him."

Mr. Andersen reached into his pocket and pulled out a small sack of coins. "Take these. You may need money along the way."

The sum amounted to little by the standards of wealth Stella had grown up with, but she had no doubt that the coins made up the man's entire savings, which he'd surely scrimped and saved for. She'd do her best to return every coin to him, but if the need arose, she would have a way to buy food or transportation.

"The boots are an eyesore," Mr. Andersen said, gesturing to them with a sardonic half smile. "But they'll keep your feet dryer and warmer than the dainty slippers you had on."

Wearing a thick coat and sturdy boots felt odd, especially having stepped in from a summer day. Yet if their guesses were correct, she would soon be freezing cold and would wish for the warmth she felt now.

"How can I ever thank you?" she said, looking from the butler to the cook and back again.

"Bring him back," Mrs. Jensen said simply.

"I'll do my best."

"That's all anyone can ask," Mr. Andersen said. "Until we meet again."

"Until we meet again," Stella replied, choking up at the thought of leaving. Though they'd only just met, she'd already begun to care for Patrick's friends.

They led her to the basement door. Mr. Andersen opened it, and she stepped back into a warm June evening. Behind her, the servants' entrance closed. The thud rang with an unsettling finality, but Stella refused to be scared into losing the man she loved.

She buttoned up the coat as if challenging the heat to overwhelm her, then lifted her chin and headed out of town along the main street. She headed north, in search of the Snow Queen.

Six

Stella headed toward the Arctic Circle, as Mrs. Jensen and Mr. Andersen knew that the Snow Queen lived in the north, almost certainly past the Arctic Circle. She had to pay her way on a ferry that crossed the narrow neck of land between her homeland and the body of the Nordic kingdoms. There she disembarked at the port of a great city. From there, she made her way ever northward through busy cobbled streets that looked much like home but were strange in their own way.

Wherever needed, she asked for guidance, though she quickly came to the point of avoiding such interactions unless absolutely necessary. People noticed her expensive gown showing between the hem of her old coat and the tops of her boots. Some pointed and laughed at her wearing winter clothing atop her summer dress. Taking off the coat and draping it over her arm didn't do much to help the situation, as the clunky boots remained loud and obvious as she walked—a far cry from satin slippers.

She didn't dispose of the coat or boots; she knew as well as the butler and cook did that where she was going, she'd need something to keep her warm. Indeed, she worried about not having more warm clothing, like a hat, scarf, and mittens—items not readily available for purchase in the summer months.

Before she left the city, she bought bread and cheese to refill the sack from Mrs. Jensen. The cobbled streets gradually changed into a dirt path with deep ruts from wagon wheels and grass growing between them. She came across fewer and fewer people, and while she felt relieved at that fact at first, she quickly came to wish she could confirm her direction with someone. She felt relatively confident that she headed northward, but she couldn't be sure, not with the summer sun, which didn't rise high from the east and then drop slowly to the west. Rather, the Nordic summer sun hovered low in the sky, appearing in the northeast at dawn then skimming the horizon along the south before setting in the northwest late at night, only to reappear in the northeast a few hours later.

She stayed on clearly worn roads, ones with signs of civilization, which meant less chance of getting hopelessly lost—or of being attacked by robbers. She was already risking her reputation; she'd never been without a chaperone for so long in her life, let alone so far from home.

The woods provided clear streams to drink from and fresh berries to eat, but three days into her journey, Stella's entire body ached. She'd never walked so far in her life. The miles had left blisters all over her feet. Her face was so sunburned that brushing a fly from her nose stung. Her dress was soiled, and the hem showed signs of wear. Though her hair was still up, the once-elegant twist now resembled a rat's nest, and it surely had pieces of leaves and twigs from her two nights of sleeping on the forest floor.

A rare wagon rumbled toward her, so she stepped to the side of the road, where she reached out to hold a thin branch out of her way. She glanced at her hand and then stared at it as if it belonged to someone else. Crescents of dirt were caked under her nails. Scratches covered her skin. Various shades of brown filled every crevice and crack.

After the wagon had passed, she stepped back onto the road and held out both hands, inspecting them by the late-afternoon sun. She was filthier than she'd ever known a person could be. Worse, her palms had blisters that would likely become calluses. They were the hands of a stranger.

How awful must the rest of me look? Mother wouldn't recognize me—or publicly admit that I'm her daughter were she to see me in such a state.

In spite of her genteel upbringing, she didn't feel ashamed of the dirt and blisters. Her thumb gently swept across a popped blister, and she found herself smiling. Daughters of wealthy merchants weren't supposed to have hands that hinted at a hard life of work, but she found the dirt, the scratches, and even the blisters to be signs that she was made of tougher mettle than others gave her credit for. She *could* do difficult things—things far greater than tatting handkerchief lace for hundreds of hours.

I am strong, she thought. She lowered her hands and noticed a torn section of her hem that hung down near her boots. One wrong misstep, and she'd step on it, then tumble to the ground in a heap. She reached down and did something that only the day before would have been unthinkable—she took her hem between her hands and ripped the cloth, tearing off a long strip along the bottom, and cast it aside.

Much better. Now she could walk without holding her dress up, which meant being able to walk much faster.

But will it be fast enough? What if Patrick is already dead?

She gritted her teeth and continued on her way. Regardless of weariness and filth, she had a mission far more important than whether she looked like a peasant. The more her limbs protested, however, the more she regretted not having done more physical work in her life to prepare her for such a task.

The sun began to set in what Stella assumed was the northwest. The road faded beneath her feet, the tracks of wheels disappearing the farther into the wild she went. Where to go next? How would she find her way home without a road to guide her?

As if a road leads to the Snow Queen, she reminded herself.

She looked about for a place to sleep, and hopefully a spring or pond where she could drink. Perhaps more berries to quell the gnawing ache of hunger in her middle. She dreaded the dark hours because she feared the wild animals, especially bears. To ease her nerves, she hummed the tune that made her happiest—the song she and Patrick always sang with their roses. Not until she'd sung the first line did she realize that, while the song made her happy under all other circumstances, tonight it made her wistful and melancholy. She missed Patrick deeply. She worried about him and wondered if they would ever again tend roses together. If their dream of eventually marrying and being seen together in public would ever become reality. If she would ever again sit beside him and simply enjoy being with him and loving him.

I'd do anything if it means being with Patrick, even if we never again touch flowers. I'd even muck out stalls in a stable.

Her song hesitated at that thought. What would her life look like when she returned home? Would it be with Patrick?

Would her family disown her for running away unchaperoned, for sullying her reputation?

As she looked for a suitable place to sleep, a glow in the distance caught her eye. She turned toward it, squinting. The light was too steady to be made by lightning or glow bugs or anything else like that. The golden-orange glow had to be a candle or a lamp.

A person lives in these woods!

With images of food and a soft bed in mind, she followed the light, eagerly increasing her pace until she stumbled upon a tiny cabin tucked in a grove. All the way, she sang, determined to remain calm and remember why she'd come so far. At the door, she hesitated, wondering if the owner of the lamp—for now she could see the shape through the window—was dangerous or kind, grouchy or welcoming.

Please be a woman, she thought. Visiting a man, in his home in the wood, no matter how kind or old he might turn out to be, was enough to smirch her reputation beyond repair completely. *Then again, how would such a rumor travel as far as my home? And who's to say I'll have any kind of reputation to salvage anyway?*

Stella's stomach gurgled, urging her on, so she raised her closed hand to knock, but before her knuckles made contact, the door swung open, revealing a small, hunched-over woman with a kerchief tied about her head.

"Oh," Stella said. "Hello."

The woman didn't appear surprised. Lines covered her face, and when she smiled knowingly, the wrinkles only deepened. "Why, hello, you young thing. I've been waiting for you. Come in. Come in."

Something rippled through Stella from the crown of her head to her toes—the sensation wasn't unpleasant, but neither could she identify what, precisely, it felt like, besides utter surprise.

"You . . . You've been . . ." She couldn't quite speak a complete thought.

"Yes, yes. Come in, come in," the old woman said, gently taking Stella's arm like a grandmother might.

Like perhaps Patrick's grandmother might, she thought, admiring the gnarled, wrinkled hand on her arm. *Certainly not like mine.*

Soon she found herself sitting at a thick table that had a stone under one leg to prop it up. The old woman brought over a steaming bowl of stew, a plate of rye bread, and a crock of butter with a wood spreader. Stella's mouth watered, and the woman chuckled as she sat down in the next chair.

"Eat up," she said. "You've been on a long journey, from what the birds have told me, and you've got a bigger one ahead."

Stella spooned the stew into her mouth, one bite after the other, in the most unladylike fashion. The woman didn't seem offended at the lack of etiquette. If anything, she was excited over it, something Stella found confusing in the brief moments between bites. When her appetite eased and her pace slowed, she thought through her arrival and the sweet grandmother who'd cared for her.

"Who are you?" Stella asked. "How did you know I was coming?" Many more questions rattled about in her mind, but those seemed to be the best place to start.

The old woman stood and poured a cup of milk, which she placed next to the now-empty cup of water Stella had drained. "Most people call me the Lap Woman," she said, easing herself back down to her chair with a slight grunt. "But I'm not a Laplander. They just don't know what else to call someone like me."

Curiosity increased in Stella's chest like a balloon building pressure. "What *are* you then, if not a Laplander?"

"You may call me Ailikki," she said coyly.

"But—" Stella had to know.

"I am a Finn," she said, smiling as if she'd given in to a child desperate for a treat. "And while Laplanders are generally Finns, not all Finns are Laplanders."

"Oh," Stella said. Nodding thoughtfully, she reached for yet another piece of hearty rye bread and spread butter on it. Her head came up suddenly. "Am I in the land of Finns, then?" Could she have traveled so far? Had she forgotten how many days she'd been gone?

"No, no," Ailikki said.

"Oh," Stella said again, unsure what else to say. Too many questions, and the ones she'd already asked had only created more.

"But we're very close." Ailikki's brow furrowed, and she lowered her chin. She was such a tiny woman that the small movement hid her expression. After a moment, she lifted her face, wearing a look of resignation. She reached out. Stella set the bread down and let the woman take her hands. Though Ailikki's were small and knotted, they felt strong wrapped about Stella's fingers. "You must go to Lapland and beyond. Much farther north."

Ailikki's intensity made Stella's breath grow shallow. "And what is beyond . . . the Laplanders?" She hardly dared speak the question, but it came out as if it had a life of its own.

"That, my dear," Ailikki said, "is where you will find the palace of the Snow Queen, and that is where you must rescue your dearest love."

"H-how?" Stella asked. For the first time since she'd embarked on her journey, her eyes welled up. She'd been so focused on heading north, on what she would eat, on where she would sleep, on making sure she found Patrick, that she hadn't given herself permission to think about how she expected to save him if she ever found him. If the Snow Queen was as powerful as Mrs. Jensen and Mr. Andersen believed, no human could defeat her. She'd taken Patrick and held him prisoner, and he was far stronger physically than she. The weight of reality fell on her shoulders—the sheer impossibility of her mission to save Patrick.

"How, indeed," Ailikki said. She placed Stella's hands on the table and gave them a couple of pats before standing and walking to the window, where she opened the shutters and gazed into the purple-gray of twilight. With her back to Stella, she said, "You love him, yes?"

"Very much."

"You must, or you couldn't have come this far." Ailikki nodded thoughtfully, arms folded, still staring outside. After a moment, she went to one side of the window and then the other, moving the shutters in place and locking them closed with a hook. She turned back to Stella, as if it was somehow safer to speak now. Perhaps it was. If word of Stella's journey had come here through the air on birds' wings, perhaps birds could carry the news to the Snow Queen herself.

Ailikki returned to the table with quick steps on her short legs. She clasped her hands and leaned forward. "I have a reindeer you may ride the rest of the way," she whispered. "His name is Remi."

Stella glanced around, instinctively wondering who else might be eavesdropping. Was it only birds who could spread messages? She'd only just learned of the existence of magic, but she wanted to know more.

"Trust Remi. He knows where"—Ailikki lowered her voice further—"*her* palace is and will deliver you safely."

"Thank you," Stella said in a matching whisper. "But why?"

"You'd never make it on your own," Ailikki said. "That coat and hat would have gotten you farther, but . . ." She clucked her tongue with a shake of her head. "You need more than that, and you need to get there quickly. The longer you stay in range of the Snow Queen's power, the more likely you are to succumb to it. Remi will help you get in quickly."

And out with Patrick?

"How will I know when I'm in the range of her power?"

"You'll know," Ailikki said. "That's when you'll need that coat or freeze in a moment. You've never experienced such cold, I assure you."

The words alone were chilling. "Why are you helping me?"

Ailikki's mouth curved into a sad half smile. "Because no one was able to help me."

Before Stella could ask or clarify anything else, Ailikki whisked her out back to a small stable, where, indeed, a handsome reindeer stood as if he had been waiting for her.

Does he have magic too?

"Here," Ailikki said, wrapping a scarf about Stella's neck and turning it into a hood. She held out wool mittens, which Stella slipped her hands into. "Now go."

"But it's dark and—"

"It'll be dark in her lair as well, broken only by the glow of snow and ice. Go now. She'll have a harder time finding you in the dark, when fewer birds are about to do her bidding."

That was all the encouragement Stella needed. She approached Remi, who lowered himself to the ground so she could climb on. She feared he'd race off into the night, but instead, he merely walked to Ailikki as if awaiting her command.

Indeed, the old woman stroked his neck and said, "Take care of her."

He dipped his head, whether in agreement or a bow, Stella did not know. It did not matter, either, as the next thing she knew, Remi was zipping through the woods so fast that they soon left all signs of summer behind. The air chilled, the ground became white, and tiny specks of ice struck her face. She fastened the coat buttons and burrowed into the collar as best she could with one hand, all the while holding on as tightly as she could with the other.

Remi didn't slacken his pace for a moment as they raced over hills and frozen lakes. At last, he jerked to a stop, and Stella woke with a start, sitting bolt upright on his back. She looked around, confused at first over where she was and what she was doing, only to feel Remi's ribcage moving beneath her as he caught his breath after their long ride. How long had it been? Days? Hours?

She had no idea, but it was still dark. She pressed her fingers against her eyelids and shook her head, trying to wake up.

The reindeer turned and pointed with his antlers. "There."

So startled was she to hear Remi speak that she nearly fell off his back. She scrambled to hang on and right herself, and she meant to ask Remi why she hadn't known he could talk. Had a spell given him the ability, or was he born of a special breed of animals?

All of her questions vanished in a blink as she looked where the reindeer indicated and she took in the unimaginably vast edifice before them. Her mouth opened, and her chin dropped.

Stretching outward and upward, more massive than Stella had ever dreamed possible, stood none other than the Snow Queen's ice palace.

Seven

An eerie blue-white glowed from the elongated towers, which disappeared in the clouds. Walls of ice had ramparts, not with square tops as Stella was used to seeing, but with sharp points like icicles that shot upward. A moat of crushed ice churned as it circled the castle. Stella wondered how far the moat stretched to go all the way around the enormous castle—surely walking around it would take days, assuming one could survive that long in these temperatures.

Already, the inside of Stella's nose froze a little more with each breath. She could scarcely move her fingers, and not without burning pain. Remi lowered himself to the ground, although unlike last time, snow blanketed the ground. Stella climbed off, her body rigid and sore from both the ride and the cold. The reindeer stood again, looking regal and strong.

If I could feel but a portion of that calm and strength, she thought.

"Now what?" she asked, as much of herself as of Remi. Finding the palace solved nothing. She had to get inside and find Patrick. And then, somehow, she had to save him. Her knees quaked, and her stomach roiled with nerves. She took a deep breath, trying to steady herself, but succeeded only in making her lungs feel half frozen.

A loud clank sounded, echoing off the ice in all directions, followed by an equally loud creaking. It sounded like the hinges of a door, only so loud it hurt. She clamped her hands over her ears and burrowed her face into Remi's neck, praying that the horrid noise would end. At last, all went quiet, but she didn't move.

After a moment, Remi spoke softly. "It's over now."

Breathing shallowly, she lifted her head and looked up at Remi, who, as before, nodded toward the palace. Stella turned and beheld a drawbridge of thick ice, straddling the deadly, churning moat.

The bridge is what made the terrible noise—it came from the hinges and chains. Yet the entire bridge, as far as she could tell, was made of nothing but ice, even the thick chains it had lowered on.

Remi nuzzled her in the back, gently moving her forward a step.

"Oh, Remi, no." Stella tried to stop herself, but her boots slid too easily. "I'm not ready."

"Yes," Remi said, "you are. You must be." He urged her forward until she stood a stone's throw from the bridge. He stepped to her side, and she laid a hand on his back. Her hand needed the warmth, but her heart needed the assurance and comfort his presence gave her. When he didn't speak, she did.

"What now?" Despite herself, the words came out timidly.

"You go inside."

"You say that as if that's the easiest thing in the world, like buttering a slice of toast."

Still staring at the expanse of the bridge ahead of them, Remi said, "I did not say it was easy. But it *is* simple."

She stared straight ahead, hand still on his back. She took a deep breath. "The first step is for us to go inside."

Remi shifted to face her. "It is for *you* to go inside."

Stella's stomach felt as if it were falling off a cliff. "I have to go alone?"

"I cannot go inside." Remi offered no explanation, but he didn't need to. Stella could sense that he genuinely wished he could accompany her, and she could feel the truth of his words.

Stella closed her eyes, balled her hands into fists, and took several deep, chilly breaths. "I can do this. I will do this." She repeated the words a few more times, trying to believe in them as much as she believed in Patrick and their love.

"Do not delay," Remi said, gently interrupting her thoughts.

Stella opened her eyes and stepped forward, right to the edge of the bridge. "It lowered for me, didn't it?" She glanced at Remi. "She knows I'm here."

"Yes," was all Remi said.

I'm about to walk into her lair.

While Stella hadn't heard all the old fables and myths, she knew enough to be aware that walking into a demon's lair without protection or a weapon amounted to foolishness. But what other choice did she have? She took a step onto the bridge. The ice cracked and webbed out from her foot. Not daring to take another step, she stood still as stone.

"Perhaps singing will ease your nerves."

Of course. She'd used song many times back home to ease the ache of missing Patrick, block out her family's criticisms, and overcome the effects of nightmares. If ever she had a time when she needed calm, it was now. Looking up at a palace tower, she hummed her and Patrick's song. To help her focus, she hummed the tune. Immediately, her anxiousness ebbed, and at the thought that Patrick was somewhere nearby, her heart sped up.

The palace was vast, but no matter its size, Patrick—her own, dear Patrick—was inside. Somehow, she'd find him. She'd see him soon.

Each note that left her mouth came out easier and clearer than the one before. She took another step. No new cracks appeared beneath her boots. Once again, she glanced over her shoulder at Remi and found him looking pleased, with what probably counted as a reindeer smile.

Emboldened, Stella abandoned humming and turned to singing, using *la* and *doo* instead of the song's words. Before she knew it, she'd reached the other side of the bridge. Her sense of victory was fleeting, however. No sooner did her boots leave the bridge than it creaked and groaned, rising from the moat. She instinctively covered her ears again, trying to blunt the volume, but this time, another emotion cut through the physical pain of the moaning ice: sickening dismay at knowing that, in moments, she would be locked inside this place.

I may freeze to death by morning. If she'd had anything left of her meal with Ailikki, it would have come back up.

Right before the rumbling bridge sealed tight, she heard Remi call, "Keep going, Stella. Keep singing."

Yes. Singing will keep me moving, which will keep me warm, so I can find Patrick.

Stella turned her back to the bridge and faced an expansive yet empty courtyard. *Nowhere out but through. Remember what Remi said: Keep going. Keep singing.*

As she walked through the courtyard, she looked about for guards or any sign of movement—signs of life or magic, either one. She found her way into the castle proper, and as she headed down a long corridor, she began the song anew. No longer needing to concentrate as hard as she had on the bridge, she let the lyrics flow. When she reached the chorus, something flashed in her periphery, making her step—and her breath—come up short.

As quickly as it appeared, it was gone. Stella whirled about in one direction and then another, trying to discover who or what she'd just seen. Was it a magical creature capable of hiding and causing trouble, like the tricksters in folklore? When no other hint of movement showed itself, Stella's pulse gradually settled from the sudden spike.

She tried to picture what she'd seen, only to realize that she *hadn't* seen anything at all—not with her eyes, at any rate. Rather, an image had come to her mind from an outside source. Such an experience should have been terrifying. Had the image been of the Snow Queen, she would have been petrified.

Instead, Stella had seen Patrick—her Patrick, but at the same time, *not* hers. In her mind's eye, she saw him sitting on the bottom step of a staircase of ice. His skin had turned pale blue and lavender. For a moment, she thought he was dead, frozen solid, but then he moved—only a blink, but enough to know that he was alive. For how much longer?

And how to find him? Was the glimpse enough for her to deduce where he might be? She couldn't remember much about the brief vision. She hadn't noticed what he wore or what he was doing besides looking down. She remembered another movement—his hands seemed to be moving an object she couldn't make out.

What about the staircase? How could she figure out how to get to it? Did it lead to another floor in the palace? A special room? She closed her eyes and tried to see the vision again.

Keep singing, she reminded herself. Perhaps her nerves had gotten the better of her again, and that's why she couldn't see Patrick again.

Stella sang again, only this time, she kept her voice soft so as not to alert the Queen of her whereabouts. She had scarcely finished the first line when the vision reappeared, clearer than before. This time, she kept singing and quickly discovered that the better her pitch and the clearer her tone, the more vivid the vision became. As she walked through the palace, she felt drawn to one turn and another. Sometimes a corridor seemed to give a slight glow, beckoning her onward. After a time, her throat grew sore, so she returned to humming, but that made the vision evaporate in the blink of an eye. The sudden loss made her step come up short.

Remi's voice urged her on: *Keep singing.*

She swallowed in hopes of moistening her raw throat and again sang every note and every word. Once more, she could envision precisely where Patrick was and how to get there. The colors were richer now, and she found herself able to move her perspective, as if she were in the room and could turn her head to look about.

If only I could reach out and touch him, call to him.

As if she were walking backward, away from Patrick, she broadened the vision so she could see more. She could see more of the room now, including where the stairs led. She'd assumed he sat at the base of a long staircase, but it had only five steps, each narrower than the previous one. At the top was a platform holding an elaborate throne with designs in ice that looked as intricate as lace.

The throne of the Snow Queen. Patrick was in the throne room.

Stella nearly sucked in another breath of fear, but she forced the air to keep outward in song. She wouldn't stop until she found Patrick, though that meant walking into the Snow Queen's throne room. At least for now, he was alone.

Farther into the bowels of the castle, snowflakes as large as dinner plates tried to attack her, but as long as she kept singing, they wilted and dropped to the icy floor. Long icicles shot down a hall toward her like rows of daggers. When she drew near, they trembled in the air, unable to finish their assault, and instead melted, dripping to the floor as she passed.

After a period that felt oddly timeless—it could have been seconds or several days, she didn't know which—she found herself face-to-face with a high-arched door. Beyond it lay a room with a floor of ice so smooth and clear that it looked like a mirror and was as large as some lakes. As awe descended on her, the song died on her lips. The sheer size of the chamber overwhelmed her, but so did the sparkling beauty of the snow and ice all around her. The perfectly reflective surface remained unmarred by a scratch, and twisting vines of ice crystals climbed the walls. Giant chandeliers hung from a ceiling so high she could not see the top of it. Everything, even the elaborate tapestries and drapes on the windows, was made of snow and ice.

Directly ahead of her in the cavernous room of ice stood the throne at the top of the staircase, just as she'd seen in vision.

Stella's awe quickly paled as her focus returned to the purpose of her journey: Patrick. She lowered her eyes to bottom step of the staircase, which she'd somehow not seen when first struck with the grandeur of the room.

When her gaze landed on him, both hands flew to her

mouth and strangled a cry. She walked toward him. Tears tumbled down her cheeks and froze on the way down, leaving icy tracks. She cared nothing for them, only about Patrick. She'd come so far, and here he was, right there, only steps away. Soon, she would hold him and kiss him. She'd warm his hands and bring him home, riding Remi.

But Patrick didn't look like himself. He'd moved from the bottom step to kneel on the icy floor, where he arranged long pieces of ice, like icicles, first one way and then another. Panic etched his blue face as if the icicles refused to cooperate—as if they were terribly important. Alarmed, Stella increased her pace to a fast walk and then to a run. Two yards from him, she slipped, which sent her sliding toward his feet. Icicles knocked against her knees as she slid, sending the pieces of ice away and knocking against the base of the staircase like balls on a billiard table. Several broke into smaller shards. When she came to a stop at the base of the stairs, she looked up at Patrick. He looked oh-so-cold and miserable, but alive.

"Patrick!" She pushed herself to a kneeling position and reached for him.

He yanked away and whirled on her, eyes dark and sinister. "Look what you did, you fool!"

If Stella had had any color left in her face after so much cold, it certainly drained right then. "Patrick, it's me, Stella." She reached out again, but he shoved her arms to the side and stormed over to the disordered ice pieces.

"Look!" he bellowed. Standing before the pile of scattered icicles, he raked his blue fingers through frosty hair and moaned with combined grief and horror, sending a chill up Stella's back.

Eight

What did I do?" She hurriedly got to her feet, losing her footing twice as she approached the figure who looked like Patrick—who had been Patrick.

"You ruined it." Pulling his hair with both hands, he raged, his eyes rimmed with red—from fear or sadness, she couldn't tell.

"I'll help you fix it." She dropped to the ice and tried to sort through what looked like a collection of random icicles. "What were you doing with them?"

"I don't *know*," he wailed. "If I did, the task would be done, and my Queen would be pleased for once. She'd stop punishing me." His voice quavered, and he wrapped his arms about his torso. "I'm . . . so . . . cold." He didn't seem to be addressing her anymore, but staring ahead vacantly.

Stella took off her coat, which made her gasp at the shock of cold. She piled the scattered ice pieces on top, careful not to break any, though she had no idea why they mattered. "See?

All cleaned up. Let's go back to the stairs, where you can tell me about you're supposed to do."

Holding her coat in one arm and gently guiding Patrick with the other, she used every drop of control to not insist he remember her. He'd clearly forgotten everything, a fact that lanced her heart in a way she could have only imagined.

I'll feel the pain another day. Not now. Not when she had to get him away from the Snow Queen and her throne room. How they'd find a way out of the palace or lower the drawbridge, she had no idea. She'd find a way. Just as she'd find a way to tell her parents about Patrick when they returned. Just as she and Patrick would find a way to make a life together, though it likely meant being disowned by her family, losing her station, and facing a life of work and poverty.

A fate I am happy to choose if he is indeed my Patrick under the frozen exterior. But that was a thought for another time, so she pushed it to the side and continued leading his cold form to the steps. When they arrived, he sank onto the bottom step and dropped his head into his hands. "She wants my magic."

Was that why the Snow Queen had taken him, because she thought he had magic? *She is as ignorant as she is evil.*

Patrick raised his head and pleaded, "I don't have any magic." As if Stella needed convincing.

"Tell her that she's mistaken," Stella said gently. "Convince her you have no magic."

"I have—a thousand times. She says I do have it, even if I don't know it, and I'm her prisoner until I give it to her. It's hopeless."

A thick, cold whoosh went through the room, like the most powerful winter storm Stella had ever felt. She knew before looking that the Snow Queen had returned. Indeed, she stood in the arched doorway, nearly filling it with her tall frame and white fur coat. Everything about her seemed cold—eyes, face, hair, even her voice as she slowly walked forward.

"Yes, my pet. It *is* hopeless."

In a panic, Patrick dropped to his knees and bowed, his arms extended and his face to the floor. For a brief second, Stella considered doing the same, but in the end refused to cow to the woman. She'd come to rescue Patrick, not to bow to evil.

The Snow Queen continued forward smoothly. Her smile was crooked, and her eyes looked mischievous. She never once looked away from Stella. For her part, Stella desperately wanted to look away. She wanted to run, pulling Patrick behind her, and never look back. But that would not succeed; she and Patrick would both end up dead. She screwed up her courage and lifted her chin in defiance, though she said nothing.

The Snow Queen stopped two paces away, her frigid eyes still locked on Stella's. "My foolish girl, it is hopeless for you both."

A sliver of cold fear slithered through her chest, but Stella kept her face impassive. "I have come to take Patrick home."

"Of course you have." The Snow Queen chuckled, throwing her head back in mirth. A nearby window shattered, sending shards of ice tinkling to the floor.

Stella glanced at Patrick and back at the Snow Queen, then balled her hands into fists. She *would* stay firm. "Release him from the spell you've put him under. Now."

She expected the Queen to laugh again, but instead, she climbed the steps to her throne, where she sat, crossed her long legs, and rested both hands on the armrests. "It's quite fortunate that you are here. When I first learned of your journey, I nearly put an end to it. While a human girl cannot usurp my power, she can become a nuisance."

"Why didn't you kill me when you had the chance?" Stella demanded, though the sliver of cold had multiplied into a dozen and seemed to dart around her body painfully.

The Snow Queen tilted her head to one side and regarded Stella for a moment before answering. "You really don't know. Fascinating."

"Know what?" Stella's confusion mixed with fear.

"Oh, how delicious," the Snow Queen said. "This will be more entertaining than I supposed."

Stella had no idea what she meant. Should she and Patrick be afraid? Was the Queen bluffing? Without a way to know, she turned to Patrick and grabbed his shoulders. "Let's go home. I have a friend outside who will take us away from this place to one where it's warm—where it's summer, with roses and gardens and beautiful sunny days."

Patrick raised his miserable, pale face to hers and furrowed his brow. "Summer. Sun." He said the words as if they were from a foreign tongue. He blinked twice, and then he spoke a single word with clear understanding. "Roses."

"Yes!" Stella took his hands and pulled him to standing. "You're starting to remember."

"No!" The Snow Queen's voice boomed, echoing off the glass-like walks, shattering columns and sending a chandelier crashing to the floor. She pointed a long fingernail at them. "He has power I need. Somehow, his power is tied to you." Still pointing, she narrowed her eyes at Stella and stood. "I am well versed in my kind of magic, but less so with human magic. You must be an amplifier of his powers. . . ." She seemed to be puzzling out a problem. "That is why his powers increased as you drew near, though he still does not understand how to control them. Very interesting."

A thousand questions tumbled about in Stella's head, but she had no time for any of them. She took Patrick's arm and tried to pull him away. He didn't budge an inch. Patrick peered into her eyes with an expression of desperation, begging for help. He opened his mouth and said more than he had since she'd arrived: "If I can spell the word that is the key to my magic, I will be free."

Perhaps the glimpse of memory that the word *roses* awakened had brought other parts of his mind back to life, and that was why he spoke so clearly to Stella, without the crazed look of a trapped animal he'd worn before.

"One word," Stella repeated. More questions crowded her mind, but this time, she had to answer one. She had to solve this puzzle. "The key to your magic." She went to her knees by the pile of icicles. Patrick joined her, and they tried to arrange them in such a way as to spell out the word that would free him.

First, she wrote *roses*. The Snow Queen shook her head.

Then *summer*. The Snow Queen smirked and folded her arms as if watching a most entertaining spectacle.

Freedom garnered an outright chortle.

"What else?" Stella asked Patrick, but though the hostility had fled from him, he seemed no closer to having understanding or insight.

He shrugged. "I don't know how to write."

He'd forgotten how. Stella turned back to the ice pieces and tried to arrange them in new ways.

"Are you quite done?" the Snow Queen asked. "We may as well get on with my plans. I'll take the magic you two share, and then you'll be on your way."

Stella straightened and turned to the throne. "You'll set us free?"

"In a manner of speaking." She sneered. "I suppose the answer depends on what you call *free*."

Surely nothing good. Stella pored over the ice pieces, but she couldn't concentrate well knowing that at any moment the Snow Queen might suck away whatever "power" she and Patrick supposedly possessed and keep them prisoner for the rest of their lives. *What I wouldn't do for a chance to sit for hours, bored, and embroider by a warm fire.* Oh, how her perspective had changed.

One more day with our roses, she thought. *If only we had that much.*

She thought of how often they'd met on the bridge they'd constructed between their two townhouses. Of how many times she'd arrived to see no properly bloomed roses, only ones in tight buds that seemed a week away from opening. Of how, when Patrick climbed through his window and joined her, she somehow found exactly the right number and type of roses she needed. Their garden thrived when they both worked in it. She'd always thought it was because they both gave their rose bushes the care they needed, but what if . . .

Stella's eyes widened. What if the two of them *did* possess magic—together? What if the magic wasn't his, amplified by her nearness, but a magic that existed only when they were together?

Yes. That must be it. But is there more? There must be.

Holding two long icicles, one in each hand, she closed her eyes and imagined being on the balcony, working at Patrick's side. She could feel her broad-brimmed bonnet protecting her face from the sun. The gloves on her hands to keep them clean. His touch as they reached for the same tool. His kisses as they sat on their bench and admired their handiwork. Their long hours together in silence.

But we weren't entirely silent. We sang. Stella's grip on the icicles tightened as realization dawned on her. With a quick movement, she shot a look at the Snow Queen. Did she know? The answer was how Stella had made her journey successfully. It was how she'd found her way through the labyrinth of passageways. How she'd found Patrick.

She swallowed, looked away, and silently moved the ice pieces into the correct positions, praying all the while that the Snow Queen wouldn't stop her or figure out the truth before Stella finished. At last, she placed the final crosspiece to a letter E.

Beside her, Patrick said, "Yes. That's it. I remember now." He reached for her hand. His skin felt warm. Stella lifted her face to his, hardly daring to hope. His cheeks indeed began to regain color—so slightly that she worried she'd imagined it, but the frozen pallor continued to fade. Her Patrick *was* beneath the ice. He remembered her. He loved her.

Hand in hand, they turned to the Queen, but before they spoke, a monstrous sound cracked the air. Columns burst all around them. Walls caved in. Chandeliers crashed against the floor and shattered into pieces.

The Snow Queen raced down the steps and looked around, sheer panic in her features. "What is this? It cannot be!" She whirled on Stella and Patrick, who ran, hand in hand, for the archway, leaping over cracks in the floor, dodging hunks of ice flying through the air around them like bombs.

"What did you do?" the Queen screamed after them. "What did you write?" Her voice grew softer as they increased their distance, but she didn't stop screeching, hurling threats their way. So many palace walls had caved in that the exterior looked like a skeleton. When they reached the moat, it was covered in pieces of the palace, which Stella and Patrick used to cross as easily as if they were walking a log to reach the other side of the river.

Faithful Remi awaited them at the edge of the forest. "You're alive," he said with relief, then bent down so the two could climb onto his back.

The reindeer bolted through the forest even faster than before if that was possible, leaving the palace behind them in ruins and the Snow Queen likely dead beneath the rubble.

Around them, the snow melted, and the day grew warm. Remi slowed to a walk and caught his breath. Patrick wrapped his arms about Stella's waist, and she leaned into his embrace.

"Stella," he said into her ear. The sound of her name was more thrilling than ever because only minutes ago, he didn't know her at all.

"Yes?" she said, pressing her ear to his chest to hear the steady thump of his heart.

"What did you write in the ice?"

Warmth flooded through her—from the sun, yes, but from being with Patrick again, safe and sound. She lifted her face to his and kissed his jawline. "The music of love."

With one thumb, Patrick stroked her cheek. He smiled, but it held a hint of confusion. "How did that make us free?"

"Our love is our magic," Stella said. Now that she understood, everything felt so clear, so simple. "When we're together, nature comes alive around us. Everything we touch blooms."

"Like our roses," he said. "And singing—"

"Increases the power—" she began.

"Of our magic," he finished.

"Exactly." Stella stroked his jawline, then reached behind his neck and pulled his face to hers. Before their lips met, she murmured, "The power of our love."

About Annette Lyon

Annette Lyon is a *USA Today* bestselling author, a four-time recipient of Utah's Best of State medal for fiction, a Whitney Award winner, and a five-time publication award winner from the League of Utah Writers. She's the author of more than a dozen novels, even more novellas, and several nonfiction books. When she's not writing, knitting, or eating chocolate, she can be found mothering and avoiding housework. Annette is a member of the Women's Fiction Writers Association and is represented by Heather Karpas at ICM Partners.

Find Annette online:
Blog: http://blog.AnnetteLyon.com
Twitter: @AnnetteLyon
Facebook: AnnetteLyon
Instagram: annette.lyon
Pinterest: AnnetteLyon
Newsletter: http://bit.ly/1n3I87y

Dear Timeless Romance Anthology Reader,

Thank you for reading our *Happily Ever After Collection.* We hoped you loved the sweet romance novellas! Heather B. Moore, Annette Lyon, and Sarah M. Eden have been indie publishing this series since 2012 through the Mirror Press imprint. For each anthology, we carefully select three guest authors. Our goal is to offer a way for our readers to discover new, favorite authors by reading these romance novellas written exclusively for our anthologies . . . all for one great price.

If you enjoyed this anthology, please consider leaving a review on Goodreads or Amazon or Barnes & Noble or any other e-book store you purchase through. Reviews and word-of-mouth is what helps us continue this fun project. For updates and notifications of sales and giveaways, please join our newsletter: TimelessRomanceAnthologies.blogspot.com or join us on Facebook: Timeless Romance Anthologies

Thank you!
The Timeless Romance Authors

MORE TIMELESS ROMANCE ANTHOLOGIES

Made in the USA
Middletown, DE
13 February 2022

61076766R00225